DRAGONS BEWARE!

**For my parents, Maria and Raul—
my biggest fans and a constant source of inspiration
—R.R.**

**For my papi, who was the first storyteller I ever knew
—J.A.**

We would like to thank our editor, Mark Siegel, for his continued support and enthusiasm for Claudette and her stories. Thank you to the amazing First Second crew: Calista Brill, Colleen AF Venable, and Gina Gagliano. Thanks also to Darlene Rosado, for her help in promoting our work and to Raul Rosado and John Novak, for their feedback. And thanks, Maggie Novak! Rafael would also like to thank Dee Dee Sue, Amelia, and Avery for their love and infinite patience. Jorge would like to thank Carla, Diego, and Pablo for their patience and impatience. Both equally important.

—Jorge & Rafael

First Second

Text Copyright © 2015 by Jorge Aguirre
Art Copyright © 2015 by Rafael Rosado
Published by First Second
First Second is an imprint of Roaring Brook Press, a division of Holtzbrinck Publishing Holdings Limited Partnership
175 Fifth Avenue, New York, New York 10010
All rights reserved

Library of Congress Cataloging-in-Publication Data
Aguirre, Jorge.
    Dragons beware! / written by Jorge Aguirre ; art by Rafael Rosado ; colors by John Novak. —First edition.
        pages cm. — (Chronicles of Claudette ; 2)
    Summary: When Claudette sets out to slay the dragon that ate her father's legs and his legendary sword, she will need more help than ever from her friend Marie and her brother Gaston.
    ISBN 978-1-59643-878-1 (trade pbk.)
    1. Graphic novels.   [1. Graphic novels.   2. Fairy tales.]   I. Rosado, Rafael, 1961– illustrator.   II. Title.

PZ7.7.A32Dr 2015
741.5'973—dc23
                                                                    2014047290

First Second books may be purchased for business or promotional use. For information on bulk purchases please contact Macmillan Corporate and Premium Sales Department at (800) 221-7945 x5442 or by email at specialmarkets@macmillan.com.

First edition 2015
Book design by Colleen AF Venable and John Green
Printed in China by 1010 Printing International Ltd., North Point, Hong Kong

10 9 8 7 6 5 4

DRAGONS BEWARE!

WRITTEN BY
JORGE AGUIRRE

ART BY
RAFAEL ROSADO

STORY BY
JORGE AGUIRRE &
RAFAEL ROSADO

COLOR BY
JOHN NOVAK

First Second
New York

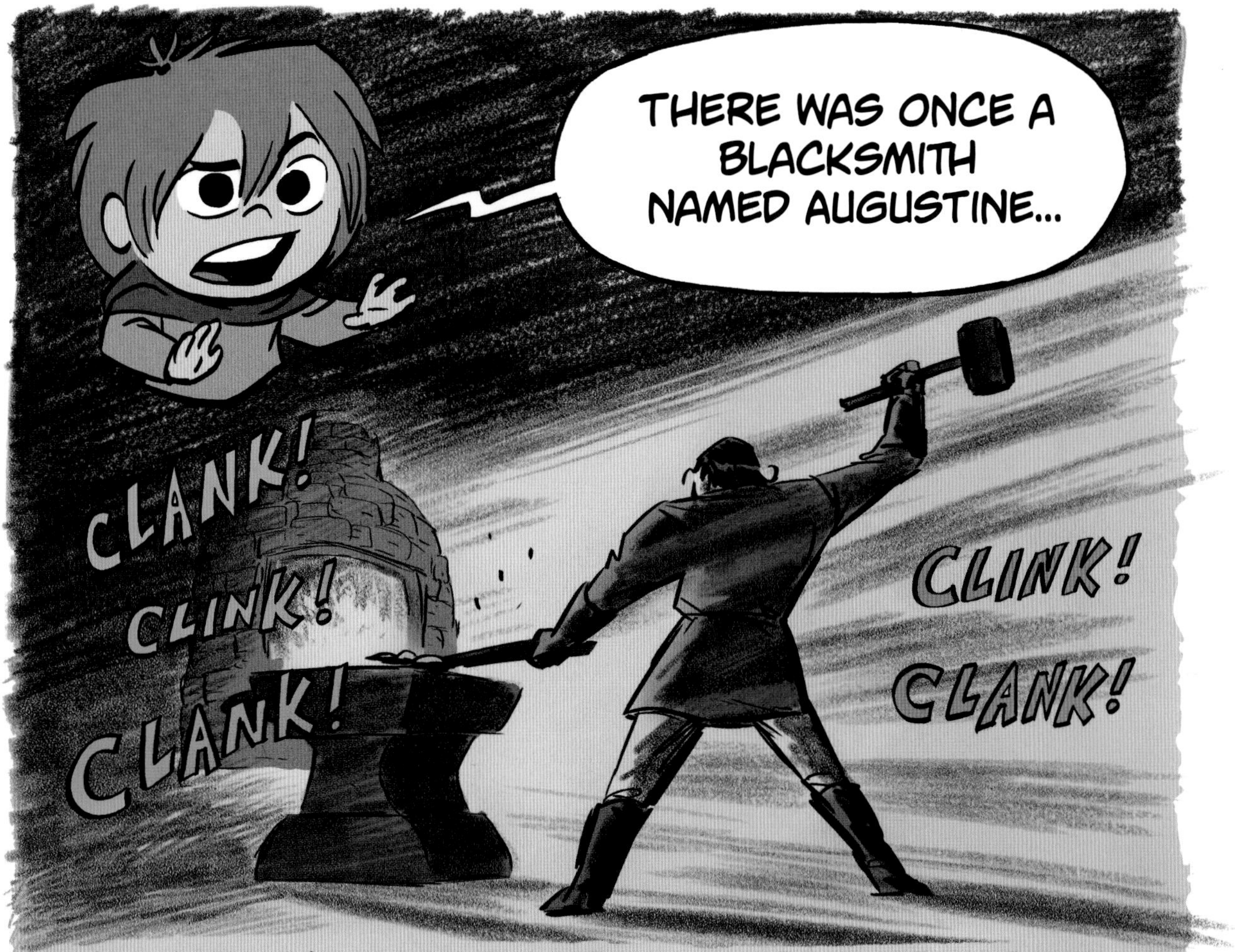
THERE WAS ONCE A BLACKSMITH NAMED AUGUSTINE...
CLANK!
CLINK!
CLANK!
CLINK!
CLANK!

HE MADE THE MOST POWERFUL SWORD EVER FORGED.

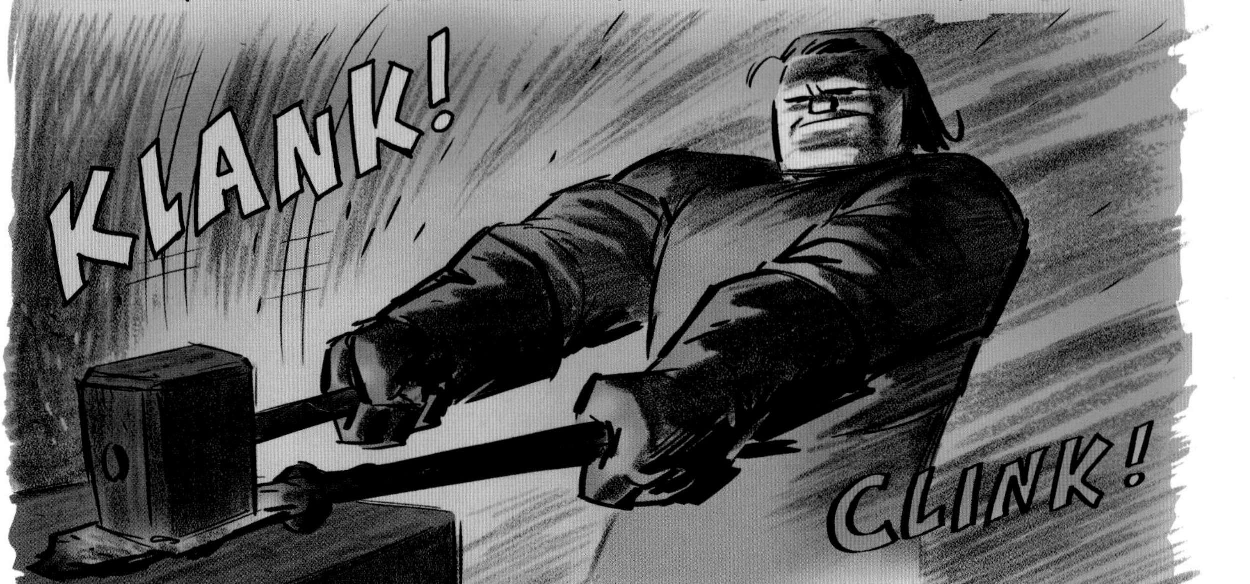
KLANK!
CLINK!
HE CALLED IT...

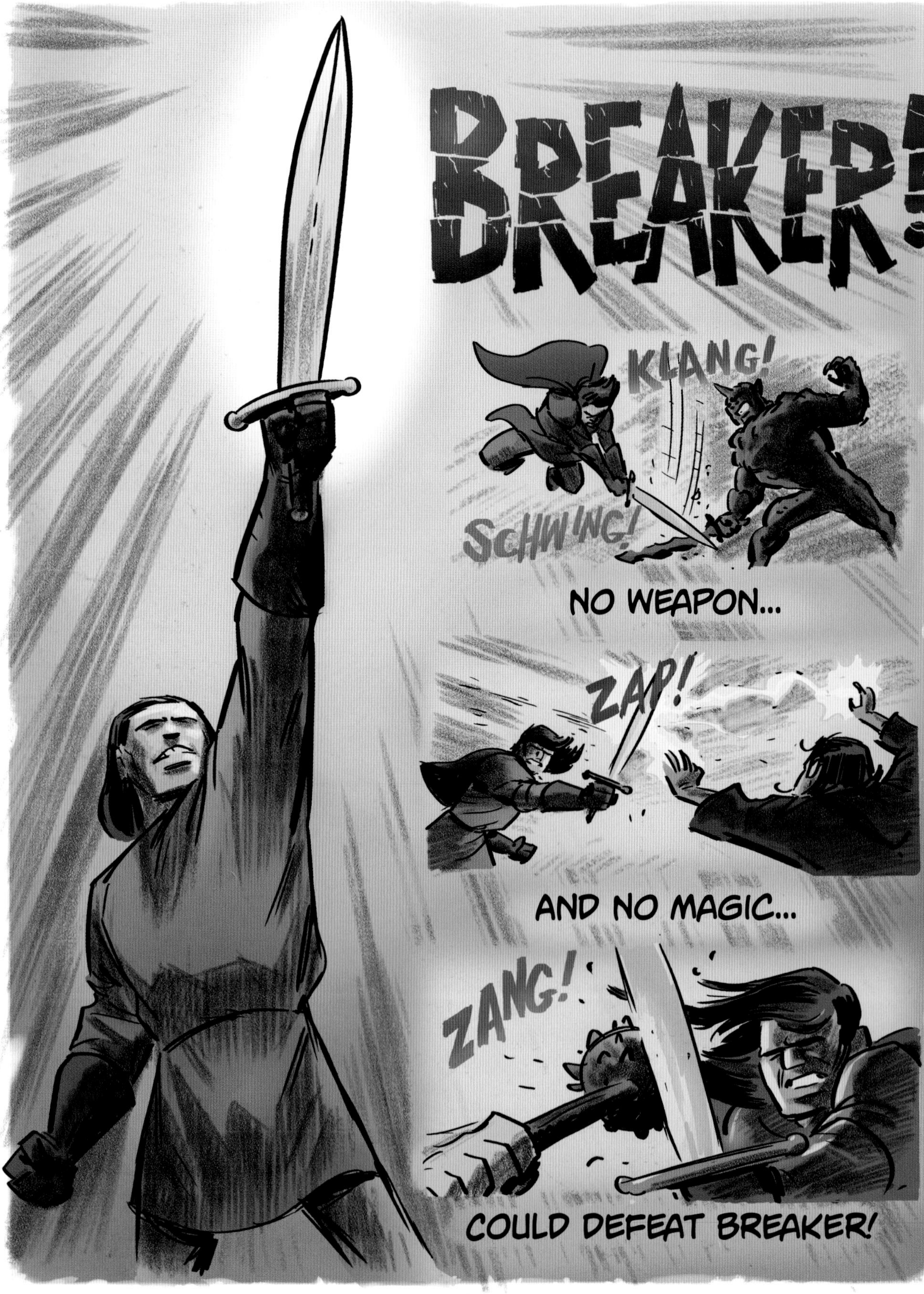
BREAKER!
KLANG!
SCHWING!
NO WEAPON...
ZAP!
AND NO MAGIC...
ZANG!
COULD DEFEAT BREAKER!

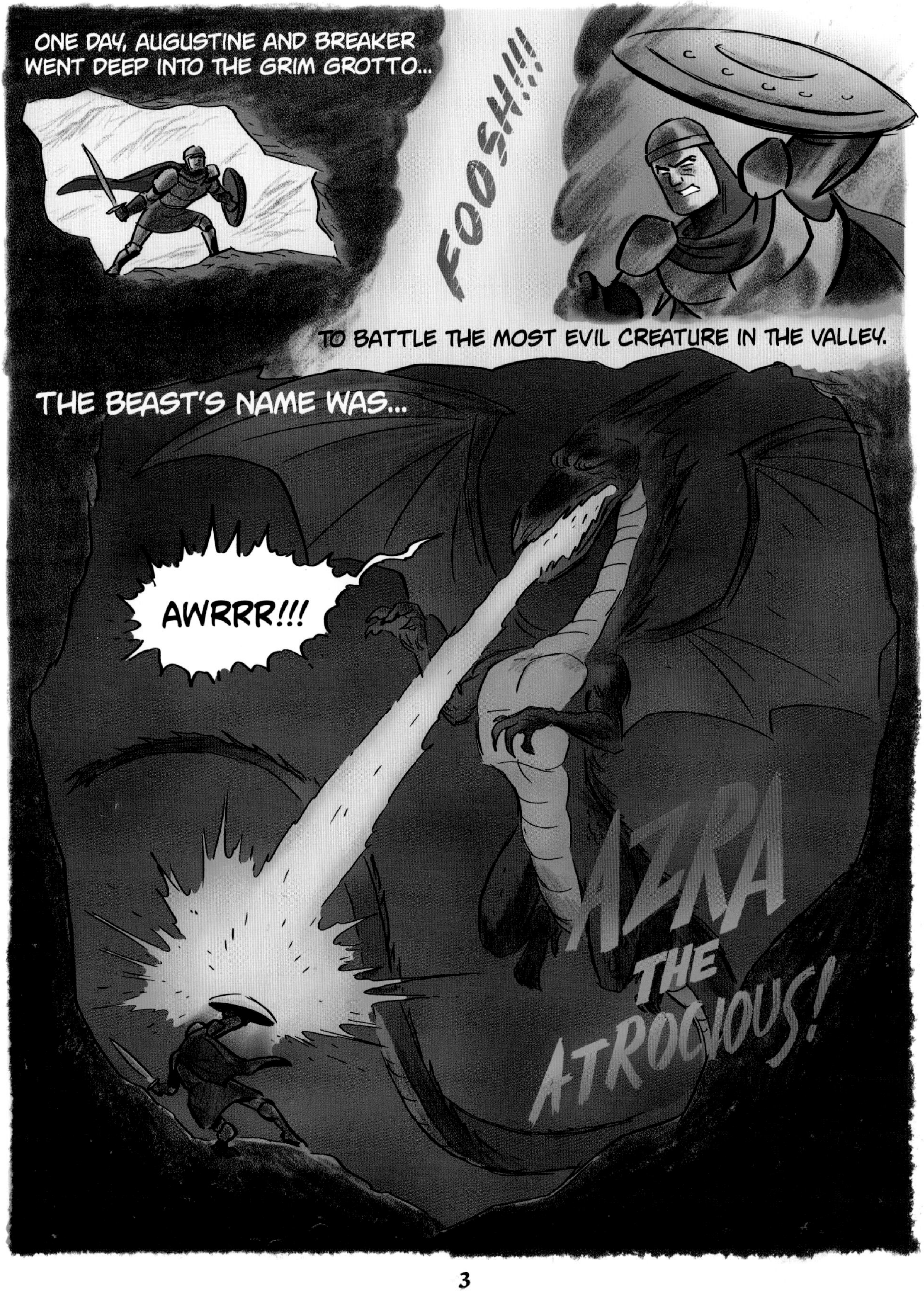
ONE DAY, AUGUSTINE AND BREAKER WENT DEEP INTO THE GRIM GROTTO...
FOOSH!!!
TO BATTLE THE MOST EVIL CREATURE IN THE VALLEY.
THE BEAST'S NAME WAS...
AWRRR!!!
AZRA THE ATROCIOUS!

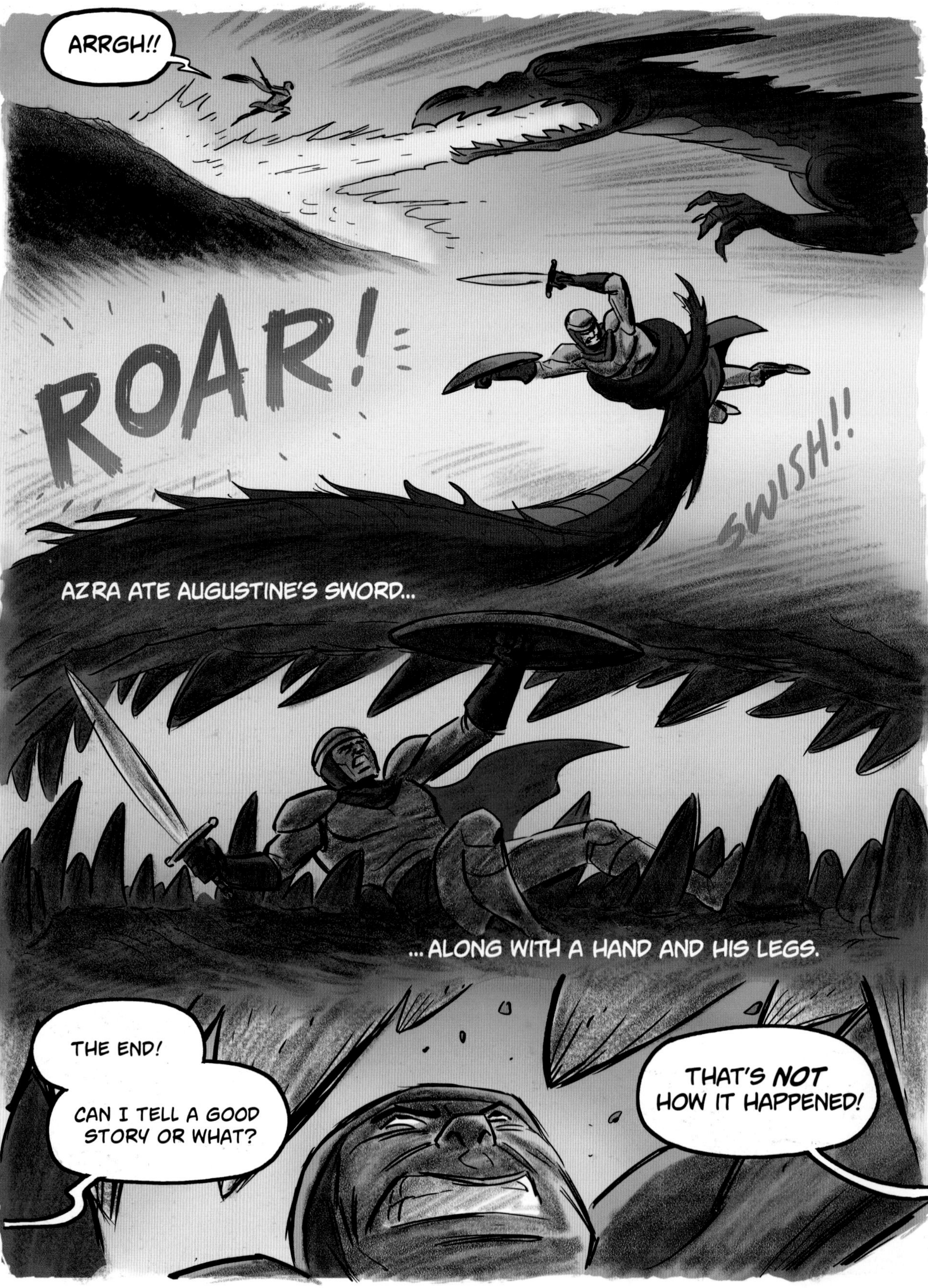
ARRGH!!
ROAR!
SWISH!!
AZRA ATE AUGUSTINE'S SWORD...
...ALONG WITH A HAND AND HIS LEGS.
THE END!
CAN I TELL A GOOD STORY OR WHAT?
THAT'S NOT HOW IT HAPPENED!

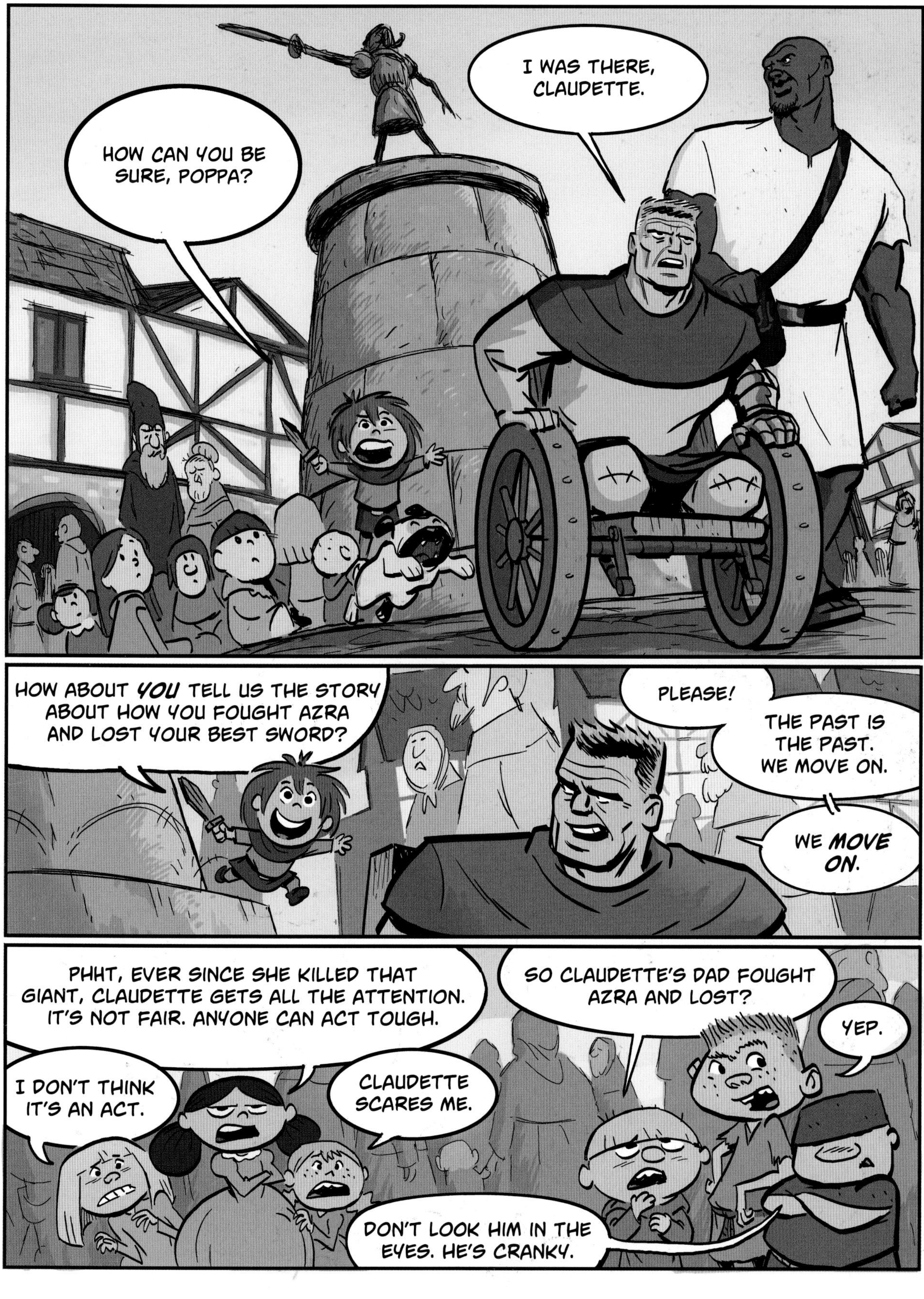
HOW CAN YOU BE SURE, POPPA?
I WAS THERE, CLAUDETTE.
HOW ABOUT YOU TELL US THE STORY ABOUT HOW YOU FOUGHT AZRA AND LOST YOUR BEST SWORD?
PLEASE!
THE PAST IS THE PAST. WE MOVE ON.
WE MOVE ON.
PHHT, EVER SINCE SHE KILLED THAT GIANT, CLAUDETTE GETS ALL THE ATTENTION. IT'S NOT FAIR. ANYONE CAN ACT TOUGH.
I DON'T THINK IT'S AN ACT.
CLAUDETTE SCARES ME.
SO CLAUDETTE'S DAD FOUGHT AZRA AND LOST?
YEP.
DON'T LOOK HIM IN THE EYES. HE'S CRANKY.

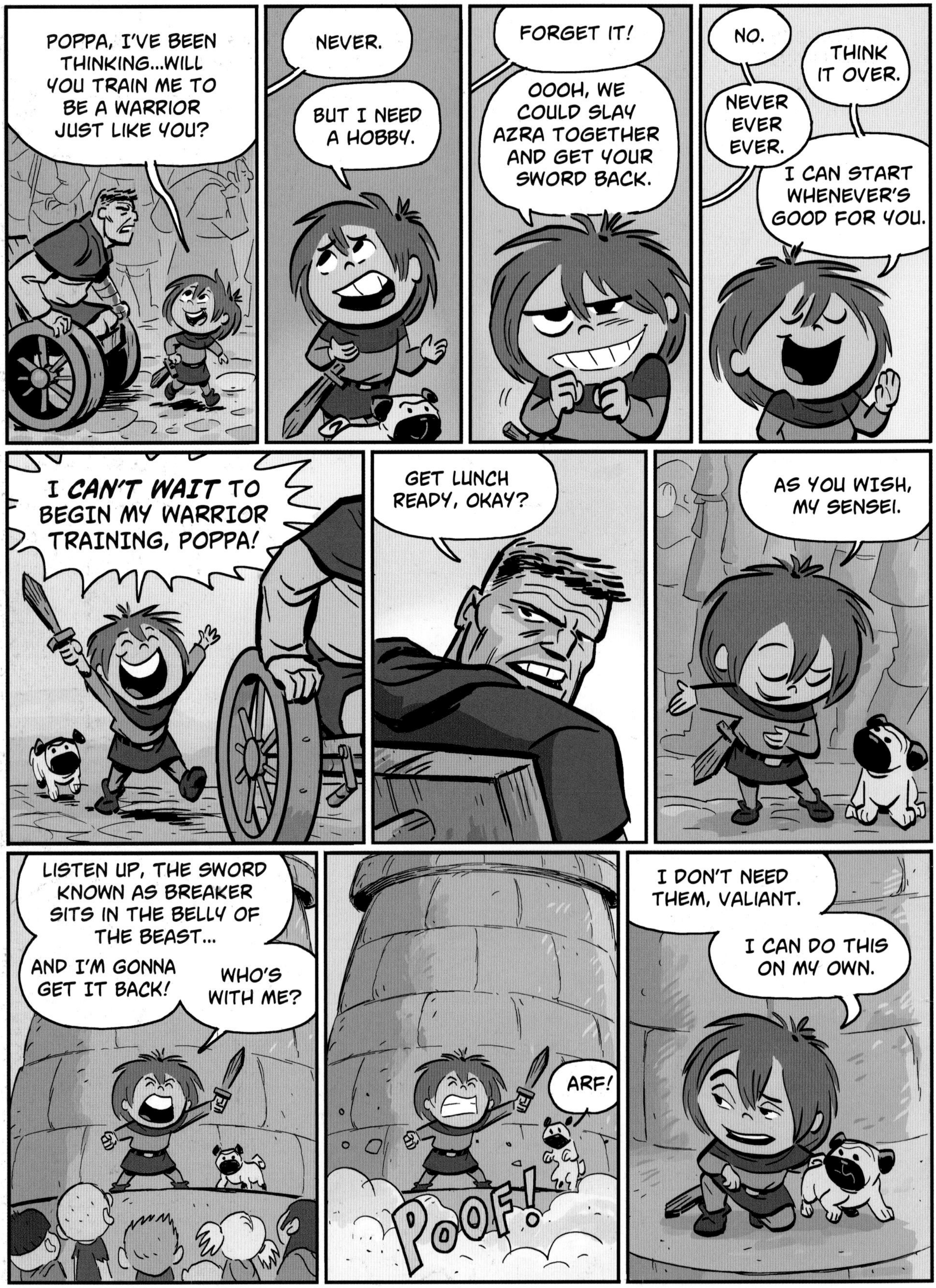
POPPA, I'VE BEEN THINKING...WILL YOU TRAIN ME TO BE A WARRIOR JUST LIKE YOU?
NEVER.
BUT I NEED A HOBBY.
FORGET IT!
OOOH, WE COULD SLAY AZRA TOGETHER AND GET YOUR SWORD BACK.
NO.
NEVER EVER EVER.
THINK IT OVER.
I CAN START WHENEVER'S GOOD FOR YOU.
I CAN'T WAIT TO BEGIN MY WARRIOR TRAINING, POPPA!
GET LUNCH READY, OKAY?
AS YOU WISH, MY SENSEI.
LISTEN UP, THE SWORD KNOWN AS BREAKER SITS IN THE BELLY OF THE BEAST...
AND I'M GONNA GET IT BACK!
WHO'S WITH ME?
ARF!
POOF!
I DON'T NEED THEM, VALIANT.
I CAN DO THIS ON MY OWN.

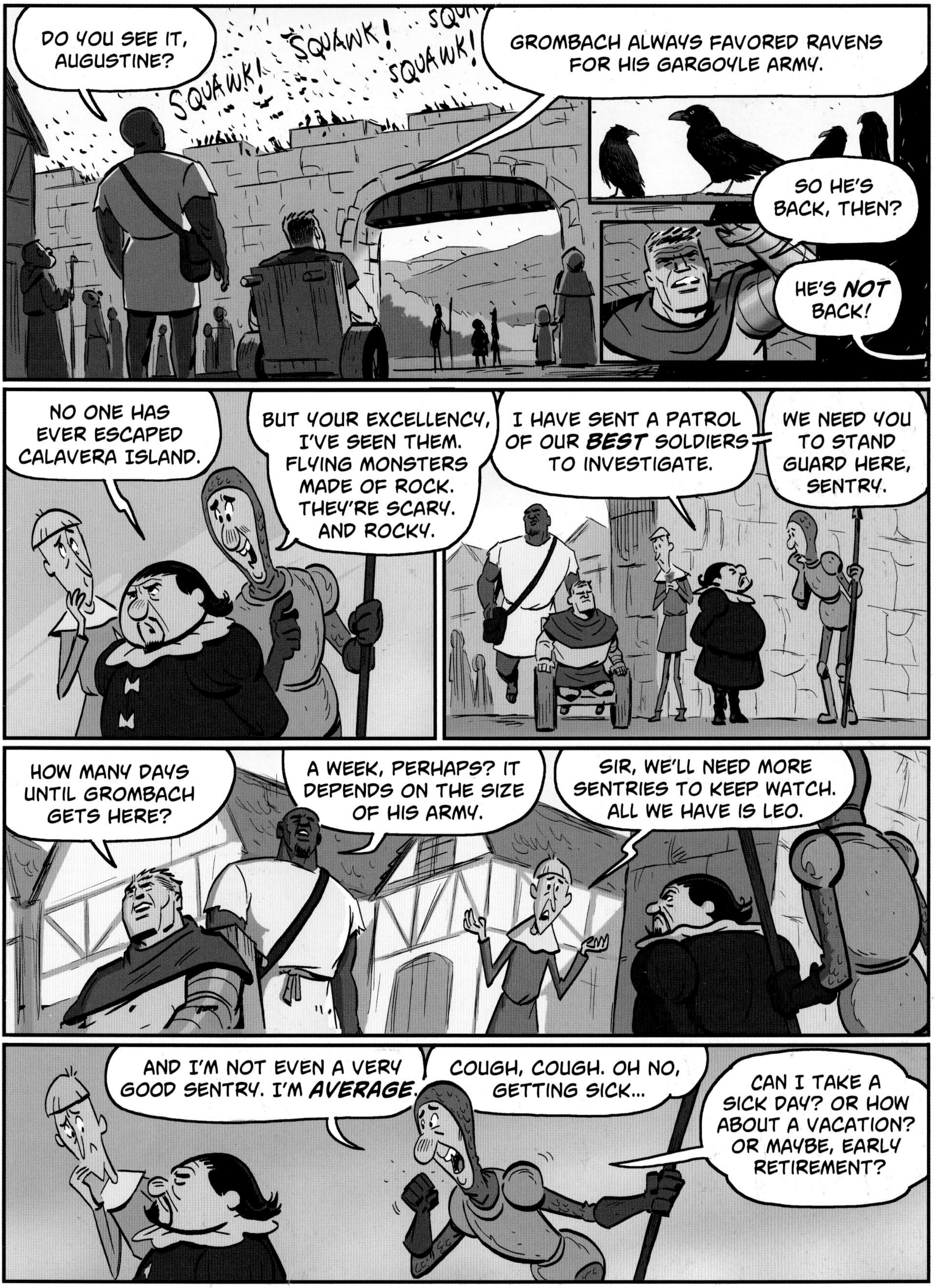
DO YOU SEE IT, AUGUSTINE?
SQUAWK! SQUAWK! SQUAWK!
GROMBACH ALWAYS FAVORED RAVENS FOR HIS GARGOYLE ARMY.
SO HE'S BACK, THEN?
HE'S NOT BACK!
NO ONE HAS EVER ESCAPED CALAVERA ISLAND.
BUT YOUR EXCELLENCY, I'VE SEEN THEM. FLYING MONSTERS MADE OF ROCK. THEY'RE SCARY. AND ROCKY.
I HAVE SENT A PATROL OF OUR BEST SOLDIERS TO INVESTIGATE.
WE NEED YOU TO STAND GUARD HERE, SENTRY.
HOW MANY DAYS UNTIL GROMBACH GETS HERE?
A WEEK, PERHAPS? IT DEPENDS ON THE SIZE OF HIS ARMY.
SIR, WE'LL NEED MORE SENTRIES TO KEEP WATCH. ALL WE HAVE IS LEO.
AND I'M NOT EVEN A VERY GOOD SENTRY. I'M AVERAGE.
COUGH, COUGH. OH NO, GETTING SICK...
CAN I TAKE A SICK DAY? OR HOW ABOUT A VACATION? OR MAYBE, EARLY RETIREMENT?

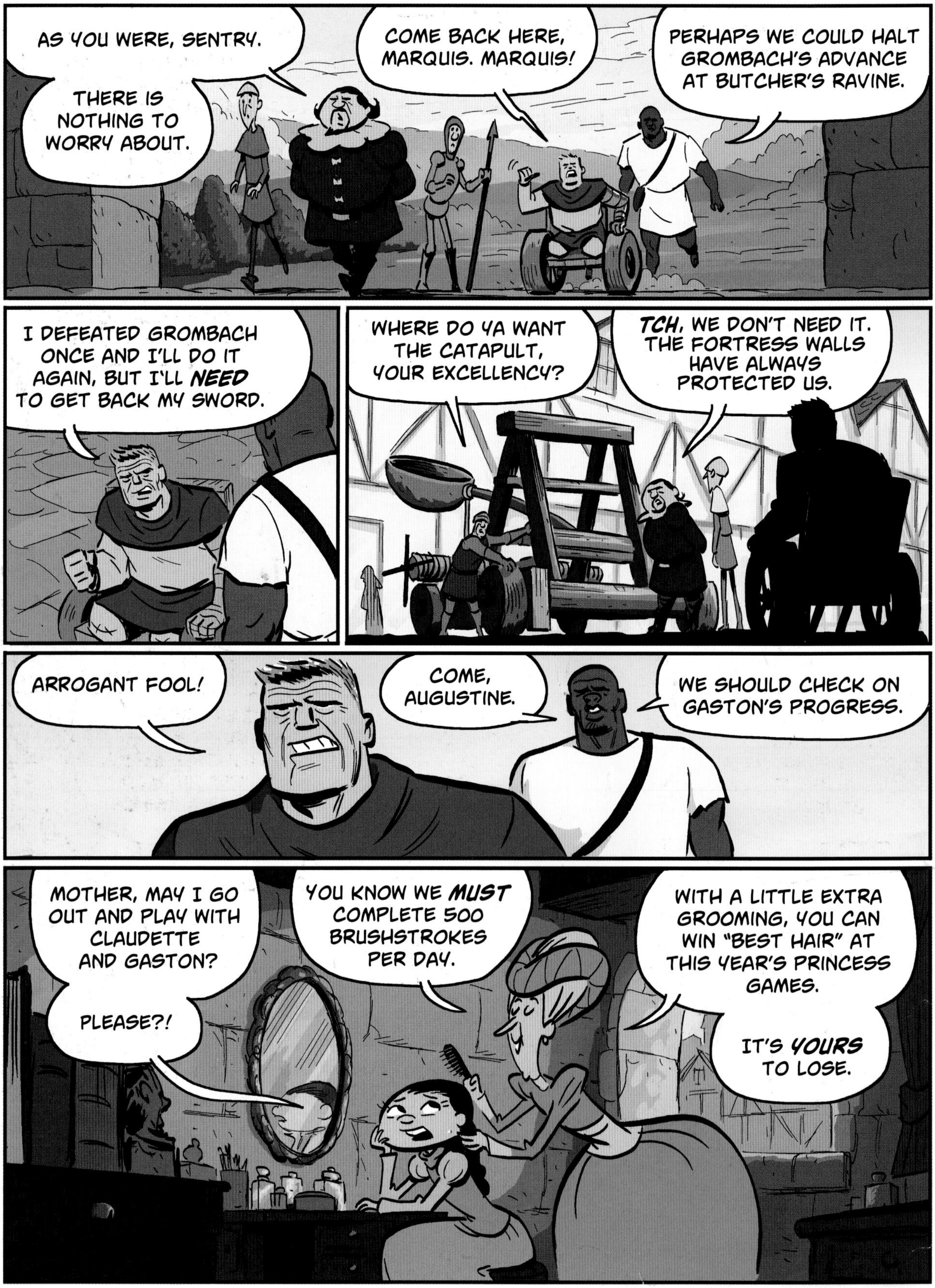
AS YOU WERE, SENTRY.
THERE IS NOTHING TO WORRY ABOUT.
COME BACK HERE, MARQUIS. MARQUIS!
PERHAPS WE COULD HALT GROMBACH'S ADVANCE AT BUTCHER'S RAVINE.
I DEFEATED GROMBACH ONCE AND I'LL DO IT AGAIN, BUT I'LL ***NEED*** TO GET BACK MY SWORD.
WHERE DO YA WANT THE CATAPULT, YOUR EXCELLENCY?
TCH, WE DON'T NEED IT. THE FORTRESS WALLS HAVE ALWAYS PROTECTED US.
ARROGANT FOOL!
COME, AUGUSTINE.
WE SHOULD CHECK ON GASTON'S PROGRESS.
MOTHER, MAY I GO OUT AND PLAY WITH CLAUDETTE AND GASTON?
PLEASE?!
YOU KNOW WE ***MUST*** COMPLETE 500 BRUSHSTROKES PER DAY.
WITH A LITTLE EXTRA GROOMING, YOU CAN WIN "BEST HAIR" AT THIS YEAR'S PRINCESS GAMES.
IT'S ***YOURS*** TO LOSE.

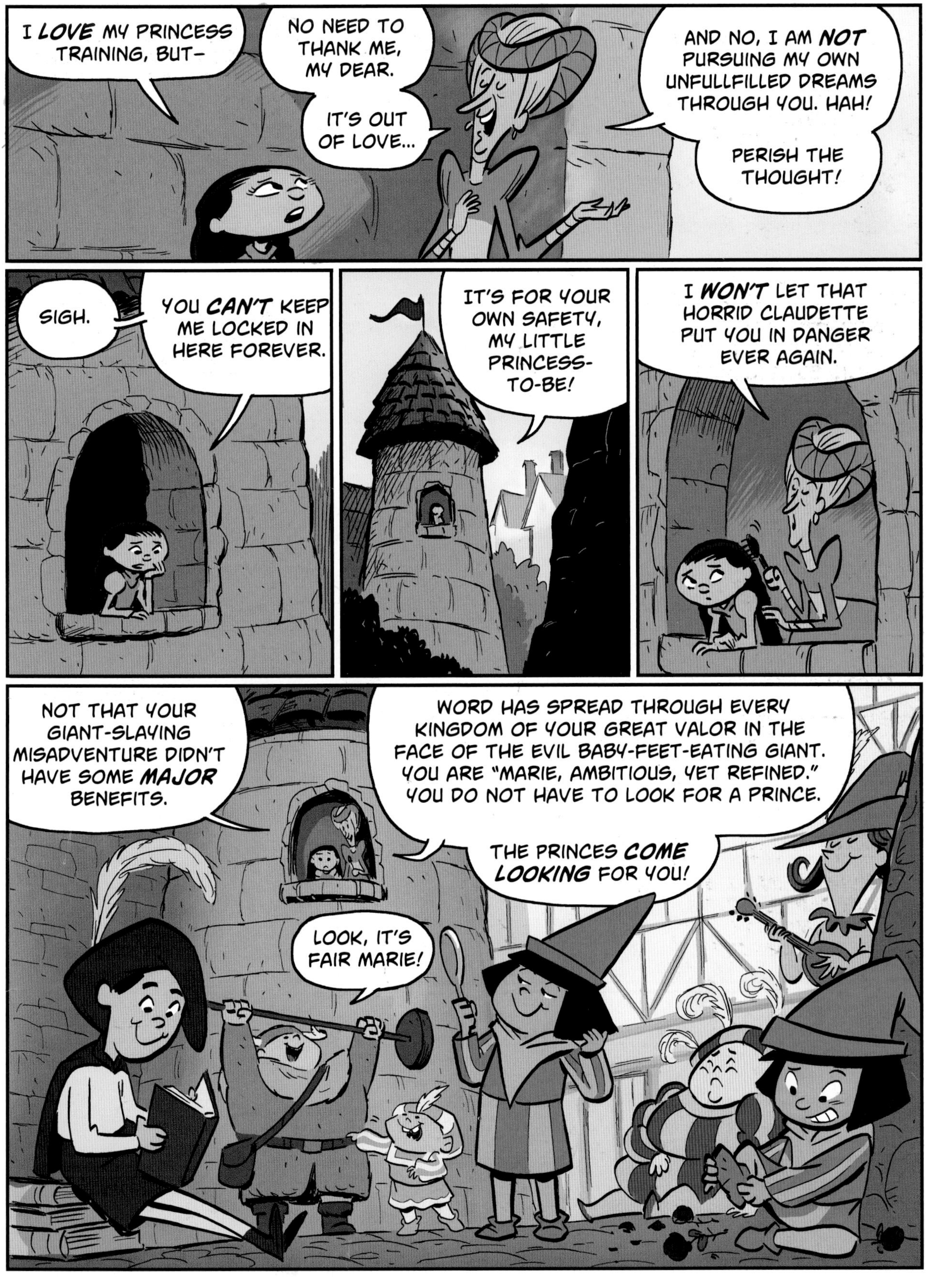
I LOVE MY PRINCESS TRAINING, BUT–
NO NEED TO THANK ME, MY DEAR.
IT'S OUT OF LOVE...
AND NO, I AM NOT PURSUING MY OWN UNFULLFILLED DREAMS THROUGH YOU. HAH!
PERISH THE THOUGHT!
SIGH.
YOU CAN'T KEEP ME LOCKED IN HERE FOREVER.
IT'S FOR YOUR OWN SAFETY, MY LITTLE PRINCESS-TO-BE!
I WON'T LET THAT HORRID CLAUDETTE PUT YOU IN DANGER EVER AGAIN.
NOT THAT YOUR GIANT-SLAYING MISADVENTURE DIDN'T HAVE SOME MAJOR BENEFITS.
WORD HAS SPREAD THROUGH EVERY KINGDOM OF YOUR GREAT VALOR IN THE FACE OF THE EVIL BABY-FEET-EATING GIANT. YOU ARE "MARIE, AMBITIOUS, YET REFINED." YOU DO NOT HAVE TO LOOK FOR A PRINCE.
THE PRINCES COME LOOKING FOR YOU!
LOOK, IT'S FAIR MARIE!

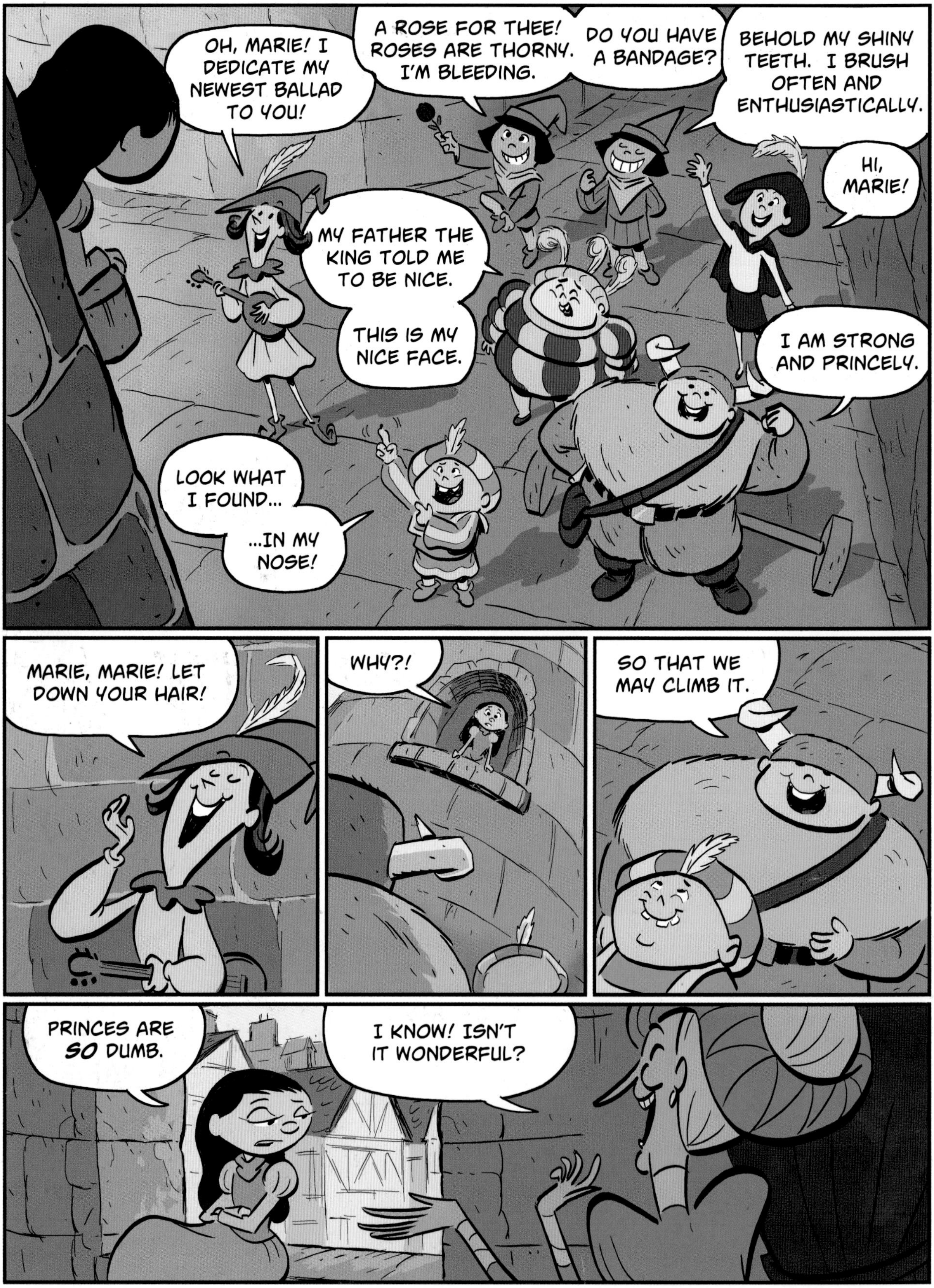
OH, MARIE! I DEDICATE MY NEWEST BALLAD TO YOU!
A ROSE FOR THEE! ROSES ARE THORNY. I'M BLEEDING.
DO YOU HAVE A BANDAGE?
BEHOLD MY SHINY TEETH. I BRUSH OFTEN AND ENTHUSIASTICALLY.
HI, MARIE!
MY FATHER THE KING TOLD ME TO BE NICE.
THIS IS MY NICE FACE.
I AM STRONG AND PRINCELY.
LOOK WHAT I FOUND...
...IN MY NOSE!
MARIE, MARIE! LET DOWN YOUR HAIR!
WHY?!
SO THAT WE MAY CLIMB IT.
PRINCES ARE *SO* DUMB.
I KNOW! ISN'T IT WONDERFUL?

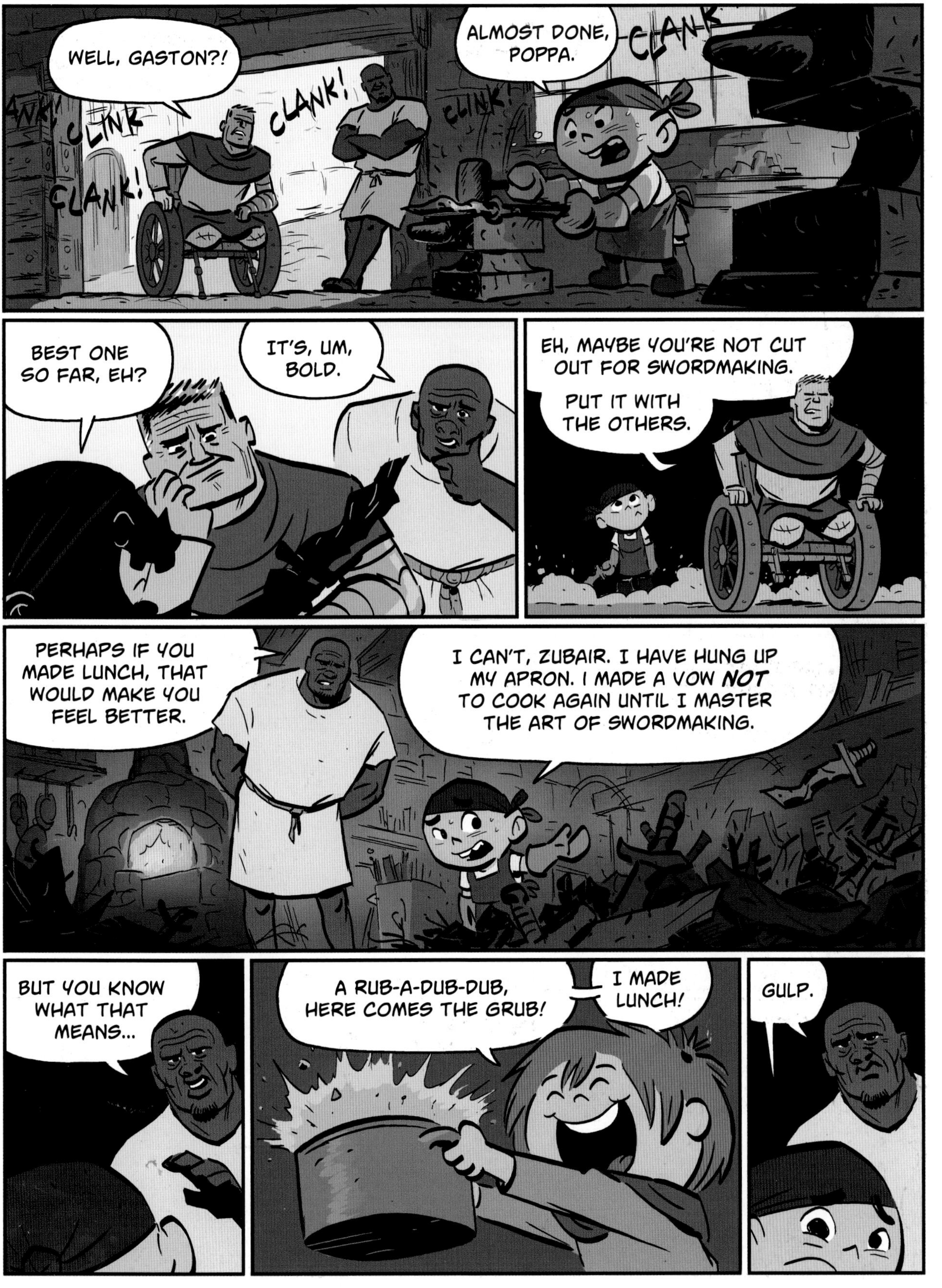
WELL, GASTON?!
ALMOST DONE, POPPA.
CLINK
CLANK!
CLANK!
CLINK!
CLANK
BEST ONE SO FAR, EH?
IT'S, UM, BOLD.
EH, MAYBE YOU'RE NOT CUT OUT FOR SWORDMAKING.
PUT IT WITH THE OTHERS.
PERHAPS IF YOU MADE LUNCH, THAT WOULD MAKE YOU FEEL BETTER.
I CAN'T, ZUBAIR. I HAVE HUNG UP MY APRON. I MADE A VOW ***NOT*** TO COOK AGAIN UNTIL I MASTER THE ART OF SWORDMAKING.
BUT YOU KNOW WHAT THAT MEANS...
A RUB-A-DUB-DUB, HERE COMES THE GRUB!
I MADE LUNCH!
GULP.

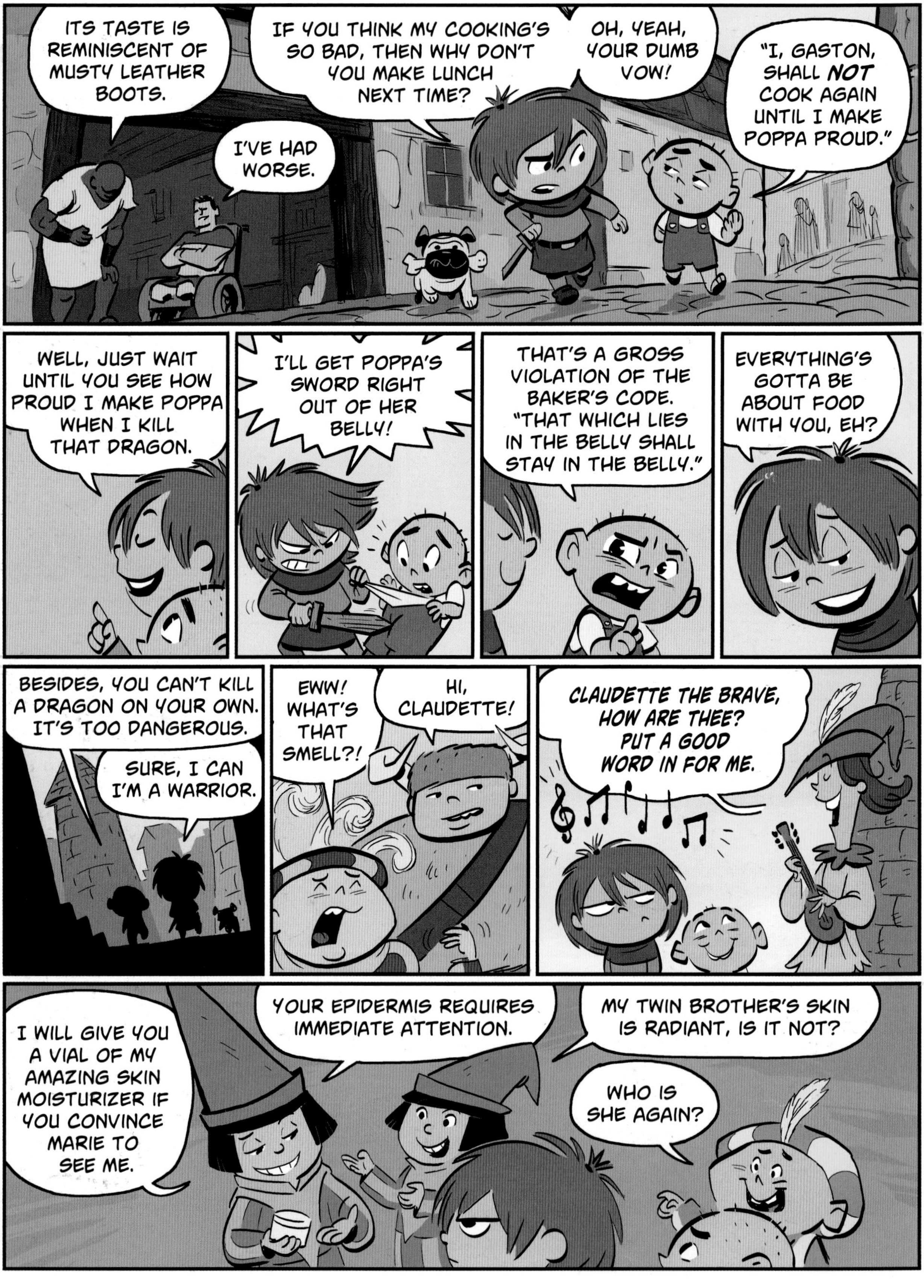

ITS TASTE IS REMINISCENT OF MUSTY LEATHER BOOTS.
I'VE HAD WORSE.
IF YOU THINK MY COOKING'S SO BAD, THEN WHY DON'T YOU MAKE LUNCH NEXT TIME?
OH, YEAH, YOUR DUMB VOW!
"I, GASTON, SHALL **NOT** COOK AGAIN UNTIL I MAKE POPPA PROUD."
WELL, JUST WAIT UNTIL YOU SEE HOW PROUD I MAKE POPPA WHEN I KILL THAT DRAGON.
I'LL GET POPPA'S SWORD RIGHT OUT OF HER BELLY!
THAT'S A GROSS VIOLATION OF THE BAKER'S CODE. "THAT WHICH LIES IN THE BELLY SHALL STAY IN THE BELLY."
EVERYTHING'S GOTTA BE ABOUT FOOD WITH YOU, EH?
BESIDES, YOU CAN'T KILL A DRAGON ON YOUR OWN. IT'S TOO DANGEROUS.
SURE, I CAN I'M A WARRIOR.
EWW! WHAT'S THAT SMELL?!
HI, CLAUDETTE!
CLAUDETTE THE BRAVE, HOW ARE THEE? PUT A GOOD WORD IN FOR ME.
I WILL GIVE YOU A VIAL OF MY AMAZING SKIN MOISTURIZER IF YOU CONVINCE MARIE TO SEE ME.
YOUR EPIDERMIS REQUIRES IMMEDIATE ATTENTION.
MY TWIN BROTHER'S SKIN IS RADIANT, IS IT NOT?
WHO IS SHE AGAIN?

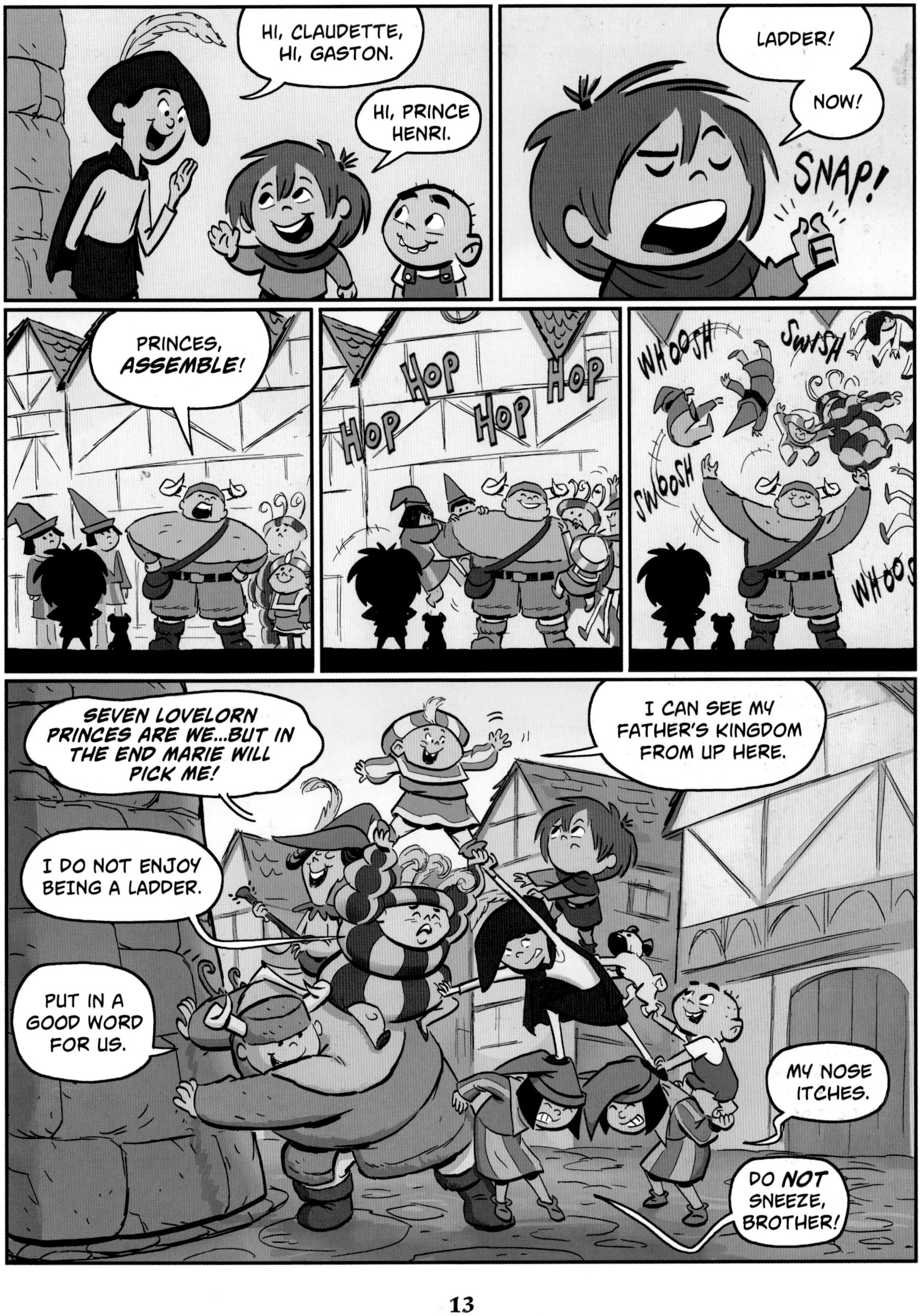
HI, CLAUDETTE, HI, GASTON.
HI, PRINCE HENRI.
LADDER!
NOW!
SNAP!
PRINCES, ASSEMBLE!
HOP
HOP
HOP
HOP
WHOOSH
SWISH
SWOOSH
WHOOS
SEVEN LOVELORN PRINCES ARE WE...BUT IN THE END MARIE WILL PICK ME!
I CAN SEE MY FATHER'S KINGDOM FROM UP HERE.
I DO NOT ENJOY BEING A LADDER.
PUT IN A GOOD WORD FOR US.
MY NOSE ITCHES.
DO NOT SNEEZE, BROTHER!

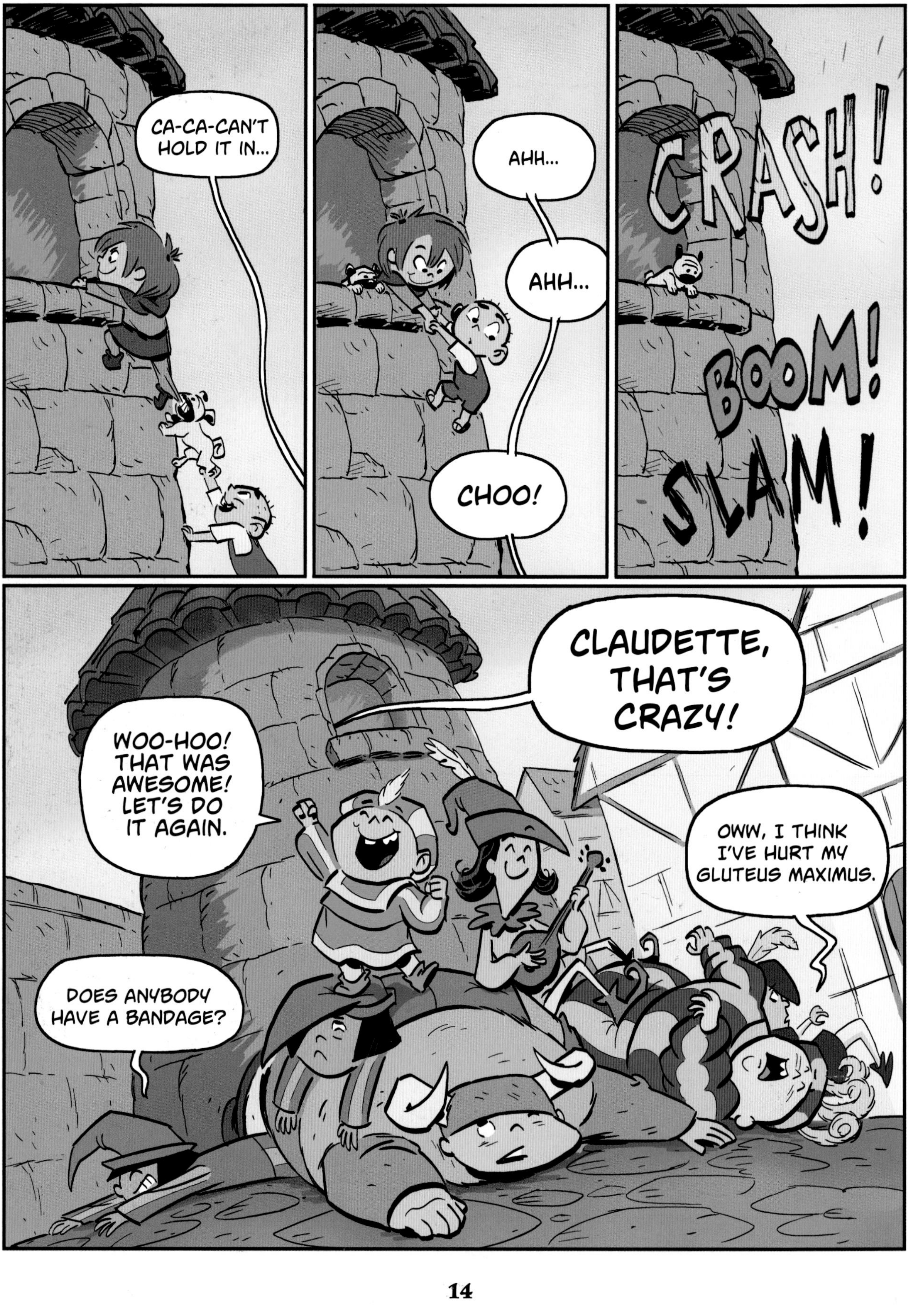
CA-CA-CAN'T HOLD IT IN...
AHH...
AHH...
CHOO!
CRASH!
BOOM!
SLAM!
CLAUDETTE, THAT'S CRAZY!
WOO-HOO! THAT WAS AWESOME! LET'S DO IT AGAIN.
OWW, I THINK I'VE HURT MY GLUTEUS MAXIMUS.
DOES ANYBODY HAVE A BANDAGE?

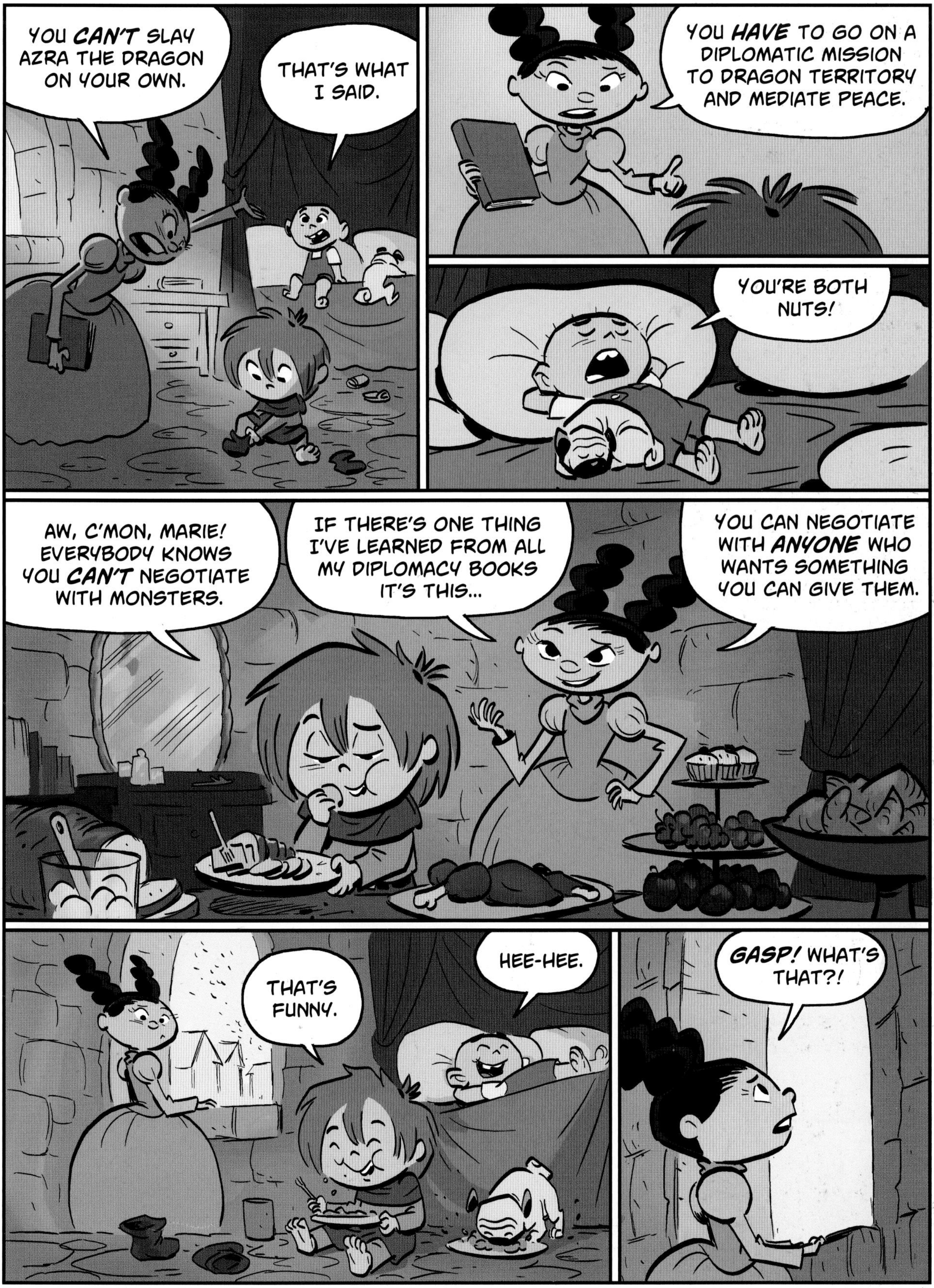
YOU ***CAN'T*** SLAY AZRA THE DRAGON ON YOUR OWN.
THAT'S WHAT I SAID.
YOU ***HAVE*** TO GO ON A DIPLOMATIC MISSION TO DRAGON TERRITORY AND MEDIATE PEACE.
YOU'RE BOTH NUTS!
AW, C'MON, MARIE! EVERYBODY KNOWS YOU ***CAN'T*** NEGOTIATE WITH MONSTERS.
IF THERE'S ONE THING I'VE LEARNED FROM ALL MY DIPLOMACY BOOKS IT'S THIS...
YOU CAN NEGOTIATE WITH ***ANYONE*** WHO WANTS SOMETHING YOU CAN GIVE THEM.
THAT'S FUNNY.
HEE-HEE.
GASP! WHAT'S THAT?!

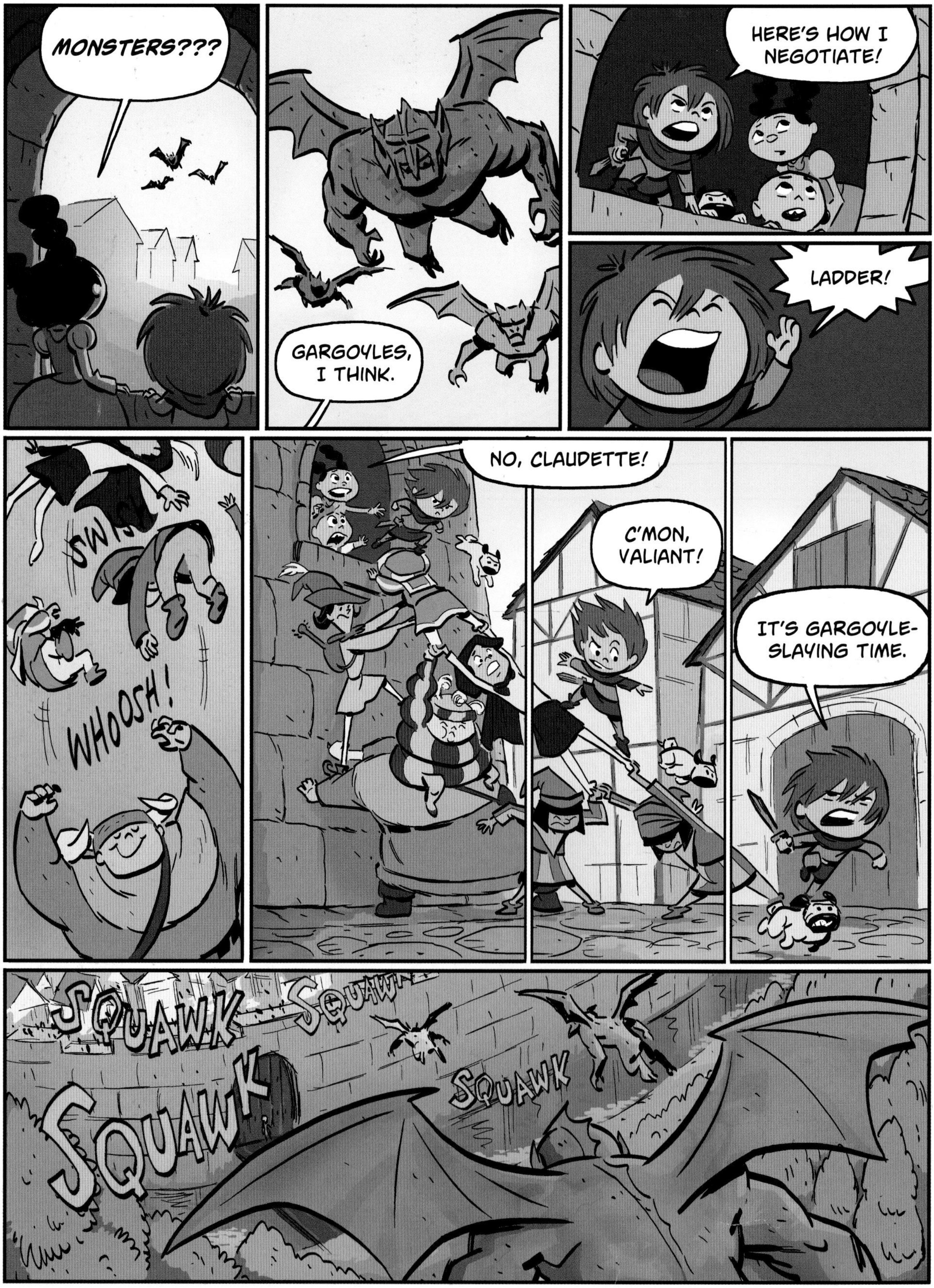
MONSTERS???
GARGOYLES, I THINK.
HERE'S HOW I NEGOTIATE!
LADDER!
SWISH
WHOOSH!
NO, CLAUDETTE!
C'MON, VALIANT!
IT'S GARGOYLE-SLAYING TIME.
SQUAWK
SQUAWK
SQUAWK
SQUAWK

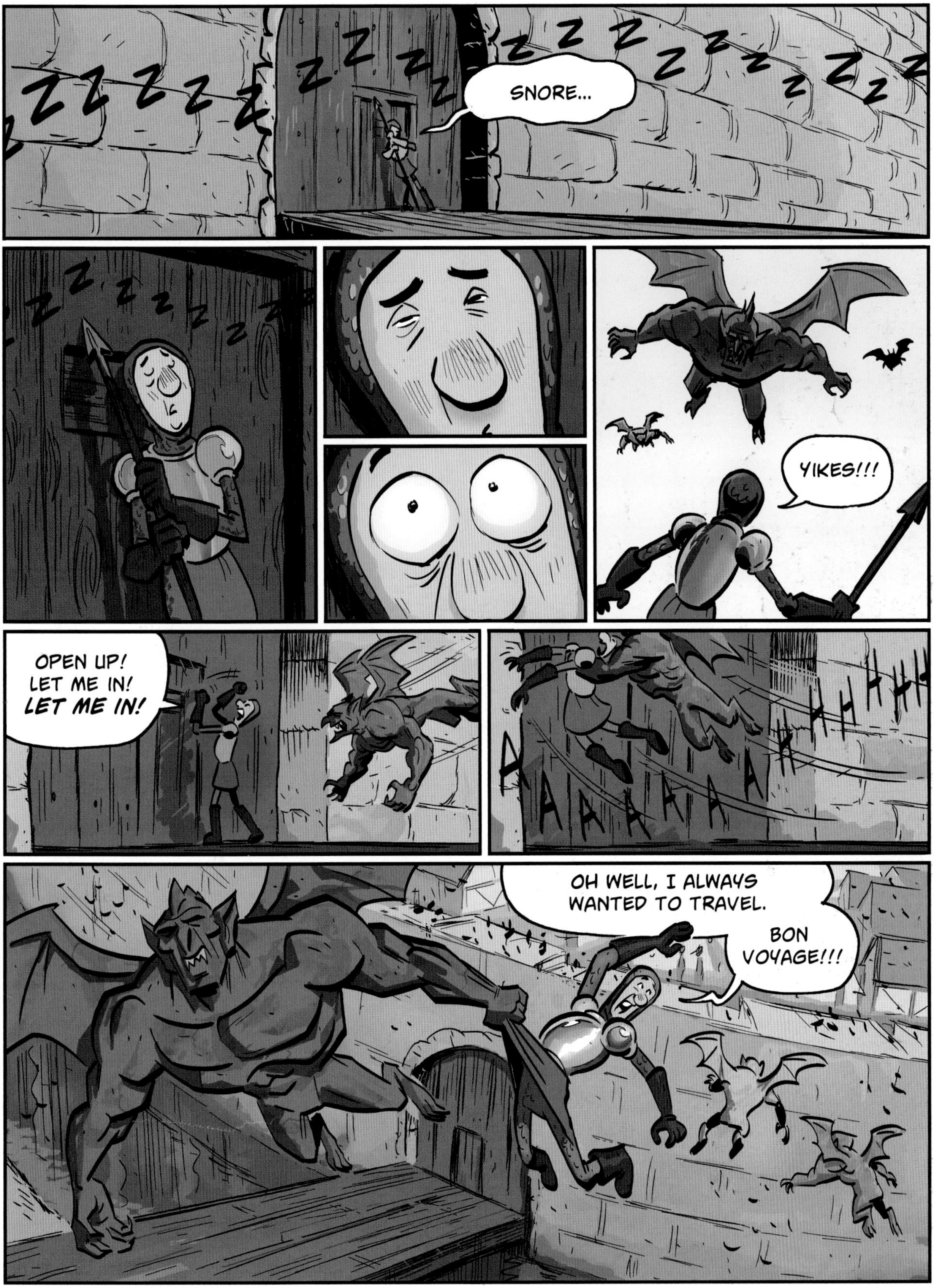
SNORE...
YIKES!!!
OPEN UP!
LET ME IN!
LET ME IN!
OH WELL, I ALWAYS WANTED TO TRAVEL.
BON VOYAGE!!!

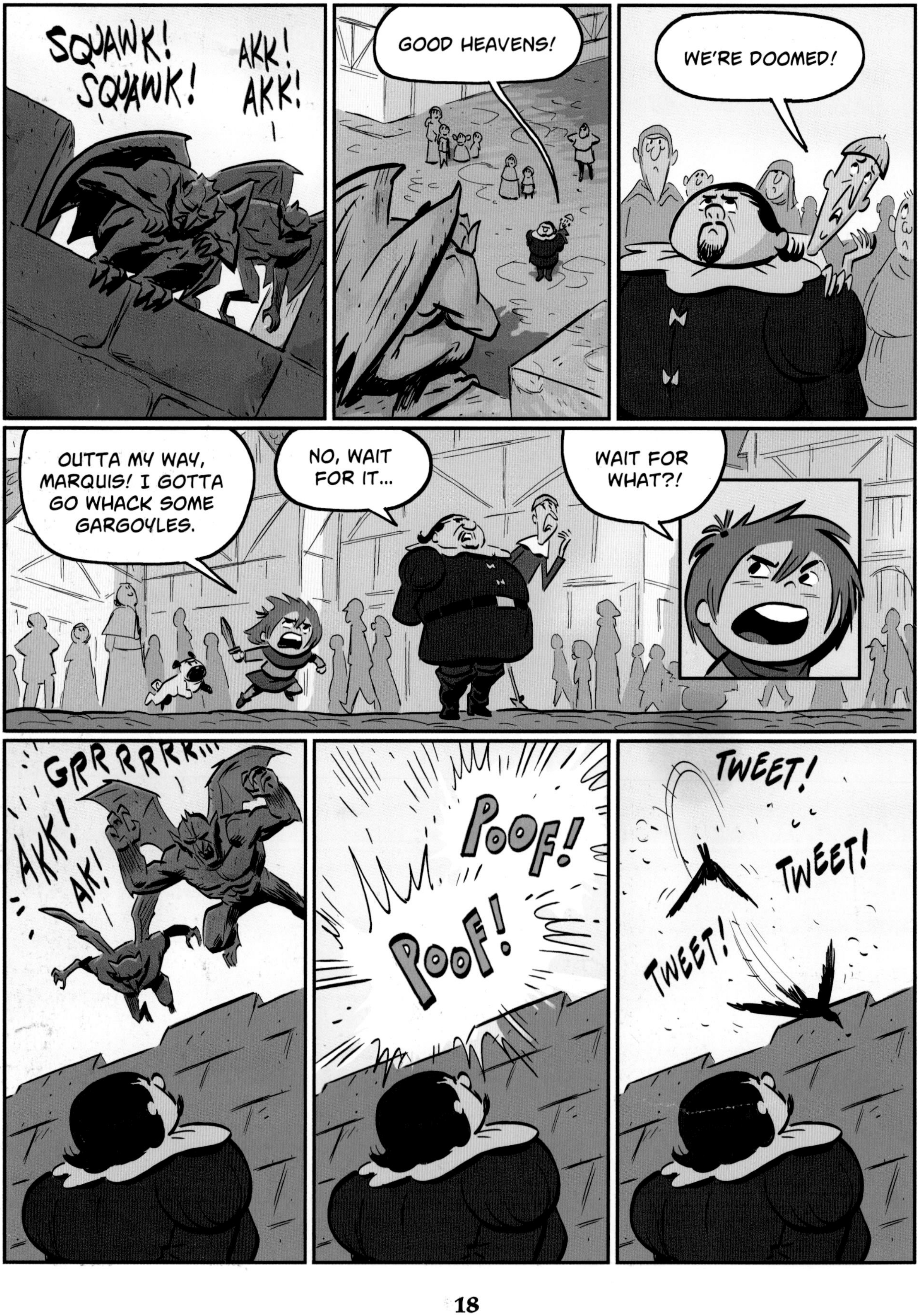
SQUAWK! SQUAWK!
AKK! AKK!
GOOD HEAVENS!
WE'RE DOOMED!
OUTTA MY WAY, MARQUIS! I GOTTA GO WHACK SOME GARGOYLES.
NO, WAIT FOR IT...
WAIT FOR WHAT?!
GRRRRRK!!!
AKK! AK!
POOF!
POOF!
TWEET!
TWEET!
TWEET!

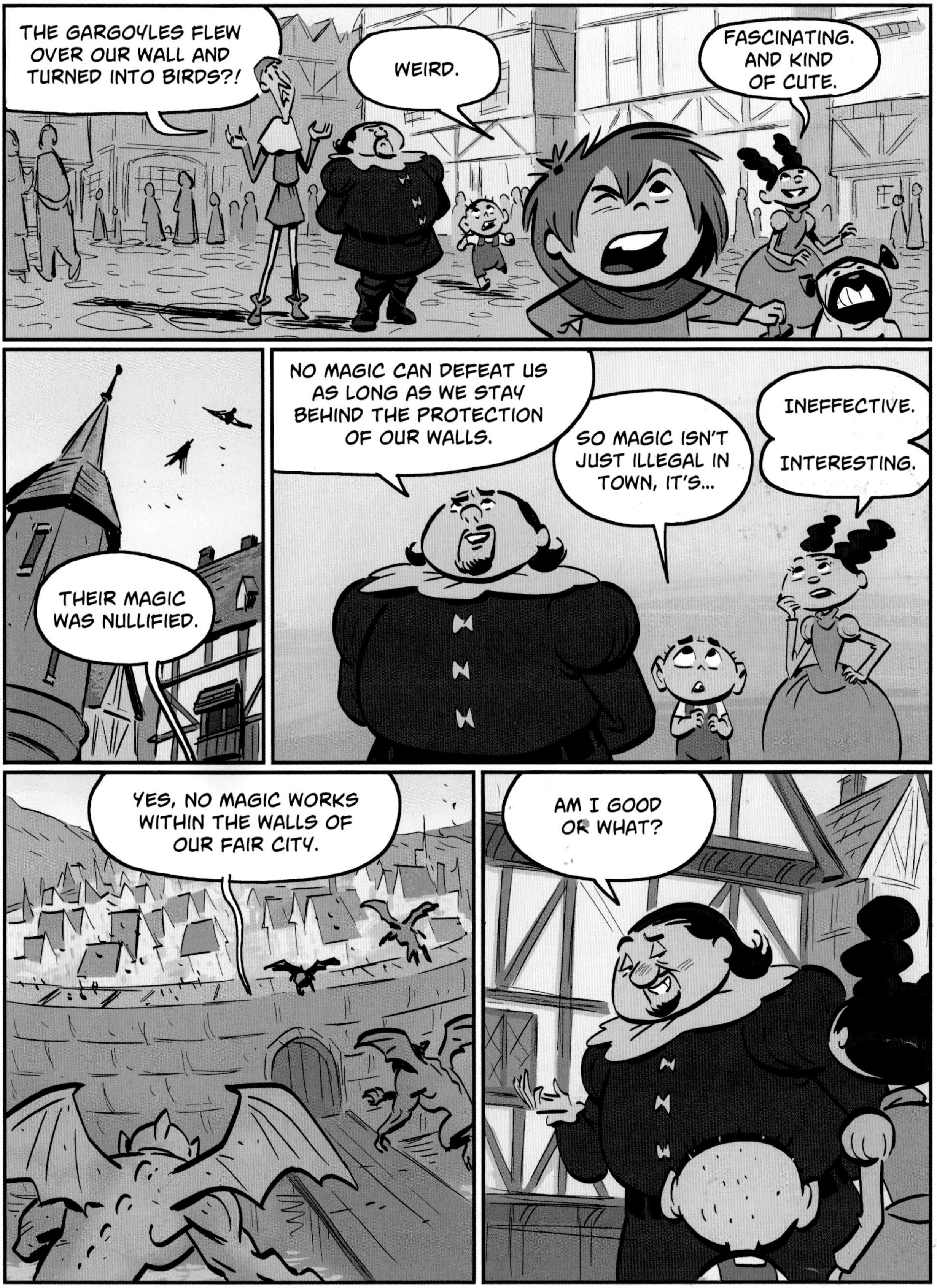
THE GARGOYLES FLEW OVER OUR WALL AND TURNED INTO BIRDS?!
WEIRD.
FASCINATING. AND KIND OF CUTE.
THEIR MAGIC WAS NULLIFIED.
NO MAGIC CAN DEFEAT US AS LONG AS WE STAY BEHIND THE PROTECTION OF OUR WALLS.
SO MAGIC ISN'T JUST ILLEGAL IN TOWN, IT'S...
INEFFECTIVE.
INTERESTING.
YES, NO MAGIC WORKS WITHIN THE WALLS OF OUR FAIR CITY.
AM I GOOD OR WHAT?

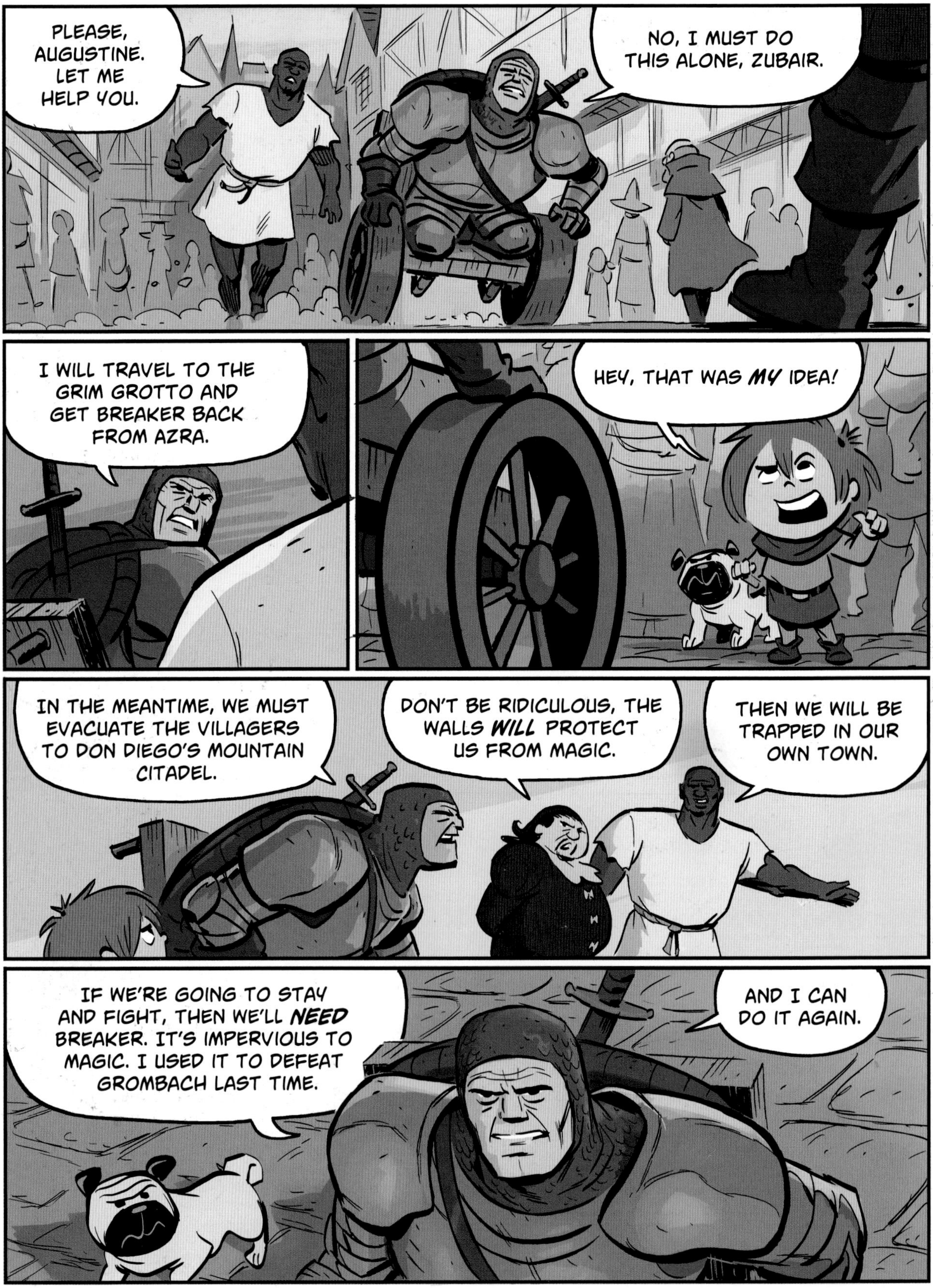
PLEASE, AUGUSTINE. LET ME HELP YOU.
NO, I MUST DO THIS ALONE, ZUBAIR.
I WILL TRAVEL TO THE GRIM GROTTO AND GET BREAKER BACK FROM AZRA.
HEY, THAT WAS MY IDEA!
IN THE MEANTIME, WE MUST EVACUATE THE VILLAGERS TO DON DIEGO'S MOUNTAIN CITADEL.
DON'T BE RIDICULOUS, THE WALLS WILL PROTECT US FROM MAGIC.
THEN WE WILL BE TRAPPED IN OUR OWN TOWN.
IF WE'RE GOING TO STAY AND FIGHT, THEN WE'LL NEED BREAKER. IT'S IMPERVIOUS TO MAGIC. I USED IT TO DEFEAT GROMBACH LAST TIME.
AND I CAN DO IT AGAIN.

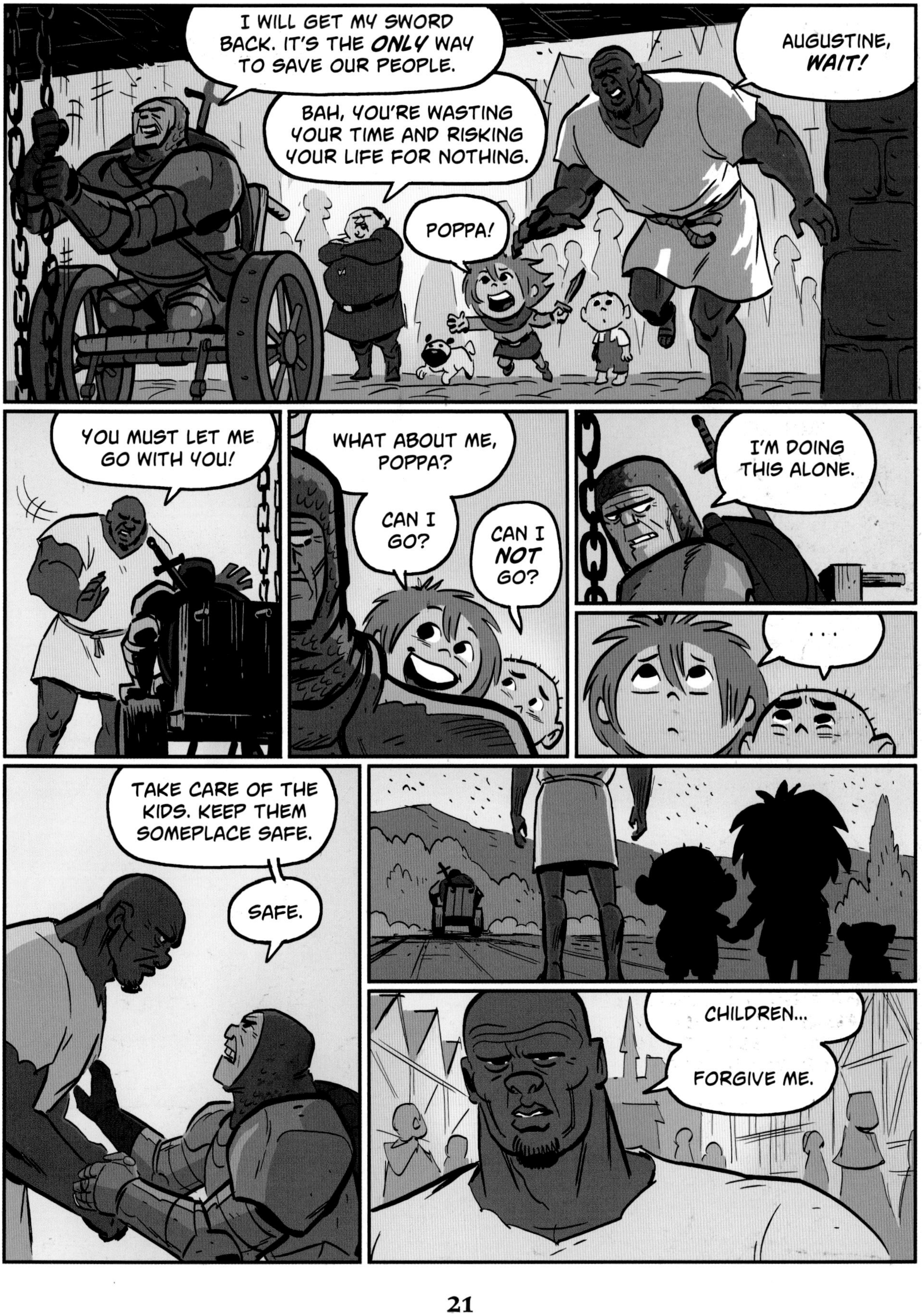
I WILL GET MY SWORD BACK. IT'S THE ONLY WAY TO SAVE OUR PEOPLE.
BAH, YOU'RE WASTING YOUR TIME AND RISKING YOUR LIFE FOR NOTHING.
AUGUSTINE, WAIT!
POPPA!
YOU MUST LET ME GO WITH YOU!
WHAT ABOUT ME, POPPA?
CAN I GO?
CAN I NOT GO?
I'M DOING THIS ALONE.
...
TAKE CARE OF THE KIDS. KEEP THEM SOMEPLACE SAFE.
SAFE.
CHILDREN...
FORGIVE ME.

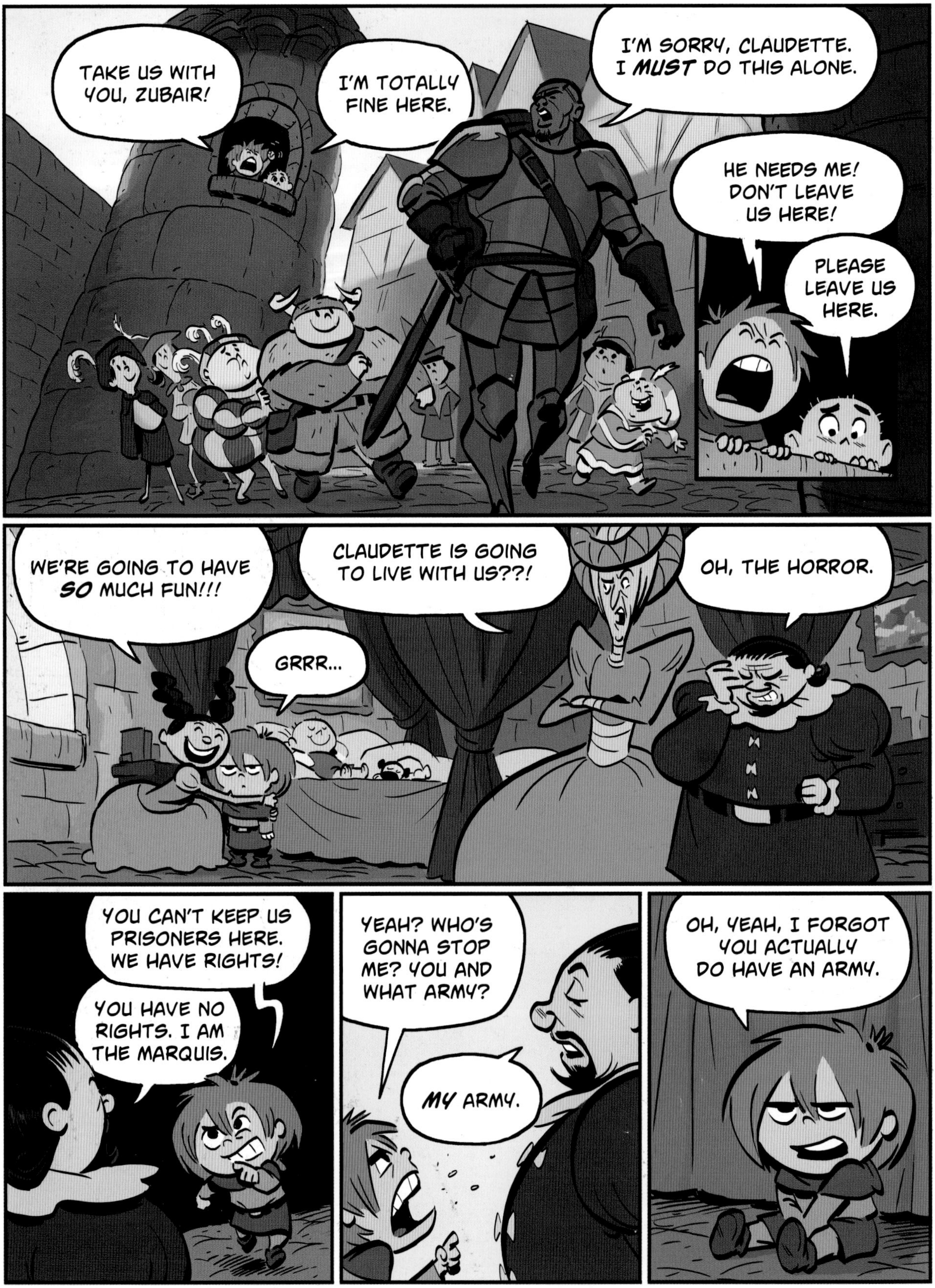
TAKE US WITH YOU, ZUBAIR!
I'M TOTALLY FINE HERE.
I'M SORRY, CLAUDETTE. I *MUST* DO THIS ALONE.
HE NEEDS ME! DON'T LEAVE US HERE!
PLEASE LEAVE US HERE.
WE'RE GOING TO HAVE *SO* MUCH FUN!!!
GRRR...
CLAUDETTE IS GOING TO LIVE WITH US??!
OH, THE HORROR.
YOU CAN'T KEEP US PRISONERS HERE. WE HAVE RIGHTS!
YOU HAVE NO RIGHTS. I AM THE MARQUIS.
YEAH? WHO'S GONNA STOP ME? YOU AND WHAT ARMY?
MY ARMY.
OH, YEAH, I FORGOT YOU ACTUALLY DO HAVE AN ARMY.

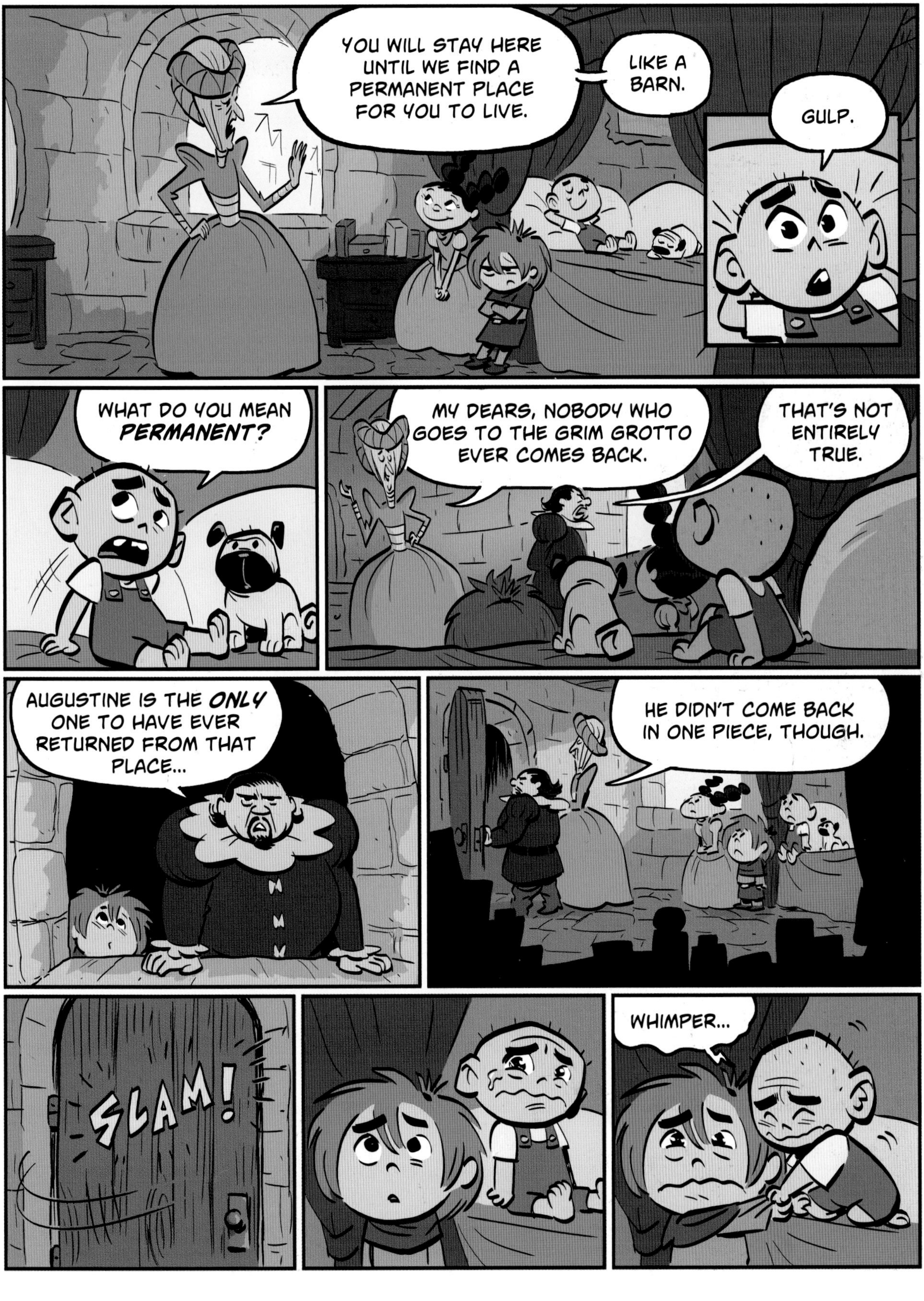
YOU WILL STAY HERE UNTIL WE FIND A PERMANENT PLACE FOR YOU TO LIVE.
LIKE A BARN.
GULP.
WHAT DO YOU MEAN *PERMANENT*?
MY DEARS, NOBODY WHO GOES TO THE GRIM GROTTO EVER COMES BACK.
THAT'S NOT ENTIRELY TRUE.
AUGUSTINE IS THE *ONLY* ONE TO HAVE EVER RETURNED FROM THAT PLACE...
HE DIDN'T COME BACK IN ONE PIECE, THOUGH.
SLAM!
WHIMPER...

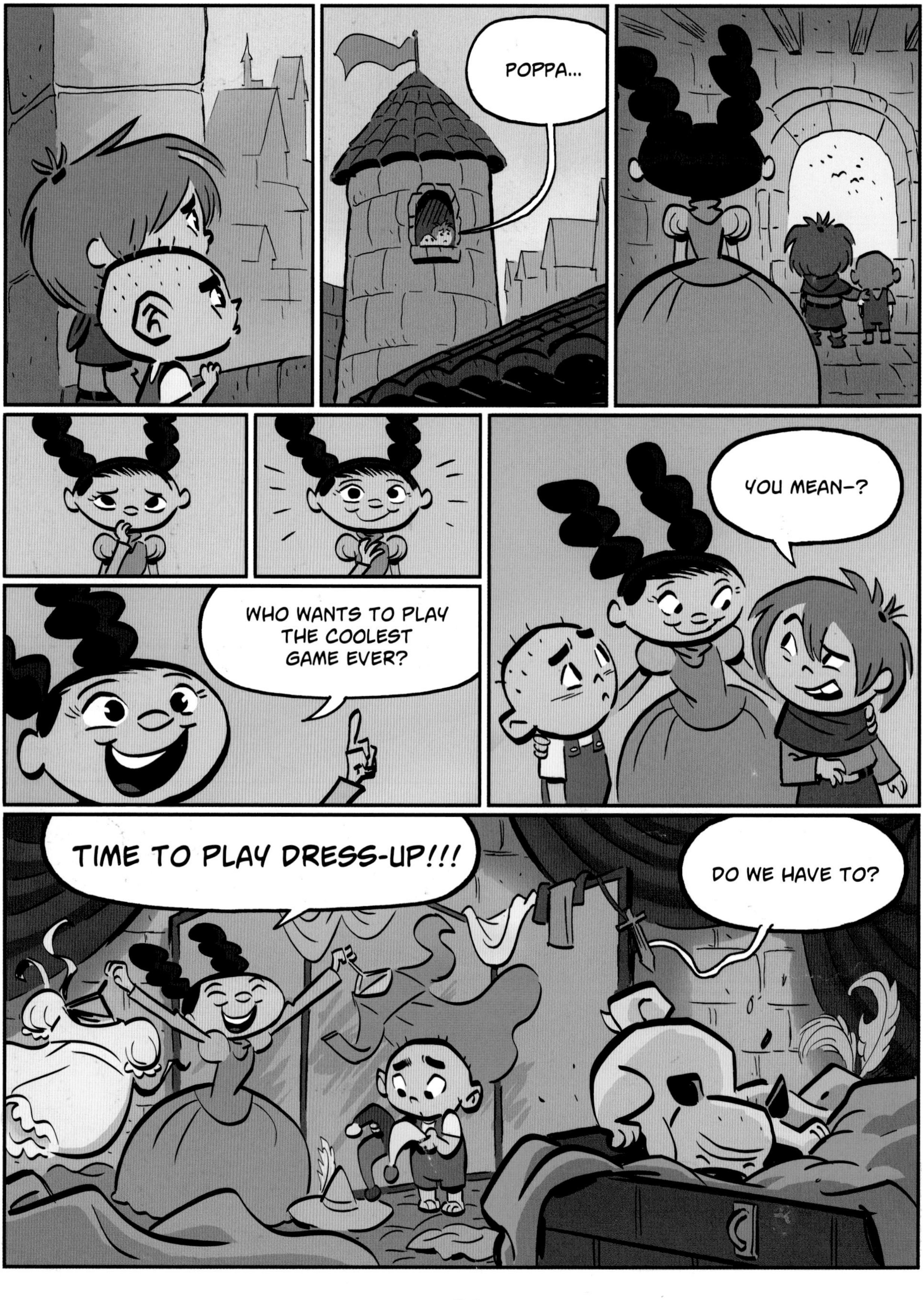
POPPA...
YOU MEAN–?
WHO WANTS TO PLAY THE COOLEST GAME EVER?
TIME TO PLAY DRESS-UP!!!
DO WE HAVE TO?

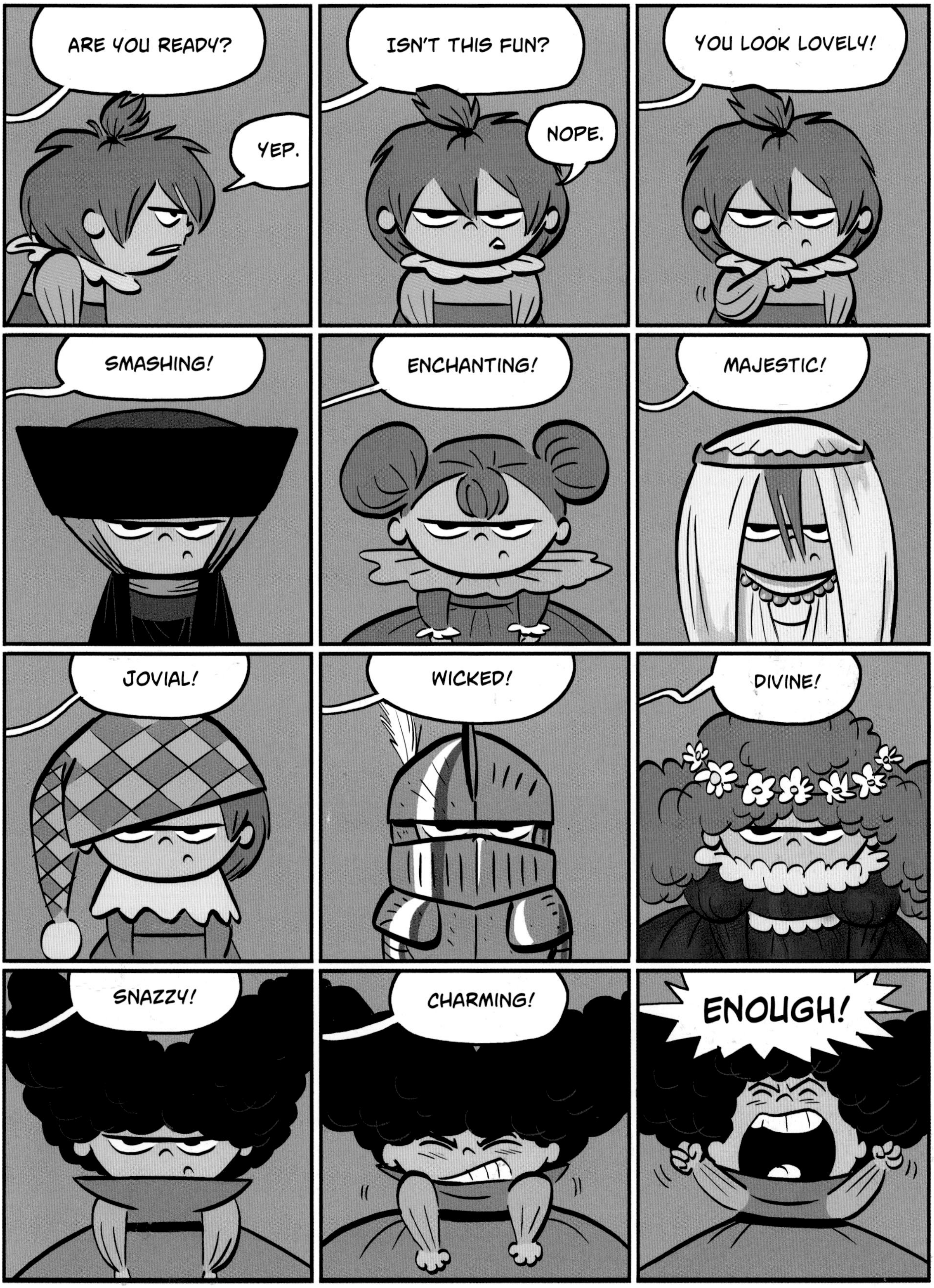
ARE YOU READY?
YEP.
ISN'T THIS FUN?
NOPE.
YOU LOOK LOVELY!
SMASHING!
ENCHANTING!
MAJESTIC!
JOVIAL!
WICKED!
DIVINE!
SNAZZY!
CHARMING!
ENOUGH!

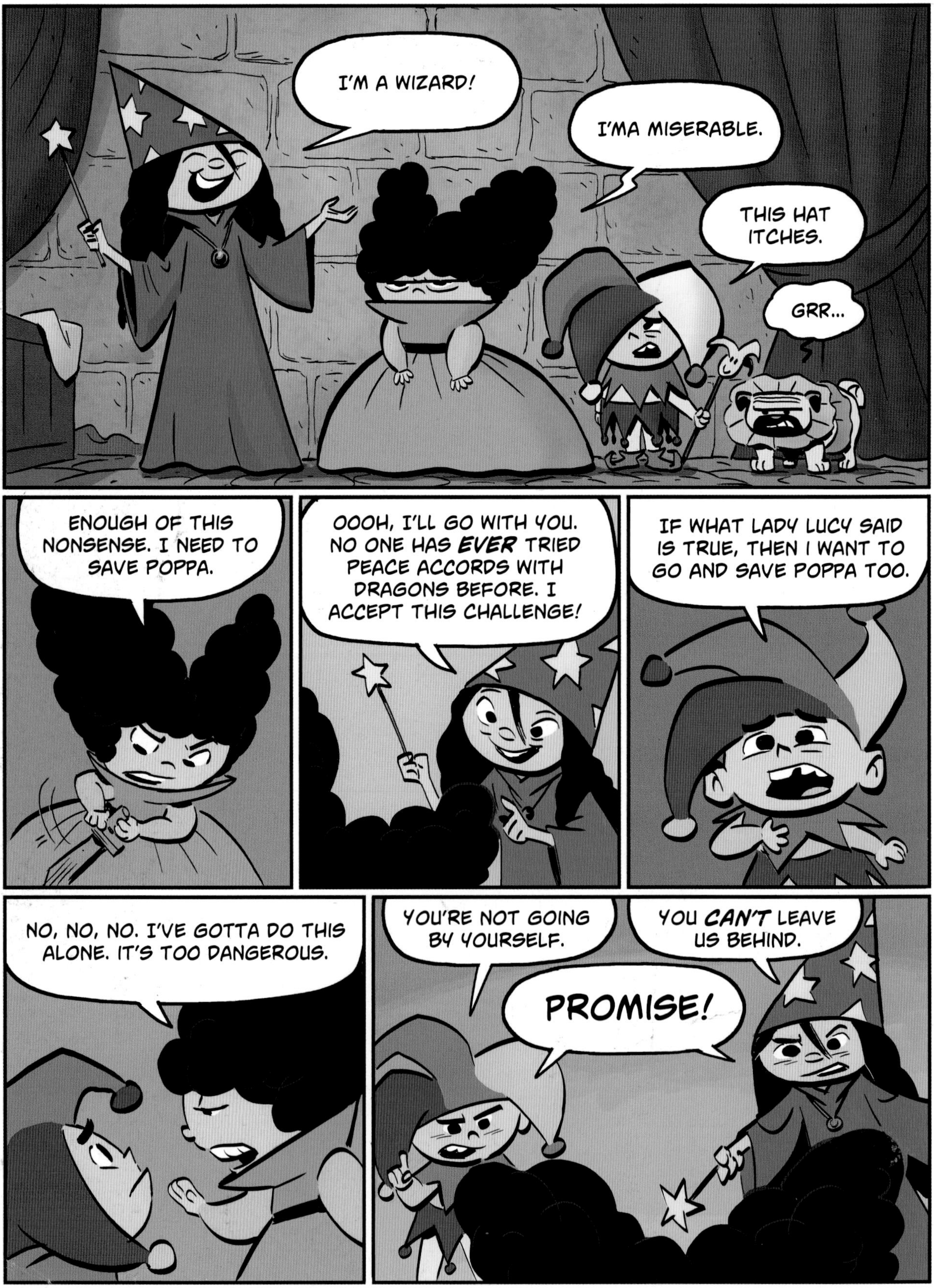
I'M A WIZARD!
I'MA MISERABLE.
THIS HAT ITCHES.
GRR...
ENOUGH OF THIS NONSENSE. I NEED TO SAVE POPPA.
OOOH, I'LL GO WITH YOU. NO ONE HAS **EVER** TRIED PEACE ACCORDS WITH DRAGONS BEFORE. I ACCEPT THIS CHALLENGE!
IF WHAT LADY LUCY SAID IS TRUE, THEN I WANT TO GO AND SAVE POPPA TOO.
NO, NO, NO. I'VE GOTTA DO THIS ALONE. IT'S TOO DANGEROUS.
YOU'RE NOT GOING BY YOURSELF.
YOU **CAN'T** LEAVE US BEHIND.
PROMISE!

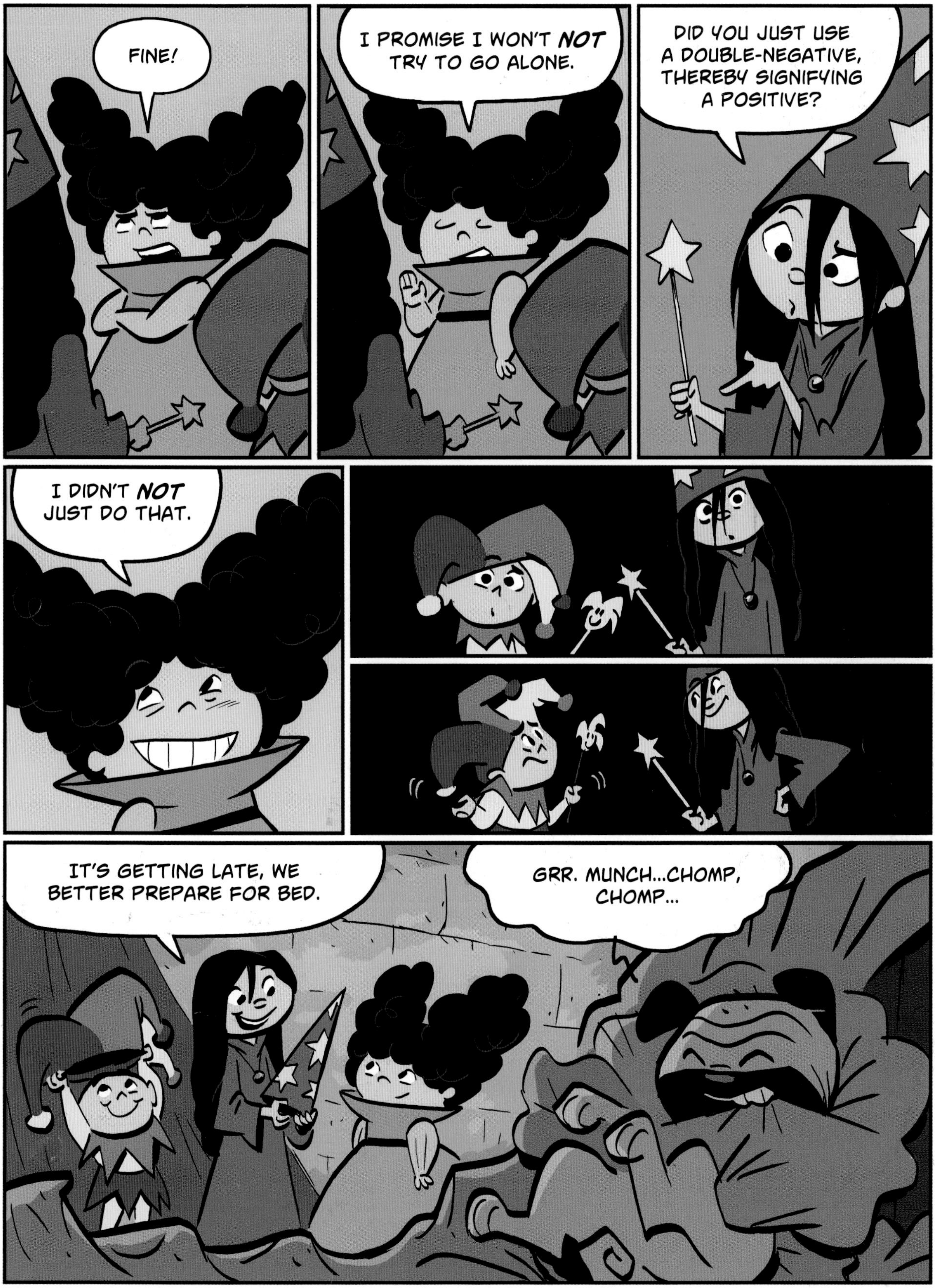
FINE!
I PROMISE I WON'T ***NOT*** TRY TO GO ALONE.
DID YOU JUST USE A DOUBLE-NEGATIVE, THEREBY SIGNIFYING A POSITIVE?
I DIDN'T ***NOT*** JUST DO THAT.
IT'S GETTING LATE, WE BETTER PREPARE FOR BED.
GRR. MUNCH...CHOMP, CHOMP...

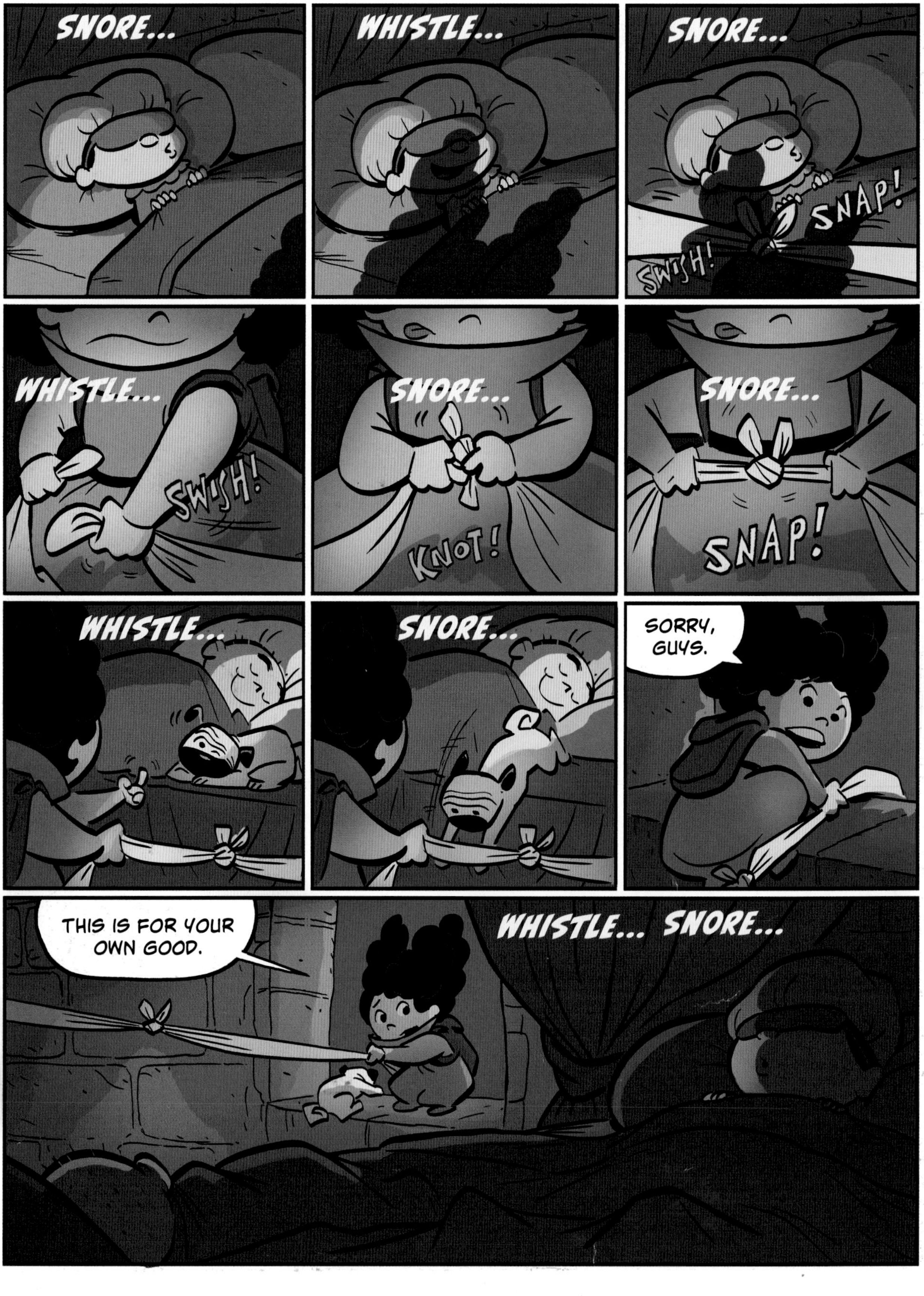
SNORE...
WHISTLE...
SNORE...
SNAP!
SWISH!
WHISTLE...
SWISH!
SNORE...
KNOT!
SNORE...
SNAP!
WHISTLE...
SNORE...
SORRY, GUYS.
THIS IS FOR YOUR OWN GOOD.
WHISTLE... SNORE...

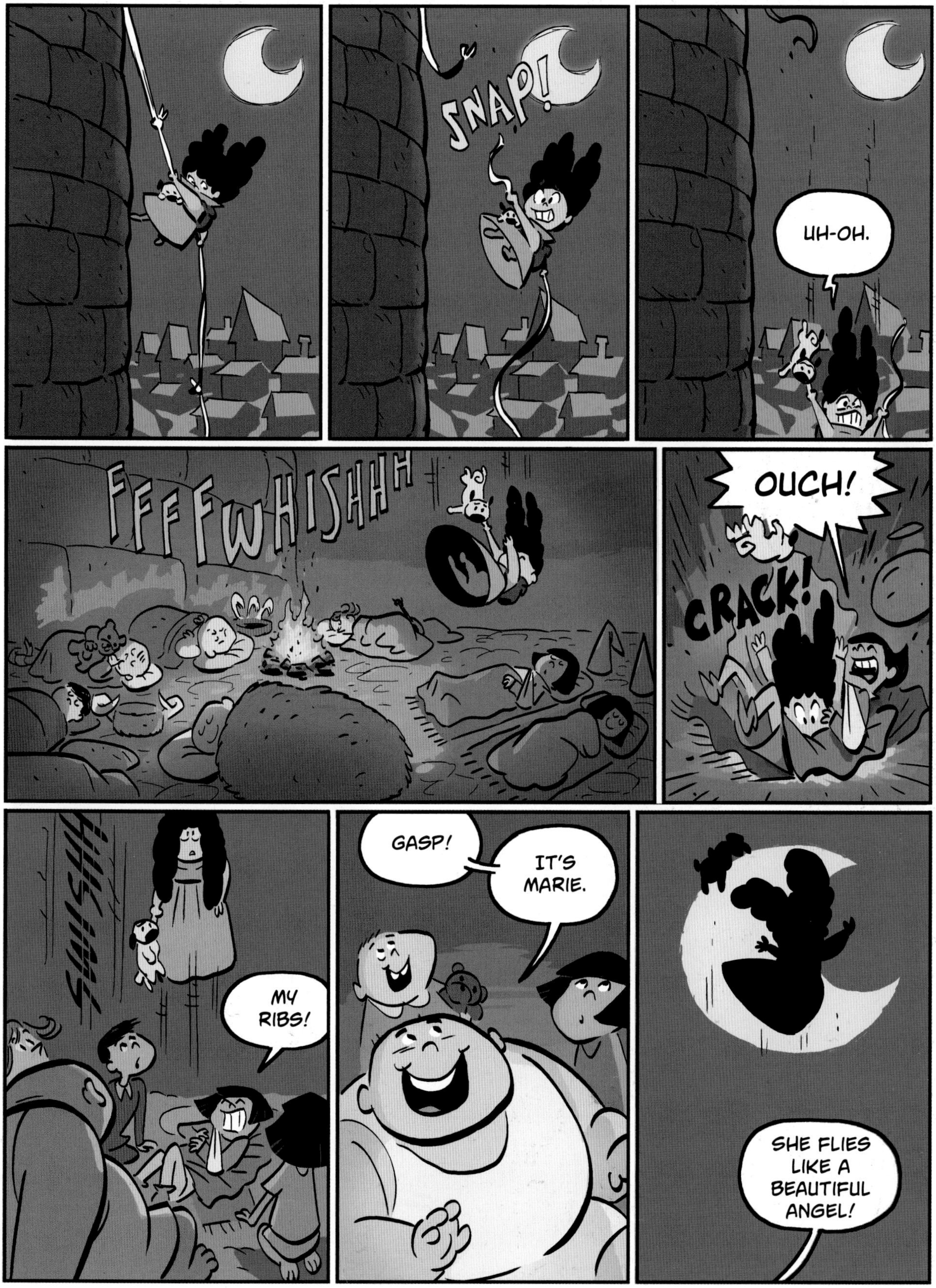
SNAP!
UH-OH.
FFFFWHISHHH
OUCH!
CRACK!
SWISHHH
MY RIBS!
GASP!
IT'S MARIE.
SHE FLIES LIKE A BEAUTIFUL ANGEL!

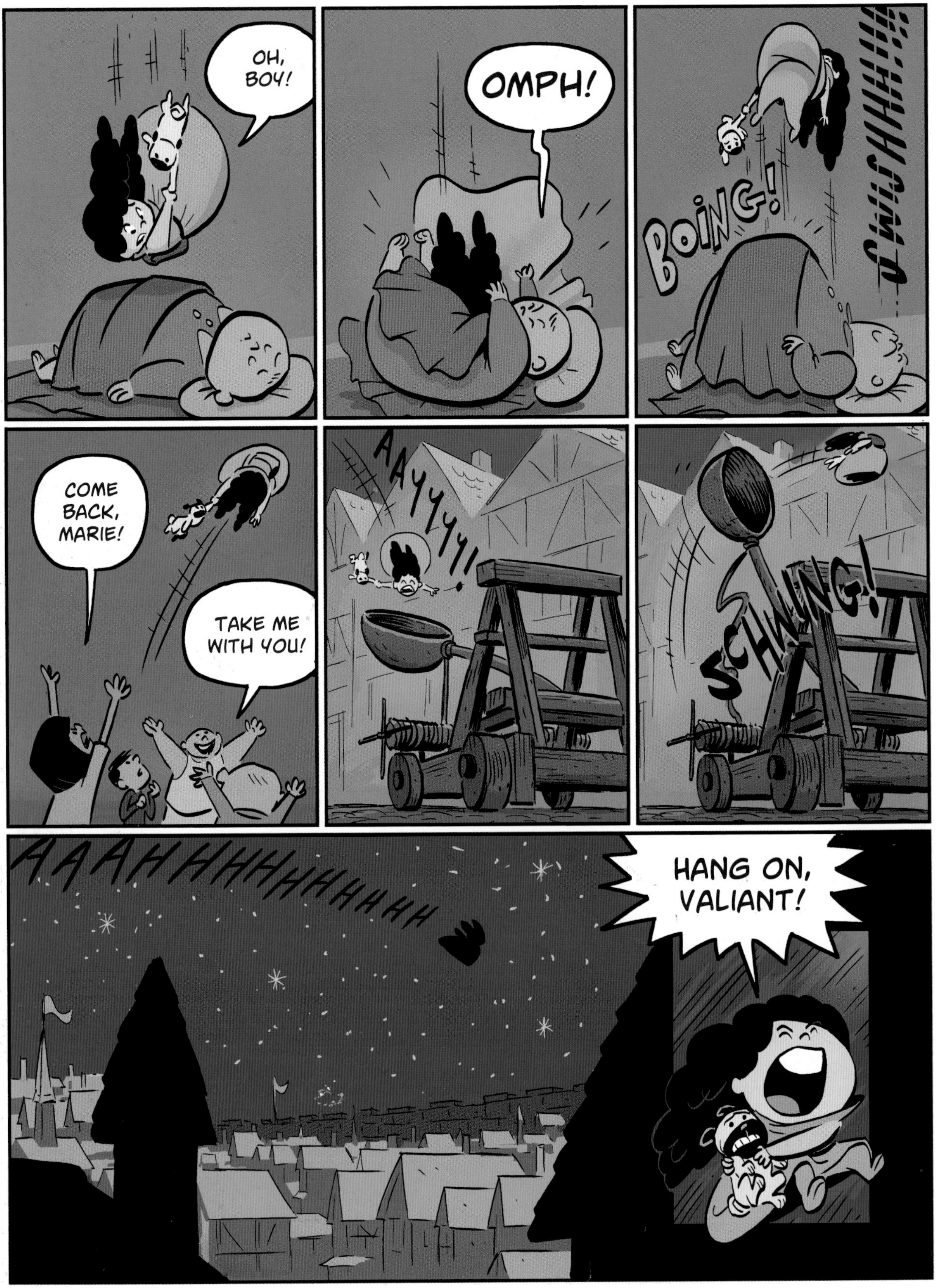
OH, BOY!
OMPH!
BOING!
SWISHHHHH!!!!
COME BACK, MARIE!
TAKE ME WITH YOU!
AAYYYY!!
SCHWING!
AAAHHHHHHHHHHHH
HANG ON, VALIANT!

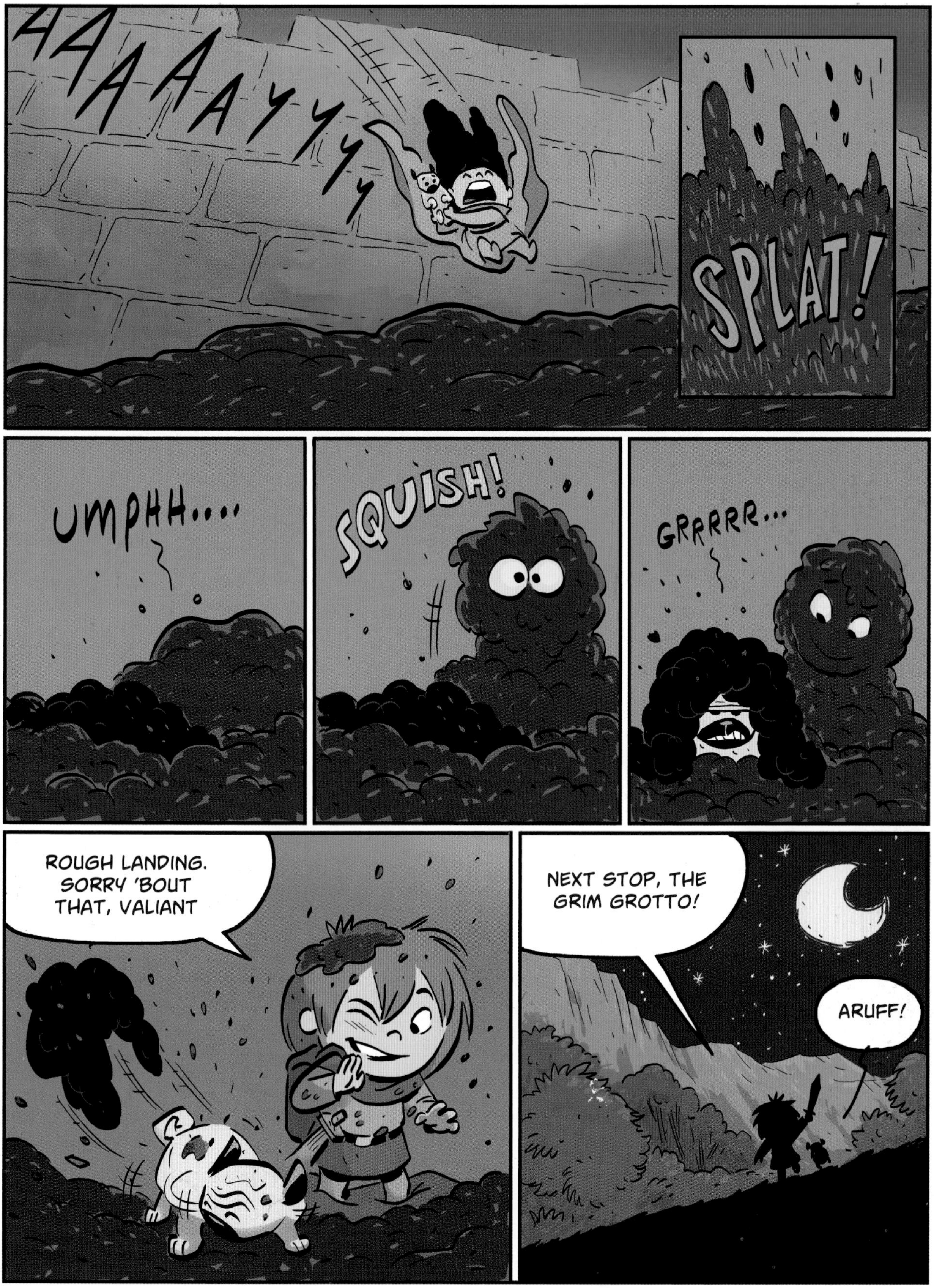
AAAAAAYYYYY
SPLAT!
UMPHH....
SQUISH!
GRRRRR...
ROUGH LANDING. SORRY 'BOUT THAT, VALIANT
NEXT STOP, THE GRIM GROTTO!
ARUFF!

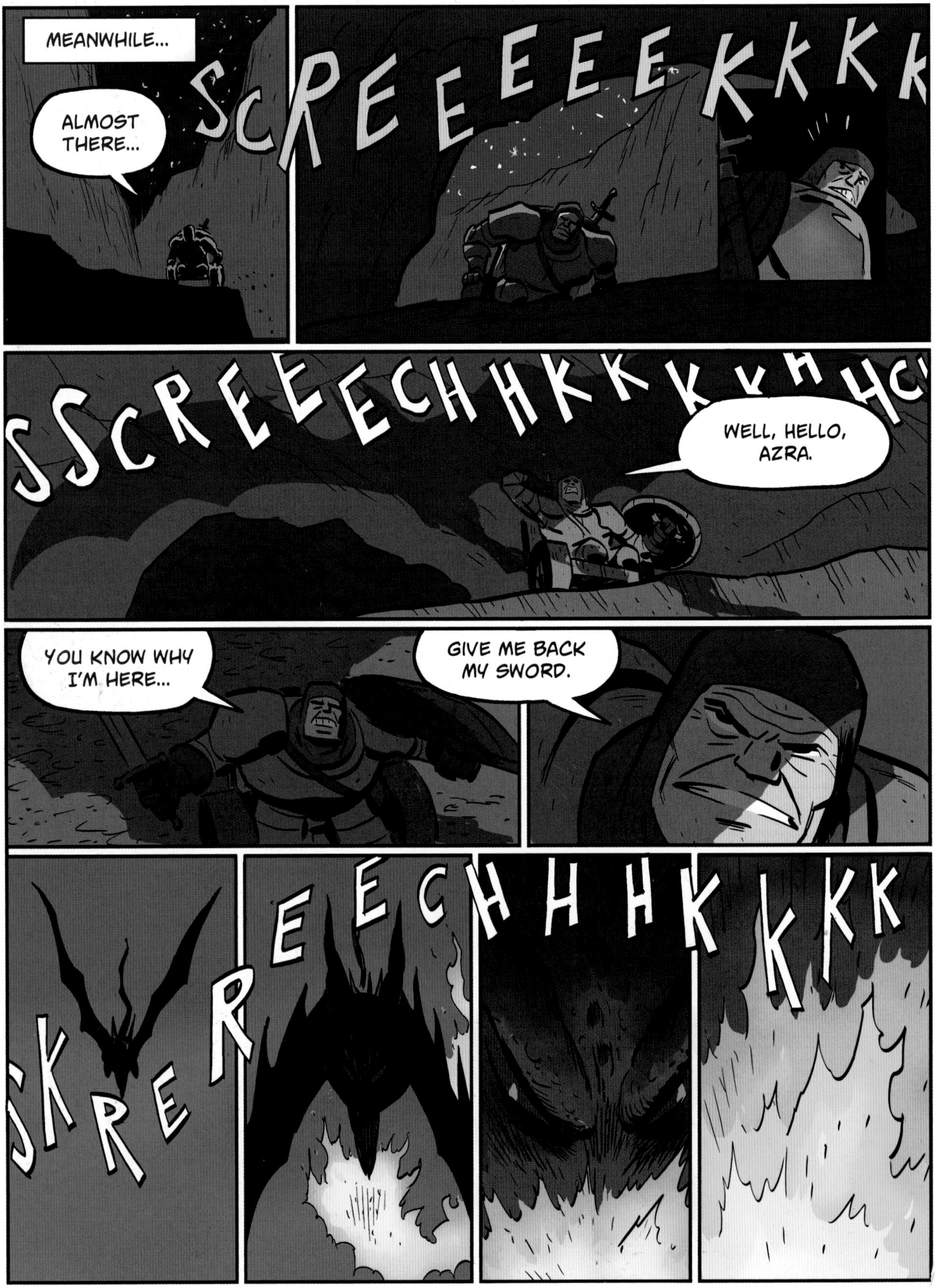
MEANWHILE...
ALMOST THERE...
SCREEEEEEKKKK
SSCREEECHHKKKKHHCH
WELL, HELLO, AZRA.
YOU KNOW WHY I'M HERE...
GIVE ME BACK MY SWORD.
SKREREEECHHHKKKK

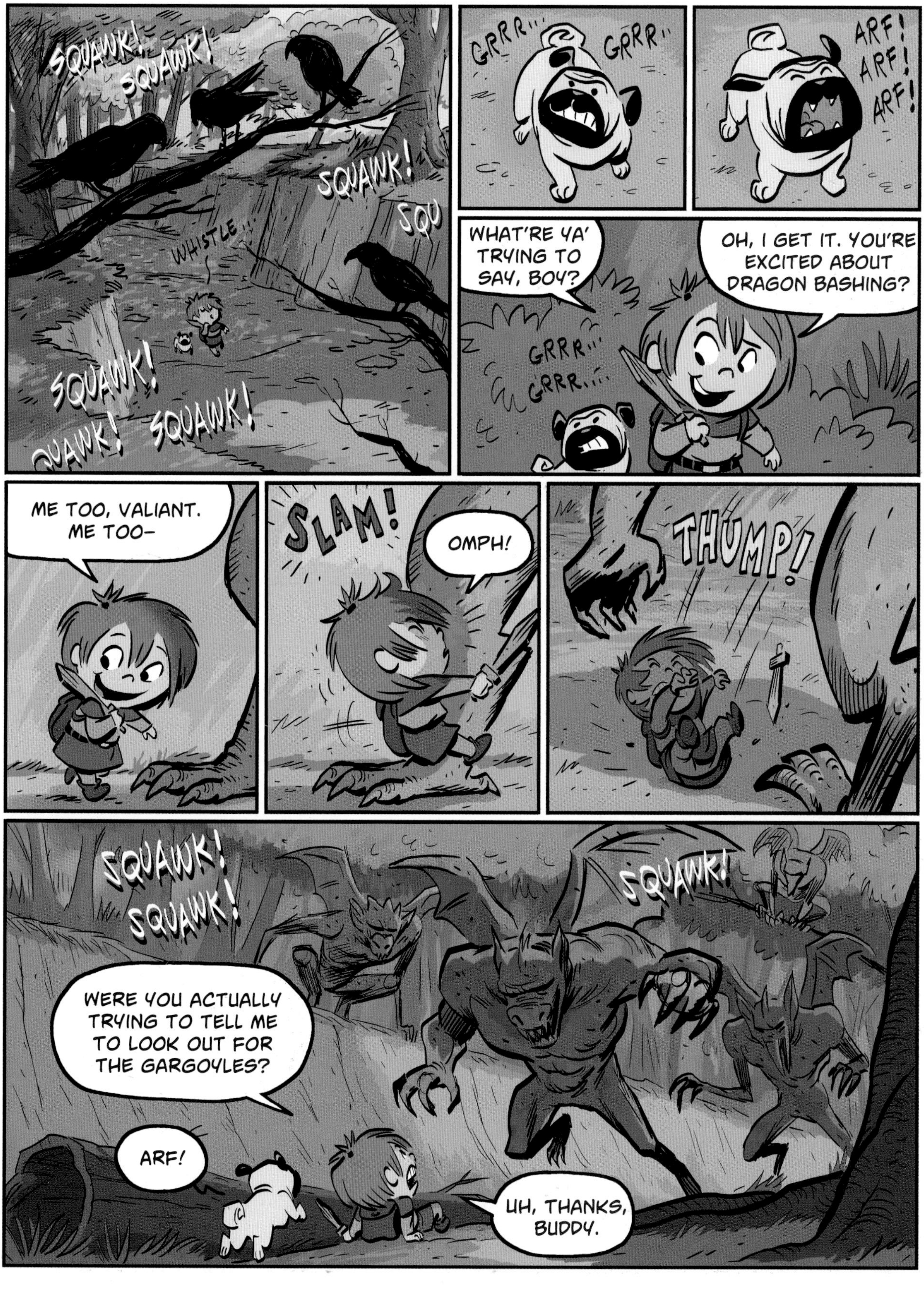
SQUAWK!
SQUAWK!
SQUAWK!
SQU
WHISTLE...
SQUAWK!
SQUAWK!
SQUAWK!
GRRR...
GRRR...
ARF!
ARF!
ARF!
WHAT'RE YA' TRYING TO SAY, BOY?
OH, I GET IT. YOU'RE EXCITED ABOUT DRAGON BASHING?
GRRR...
GRRR...
ME TOO, VALIANT. ME TOO–
SLAM!
OMPH!
THUMP!
SQUAWK!
SQUAWK!
SQUAWK!
WERE YOU ACTUALLY TRYING TO TELL ME TO LOOK OUT FOR THE GARGOYLES?
ARF!
UH, THANKS, BUDDY.

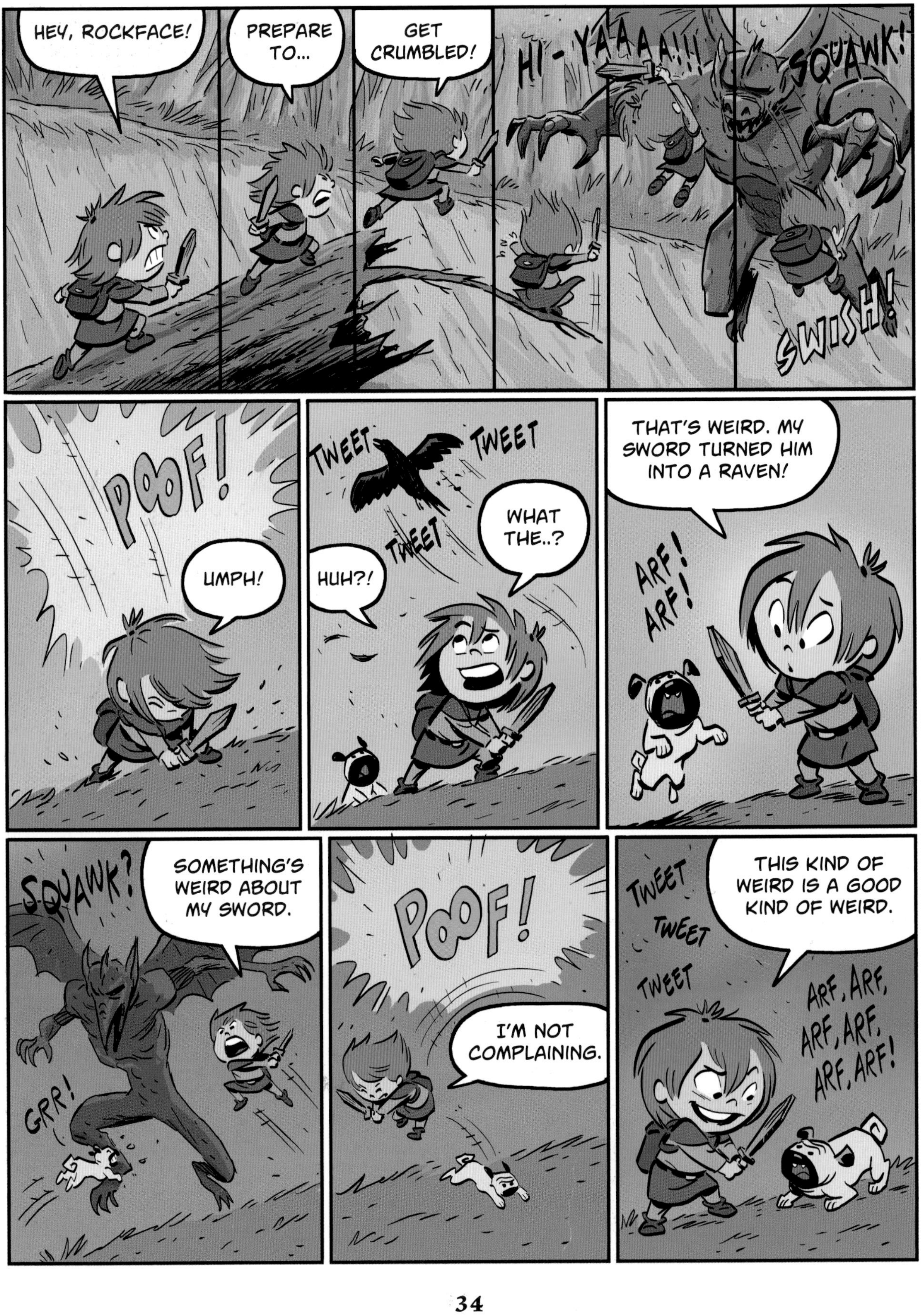
HEY, ROCKFACE!
PREPARE TO...
GET CRUMBLED!
HI - YAAAA!!!
SQUAWK!
SWISH!
POOF!
UMPH!
TWEET
TWEET
TWEET
WHAT THE..?
HUH?!
THAT'S WEIRD. MY SWORD TURNED HIM INTO A RAVEN!
ARF! ARF!
SQUAWK?
SOMETHING'S WEIRD ABOUT MY SWORD.
GRR!
POOF!
I'M NOT COMPLAINING.
TWEET
TWEET
TWEET
THIS KIND OF WEIRD IS A GOOD KIND OF WEIRD.
ARF, ARF, ARF, ARF, ARF, ARF!

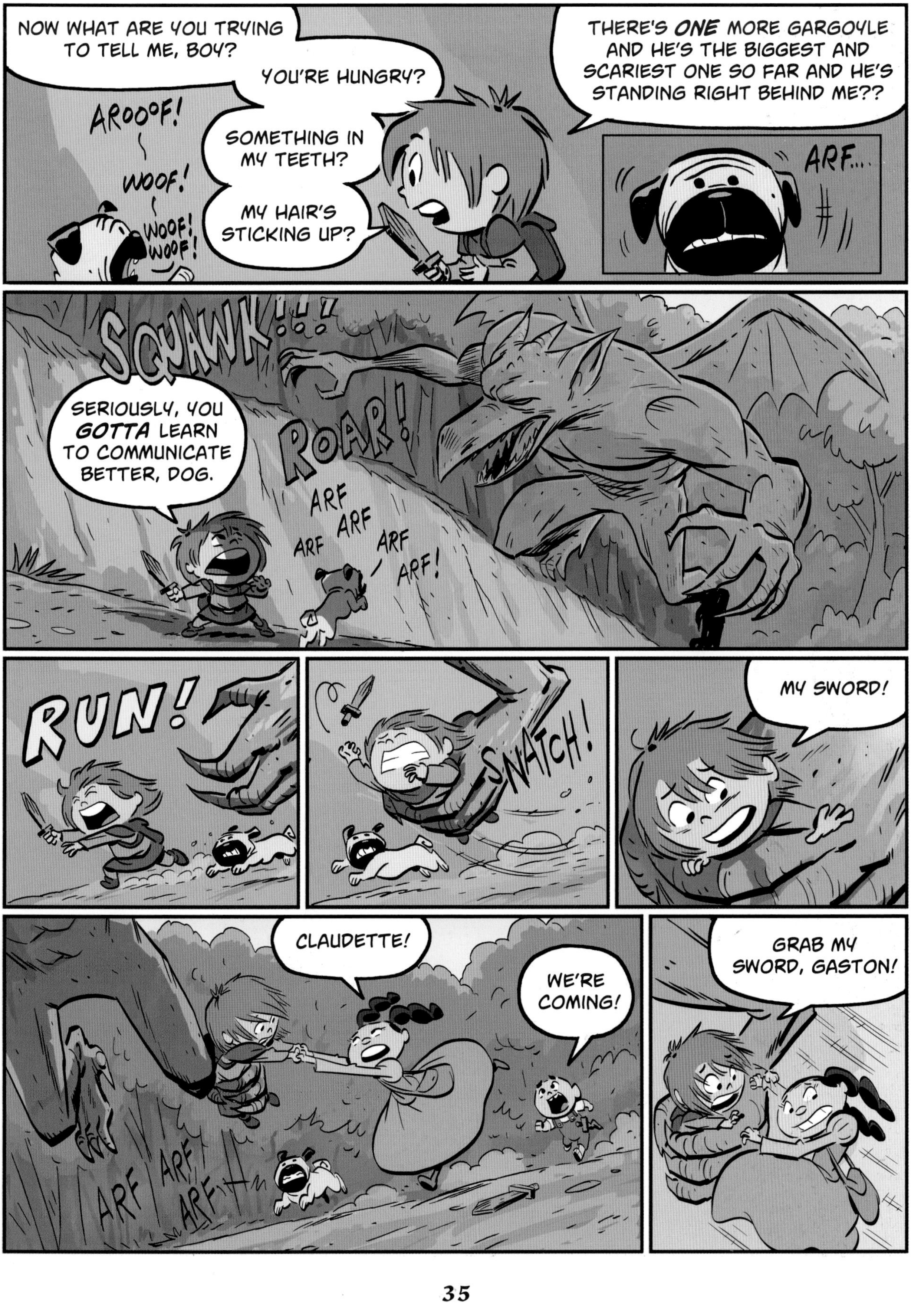

NOW WHAT ARE YOU TRYING TO TELL ME, BOY?
AROOOF!
WOOF!
WOOF! WOOF!
YOU'RE HUNGRY?
SOMETHING IN MY TEETH?
MY HAIR'S STICKING UP?
THERE'S ***ONE*** MORE GARGOYLE AND HE'S THE BIGGEST AND SCARIEST ONE SO FAR AND HE'S STANDING RIGHT BEHIND ME??
ARF...
SQUAWK!!!
SERIOUSLY, YOU ***GOTTA*** LEARN TO COMMUNICATE BETTER, DOG.
ROAR!
ARF ARF ARF ARF ARF!
RUN!
SNATCH!
MY SWORD!
CLAUDETTE!
WE'RE COMING!
ARF ARF ARF
GRAB MY SWORD, GASTON!

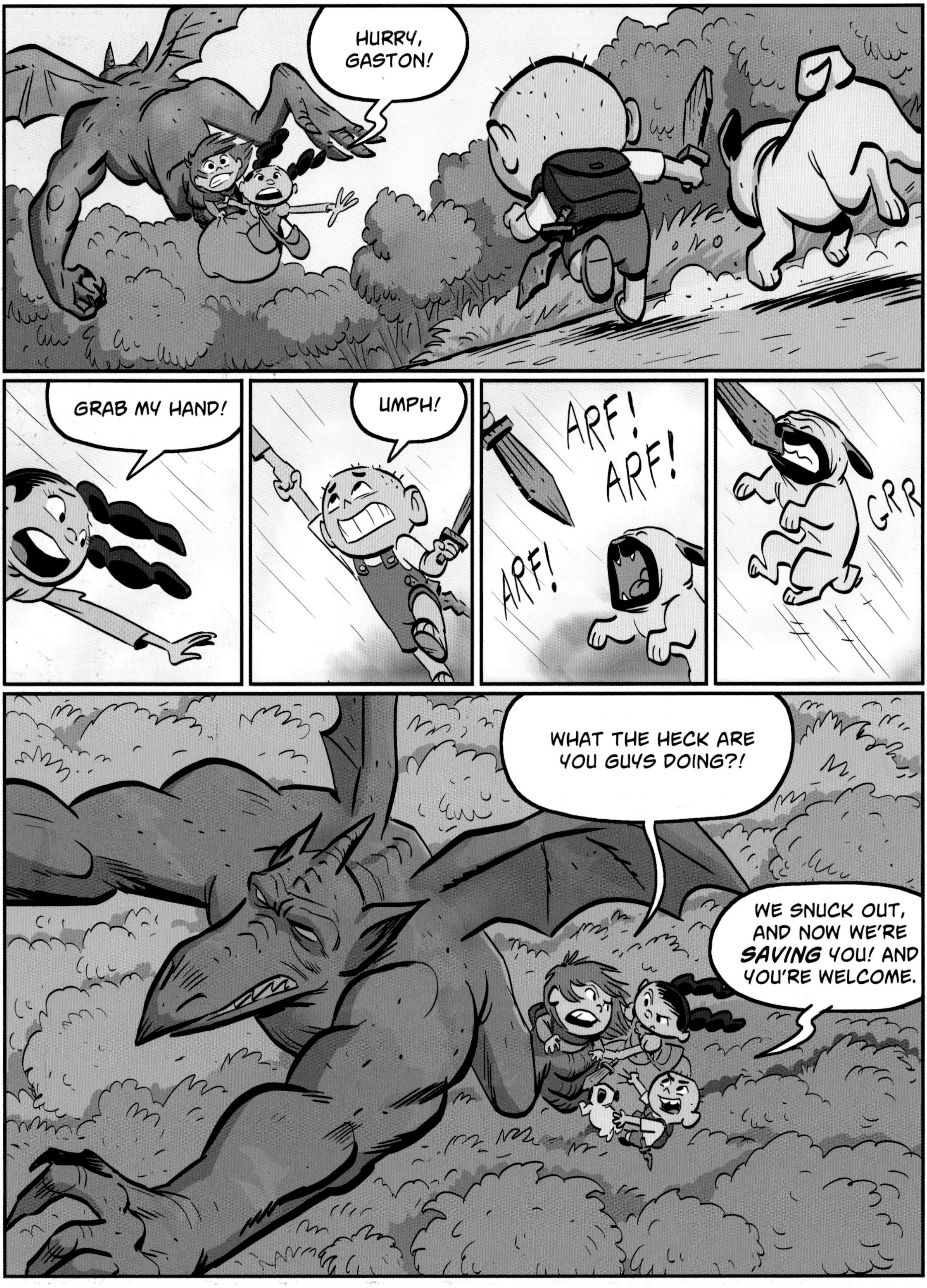
HURRY, GASTON!
GRAB MY HAND!
UMPH!
ARF! ARF!
ARF!
GRR
WHAT THE HECK ARE YOU GUYS DOING?!
WE SNUCK OUT, AND NOW WE'RE *SAVING* YOU! AND YOU'RE WELCOME.

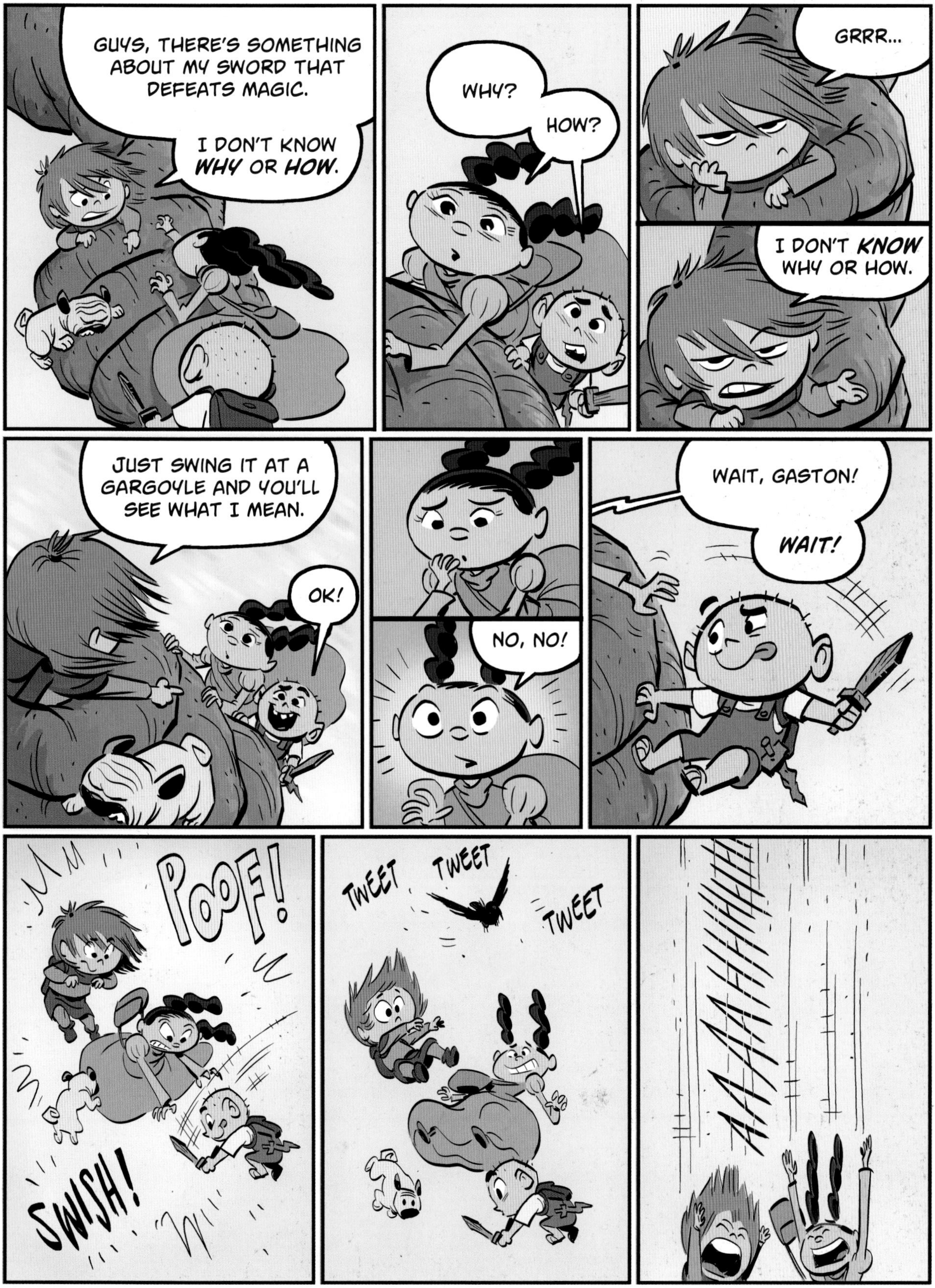
GUYS, THERE'S SOMETHING ABOUT MY SWORD THAT DEFEATS MAGIC.
I DON'T KNOW *WHY* OR *HOW*.
WHY?
HOW?
GRRR...
I DON'T *KNOW* WHY OR HOW.
JUST SWING IT AT A GARGOYLE AND YOU'LL SEE WHAT I MEAN.
OK!
NO, NO!
WAIT, GASTON!
WAIT!
POOF!
SWISH!
TWEET
TWEET
TWEET
AAAAHHHHH

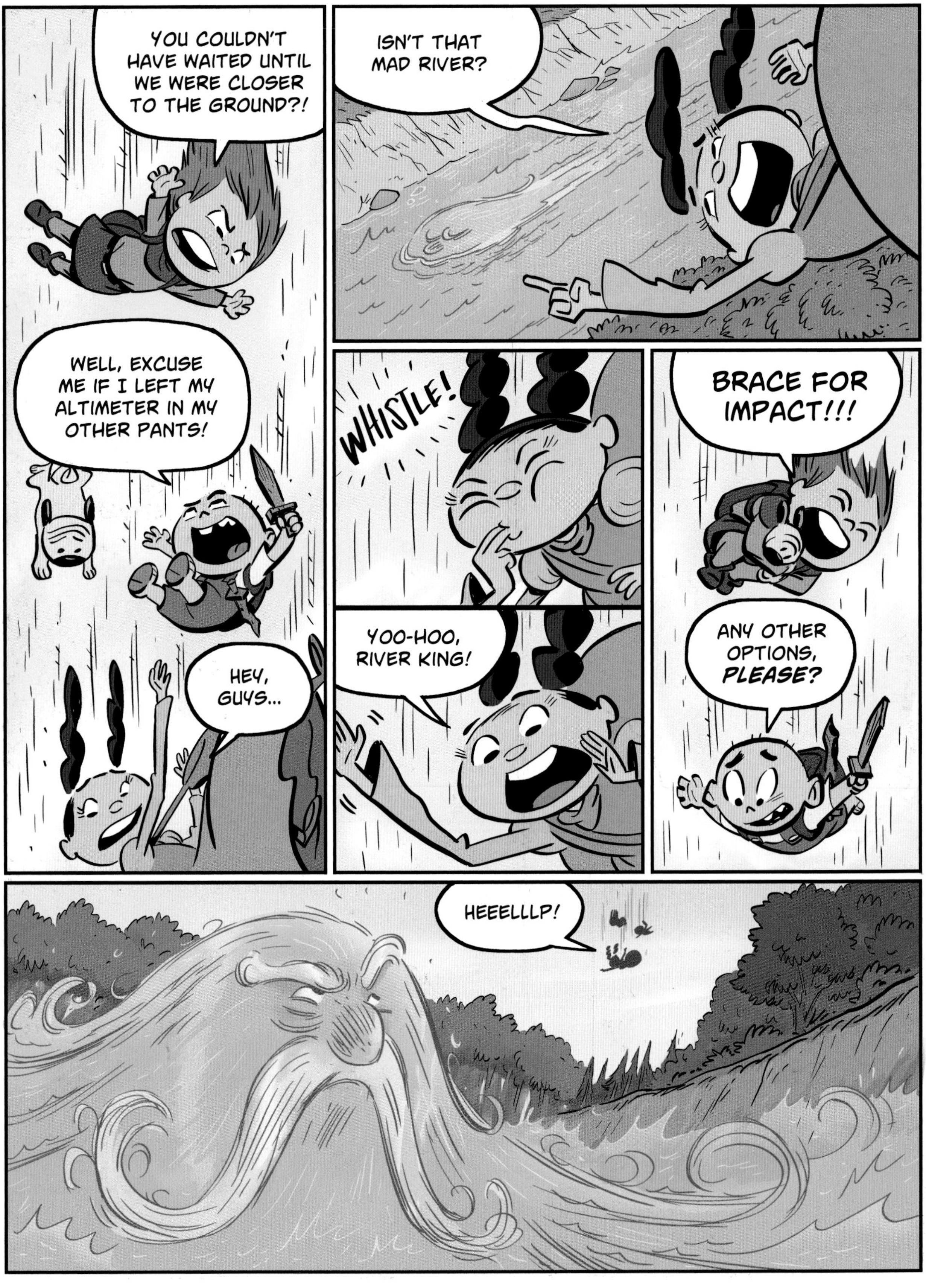
YOU COULDN'T HAVE WAITED UNTIL WE WERE CLOSER TO THE GROUND?!
ISN'T THAT MAD RIVER?
WELL, EXCUSE ME IF I LEFT MY ALTIMETER IN MY OTHER PANTS!
WHISTLE!
BRACE FOR IMPACT!!!
HEY, GUYS...
YOO-HOO, RIVER KING!
ANY OTHER OPTIONS, *PLEASE?*
HEEELLLP!

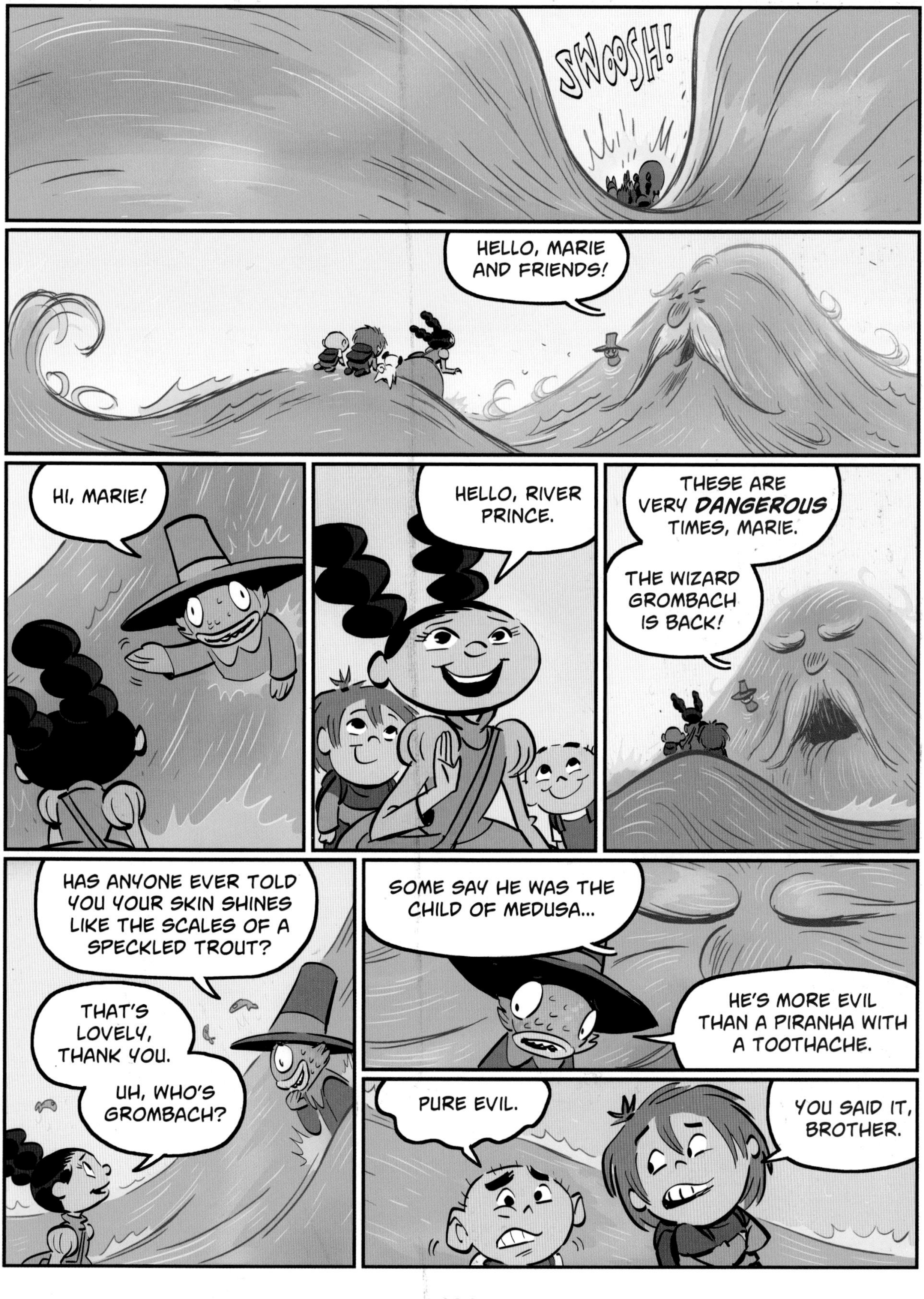
SWOOSH!
HELLO, MARIE AND FRIENDS!
HI, MARIE!
HELLO, RIVER PRINCE.
THESE ARE VERY **DANGEROUS** TIMES, MARIE.
THE WIZARD GROMBACH IS BACK!
HAS ANYONE EVER TOLD YOU YOUR SKIN SHINES LIKE THE SCALES OF A SPECKLED TROUT?
THAT'S LOVELY, THANK YOU.
UH, WHO'S GROMBACH?
SOME SAY HE WAS THE CHILD OF MEDUSA...
HE'S MORE EVIL THAN A PIRANHA WITH A TOOTHACHE.
PURE EVIL.
YOU SAID IT, BROTHER.

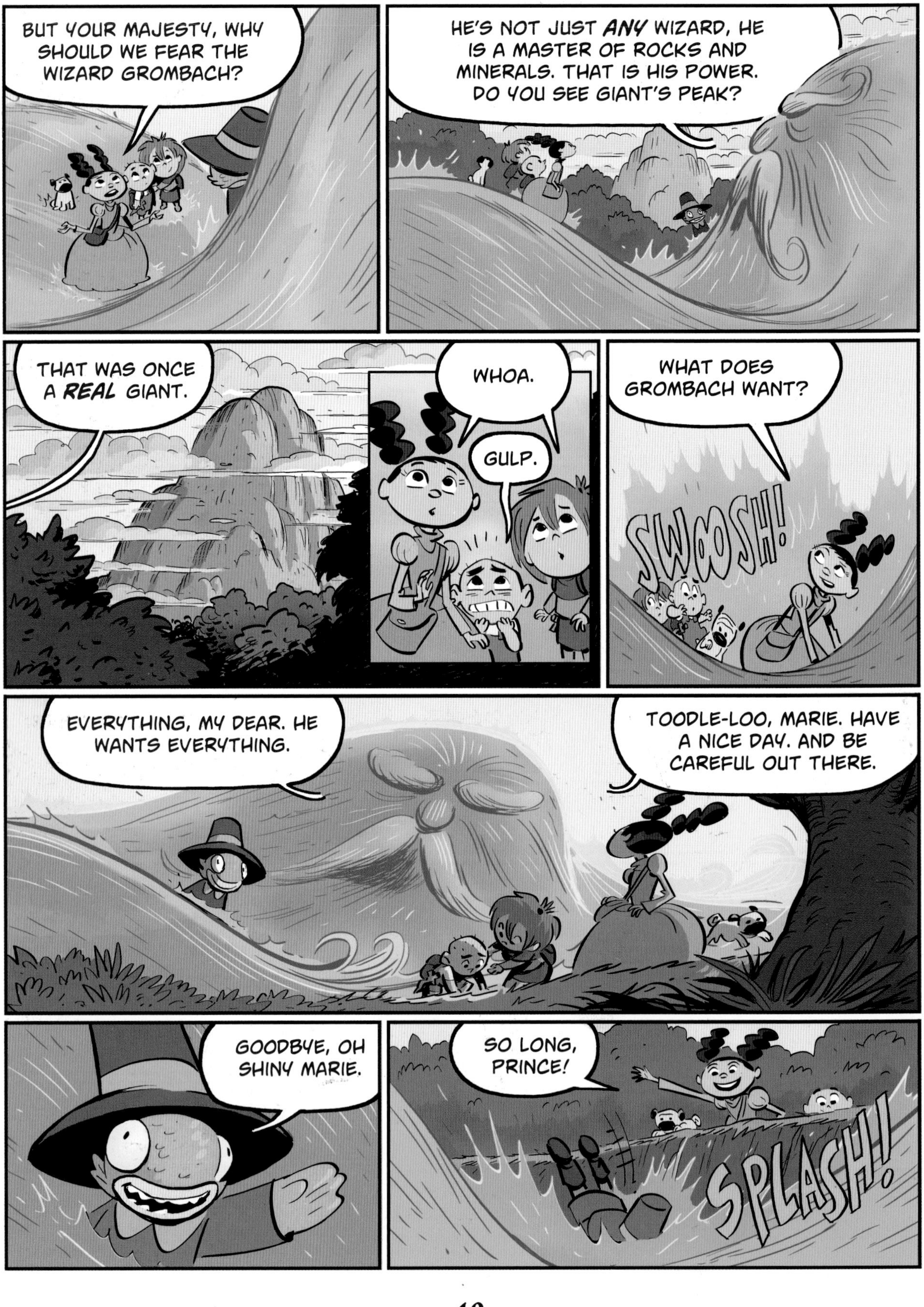
BUT YOUR MAJESTY, WHY SHOULD WE FEAR THE WIZARD GROMBACH?
HE'S NOT JUST ANY WIZARD, HE IS A MASTER OF ROCKS AND MINERALS. THAT IS HIS POWER. DO YOU SEE GIANT'S PEAK?
THAT WAS ONCE A REAL GIANT.
WHOA.
GULP.
WHAT DOES GROMBACH WANT?
SWOOSH!
EVERYTHING, MY DEAR. HE WANTS EVERYTHING.
TOODLE-LOO, MARIE. HAVE A NICE DAY. AND BE CAREFUL OUT THERE.
GOODBYE, OH SHINY MARIE.
SO LONG, PRINCE!
SPLASH!

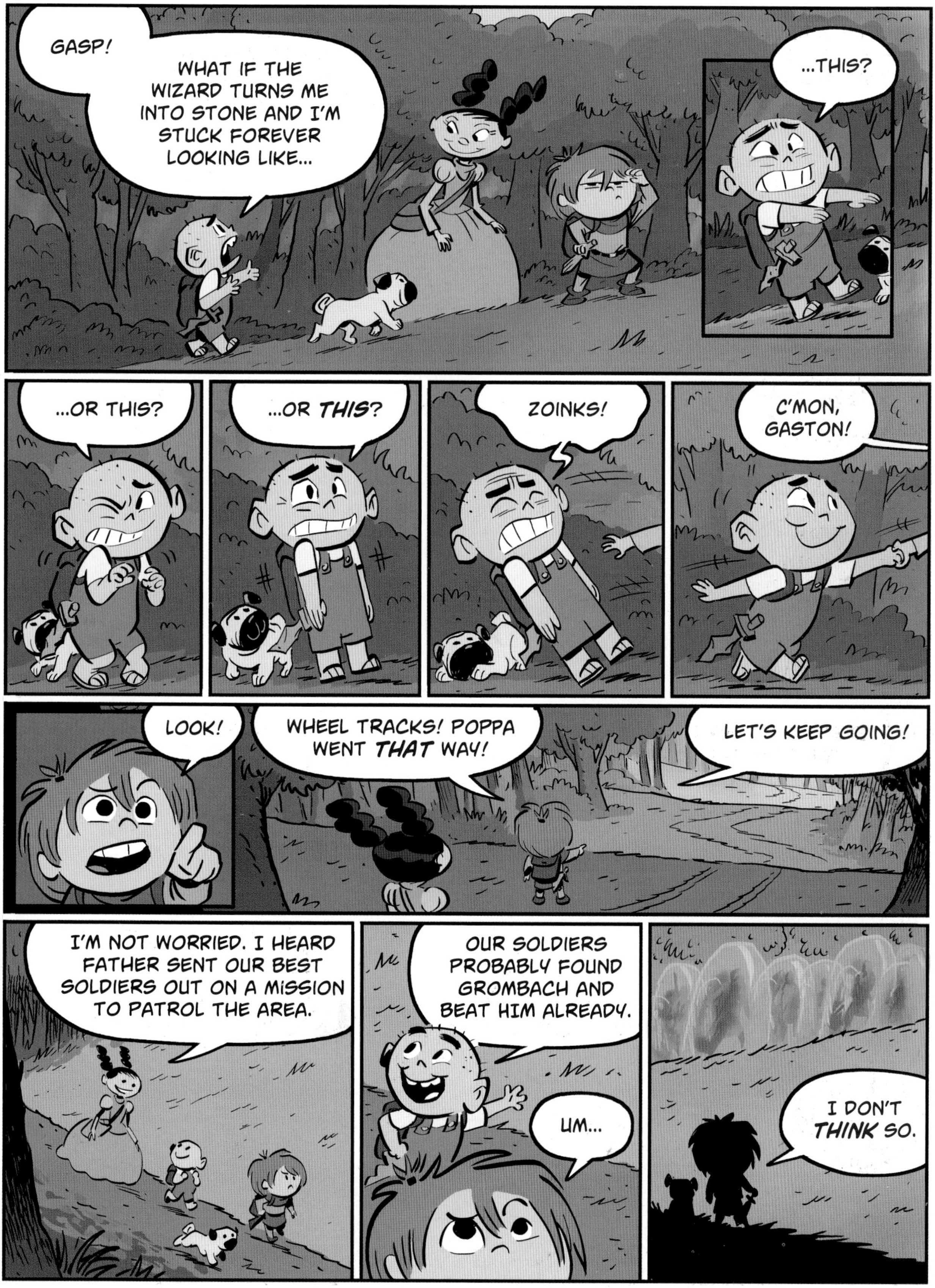
GASP!
WHAT IF THE WIZARD TURNS ME INTO STONE AND I'M STUCK FOREVER LOOKING LIKE...
...THIS?
...OR THIS?
...OR *THIS*?
ZOINKS!
C'MON, GASTON!
LOOK!
WHEEL TRACKS! POPPA WENT *THAT* WAY!
LET'S KEEP GOING!
I'M NOT WORRIED. I HEARD FATHER SENT OUR BEST SOLDIERS OUT ON A MISSION TO PATROL THE AREA.
OUR SOLDIERS PROBABLY FOUND GROMBACH AND BEAT HIM ALREADY.
UM...
I DON'T *THINK* SO.

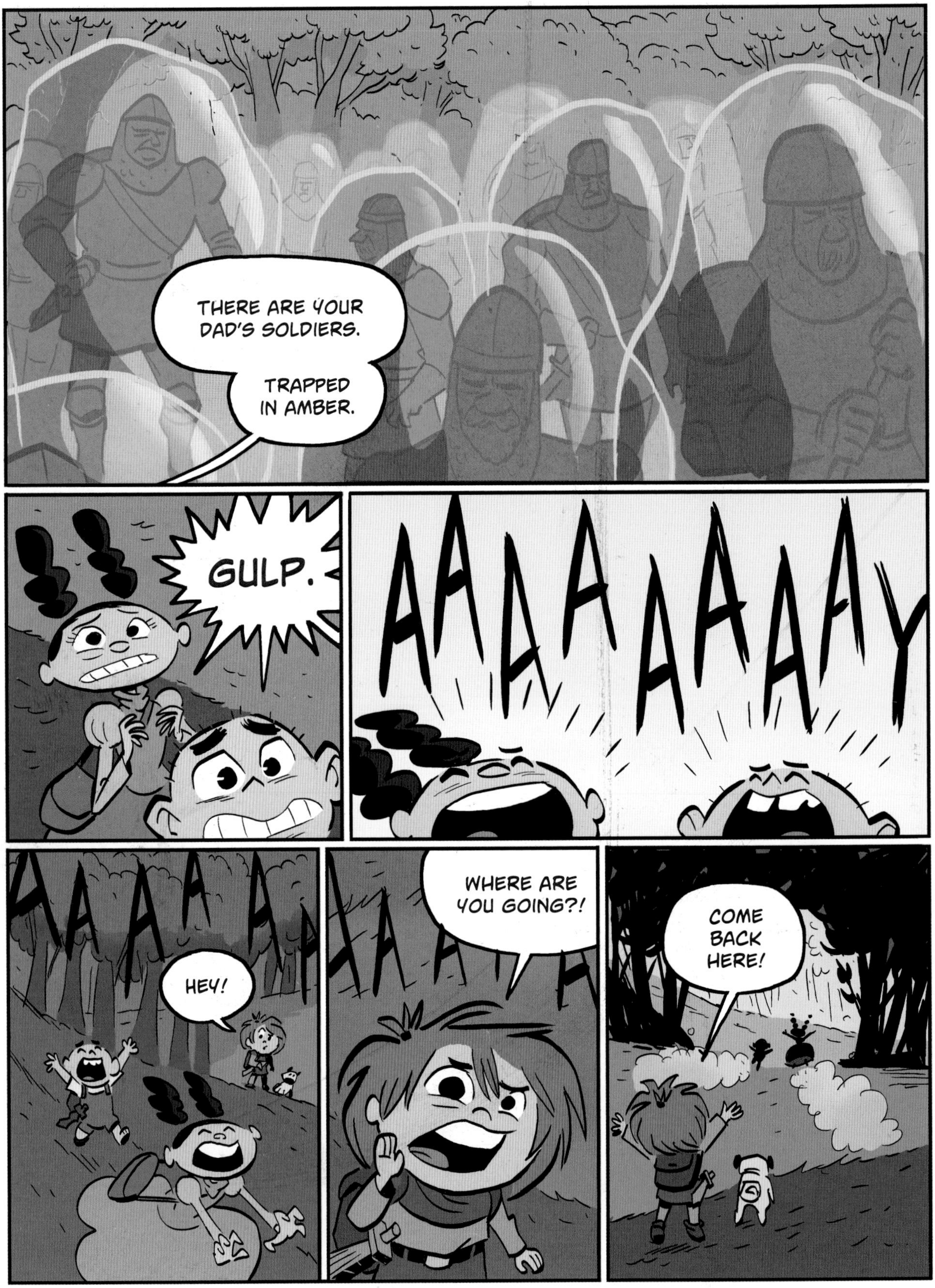
THERE ARE YOUR DAD'S SOLDIERS.
TRAPPED IN AMBER.
GULP.
AAAAAAAY
AAAAA
HEY!
WHERE ARE YOU GOING?!
COME BACK HERE!

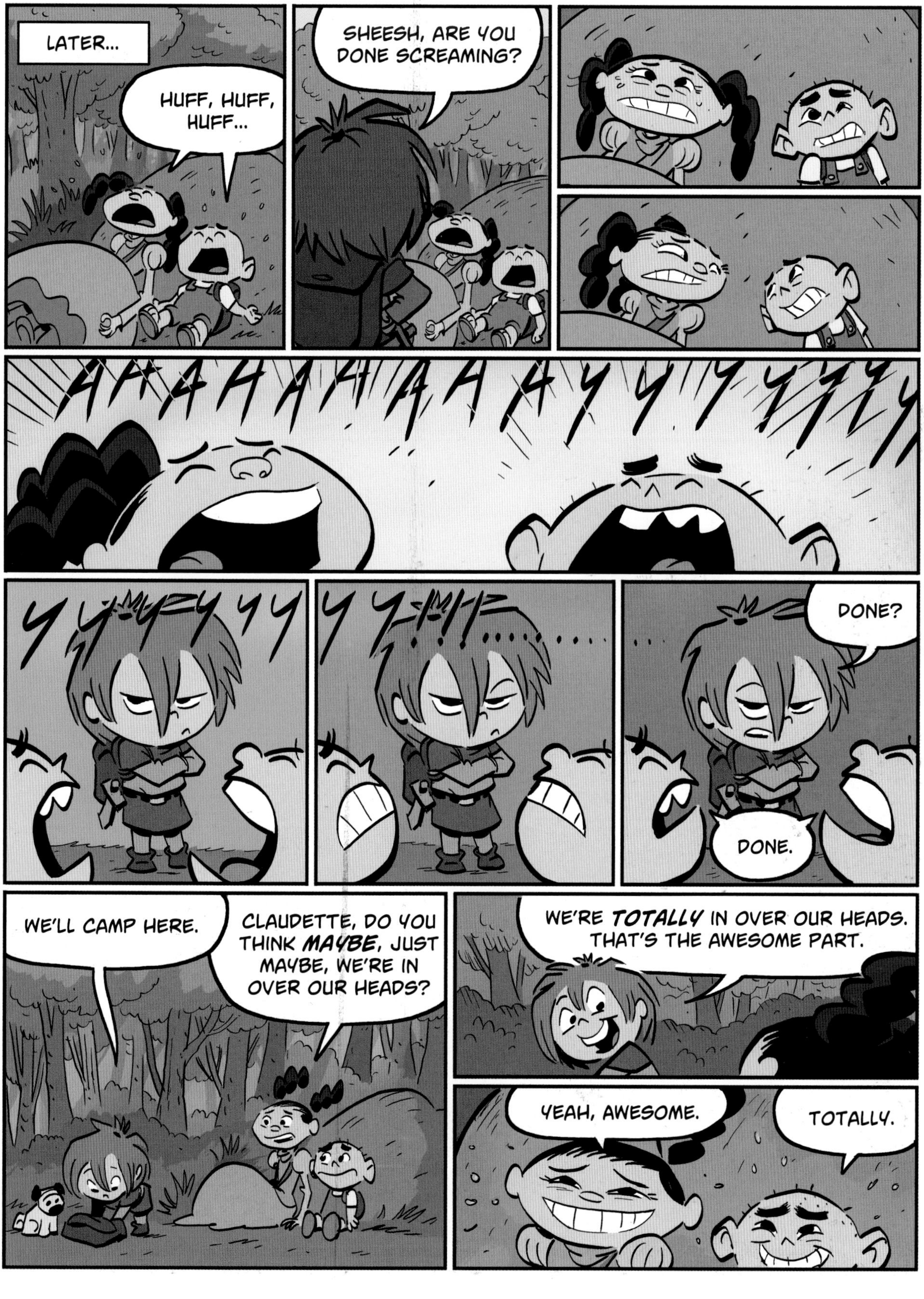
LATER...
HUFF, HUFF, HUFF...
SHEESH, ARE YOU DONE SCREAMING?
AAAAAAAAAAAAYYYYYYYYY
YYYYYYY
YYYY!!!....
....
DONE?
DONE.
WE'LL CAMP HERE.
CLAUDETTE, DO YOU THINK MAYBE, JUST MAYBE, WE'RE IN OVER OUR HEADS?
WE'RE TOTALLY IN OVER OUR HEADS. THAT'S THE AWESOME PART.
YEAH, AWESOME.
TOTALLY.

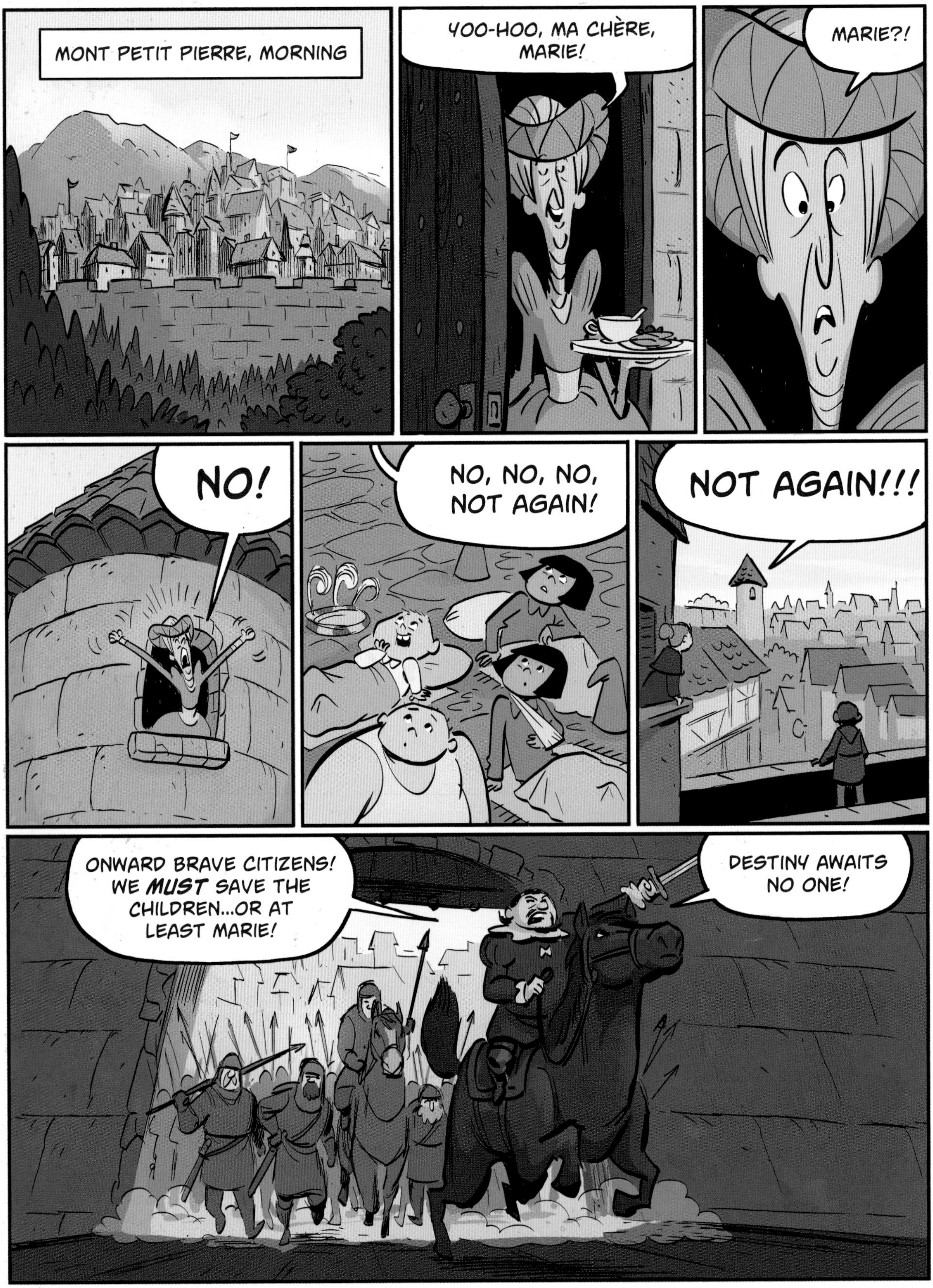
MONT PETIT PIERRE, MORNING
YOO-HOO, MA CHÈRE, MARIE!
MARIE?!
NO!
NO, NO, NO, NOT AGAIN!
NOT AGAIN!!!
ONWARD BRAVE CITIZENS! WE MUST SAVE THE CHILDREN...OR AT LEAST MARIE!
DESTINY AWAITS NO ONE!

NOTHING COULD POSSIBLY IMPEDE OUR PATH TO VICTORY!

WHY ARE WE RISKING OUR NECKS TO SAVE THOSE DUMB KIDS AGAIN?

YEAH, WHY?

SQUAWK! SQUAWK! SQUA WK! SQUAWK! SQUAWK! SQUAWK! SQUAWK!

SQUAWK!

UH-OH.

WK! SQUAWK! SQU SQUAWK! SQUAWK! SQUAWK! SQUAWK! SQUA

IT'S AN AMBUSH!

SQUAWK! SQUAWK! SQUAWK! SQUAWK! SQUAWK! SQUAWK! SQUAWK! SQUAWK! SQUAWK! SQ

SIGH. I GUESS I'LL BE HANDLING THIS RESCUE MISSION.

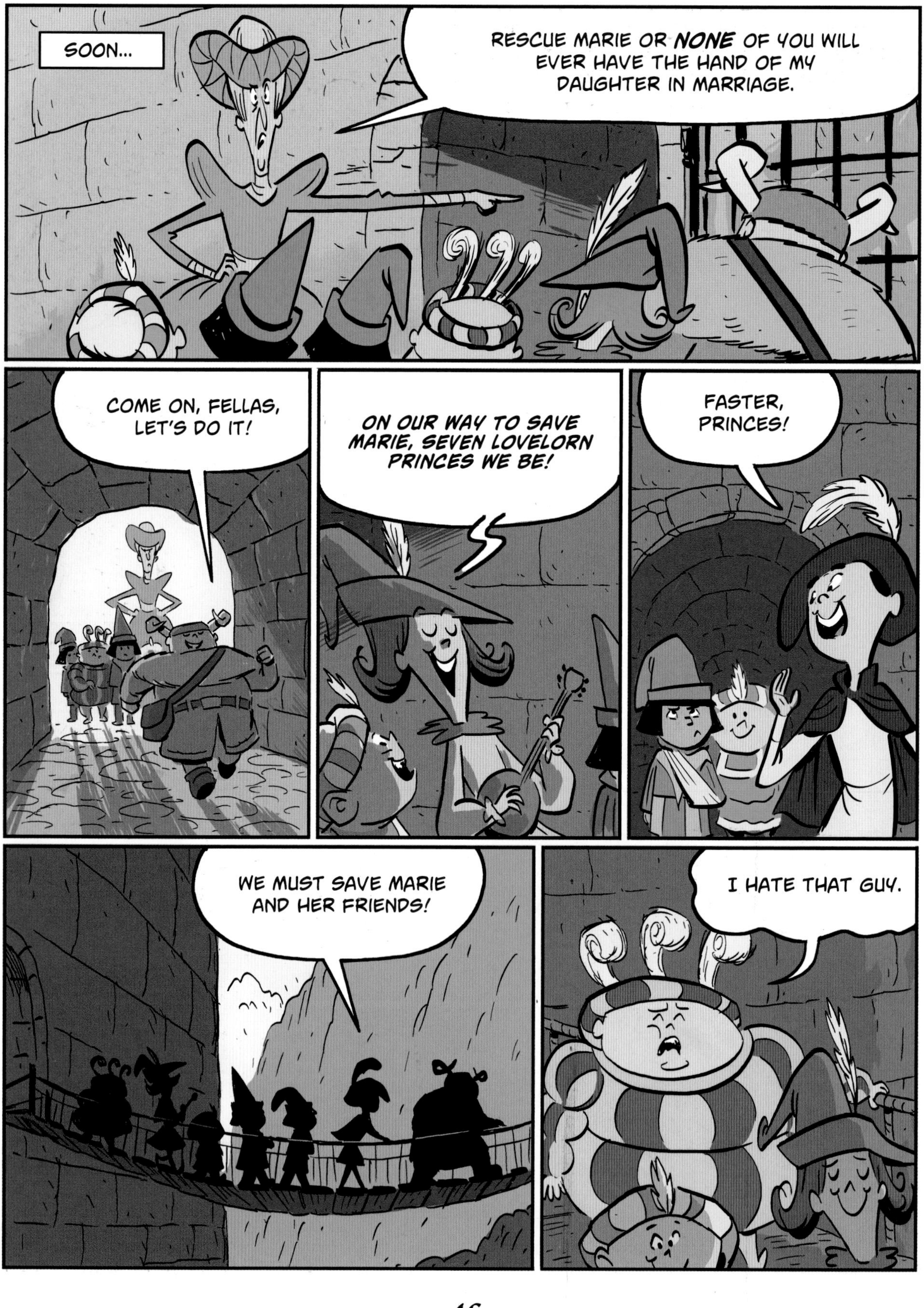
SOON...
RESCUE MARIE OR NONE OF YOU WILL EVER HAVE THE HAND OF MY DAUGHTER IN MARRIAGE.
COME ON, FELLAS, LET'S DO IT!
ON OUR WAY TO SAVE MARIE, SEVEN LOVELORN PRINCES WE BE!
FASTER, PRINCES!
WE MUST SAVE MARIE AND HER FRIENDS!
I HATE THAT GUY.

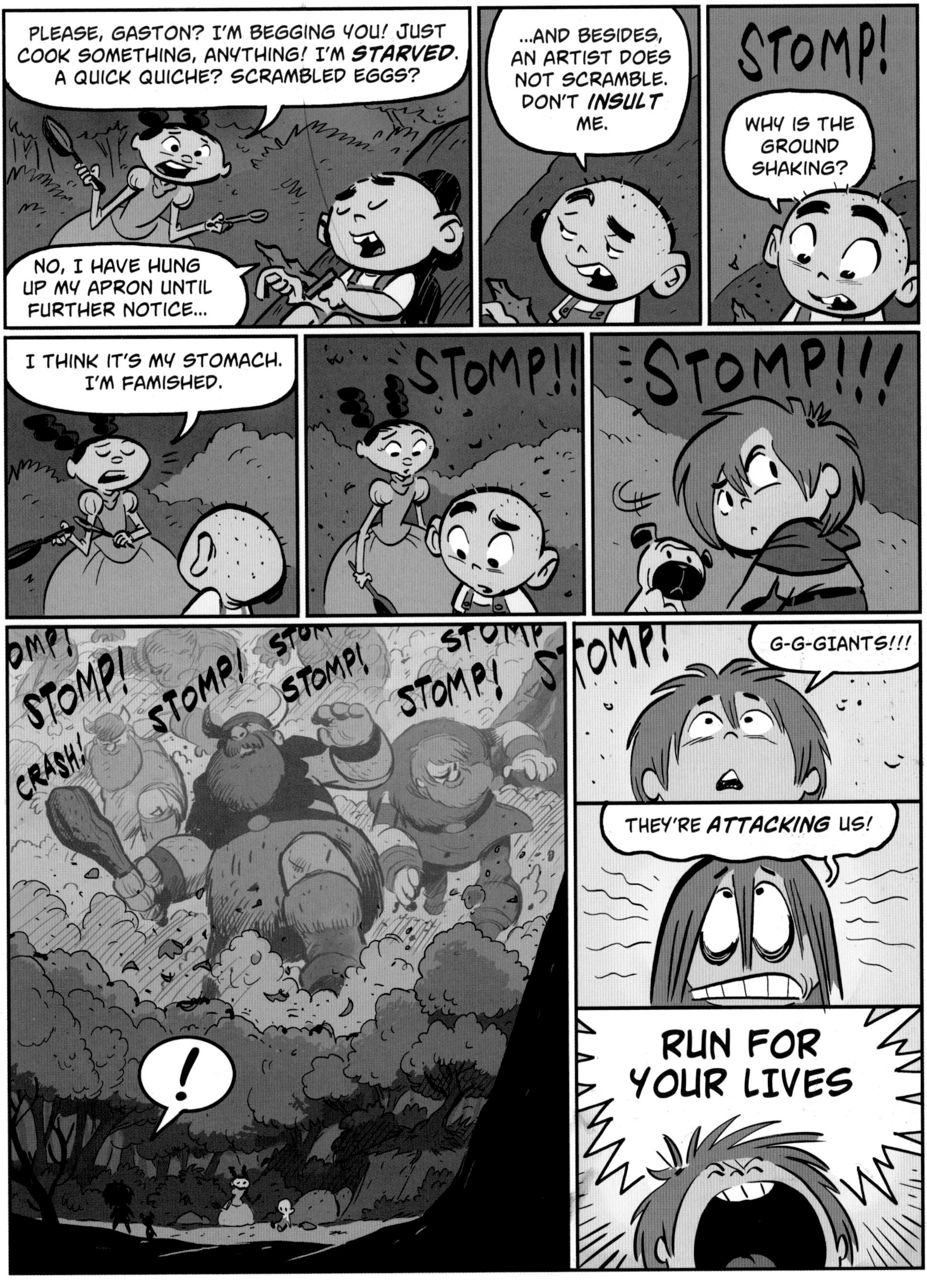
PLEASE, GASTON? I'M BEGGING YOU! JUST COOK SOMETHING, ANYTHING! I'M STARVED. A QUICK QUICHE? SCRAMBLED EGGS?
NO, I HAVE HUNG UP MY APRON UNTIL FURTHER NOTICE...
...AND BESIDES, AN ARTIST DOES NOT SCRAMBLE. DON'T INSULT ME.
STOMP!
WHY IS THE GROUND SHAKING?
I THINK IT'S MY STOMACH. I'M FAMISHED.
STOMP!!
STOMP!!!
STOMP!
STOMP!
CRASH!
STOMP!
STOMP!
STOMP!
STOMP!
!
STOMP!
G-G-GIANTS!!!
THEY'RE ATTACKING US!
RUN FOR YOUR LIVES

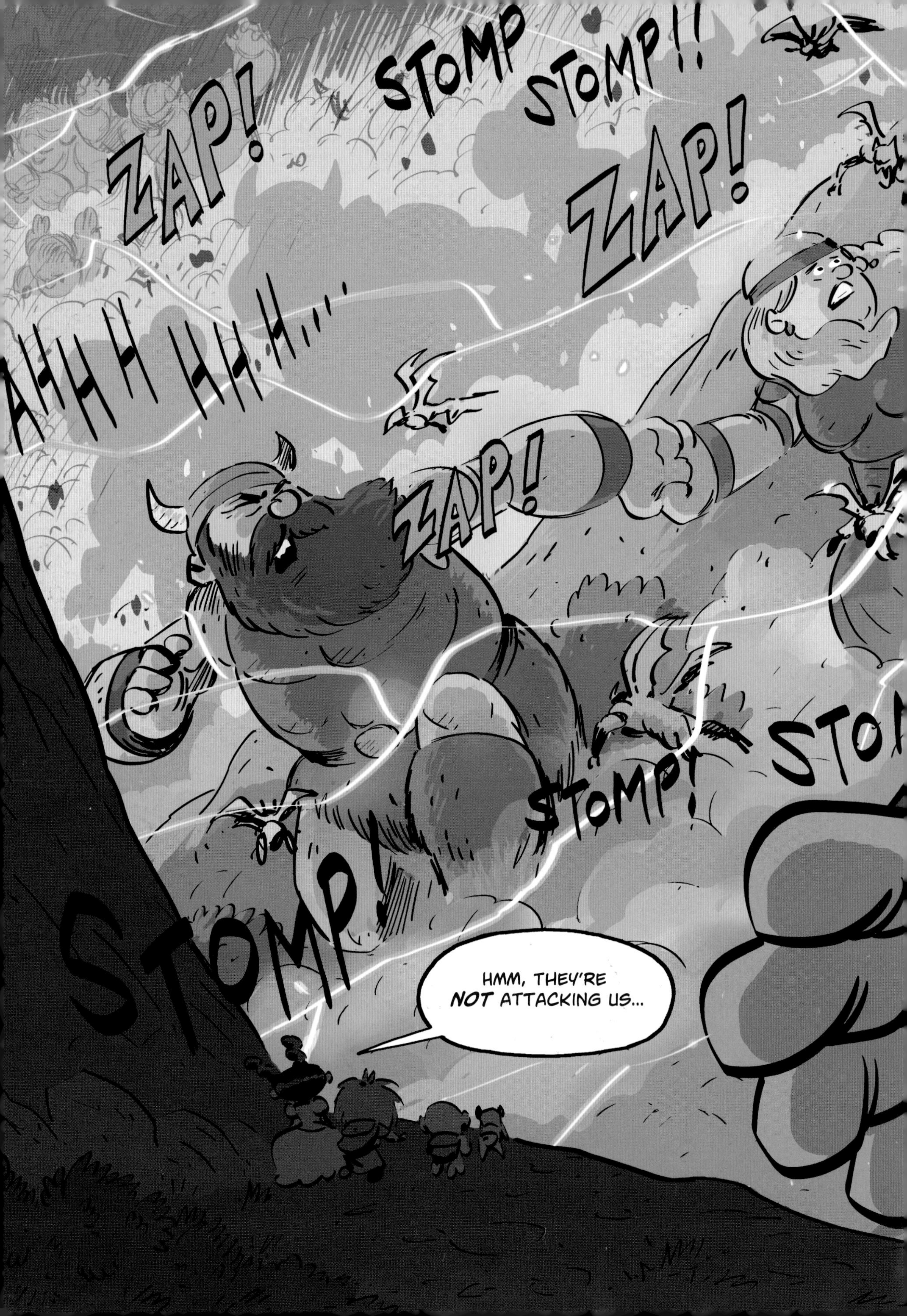
ZAP!
STOMP
STOMP!!
ZAP!
AHHH HHH...
ZAP!
STOMP!
STOMP!
HMM, THEY'RE *NOT* ATTACKING US...

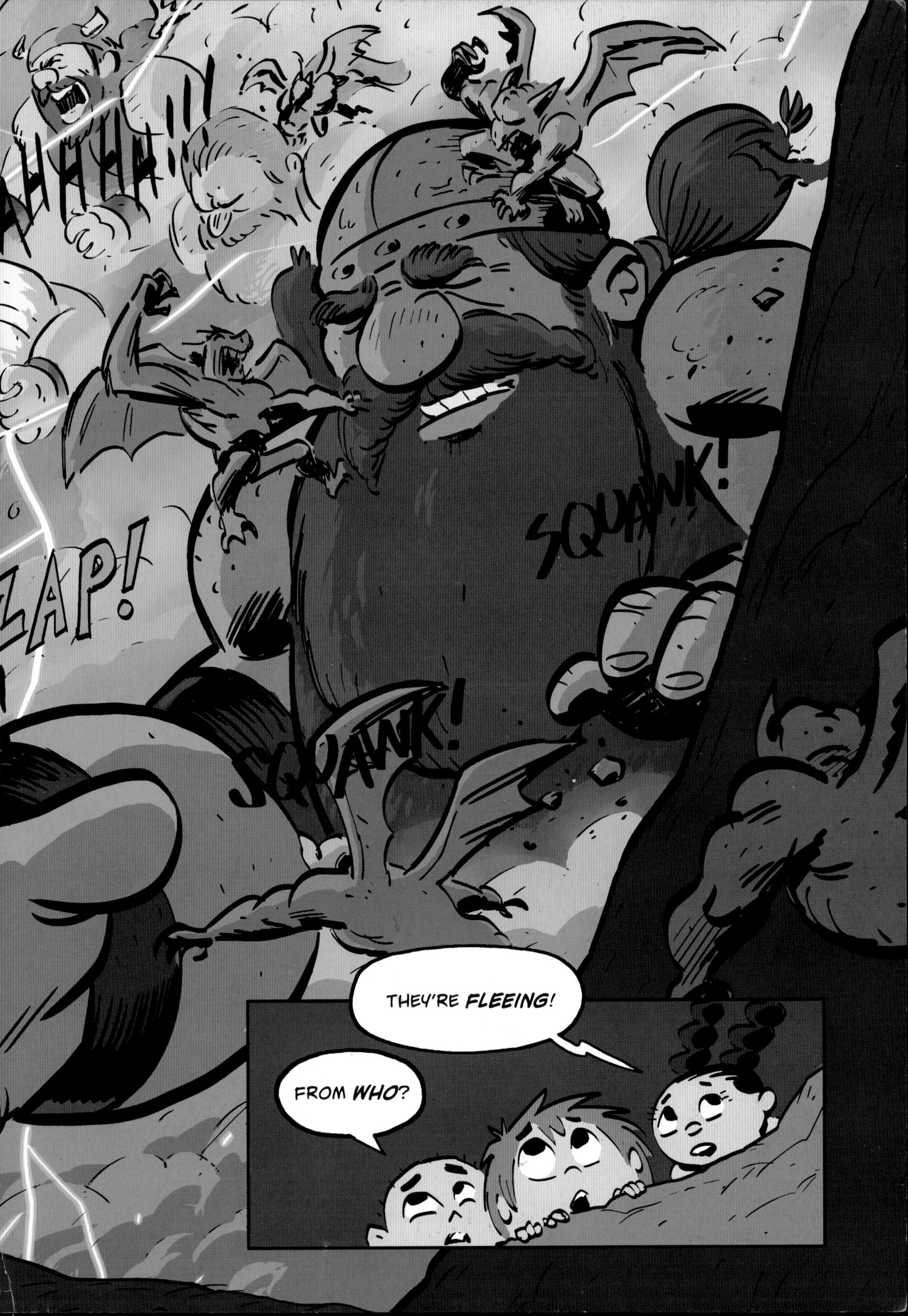
ZAP!
SQUAWK!
SQUAWK!
THEY'RE FLEEING!
FROM WHO?

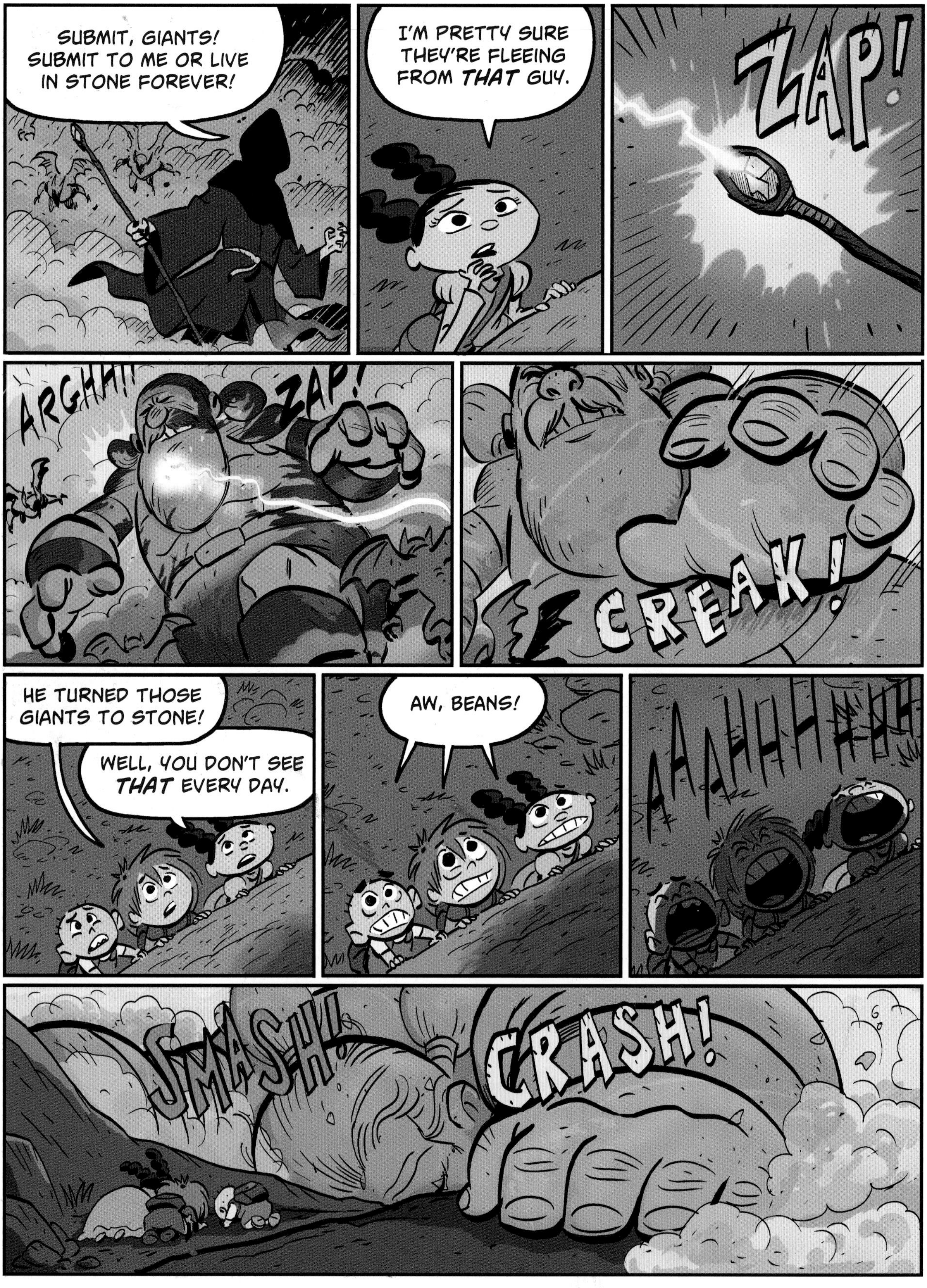
SUBMIT, GIANTS! SUBMIT TO ME OR LIVE IN STONE FOREVER!
I'M PRETTY SURE THEY'RE FLEEING FROM THAT GUY.
ZAP!
ARGHH!!
ZAP!
CREAK!
HE TURNED THOSE GIANTS TO STONE!
WELL, YOU DON'T SEE THAT EVERY DAY.
AW, BEANS!
AAAHHHHHH!
SMASH!
CRASH!

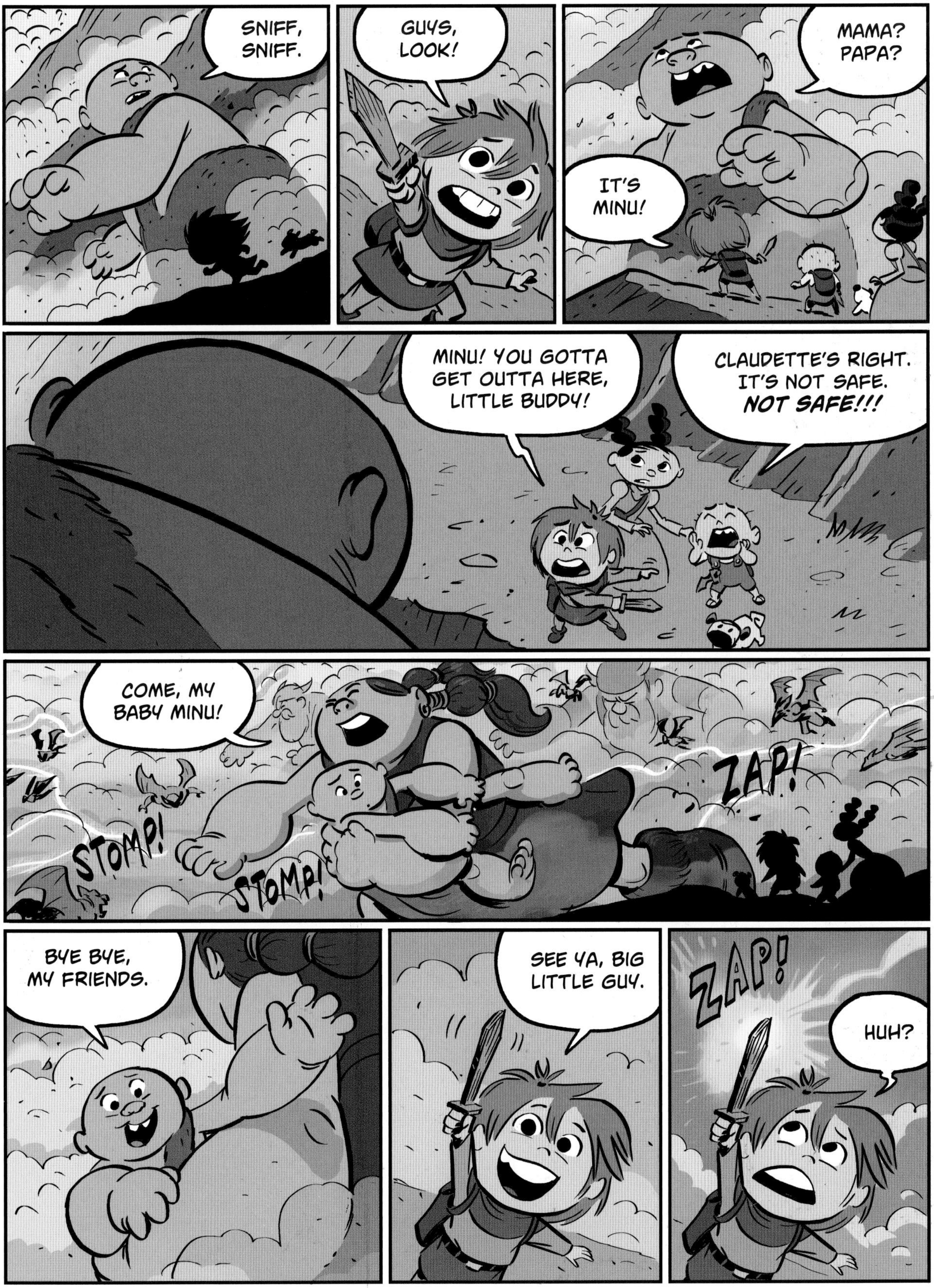
SNIFF, SNIFF.
GUYS, LOOK!
MAMA? PAPA?
IT'S MINU!
MINU! YOU GOTTA GET OUTTA HERE, LITTLE BUDDY!
CLAUDETTE'S RIGHT. IT'S NOT SAFE. ***NOT SAFE!!!***
COME, MY BABY MINU!
ZAP!
STOMP!
STOMP!
BYE BYE, MY FRIENDS.
SEE YA, BIG LITTLE GUY.
ZAP!
HUH?

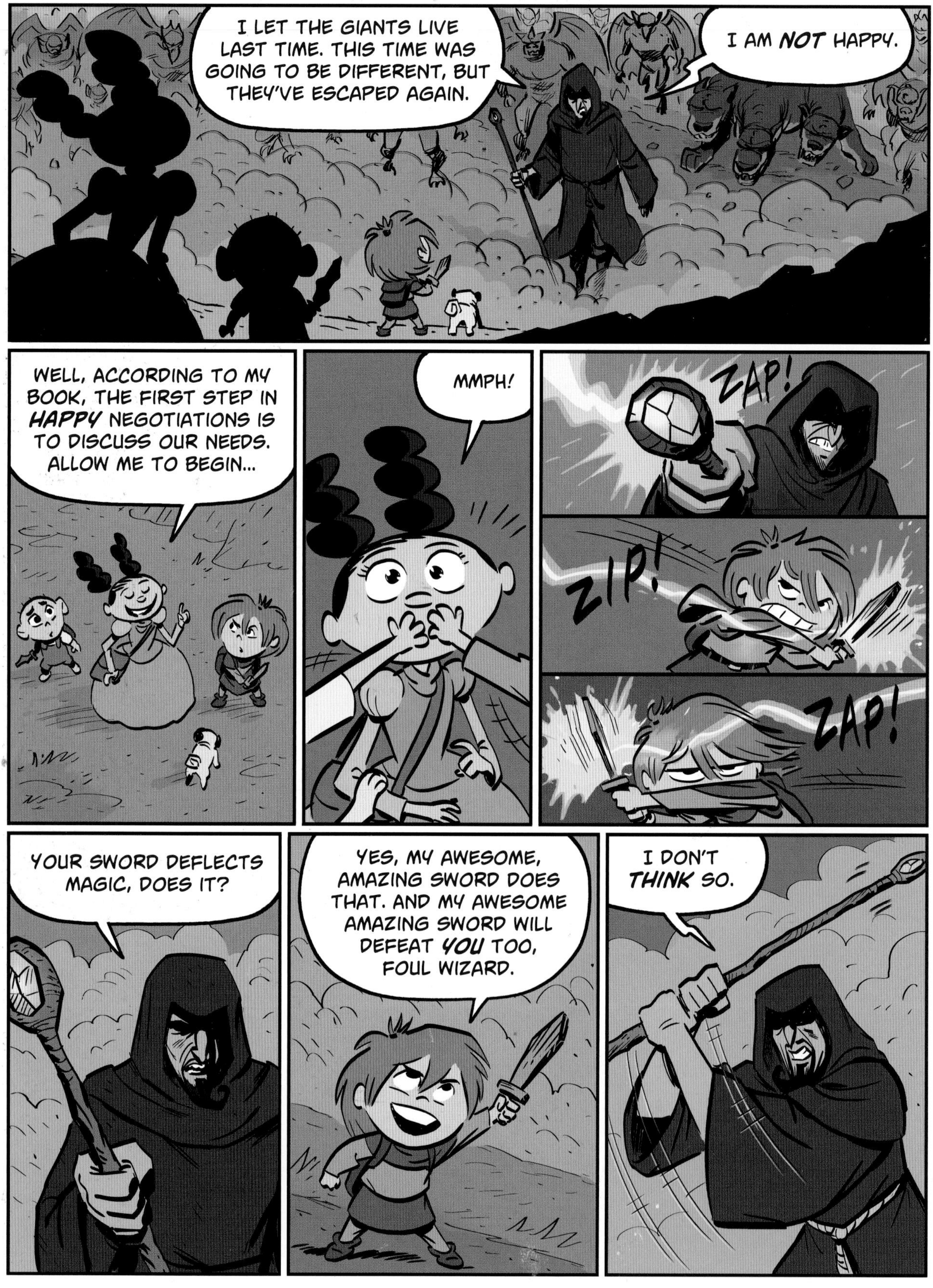

I LET THE GIANTS LIVE LAST TIME. THIS TIME WAS GOING TO BE DIFFERENT, BUT THEY'VE ESCAPED AGAIN.
I AM **NOT** HAPPY.
WELL, ACCORDING TO MY BOOK, THE FIRST STEP IN **HAPPY** NEGOTIATIONS IS TO DISCUSS OUR NEEDS. ALLOW ME TO BEGIN...
MMPH!
ZAP!
ZIP!
ZAP!
YOUR SWORD DEFLECTS MAGIC, DOES IT?
YES, MY AWESOME, AMAZING SWORD DOES THAT. AND MY AWESOME AMAZING SWORD WILL DEFEAT **YOU** TOO, FOUL WIZARD.
I DON'T **THINK** SO.

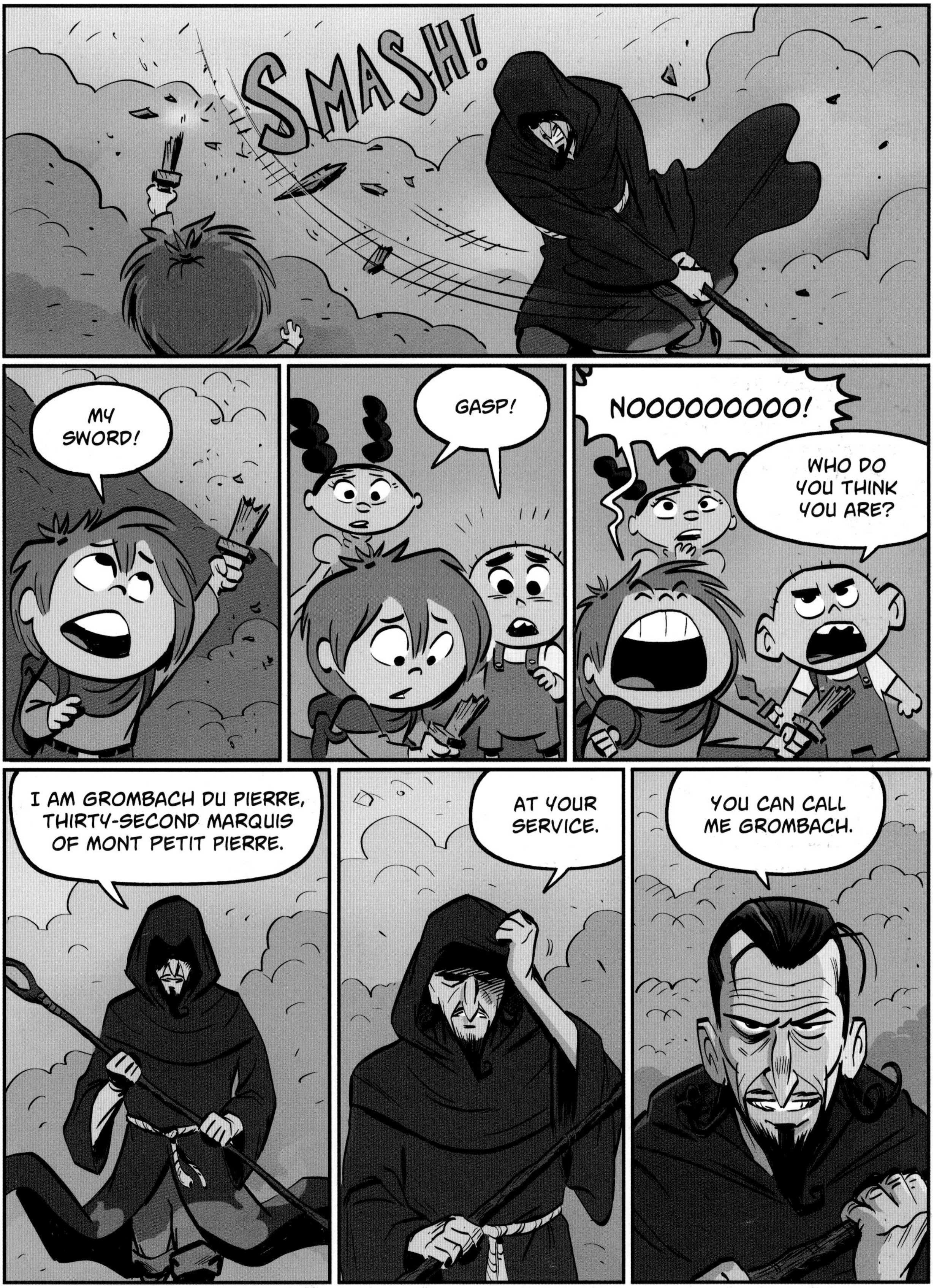
SMASH!
MY SWORD!
GASP!
NOOOOOOOOO!
WHO DO YOU THINK YOU ARE?
I AM GROMBACH DU PIERRE, THIRTY-SECOND MARQUIS OF MONT PETIT PIERRE.
AT YOUR SERVICE.
YOU CAN CALL ME GROMBACH.

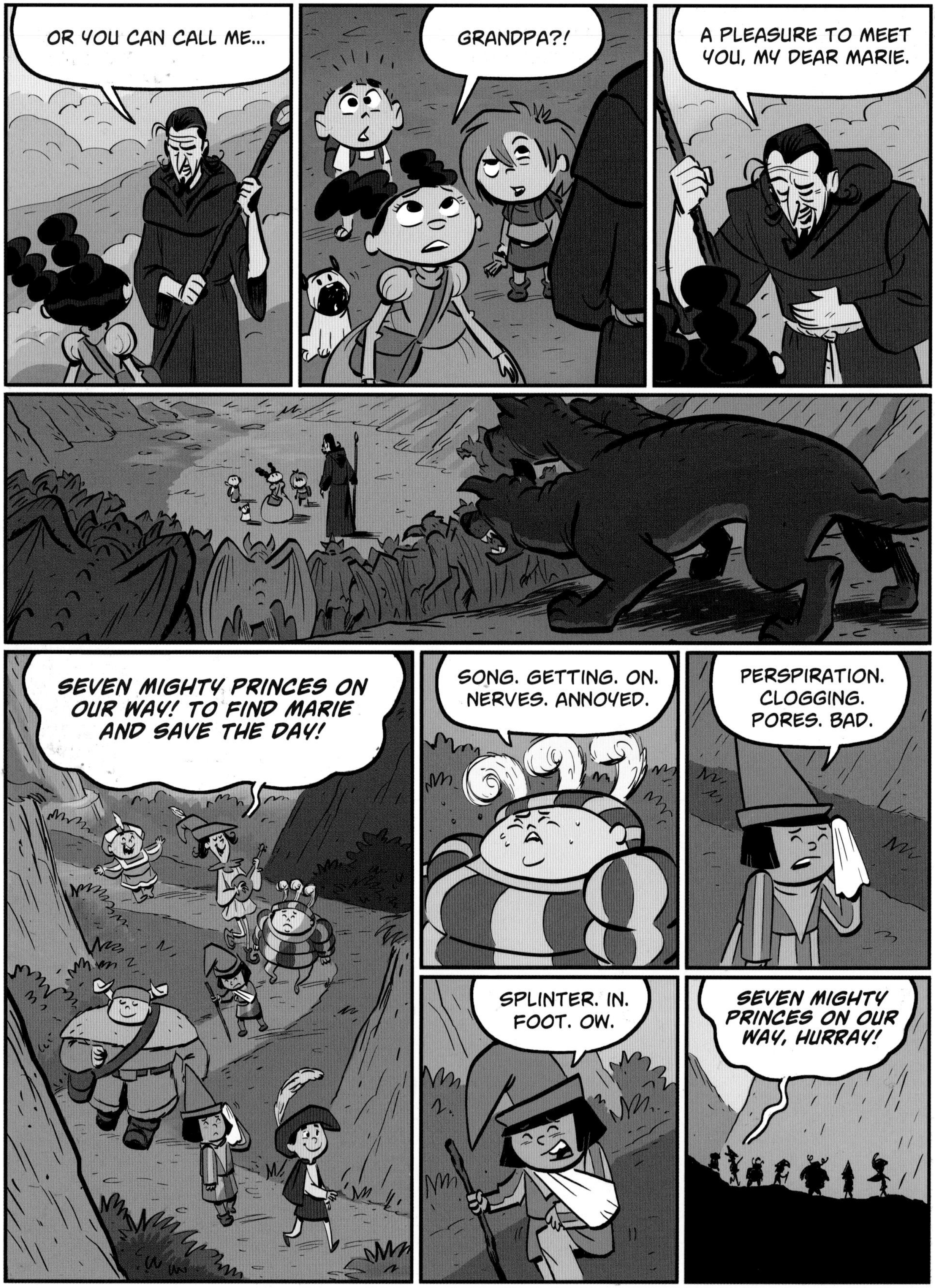

OR YOU CAN CALL ME...
GRANDPA?!
A PLEASURE TO MEET YOU, MY DEAR MARIE.
SEVEN MIGHTY PRINCES ON OUR WAY! TO FIND MARIE AND SAVE THE DAY!
SONG. GETTING. ON. NERVES. ANNOYED.
PERSPIRATION. CLOGGING. PORES. BAD.
SPLINTER. IN. FOOT. OW.
SEVEN MIGHTY PRINCES ON OUR WAY, HURRAY!

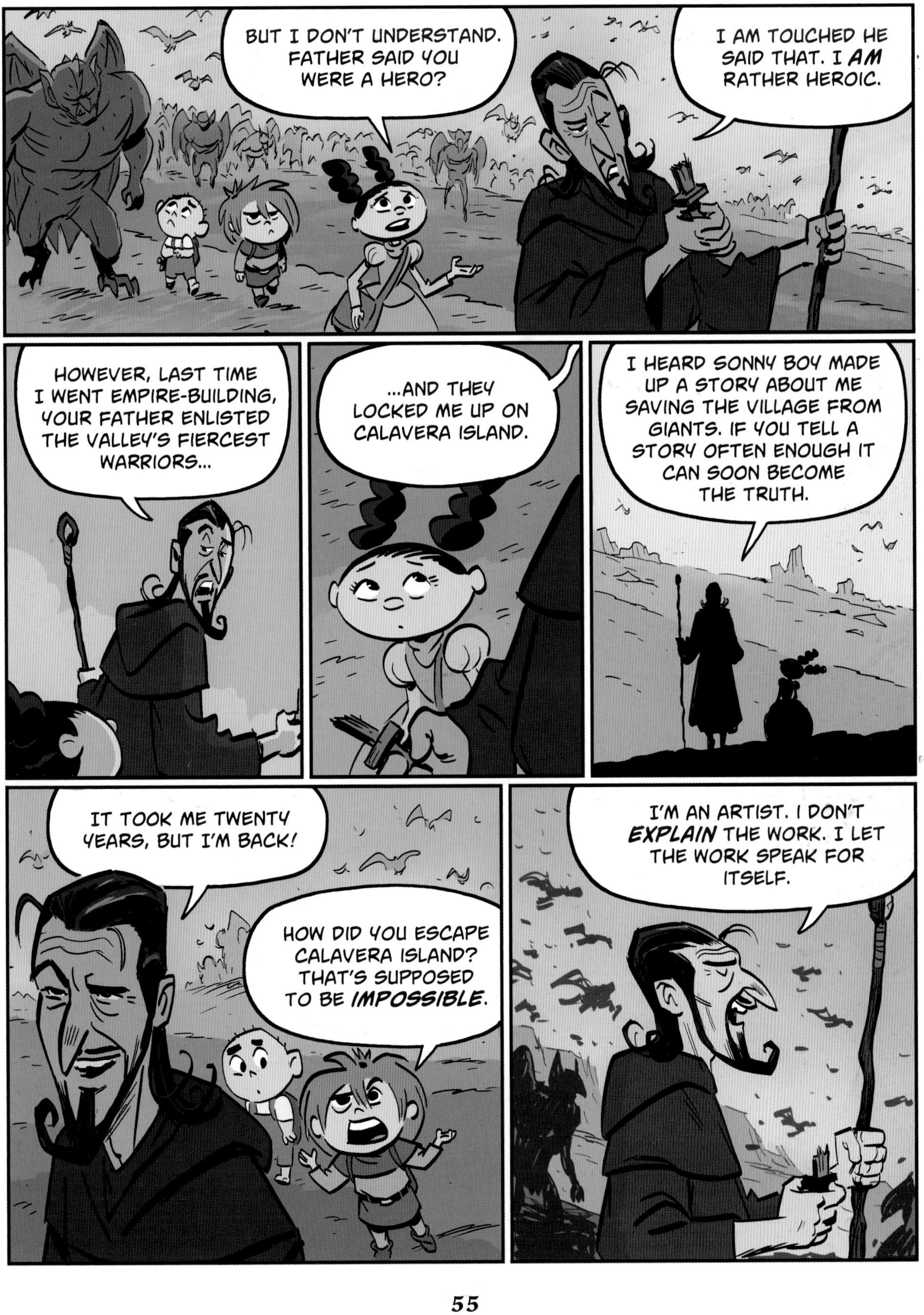
BUT I DON'T UNDERSTAND. FATHER SAID YOU WERE A HERO?
I AM TOUCHED HE SAID THAT. I *AM* RATHER HEROIC.
HOWEVER, LAST TIME I WENT EMPIRE-BUILDING, YOUR FATHER ENLISTED THE VALLEY'S FIERCEST WARRIORS...
...AND THEY LOCKED ME UP ON CALAVERA ISLAND.
I HEARD SONNY BOY MADE UP A STORY ABOUT ME SAVING THE VILLAGE FROM GIANTS. IF YOU TELL A STORY OFTEN ENOUGH IT CAN SOON BECOME THE TRUTH.
IT TOOK ME TWENTY YEARS, BUT I'M BACK!
HOW DID YOU ESCAPE CALAVERA ISLAND? THAT'S SUPPOSED TO BE *IMPOSSIBLE*.
I'M AN ARTIST. I DON'T *EXPLAIN* THE WORK. I LET THE WORK SPEAK FOR ITSELF.

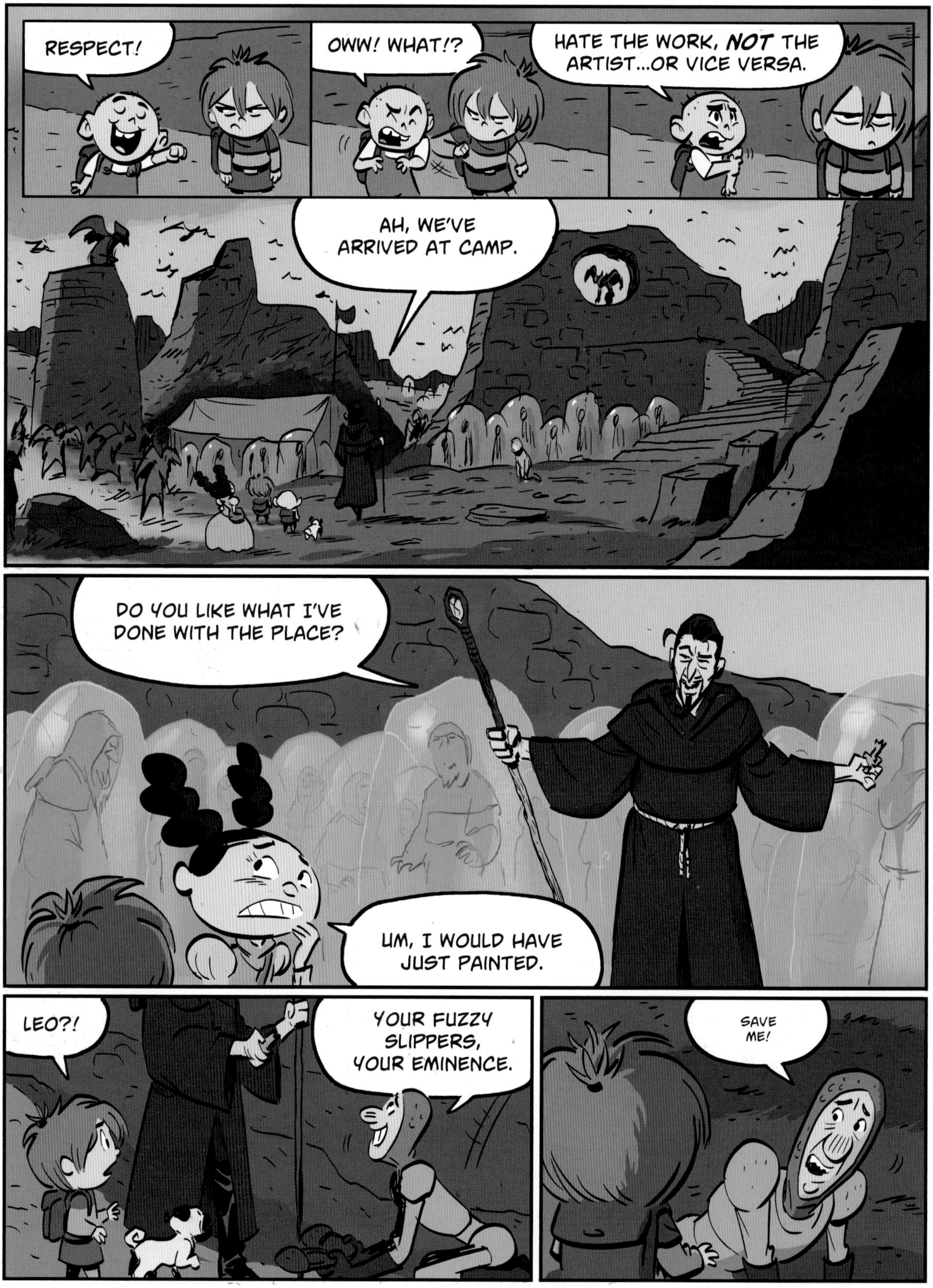
RESPECT!
OWW! WHAT!?
HATE THE WORK, **NOT** THE ARTIST...OR VICE VERSA.
AH, WE'VE ARRIVED AT CAMP.
DO YOU LIKE WHAT I'VE DONE WITH THE PLACE?
UM, I WOULD HAVE JUST PAINTED.
LEO?!
YOUR FUZZY SLIPPERS, YOUR EMINENCE.
SAVE ME!

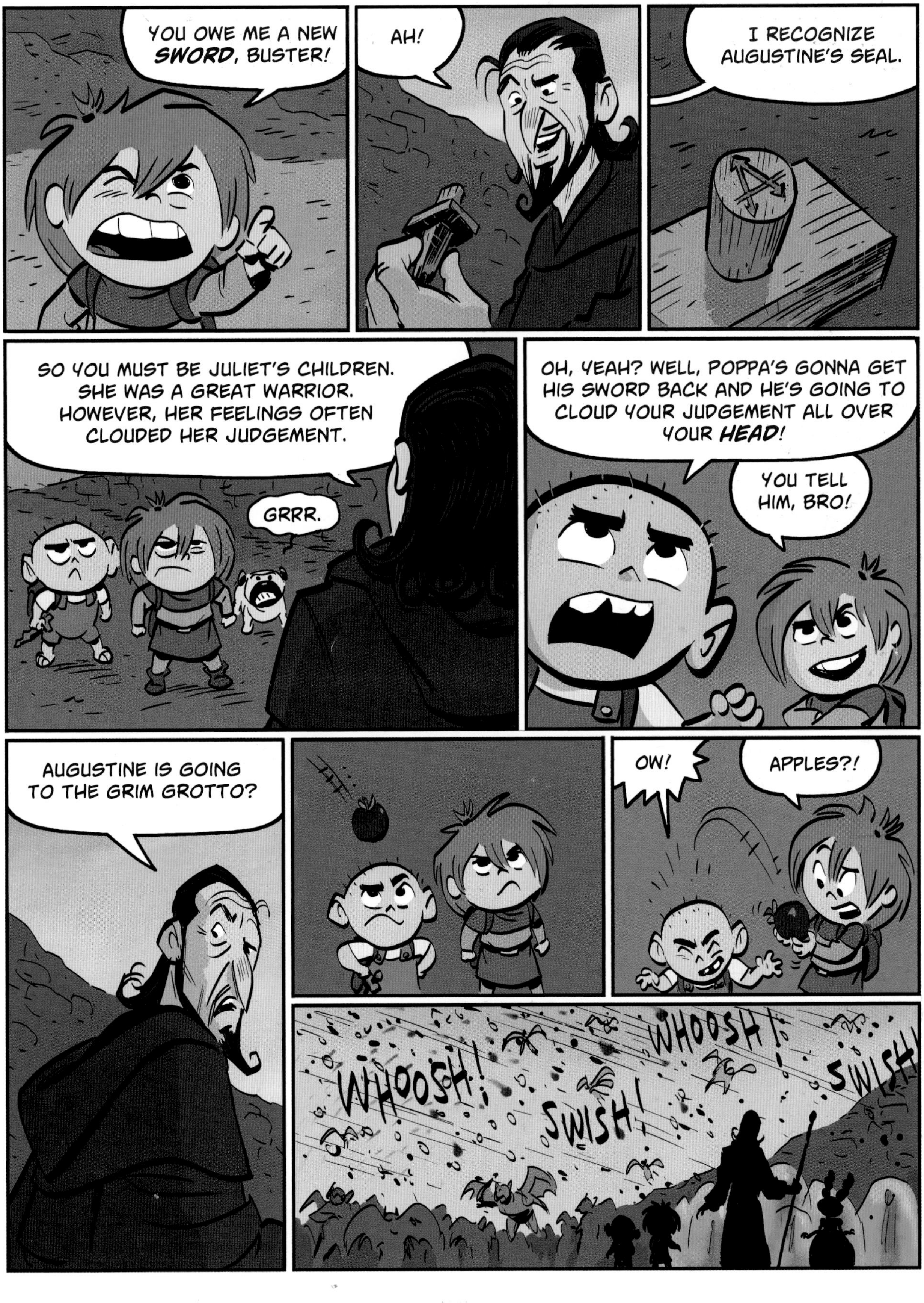
YOU OWE ME A NEW SWORD, BUSTER!
AH!
I RECOGNIZE AUGUSTINE'S SEAL.
SO YOU MUST BE JULIET'S CHILDREN. SHE WAS A GREAT WARRIOR. HOWEVER, HER FEELINGS OFTEN CLOUDED HER JUDGEMENT.
GRRR.
OH, YEAH? WELL, POPPA'S GONNA GET HIS SWORD BACK AND HE'S GOING TO CLOUD YOUR JUDGEMENT ALL OVER YOUR HEAD!
YOU TELL HIM, BRO!
AUGUSTINE IS GOING TO THE GRIM GROTTO?
OW!
APPLES?!
WHOOSH!
WHOOSH!
SWISH!
SWISH

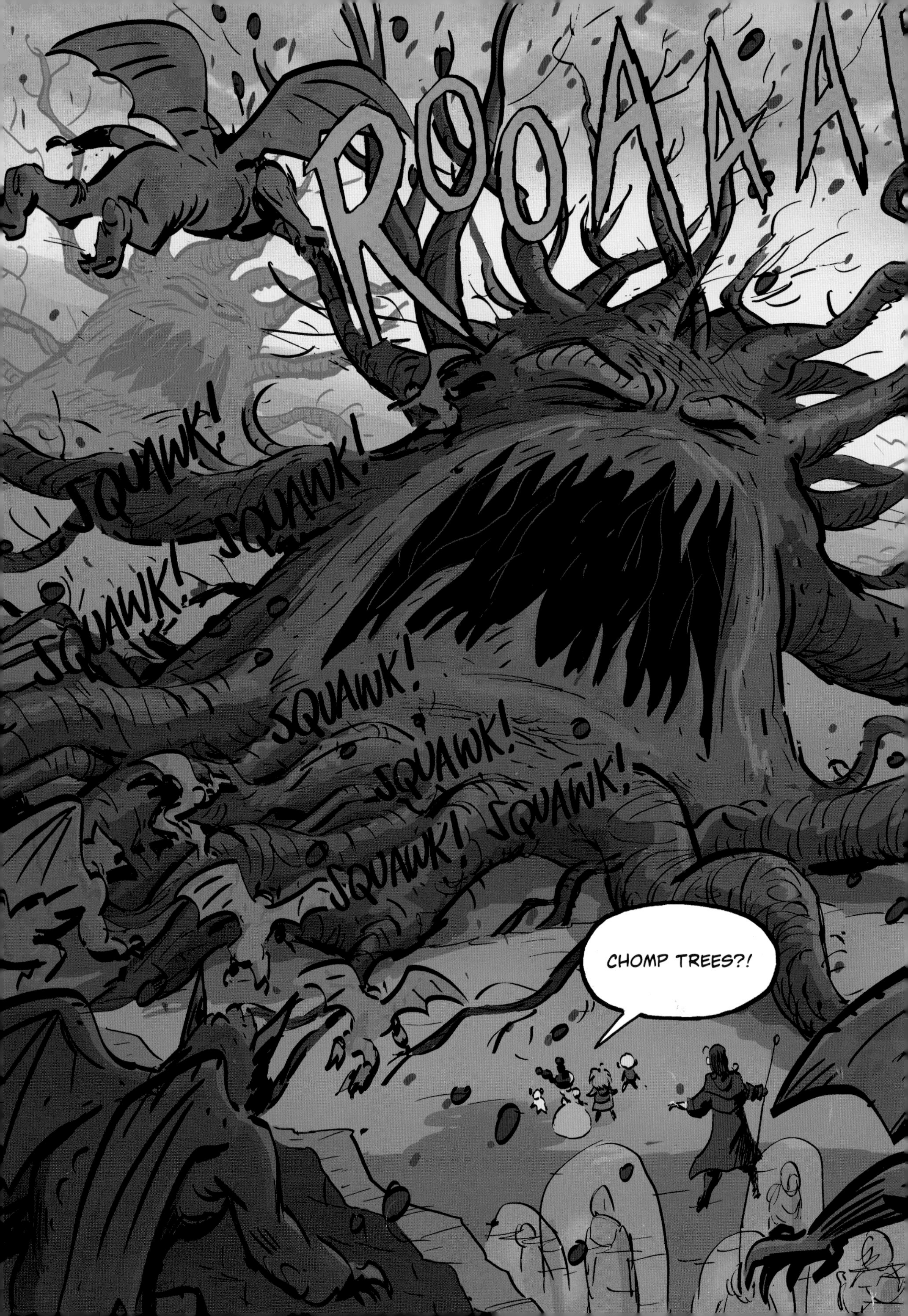
ROOOAAAA
SQUAWK!
SQUAWK!
SQUAWK!
SQUAWK!
SQUAWK!
SQUAWK!
SQUAWK!
CHOMP TREES?!

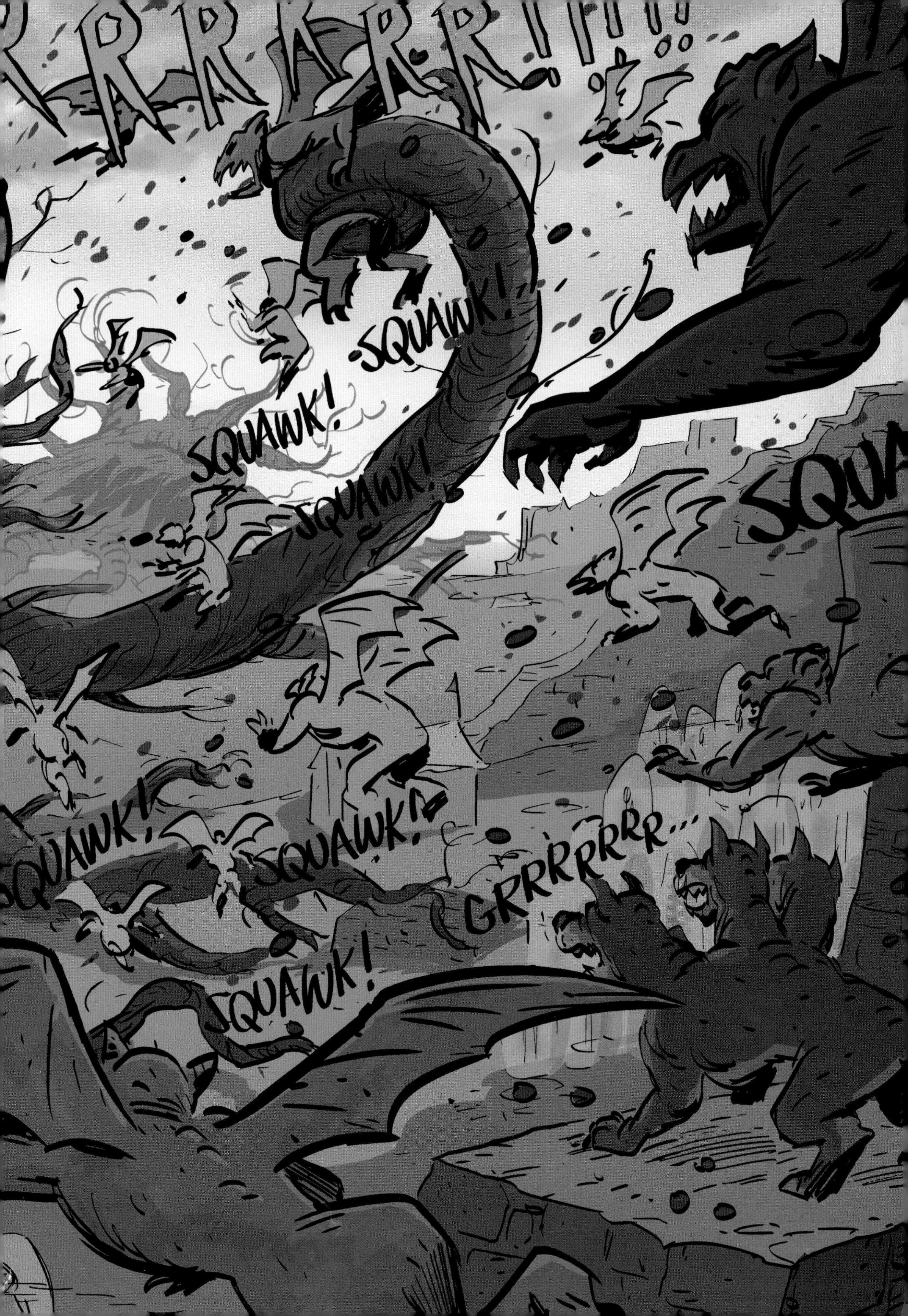
RRRARRR!!!!
SQUAWK!
SQUAWK!
SQUAWK!
SQUAWK!
SQUA
SQUAWK!
SQUAWK!
GRRRRRRR...
SQUAWK!

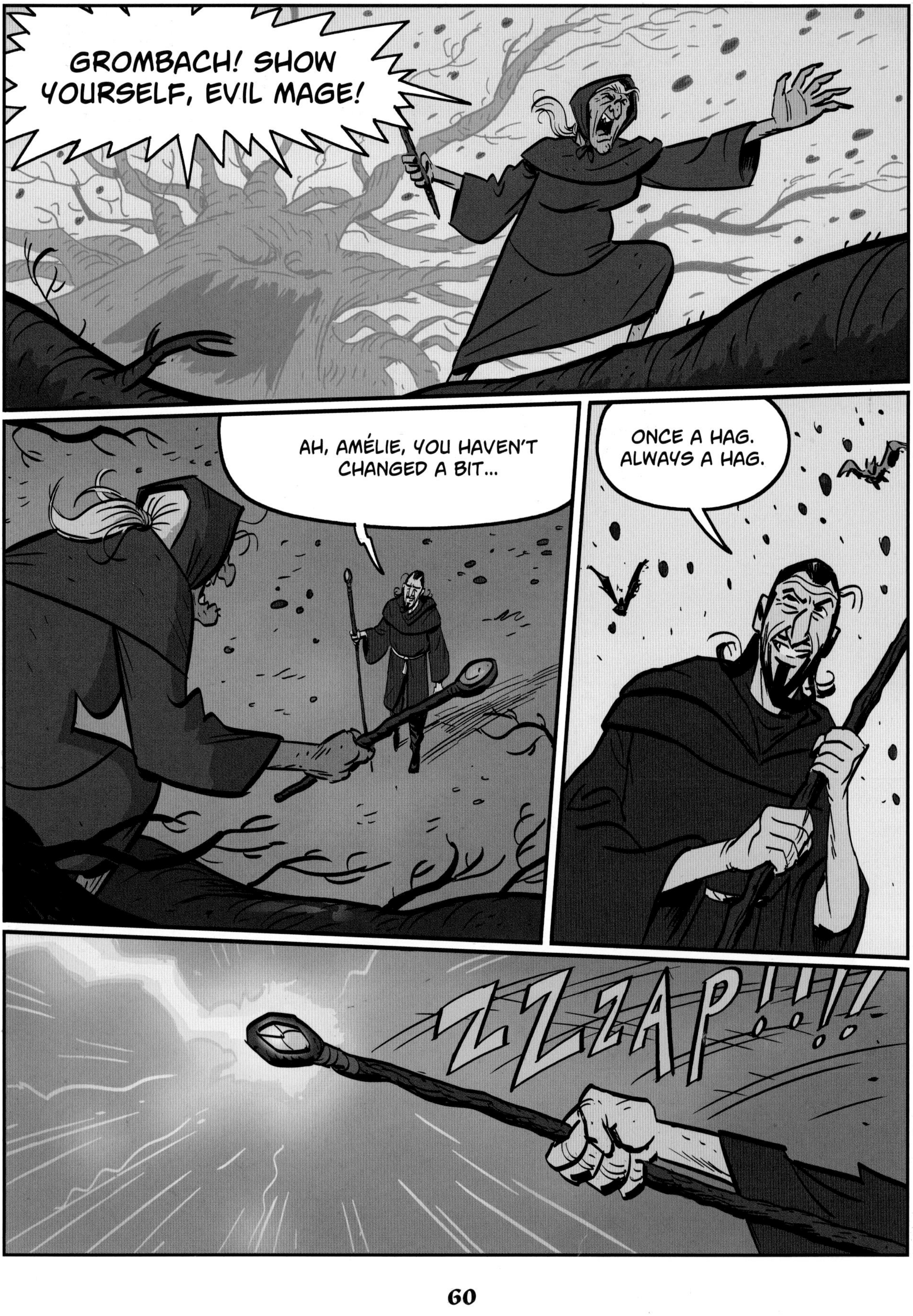
GROMBACH! SHOW YOURSELF, EVIL MAGE!
AH, AMÉLIE, YOU HAVEN'T CHANGED A BIT...
ONCE A HAG. ALWAYS A HAG.
ZZZAP!!!!

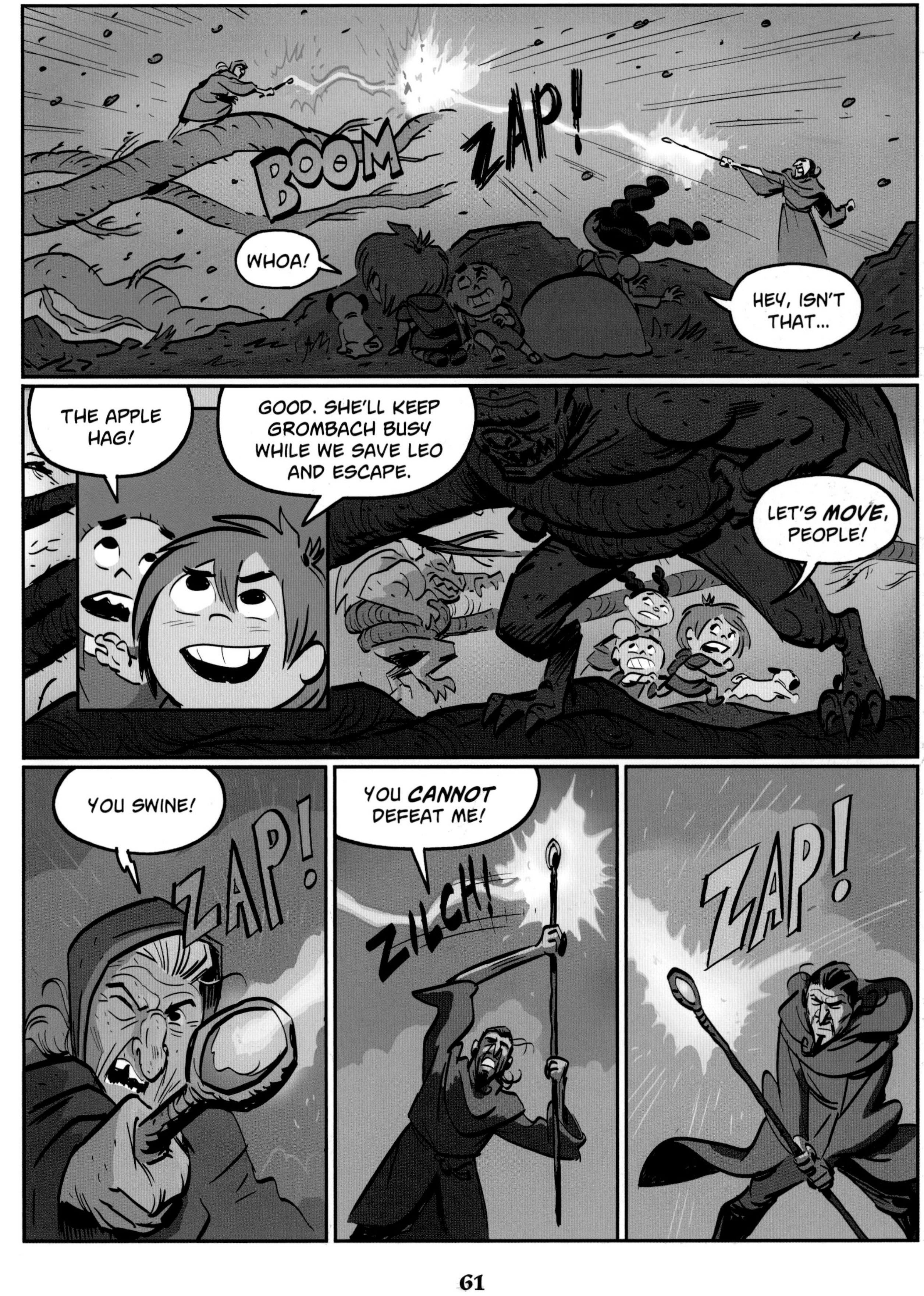
BOOM
ZAP!
WHOA!
HEY, ISN'T THAT...
THE APPLE HAG!
GOOD. SHE'LL KEEP GROMBACH BUSY WHILE WE SAVE LEO AND ESCAPE.
LET'S MOVE, PEOPLE!
YOU SWINE!
ZAP!
YOU CANNOT DEFEAT ME!
ZILCH!
ZAP!

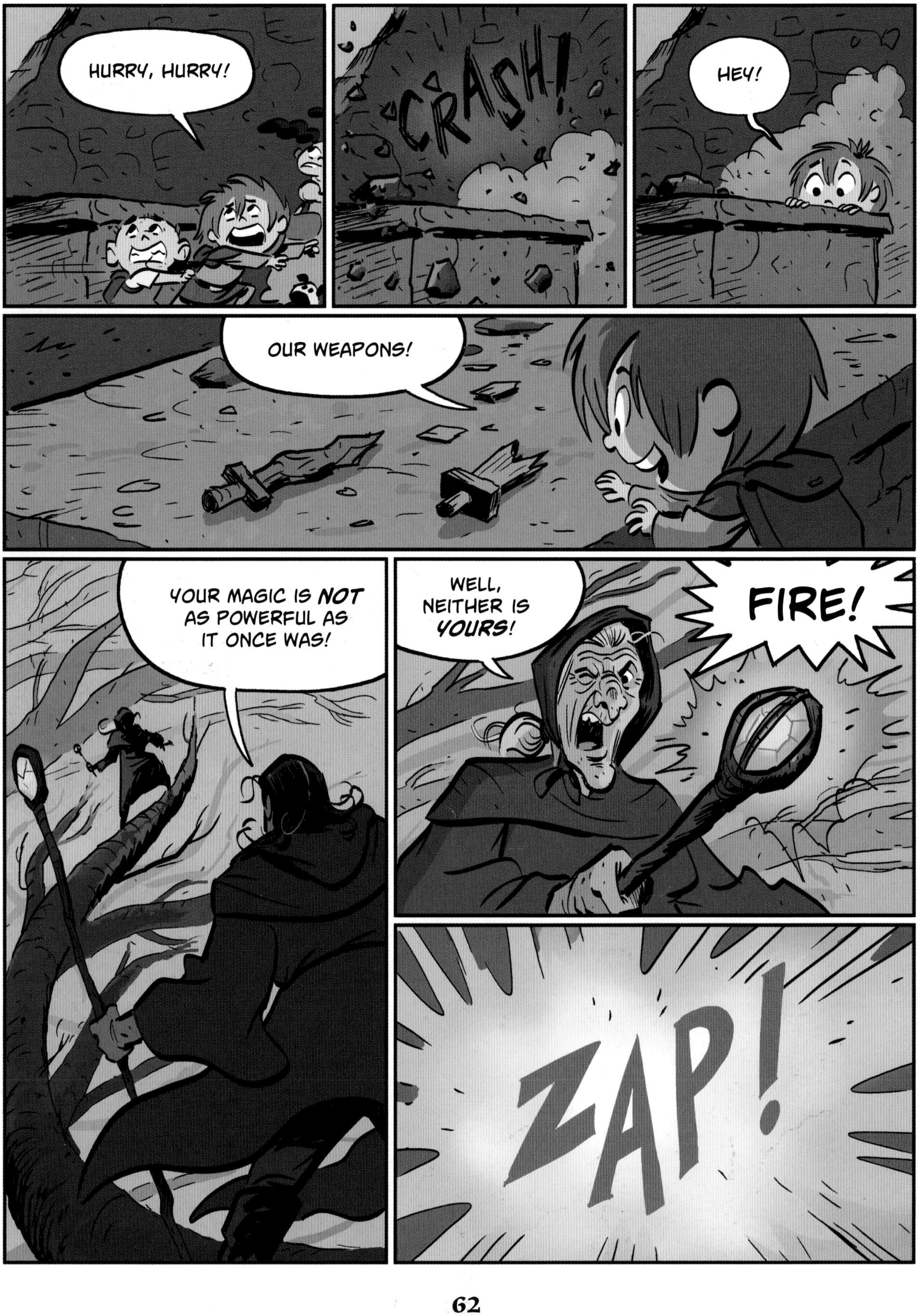
HURRY, HURRY!
CRASH!
HEY!
OUR WEAPONS!
YOUR MAGIC IS NOT AS POWERFUL AS IT ONCE WAS!
WELL, NEITHER IS YOURS!
FIRE!
ZAP!

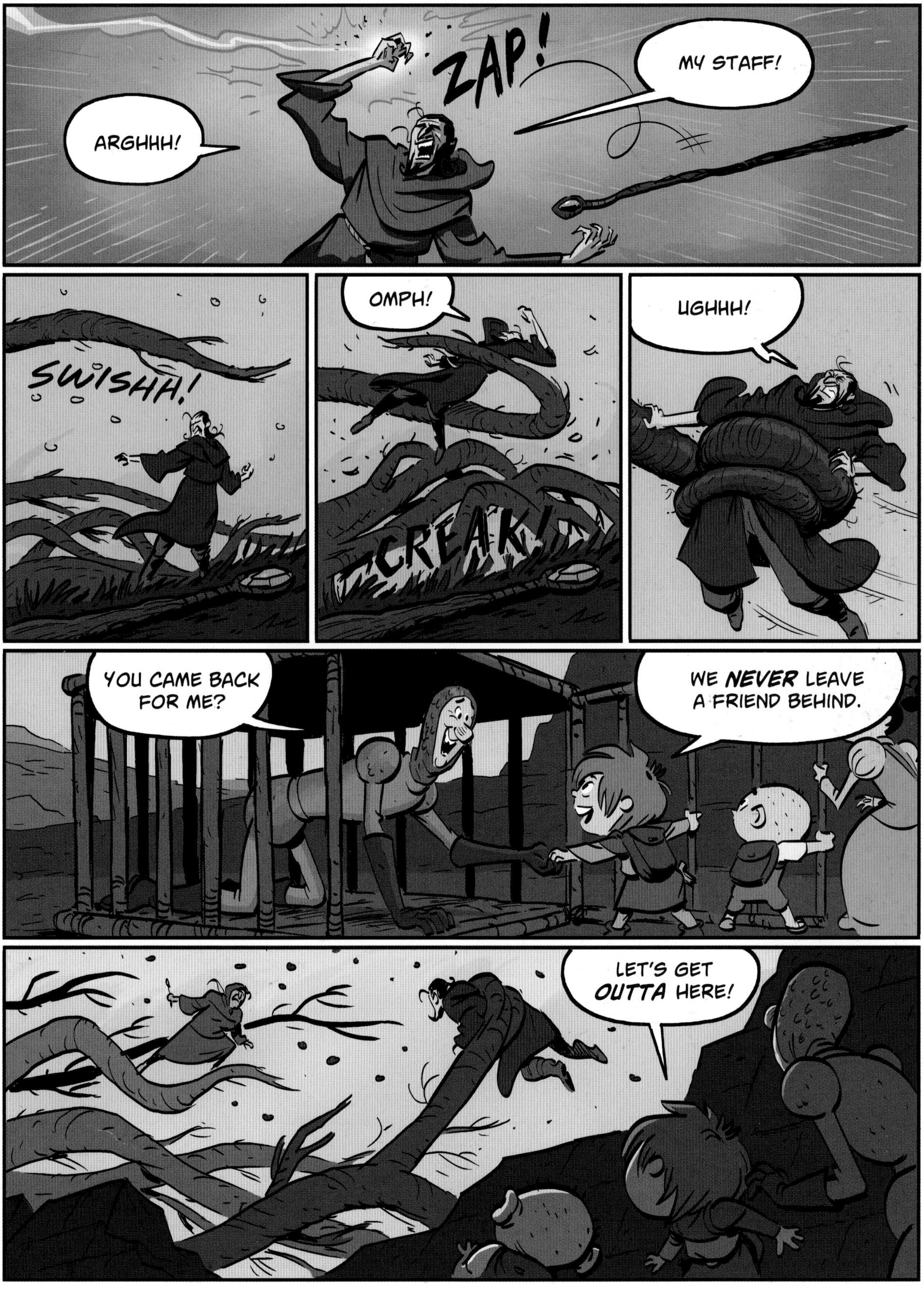
ZAP!
MY STAFF!
ARGHHH!
SWISHH!
OMPH!
CREAK!
UGHHH!
YOU CAME BACK FOR ME?
WE NEVER LEAVE A FRIEND BEHIND.
LET'S GET OUTTA HERE!

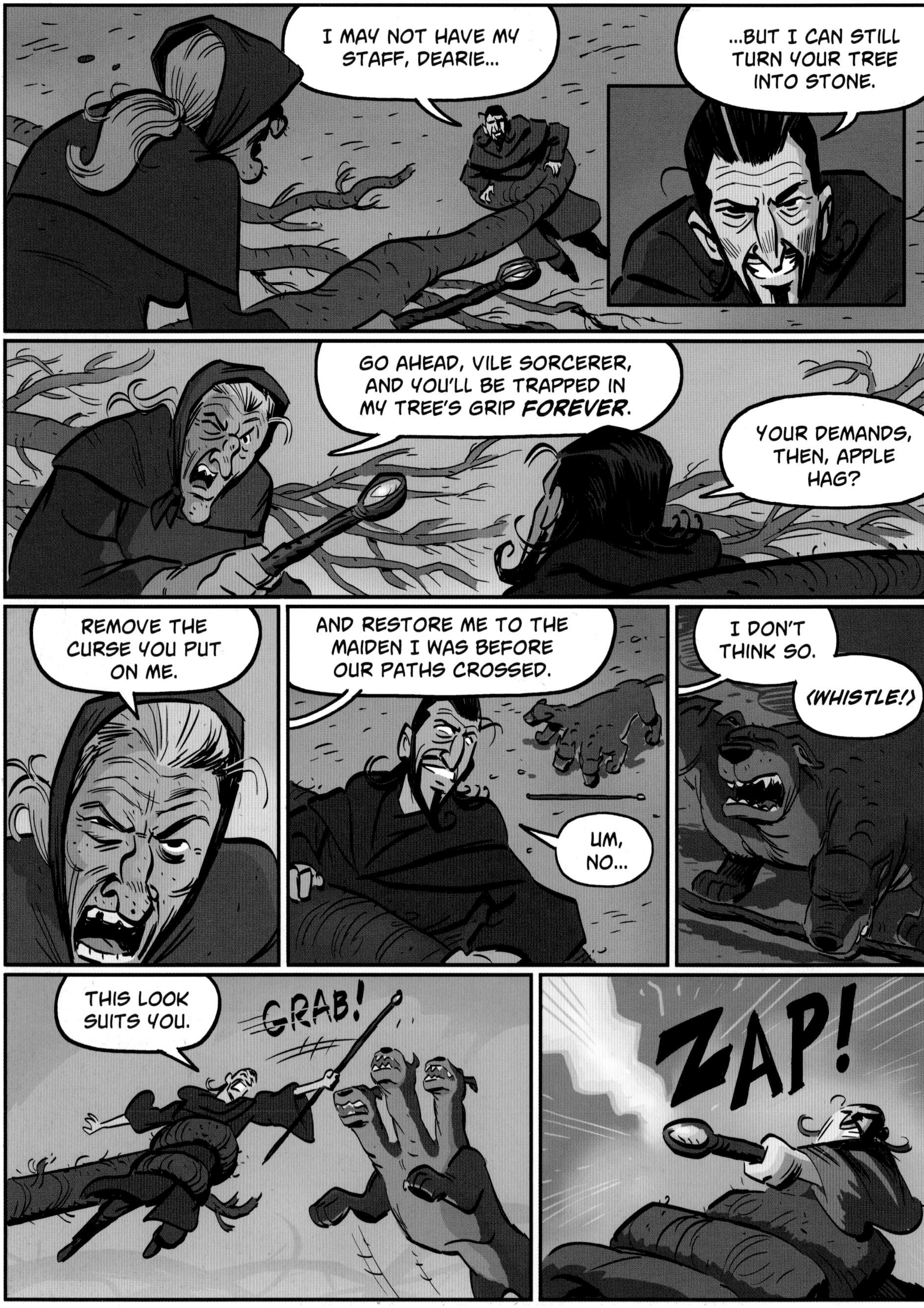
I MAY NOT HAVE MY STAFF, DEARIE...
...BUT I CAN STILL TURN YOUR TREE INTO STONE.
GO AHEAD, VILE SORCERER, AND YOU'LL BE TRAPPED IN MY TREE'S GRIP *FOREVER*.
YOUR DEMANDS, THEN, APPLE HAG?
REMOVE THE CURSE YOU PUT ON ME.
AND RESTORE ME TO THE MAIDEN I WAS BEFORE OUR PATHS CROSSED.
UM, NO...
I DON'T THINK SO.
(WHISTLE!)
THIS LOOK SUITS YOU.
GRAB!
ZAP!

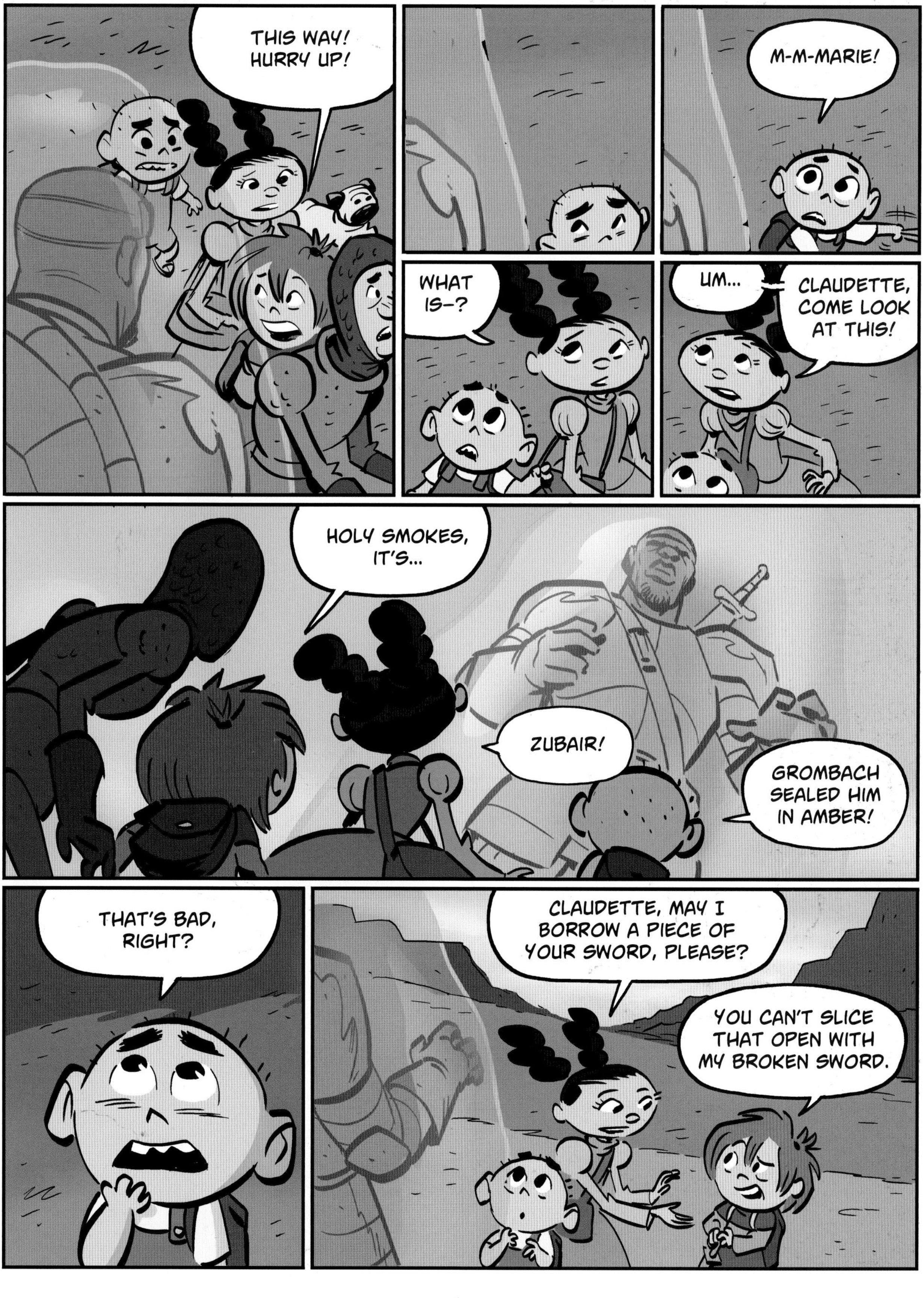
THIS WAY! HURRY UP!
M-M-MARIE!
WHAT IS–?
UM...
CLAUDETTE, COME LOOK AT THIS!
HOLY SMOKES, IT'S...
ZUBAIR!
GROMBACH SEALED HIM IN AMBER!
THAT'S BAD, RIGHT?
CLAUDETTE, MAY I BORROW A PIECE OF YOUR SWORD, PLEASE?
YOU CAN'T SLICE THAT OPEN WITH MY BROKEN SWORD.

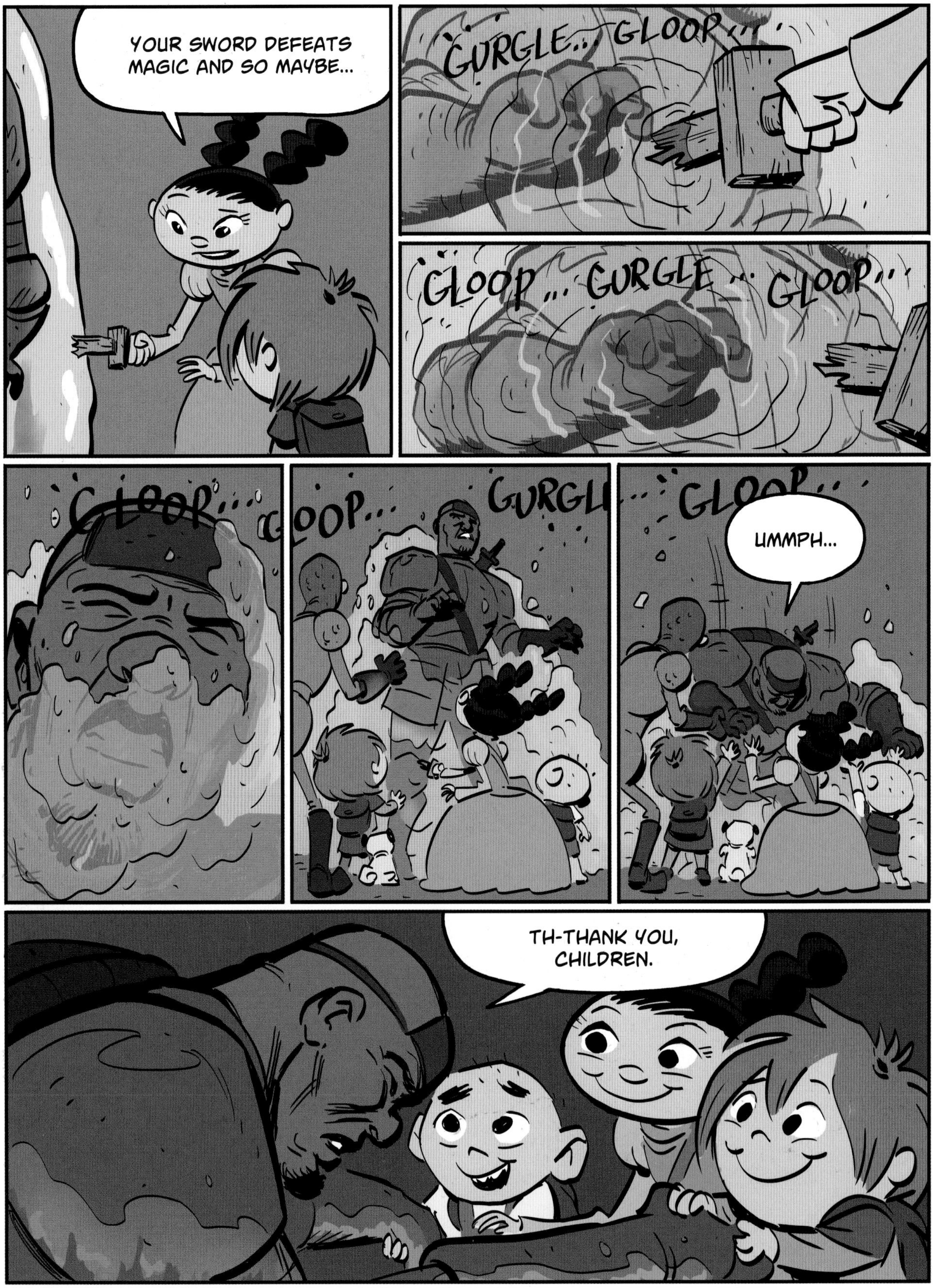

YOUR SWORD DEFEATS MAGIC AND SO MAYBE...
GURGLE... GLOOP...
GLOOP... GURGLE... GLOOP...
GLOOP... GLOOP...
GURGLE...
GLOOP...
UMMPH...
TH-THANK YOU, CHILDREN.

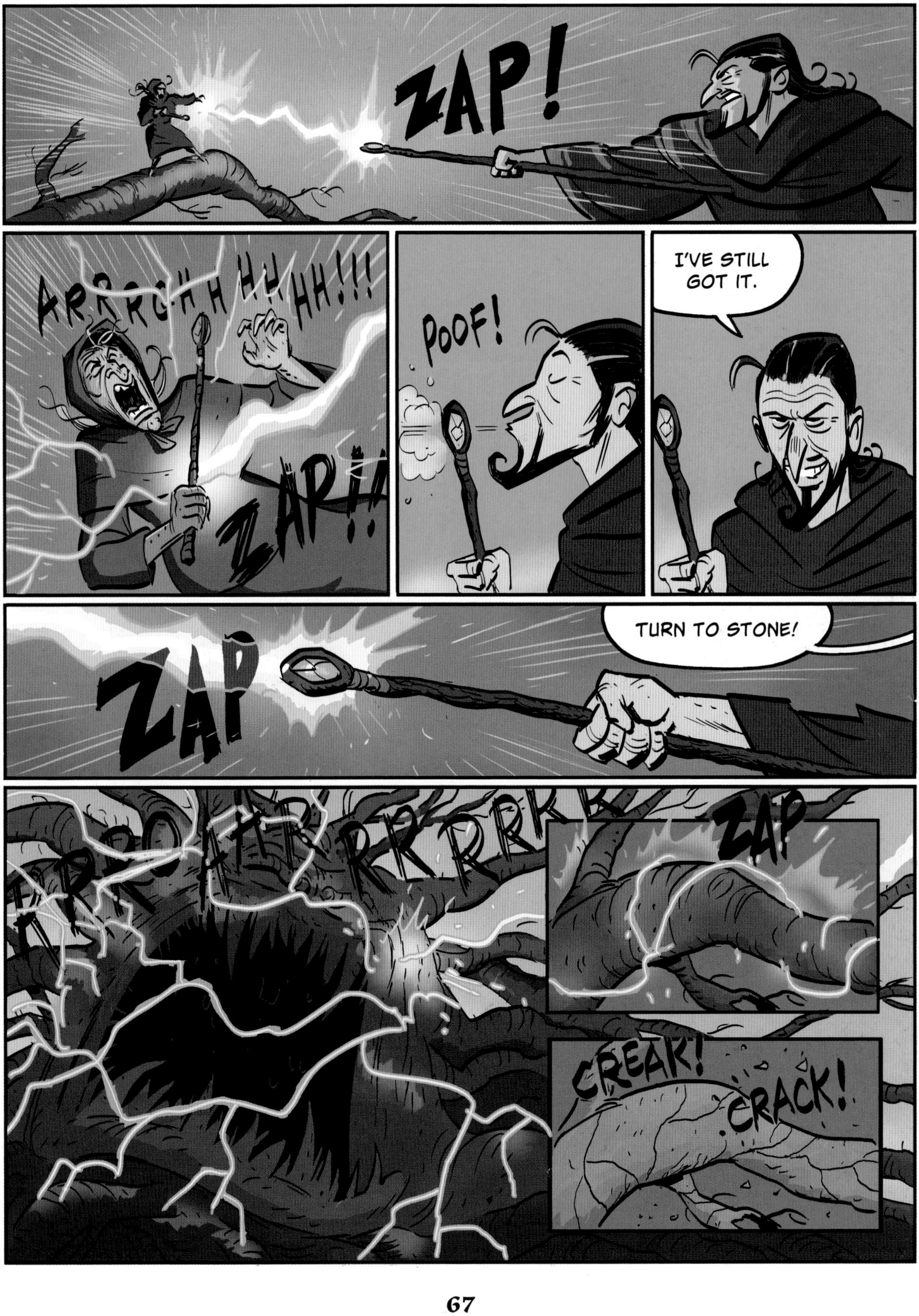
ZAP!
ARRRGHHHHHH!!!
ZAP!!!
POOF!
I'VE STILL GOT IT.
TURN TO STONE!
ZAP
ZAP
CREAK!
CRACK!

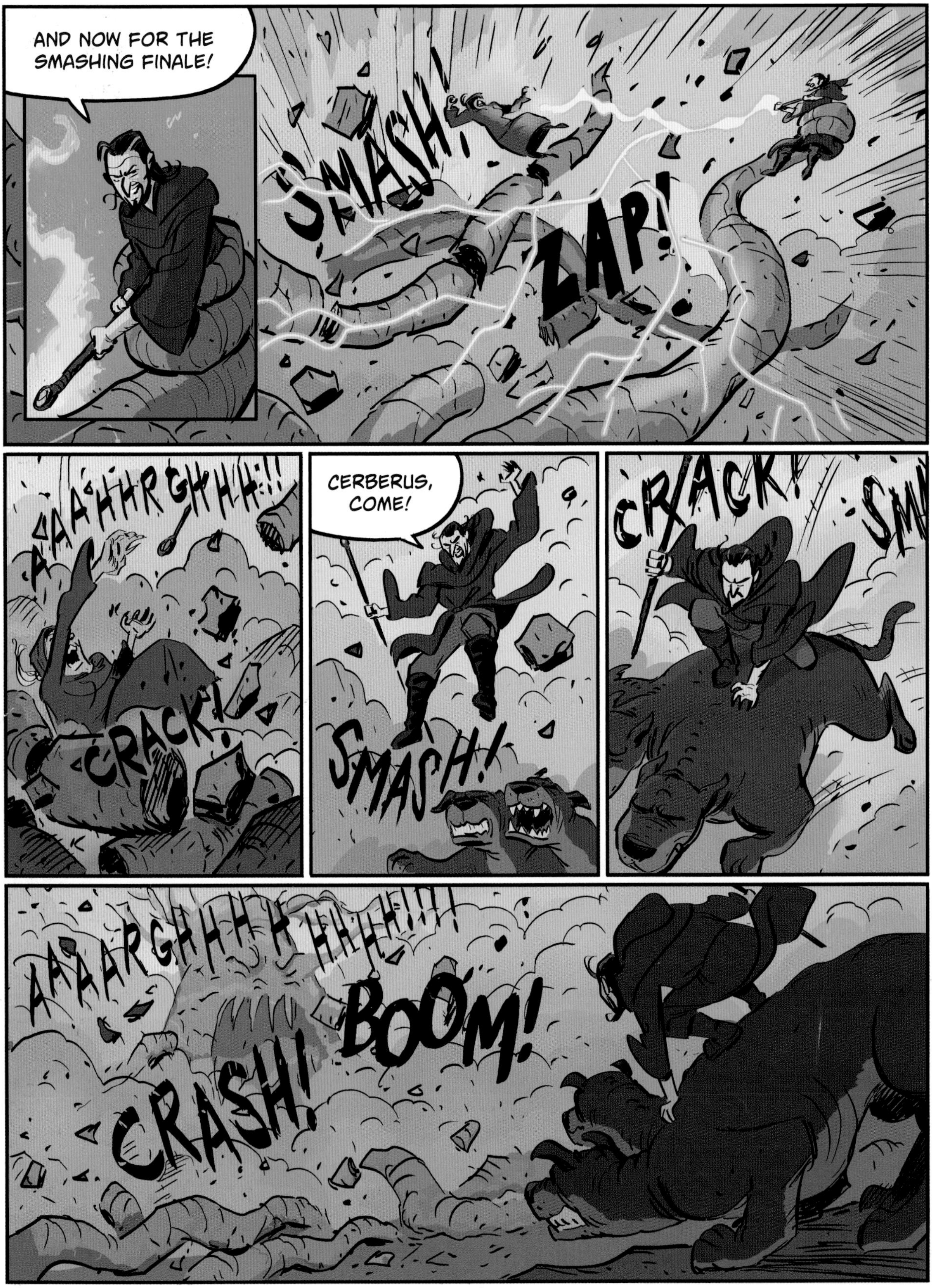
AND NOW FOR THE SMASHING FINALE!
SMASH!
ZAP!
AAAHHRGHHH!!!
CRACK!
CERBERUS, COME!
SMASH!
CRACK!
AAAARGHHHHHHHH!!!!
BOOM!
CRASH!

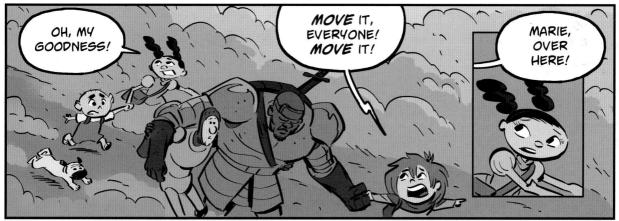

OH, MY GOODNESS!

MOVE IT, EVERYONE! MOVE IT!

MARIE, OVER HERE!

WE, THE SEVEN MIGHTY PRINCES, HAVE COME TO RESCUE YOU!

WE'LL BE RIGHT THERE, MARIE!

IT'S FAR TOO DANGEROUS!

NO, PLEASE, GO BACK!

SLAM!

AAAAHHHHHH!

SQUAWK! SQUAWK!

AAHHHHHHHAAHHH!

MY FELLOW PRINCES, MARIE MAKES A VALID POINT.

I WANT TO GO HOME.

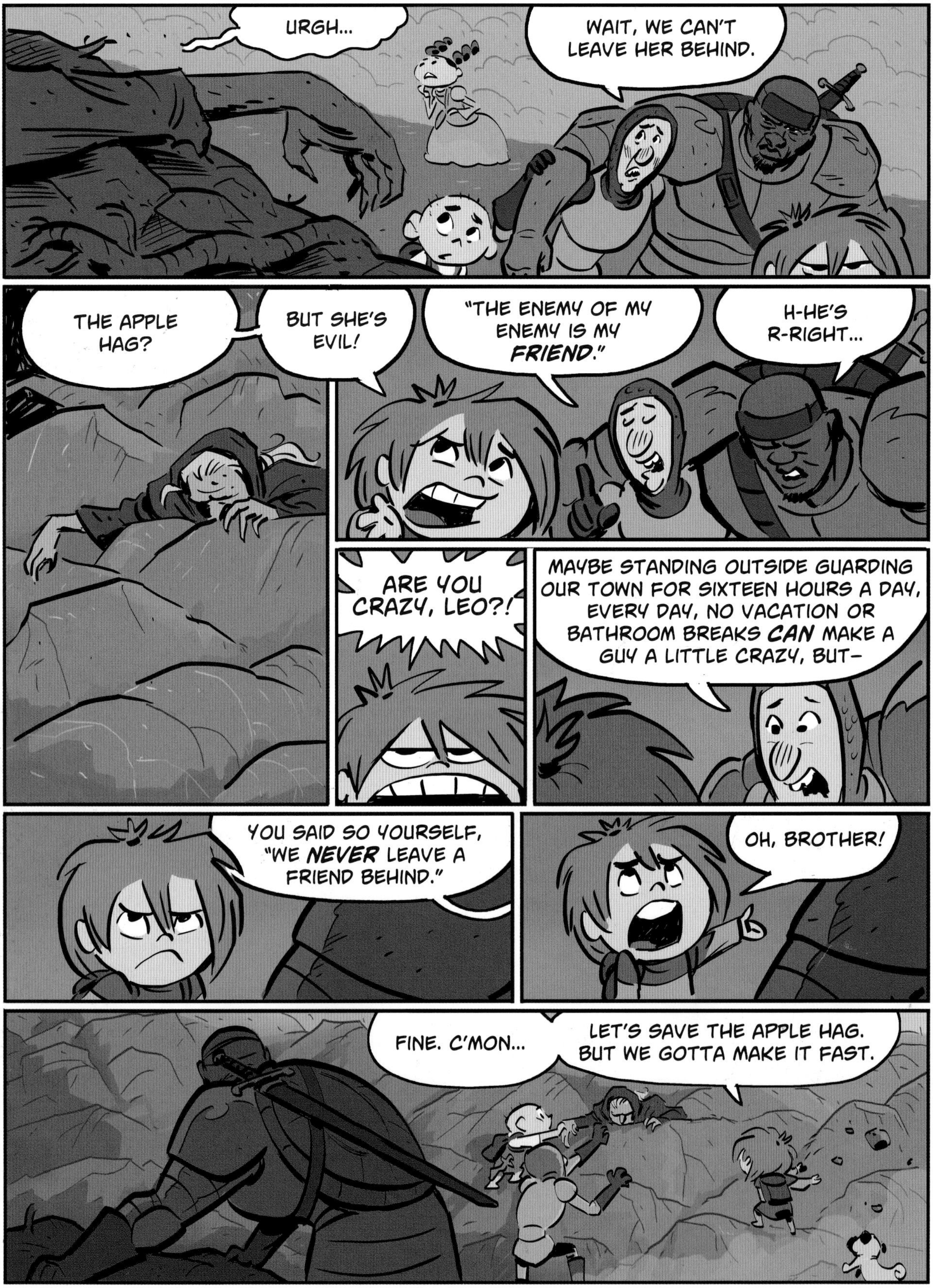
URGH...
WAIT, WE CAN'T LEAVE HER BEHIND.
THE APPLE HAG?
BUT SHE'S EVIL!
"THE ENEMY OF MY ENEMY IS MY *FRIEND*."
H-HE'S R-RIGHT...
ARE YOU CRAZY, LEO?!
MAYBE STANDING OUTSIDE GUARDING OUR TOWN FOR SIXTEEN HOURS A DAY, EVERY DAY, NO VACATION OR BATHROOM BREAKS *CAN* MAKE A GUY A LITTLE CRAZY, BUT–
YOU SAID SO YOURSELF, "WE *NEVER* LEAVE A FRIEND BEHIND."
OH, BROTHER!
FINE. C'MON...
LET'S SAVE THE APPLE HAG. BUT WE GOTTA MAKE IT FAST.

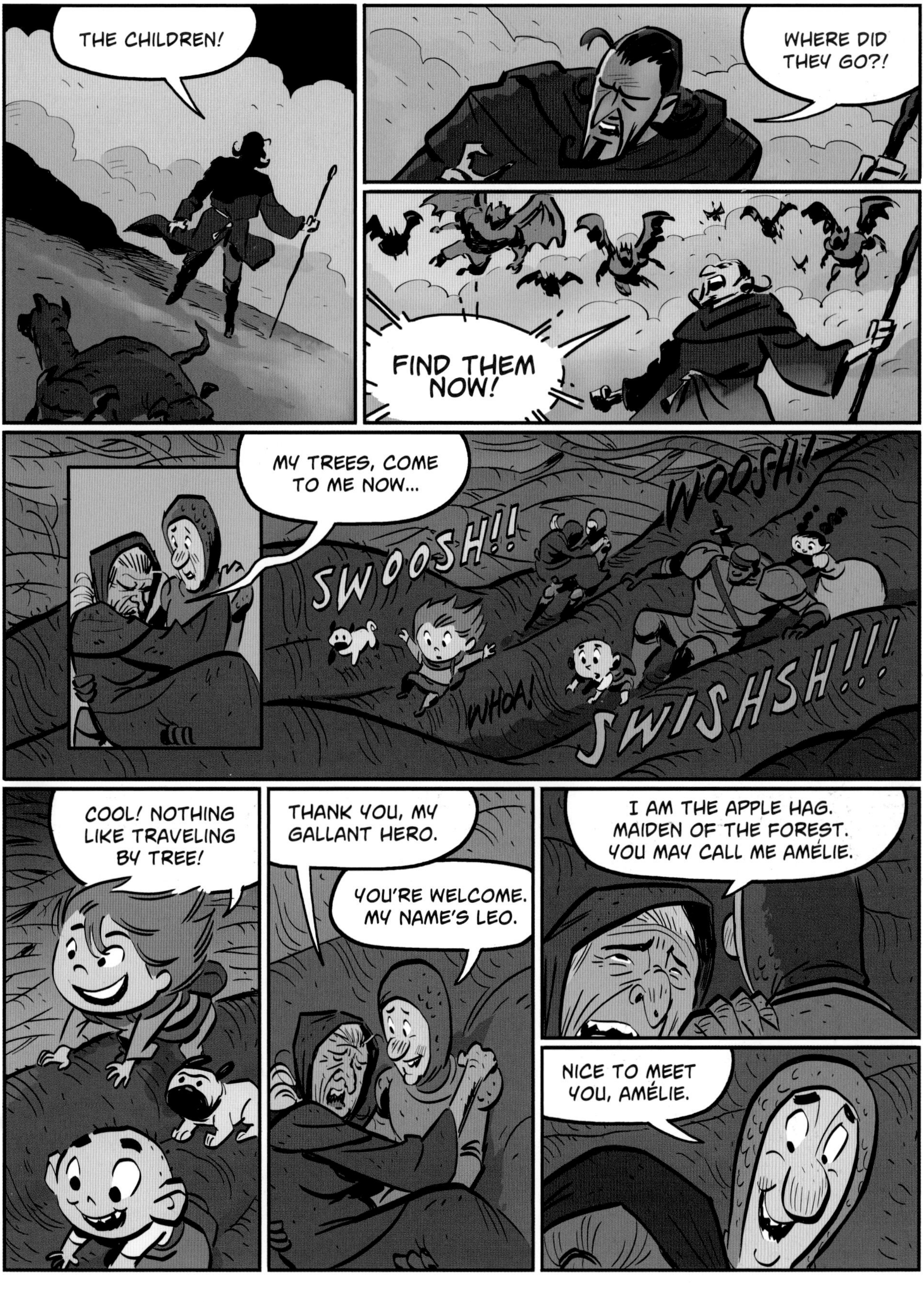
THE CHILDREN!
WHERE DID THEY GO?!
FIND THEM NOW!
MY TREES, COME TO ME NOW...
SWOOSH!!
WOOSH!
WHOA!
SWISHSH!!!
COOL! NOTHING LIKE TRAVELING BY TREE!
THANK YOU, MY GALLANT HERO.
YOU'RE WELCOME. MY NAME'S LEO.
I AM THE APPLE HAG. MAIDEN OF THE FOREST. YOU MAY CALL ME AMÉLIE.
NICE TO MEET YOU, AMÉLIE.

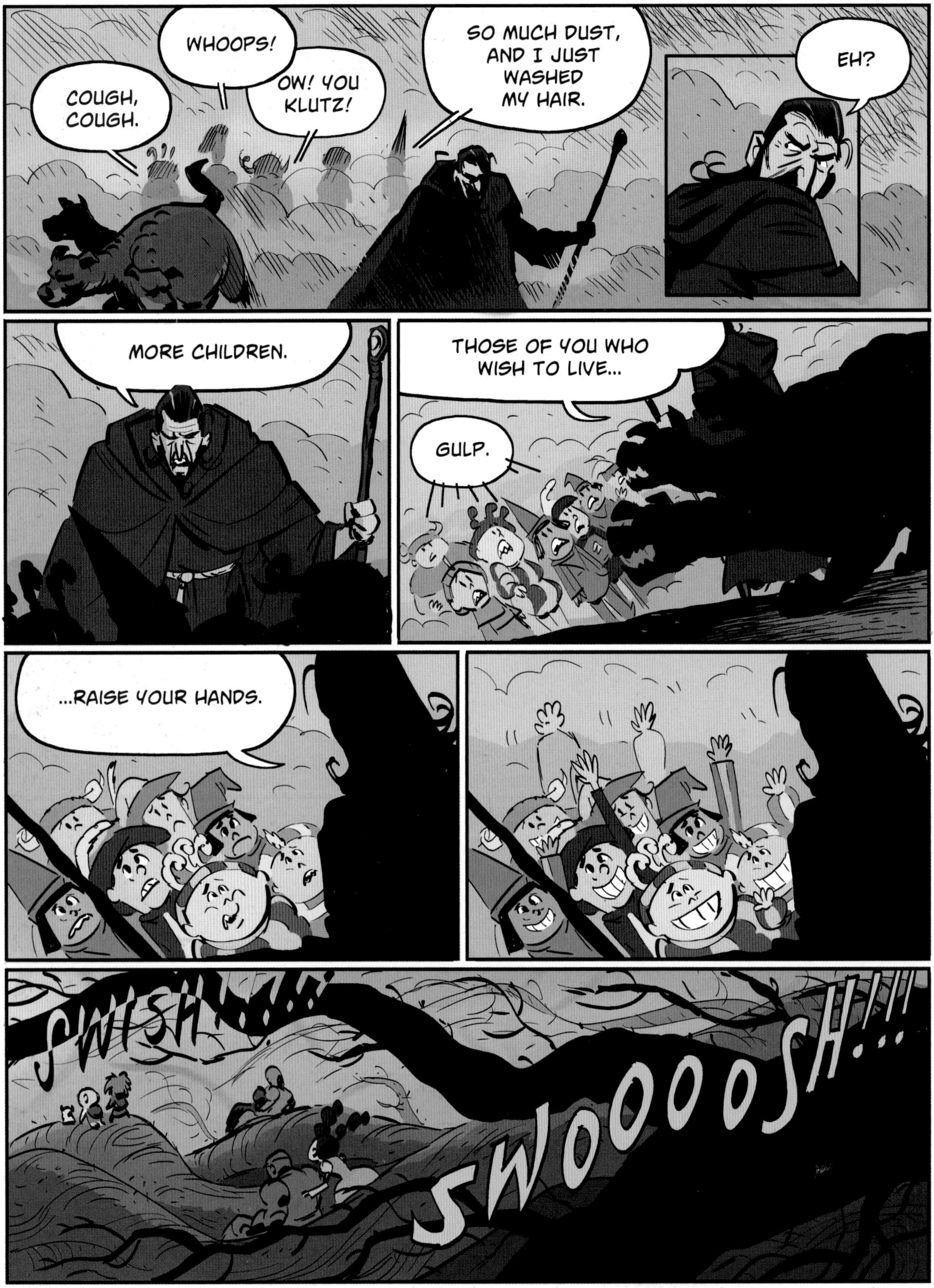
COUGH, COUGH.
WHOOPS!
OW! YOU KLUTZ!
SO MUCH DUST, AND I JUST WASHED MY HAIR.
EH?
MORE CHILDREN.
THOSE OF YOU WHO WISH TO LIVE...
GULP.
...RAISE YOUR HANDS.
SWISH!!!
SWOOOOSH!!!

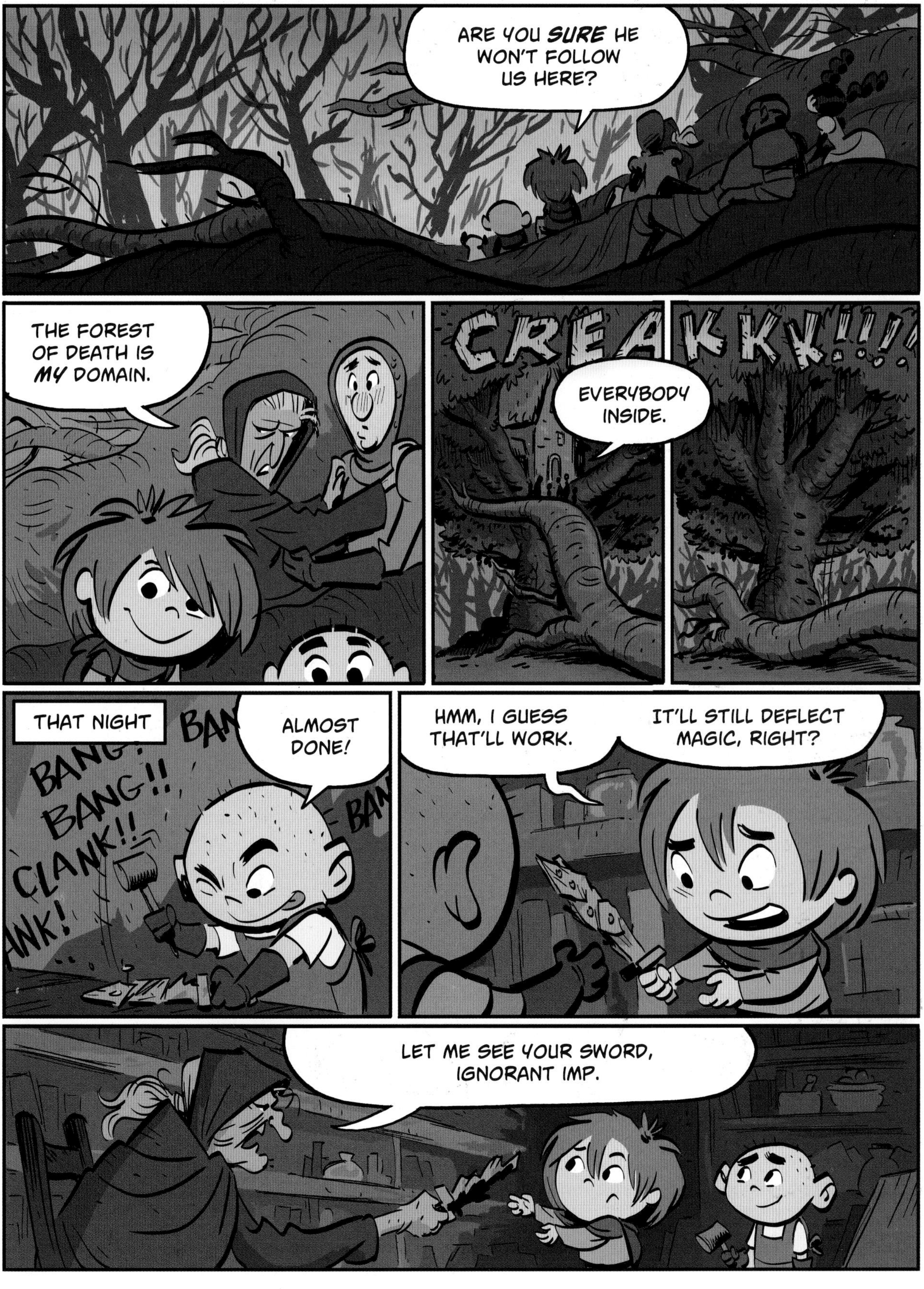
ARE YOU SURE HE WON'T FOLLOW US HERE?
THE FOREST OF DEATH IS MY DOMAIN.
CREAKK!!!!
EVERYBODY INSIDE.
THAT NIGHT
BANG! BANG!! CLANK!!
ALMOST DONE!
HMM, I GUESS THAT'LL WORK.
IT'LL STILL DEFLECT MAGIC, RIGHT?
LET ME SEE YOUR SWORD, IGNORANT IMP.

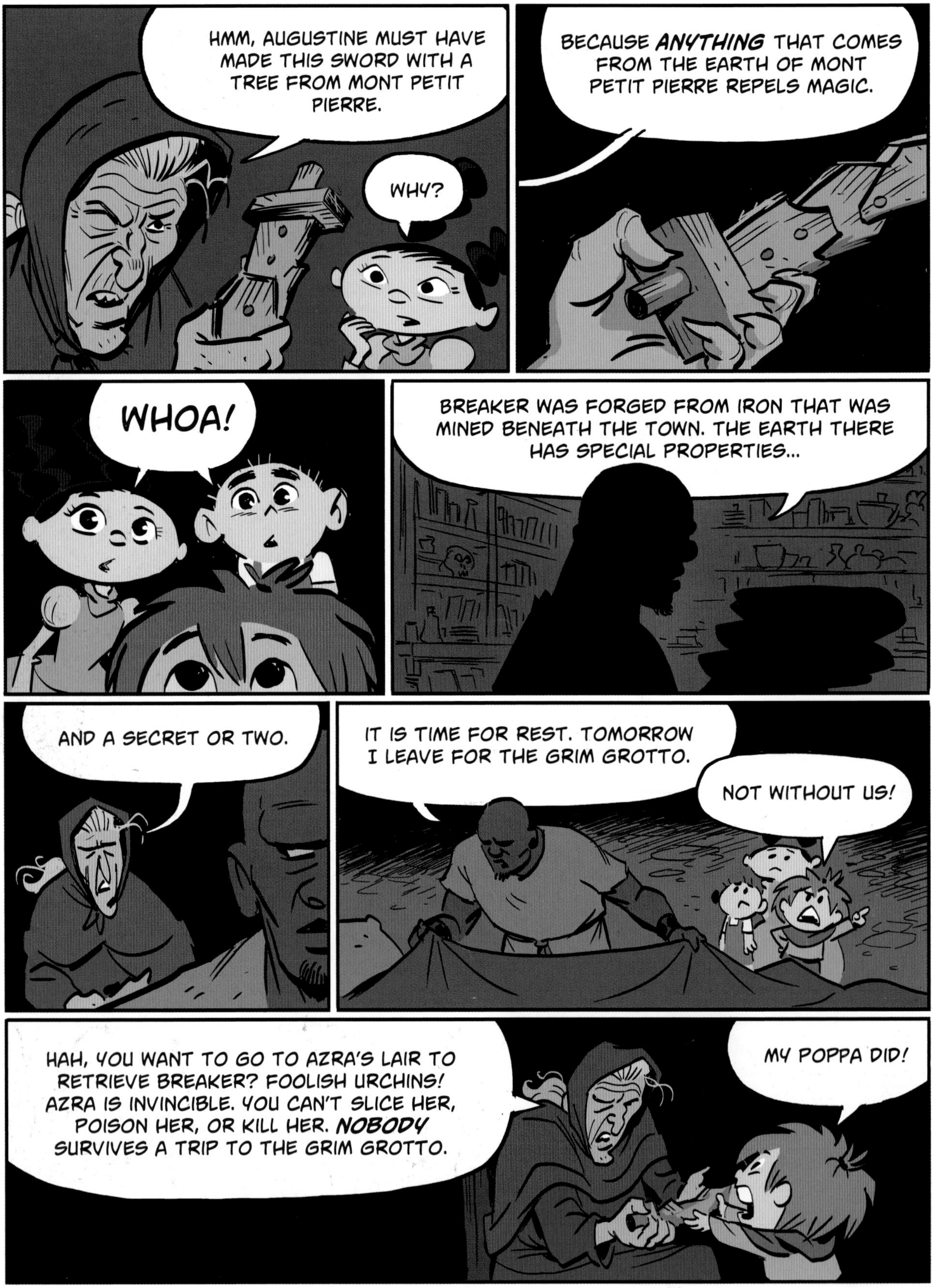
HMM, AUGUSTINE MUST HAVE MADE THIS SWORD WITH A TREE FROM MONT PETIT PIERRE.
WHY?
BECAUSE ***ANYTHING*** THAT COMES FROM THE EARTH OF MONT PETIT PIERRE REPELS MAGIC.
WHOA!
BREAKER WAS FORGED FROM IRON THAT WAS MINED BENEATH THE TOWN. THE EARTH THERE HAS SPECIAL PROPERTIES...
AND A SECRET OR TWO.
IT IS TIME FOR REST. TOMORROW I LEAVE FOR THE GRIM GROTTO.
NOT WITHOUT US!
HAH, YOU WANT TO GO TO AZRA'S LAIR TO RETRIEVE BREAKER? FOOLISH URCHINS! AZRA IS INVINCIBLE. YOU CAN'T SLICE HER, POISON HER, OR KILL HER. ***NOBODY*** SURVIVES A TRIP TO THE GRIM GROTTO.
MY POPPA DID!

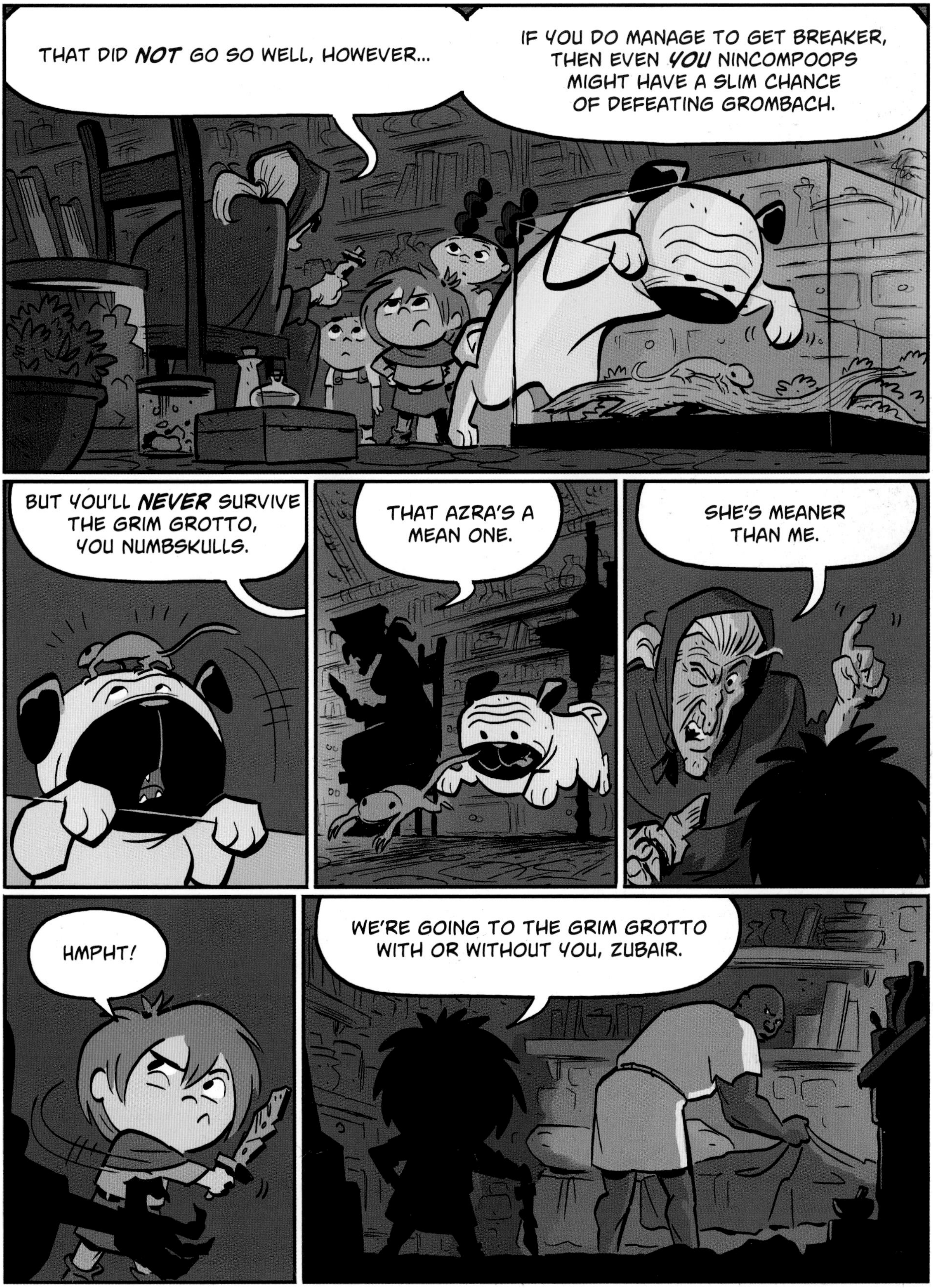
THAT DID NOT GO SO WELL, HOWEVER...
IF YOU DO MANAGE TO GET BREAKER, THEN EVEN YOU NINCOMPOOPS MIGHT HAVE A SLIM CHANCE OF DEFEATING GROMBACH.
BUT YOU'LL NEVER SURVIVE THE GRIM GROTTO, YOU NUMBSKULLS.
THAT AZRA'S A MEAN ONE.
SHE'S MEANER THAN ME.
HMPHT!
WE'RE GOING TO THE GRIM GROTTO WITH OR WITHOUT YOU, ZUBAIR.

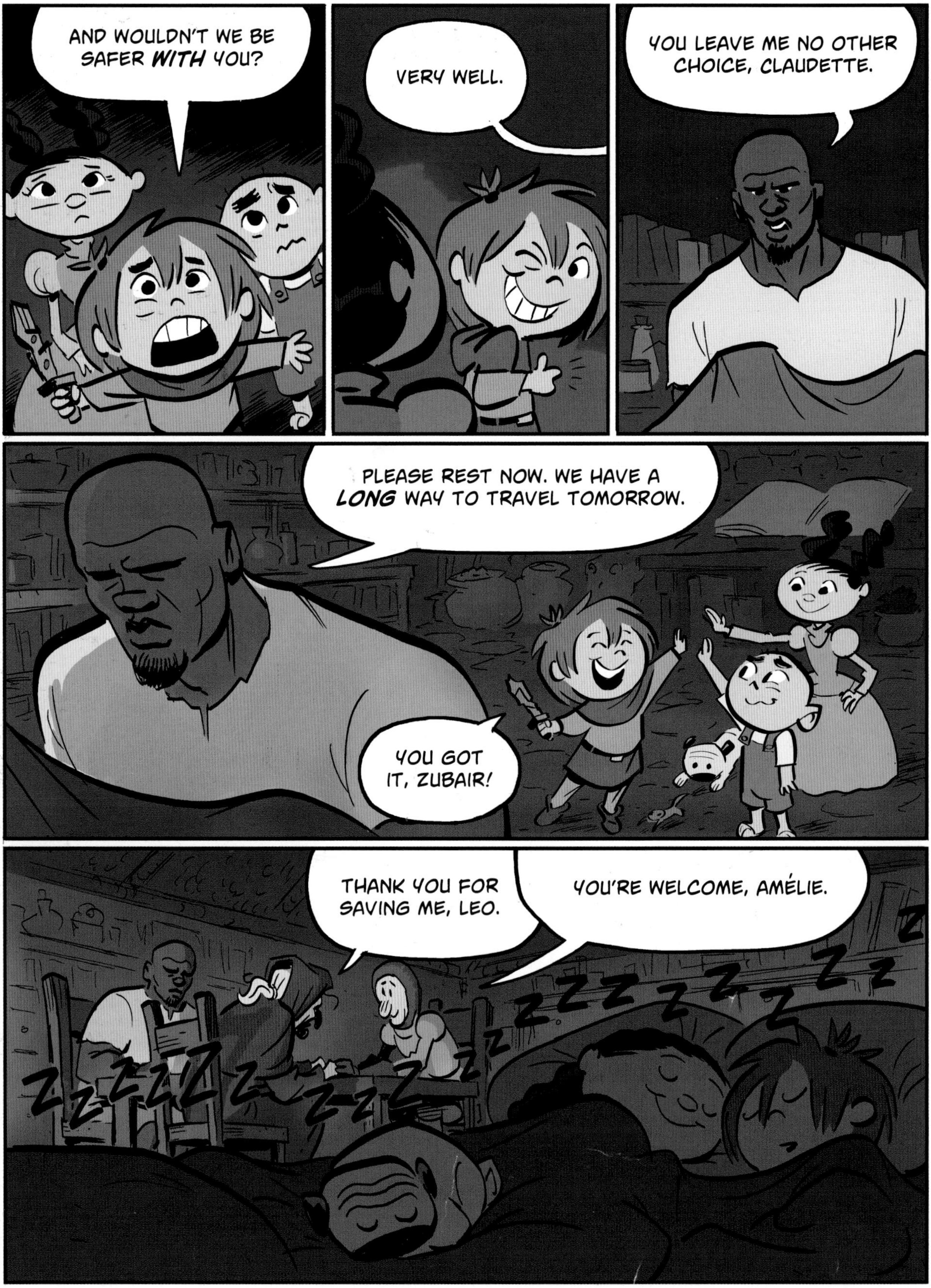
AND WOULDN'T WE BE SAFER *WITH* YOU?
VERY WELL.
YOU LEAVE ME NO OTHER CHOICE, CLAUDETTE.
PLEASE REST NOW. WE HAVE A *LONG* WAY TO TRAVEL TOMORROW.
YOU GOT IT, ZUBAIR!
THANK YOU FOR SAVING ME, LEO.
YOU'RE WELCOME, AMÉLIE.

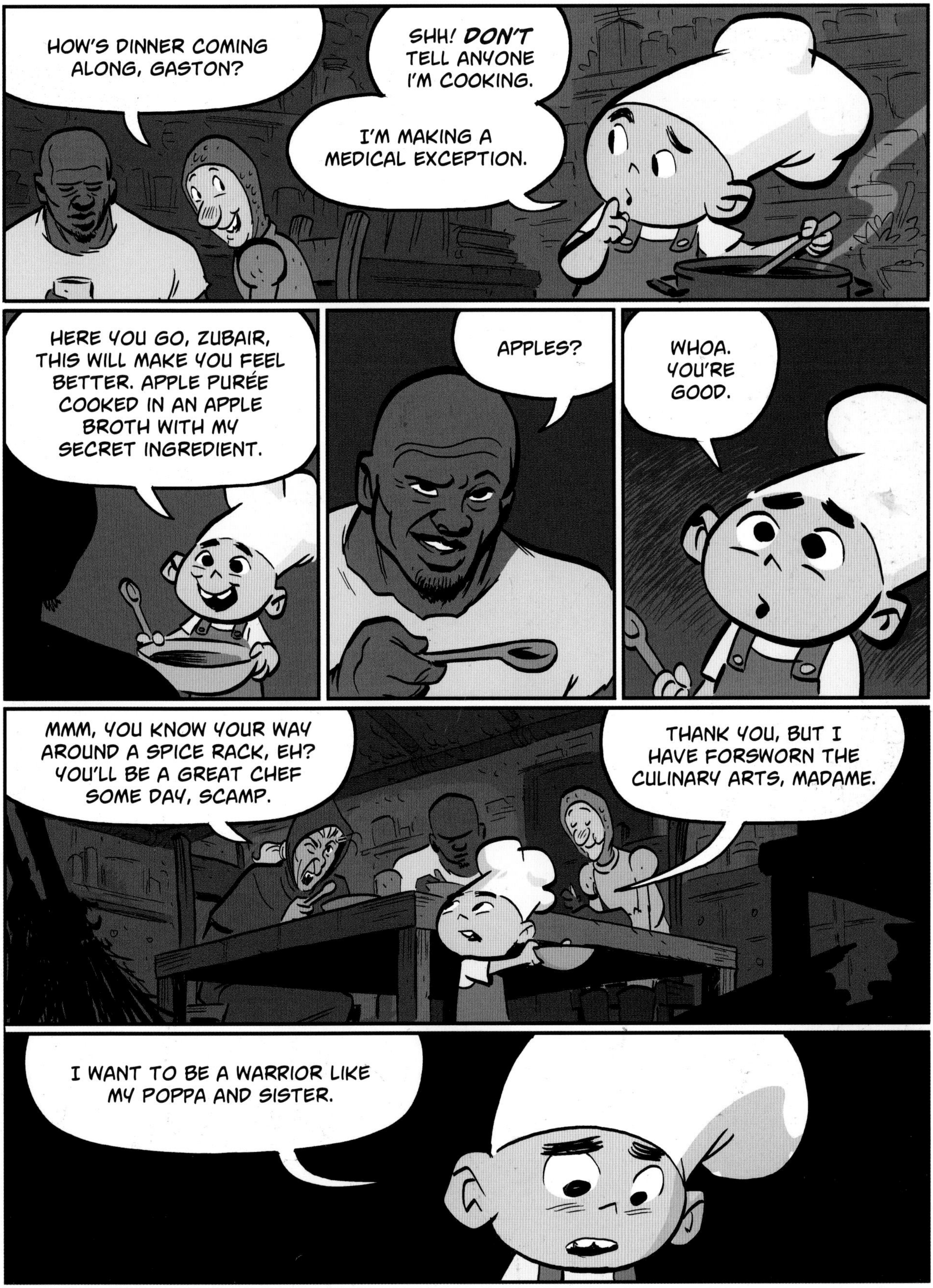
HOW'S DINNER COMING ALONG, GASTON?
SHH! ***DON'T*** TELL ANYONE I'M COOKING.
I'M MAKING A MEDICAL EXCEPTION.
HERE YOU GO, ZUBAIR, THIS WILL MAKE YOU FEEL BETTER. APPLE PURÉE COOKED IN AN APPLE BROTH WITH MY SECRET INGREDIENT.
APPLES?
WHOA. YOU'RE GOOD.
MMM, YOU KNOW YOUR WAY AROUND A SPICE RACK, EH? YOU'LL BE A GREAT CHEF SOME DAY, SCAMP.
THANK YOU, BUT I HAVE FORSWORN THE CULINARY ARTS, MADAME.
I WANT TO BE A WARRIOR LIKE MY POPPA AND SISTER.

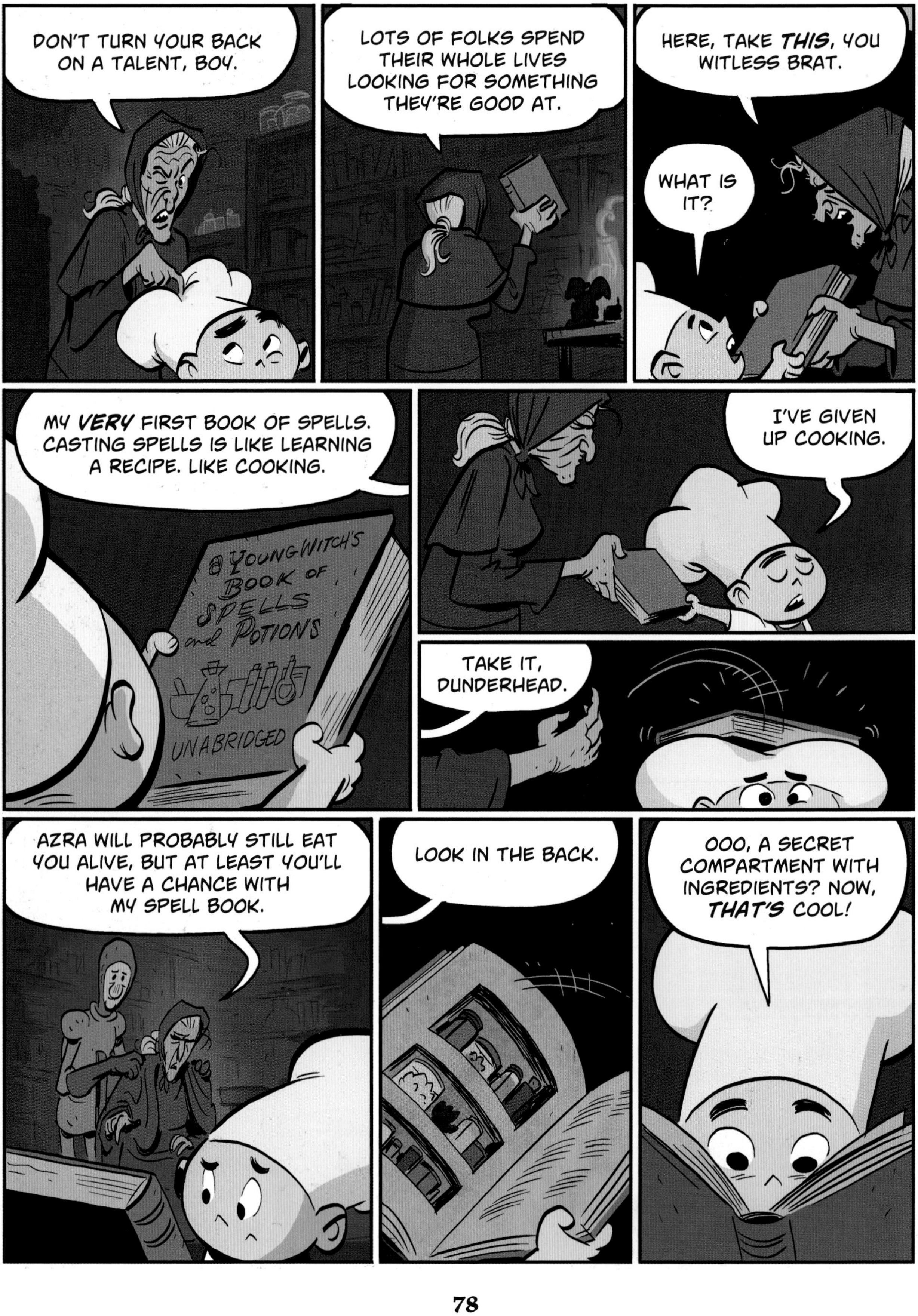
DON'T TURN YOUR BACK ON A TALENT, BOY.
LOTS OF FOLKS SPEND THEIR WHOLE LIVES LOOKING FOR SOMETHING THEY'RE GOOD AT.
HERE, TAKE *THIS*, YOU WITLESS BRAT.
WHAT IS IT?
MY *VERY* FIRST BOOK OF SPELLS. CASTING SPELLS IS LIKE LEARNING A RECIPE. LIKE COOKING.
A YOUNG WITCH'S BOOK OF SPELLS and POTIONS
UNABRIDGED
I'VE GIVEN UP COOKING.
TAKE IT, DUNDERHEAD.
AZRA WILL PROBABLY STILL EAT YOU ALIVE, BUT AT LEAST YOU'LL HAVE A CHANCE WITH MY SPELL BOOK.
LOOK IN THE BACK.
OOO, A SECRET COMPARTMENT WITH INGREDIENTS? NOW, *THAT'S* COOL!

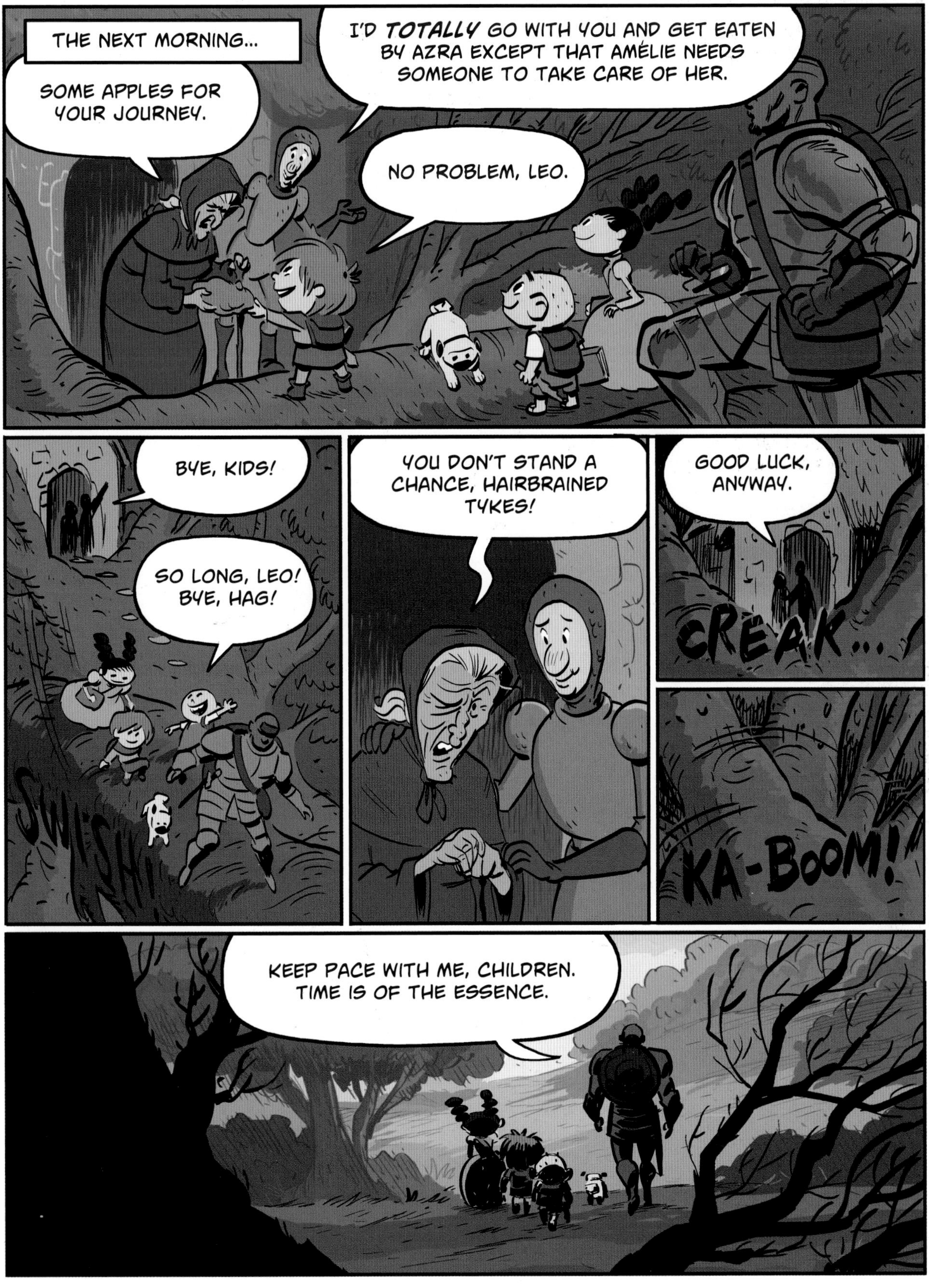
THE NEXT MORNING...
SOME APPLES FOR YOUR JOURNEY.
I'D **TOTALLY** GO WITH YOU AND GET EATEN BY AZRA EXCEPT THAT AMÉLIE NEEDS SOMEONE TO TAKE CARE OF HER.
NO PROBLEM, LEO.
BYE, KIDS!
SO LONG, LEO! BYE, HAG!
SWISH
YOU DON'T STAND A CHANCE, HAIRBRAINED TYKES!
GOOD LUCK, ANYWAY.
CREAK...
KA-BOOM!
KEEP PACE WITH ME, CHILDREN. TIME IS OF THE ESSENCE.

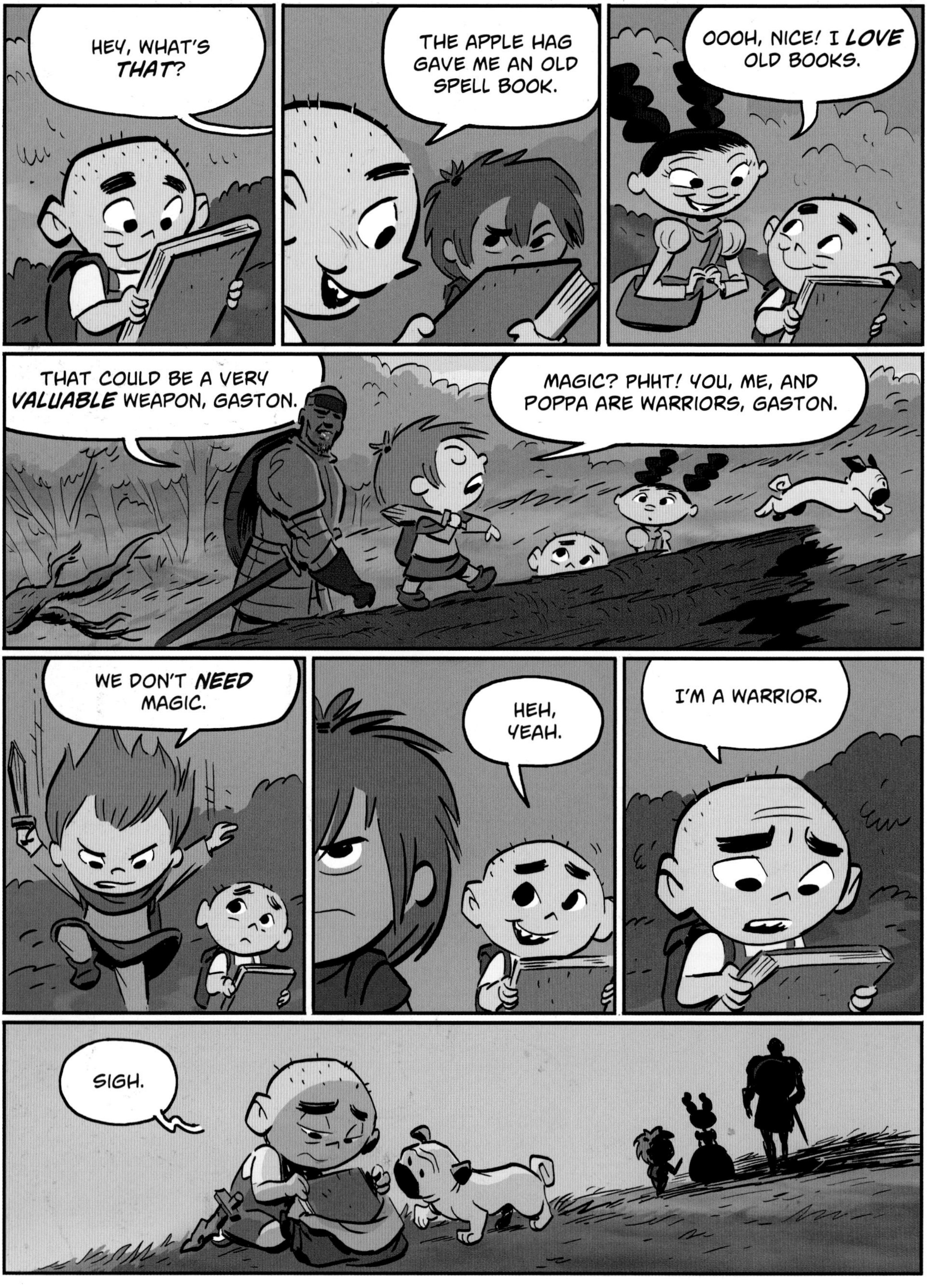
HEY, WHAT'S *THAT*?
THE APPLE HAG GAVE ME AN OLD SPELL BOOK.
OOOH, NICE! I **LOVE** OLD BOOKS.
THAT COULD BE A VERY **VALUABLE** WEAPON, GASTON.
MAGIC? PHHT! YOU, ME, AND POPPA ARE WARRIORS, GASTON.
WE DON'T **NEED** MAGIC.
HEH, YEAH.
I'M A WARRIOR.
SIGH.

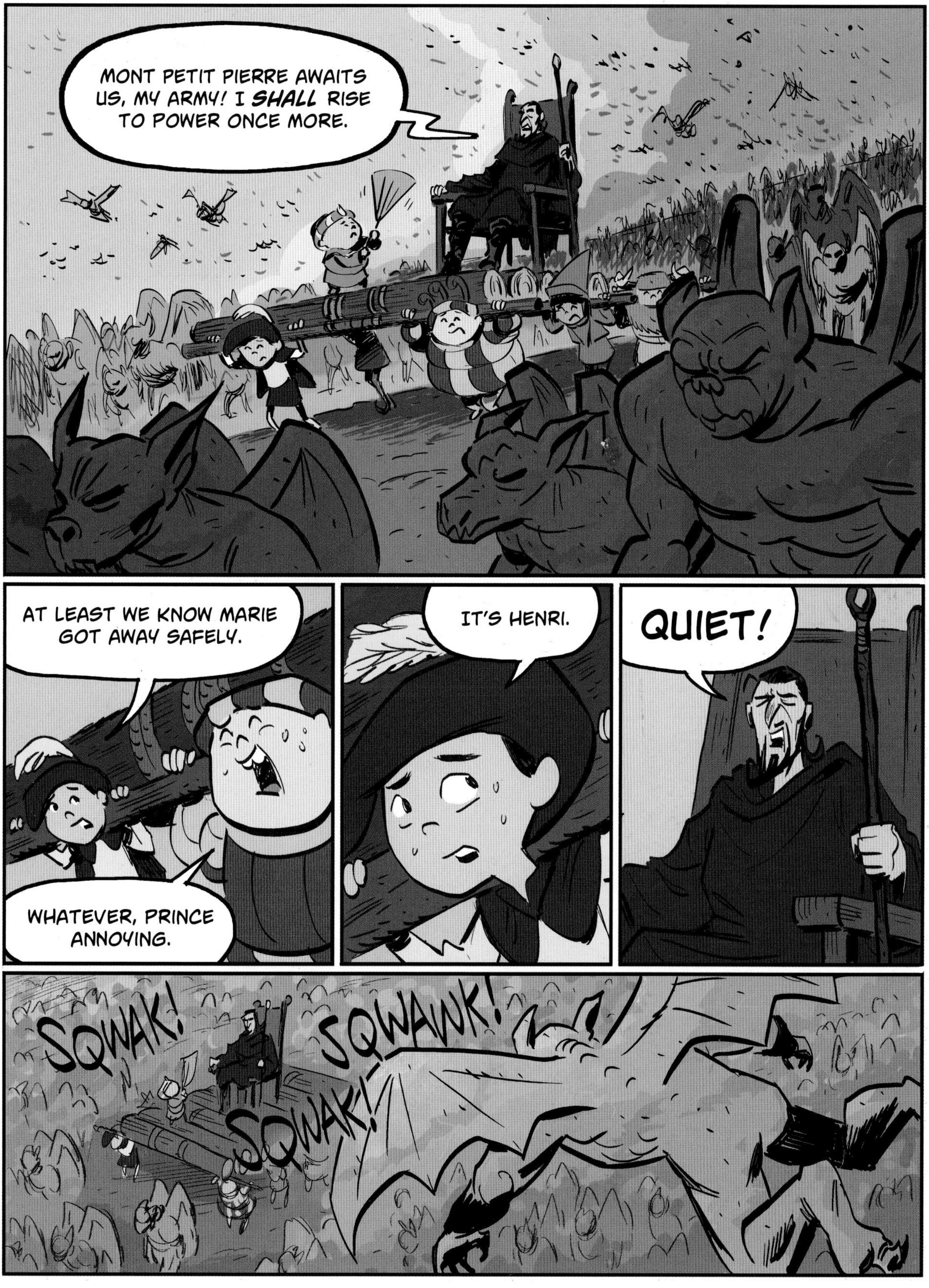
MONT PETIT PIERRE AWAITS US, MY ARMY! I SHALL RISE TO POWER ONCE MORE.
AT LEAST WE KNOW MARIE GOT AWAY SAFELY.
WHATEVER, PRINCE ANNOYING.
IT'S HENRI.
QUIET!
SQWAK!
SQWANK!
SQWAK!

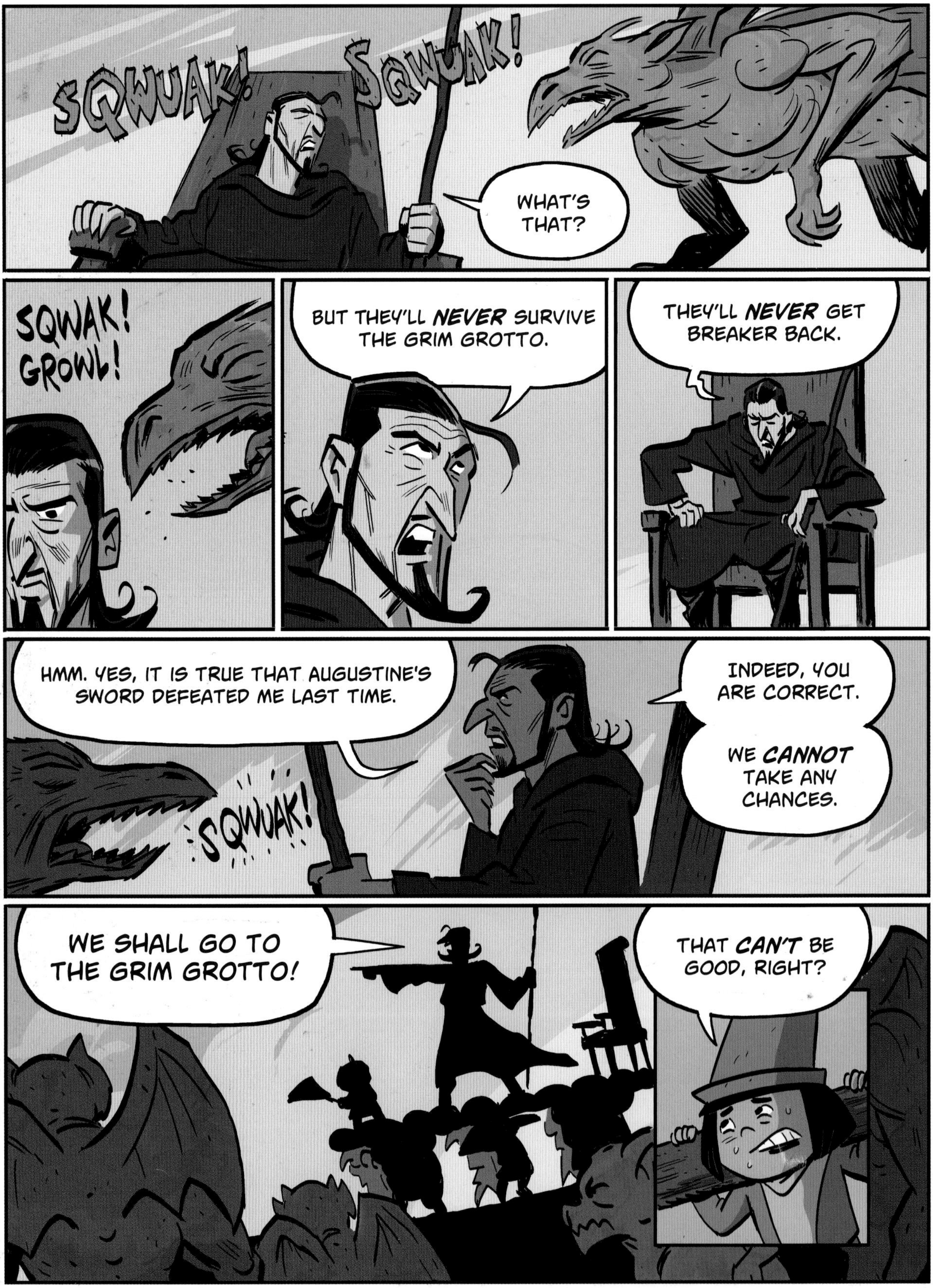
SQWUAK! SQWUAK!
WHAT'S THAT?
SQWAK! GROWL!
BUT THEY'LL NEVER SURVIVE THE GRIM GROTTO.
THEY'LL NEVER GET BREAKER BACK.
HMM. YES, IT IS TRUE THAT AUGUSTINE'S SWORD DEFEATED ME LAST TIME.
SQWUAK!
INDEED, YOU ARE CORRECT.
WE CANNOT TAKE ANY CHANCES.
WE SHALL GO TO THE GRIM GROTTO!
THAT CAN'T BE GOOD, RIGHT?

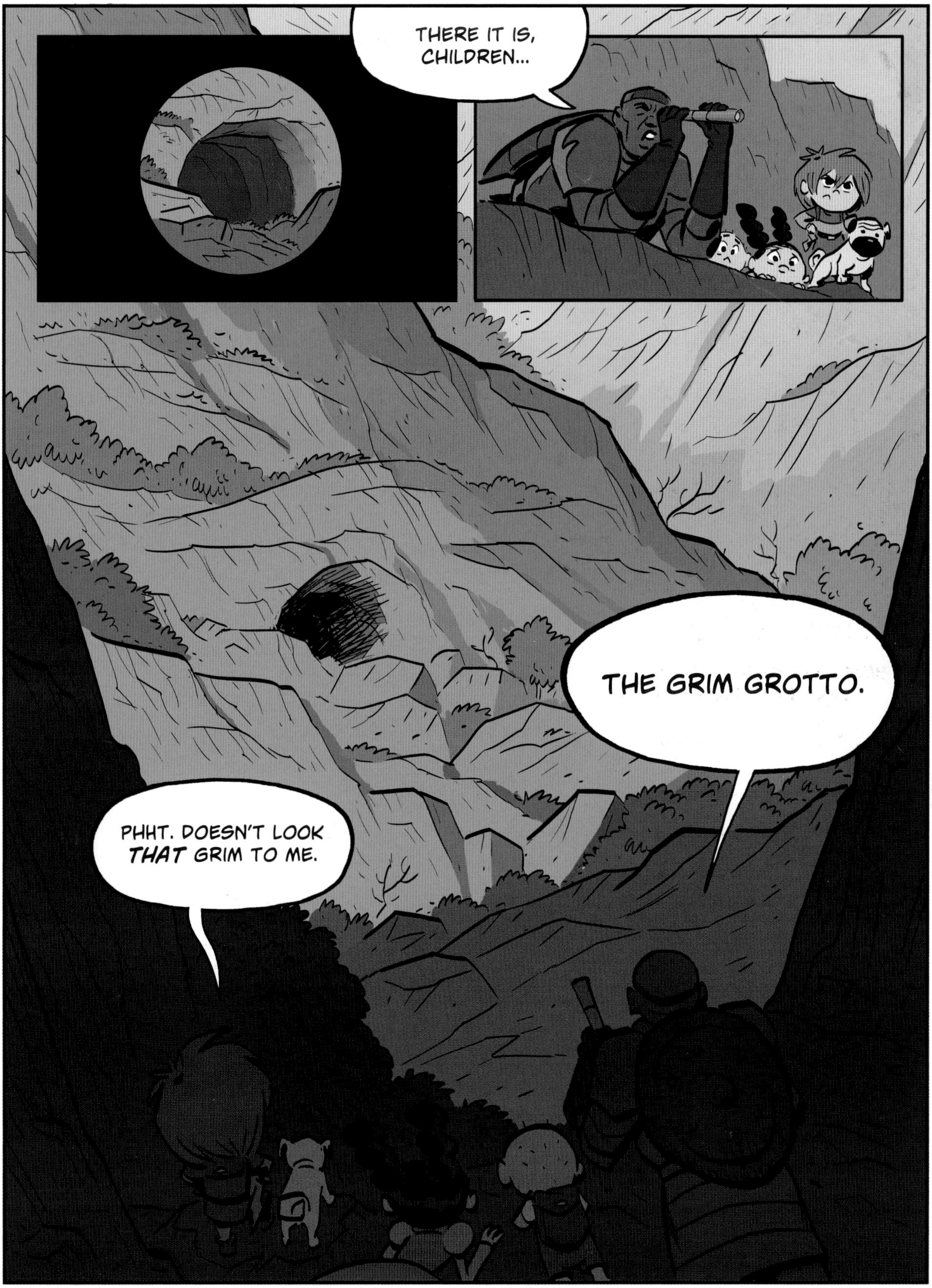
THERE IT IS, CHILDREN...
THE GRIM GROTTO.
PHHT. DOESN'T LOOK *THAT* GRIM TO ME.

I'LL GIVE AZRA SOMETHING TO BE GRIM ABOUT!

GRAB!

HEY, WHAT GIVES?!

PATIENCE, CLAUDETTE. PATIENCE.

AZRA DOES *NOT* LIVE ALONE. SHE HAS OFFSPRING. AND THEY *WILL* PROTECT HER.

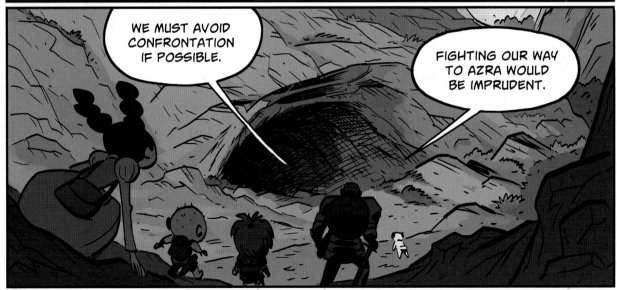
WE MUST AVOID CONFRONTATION IF POSSIBLE.

FIGHTING OUR WAY TO AZRA WOULD BE IMPRUDENT.

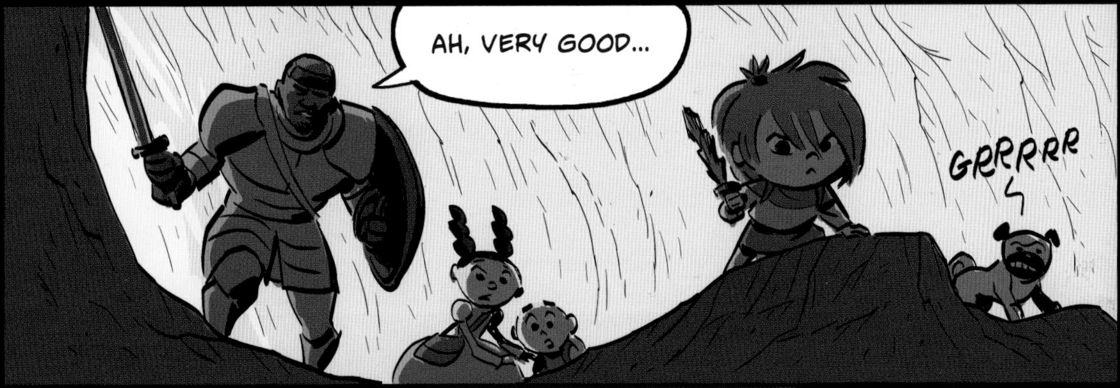
AH, VERY GOOD...
GRRRRR

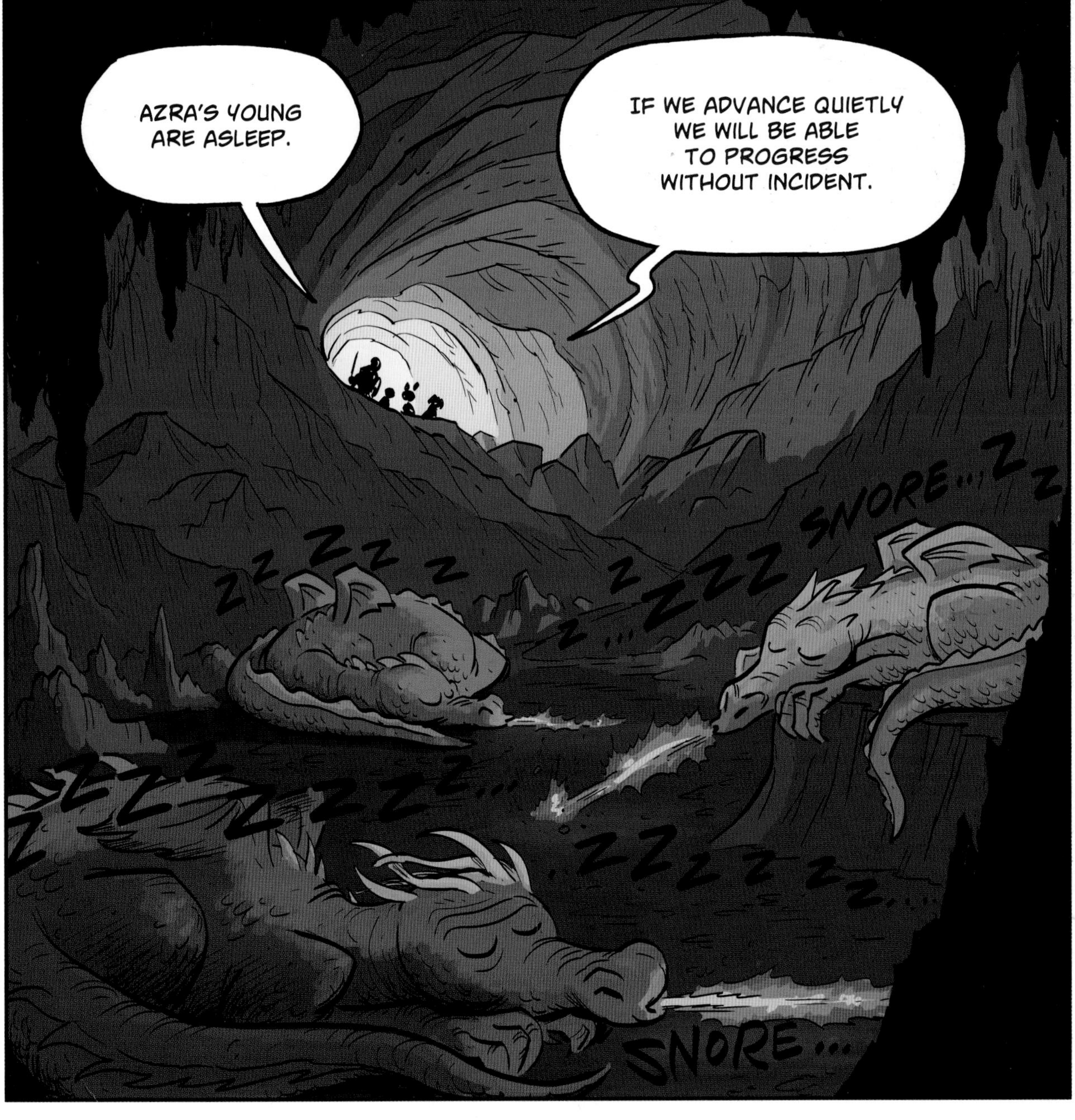
AZRA'S YOUNG ARE ASLEEP.
IF WE ADVANCE QUIETLY WE WILL BE ABLE TO PROGRESS WITHOUT INCIDENT.
SNORE...
SNORE...

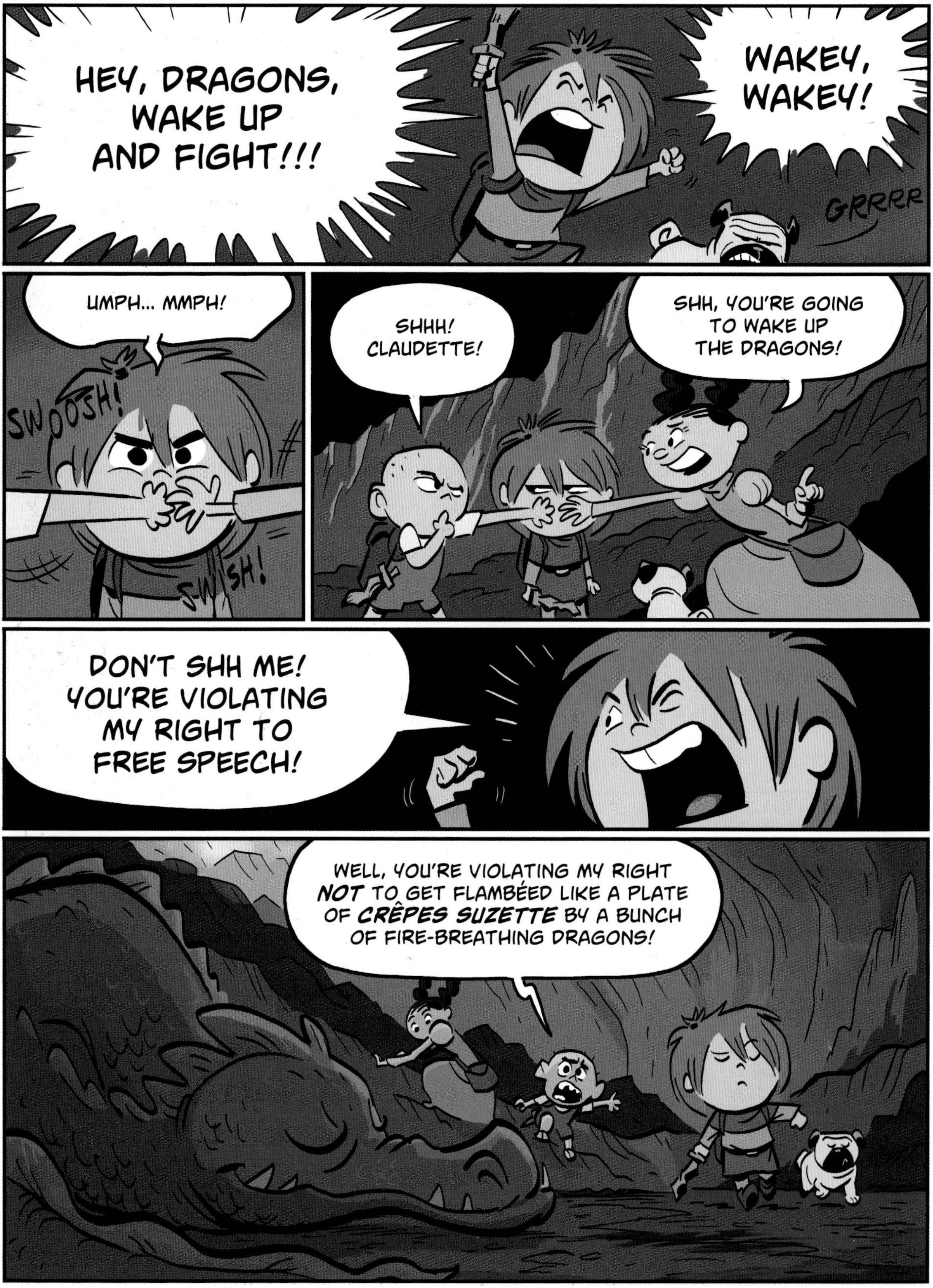

HEY, DRAGONS, WAKE UP AND FIGHT!!!
WAKEY, WAKEY!
GRRRR
UMPH... MMPH!
SWOOSH!
S-WISH!
SHHH! CLAUDETTE!
SHH, YOU'RE GOING TO WAKE UP THE DRAGONS!
DON'T SHH ME! YOU'RE VIOLATING MY RIGHT TO FREE SPEECH!
WELL, YOU'RE VIOLATING MY RIGHT *NOT* TO GET FLAMBÉED LIKE A PLATE OF *CRÊPES SUZETTE* BY A BUNCH OF FIRE-BREATHING DRAGONS!

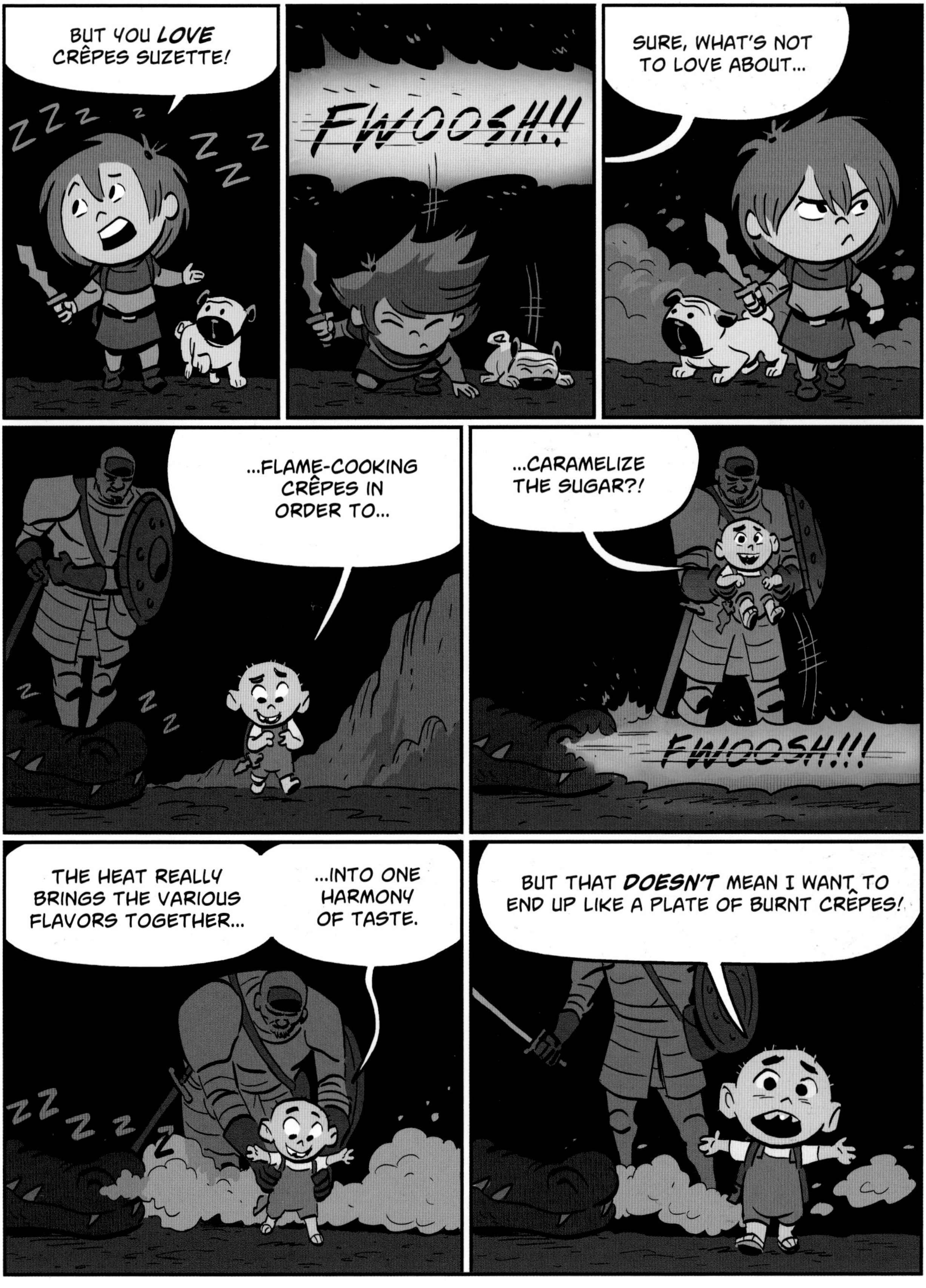
BUT YOU LOVE CRÊPES SUZETTE!
FWOOSH!!
SURE, WHAT'S NOT TO LOVE ABOUT...
...FLAME-COOKING CRÊPES IN ORDER TO...
...CARAMELIZE THE SUGAR?!
FWOOSH!!!
THE HEAT REALLY BRINGS THE VARIOUS FLAVORS TOGETHER...
...INTO ONE HARMONY OF TASTE.
BUT THAT DOESN'T MEAN I WANT TO END UP LIKE A PLATE OF BURNT CRÊPES!

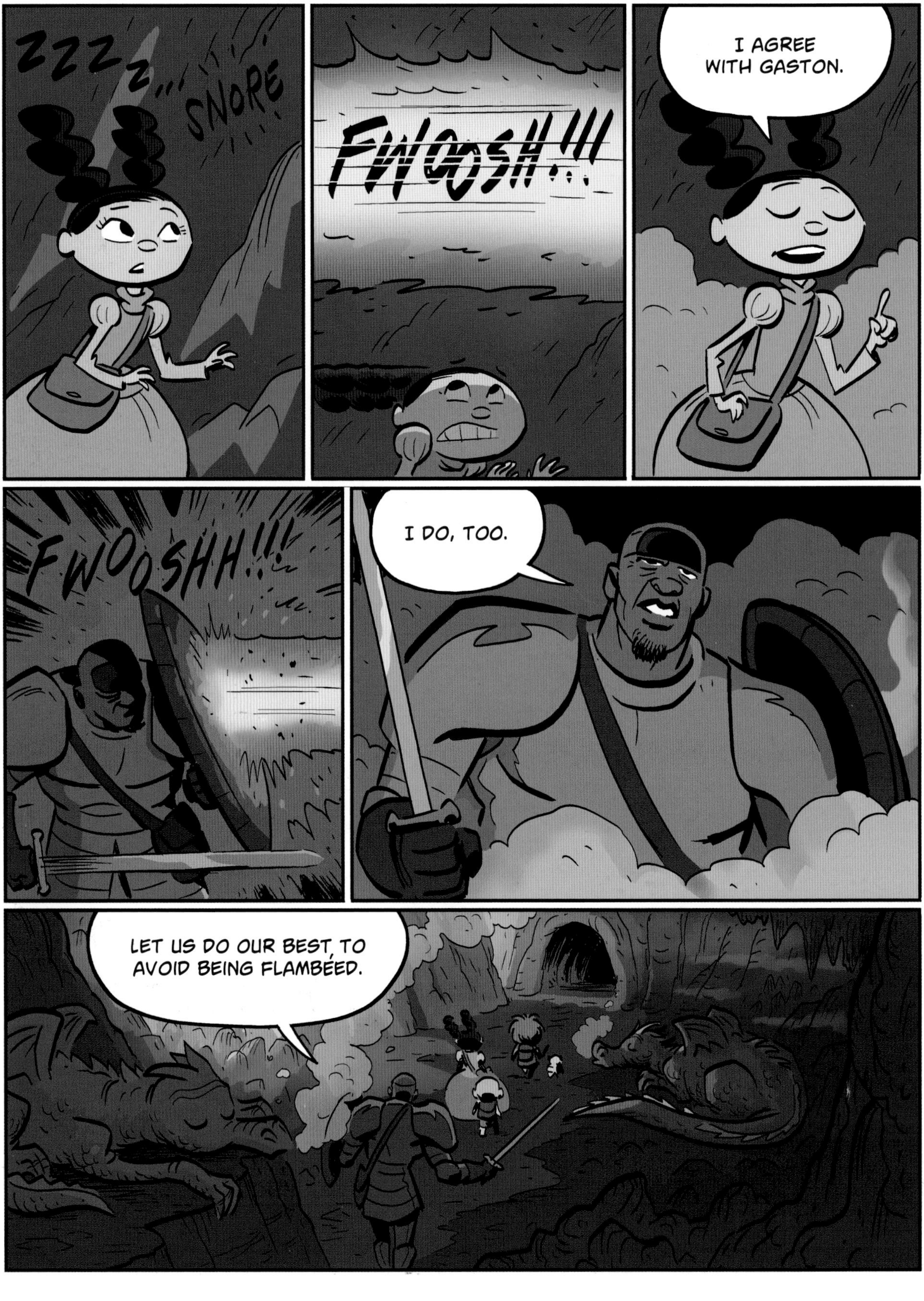
ZZZZ... SNORE
FWOOSH!!!
I AGREE WITH GASTON.
FWOOSHH!!!
I DO, TOO.
LET US DO OUR BEST, TO AVOID BEING FLAMBÉED.

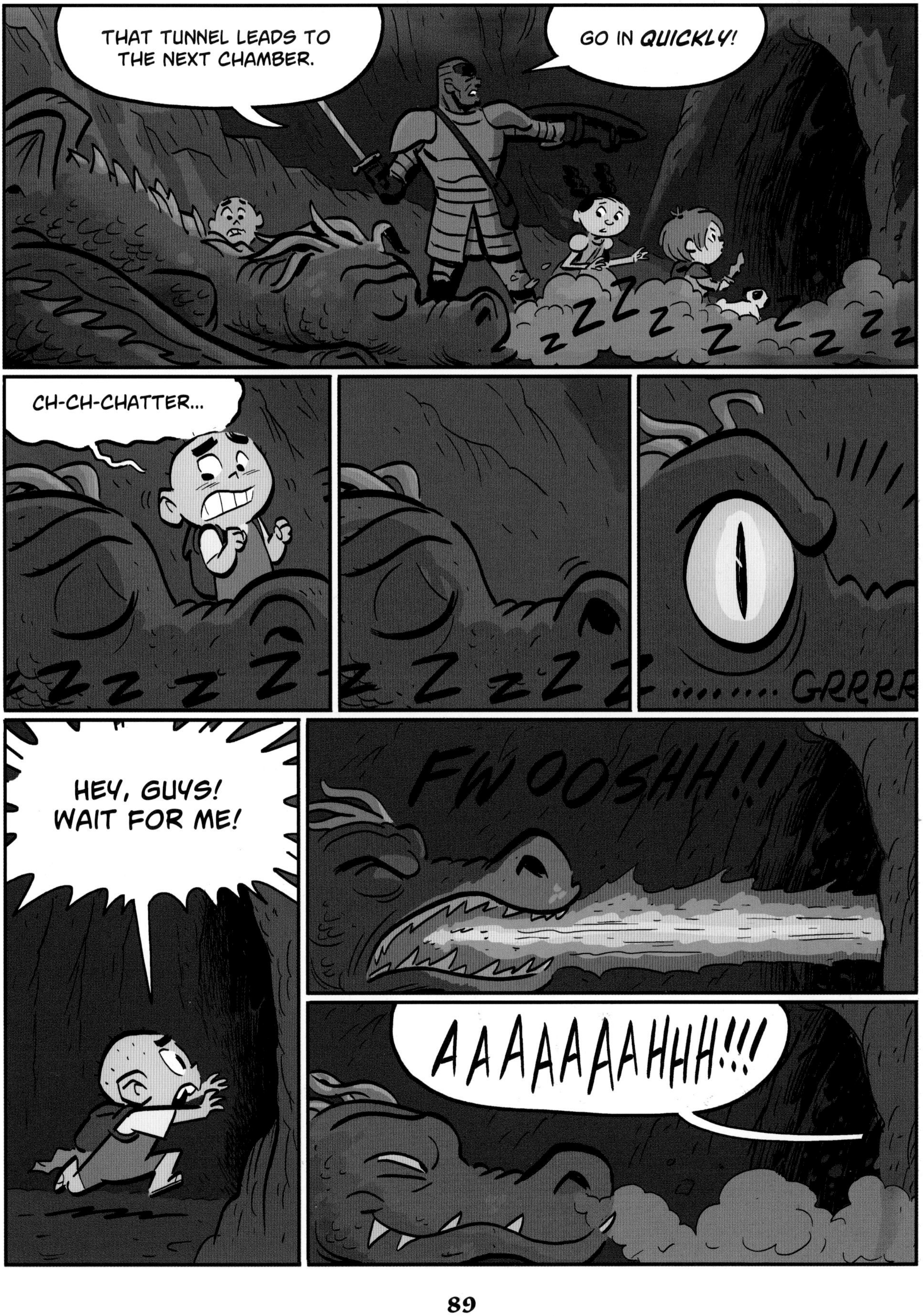
THAT TUNNEL LEADS TO THE NEXT CHAMBER.
GO IN QUICKLY!
ZZZ Z Z Z Z Z Z
CH-CH-CHATTER...
ZZZZZ
ZZZZZ
.......GRRRR
HEY, GUYS! WAIT FOR ME!
FWOOSHH!!
AAAAAAAHHH!!!

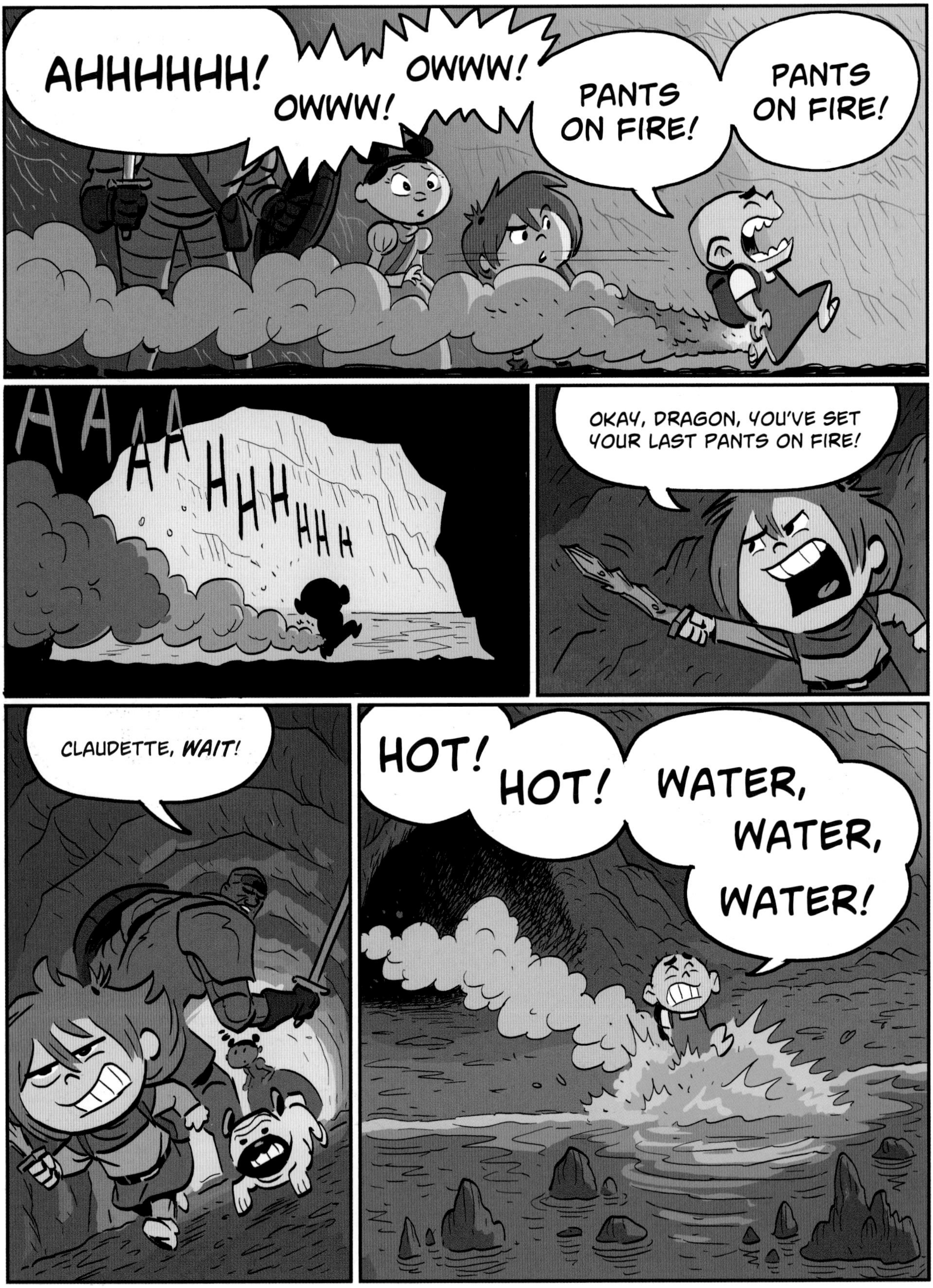
AHHHHHH!
OWWW!
OWWW!
PANTS ON FIRE!
PANTS ON FIRE!
AAAAAHHHHHH
OKAY, DRAGON, YOU'VE SET YOUR LAST PANTS ON FIRE!
CLAUDETTE, *WAIT!*
HOT!
HOT!
WATER, WATER, WATER!

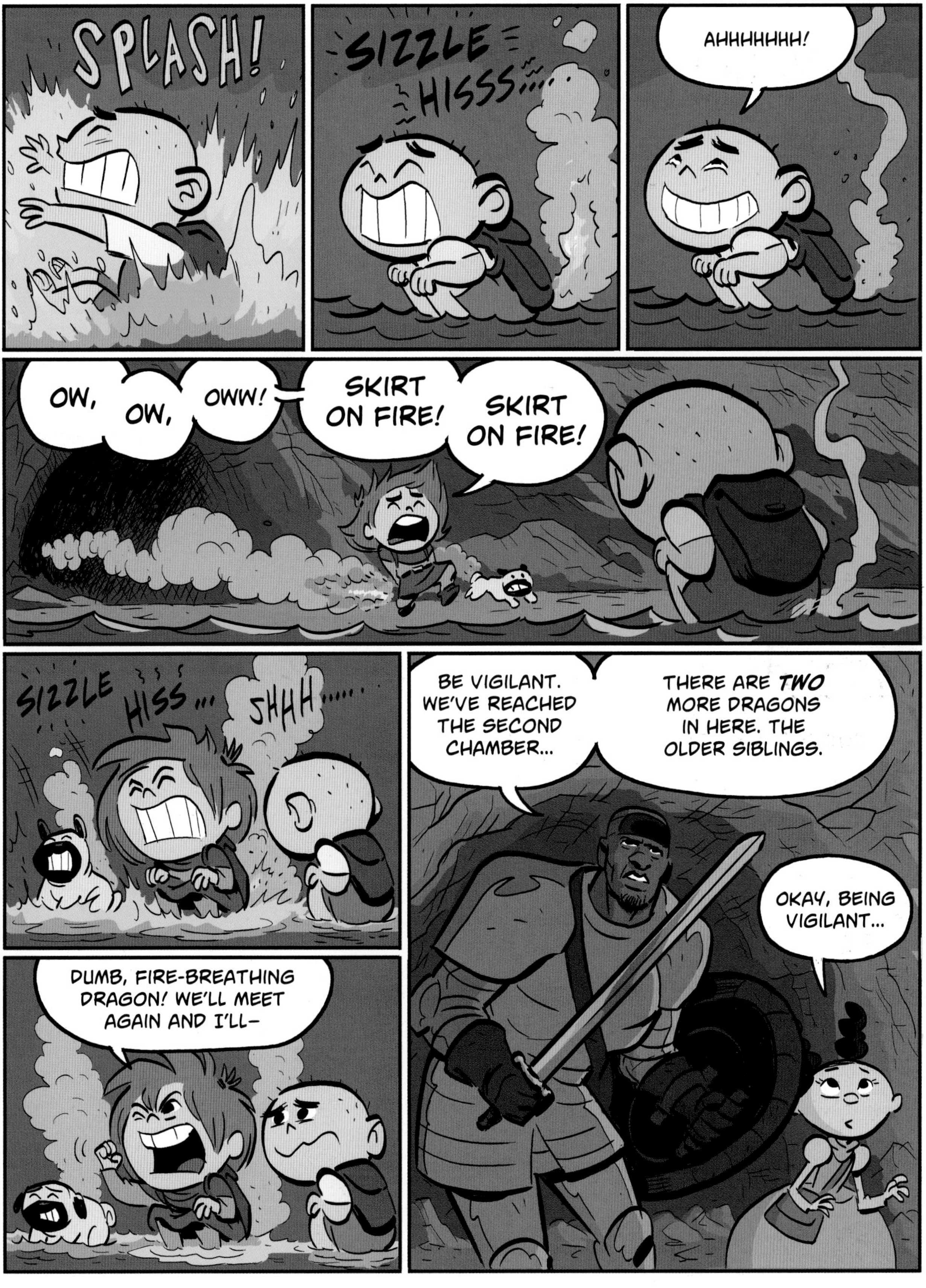
SPLASH!
SIZZLE
HISSS...
AHHHHHHH!
OW,
OW,
OWW!
SKIRT ON FIRE!
SKIRT ON FIRE!
SIZZLE
HISS...
SHHH......
DUMB, FIRE-BREATHING DRAGON! WE'LL MEET AGAIN AND I'LL–
BE VIGILANT. WE'VE REACHED THE SECOND CHAMBER...
THERE ARE *TWO* MORE DRAGONS IN HERE. THE OLDER SIBLINGS.
OKAY, BEING VIGILANT...

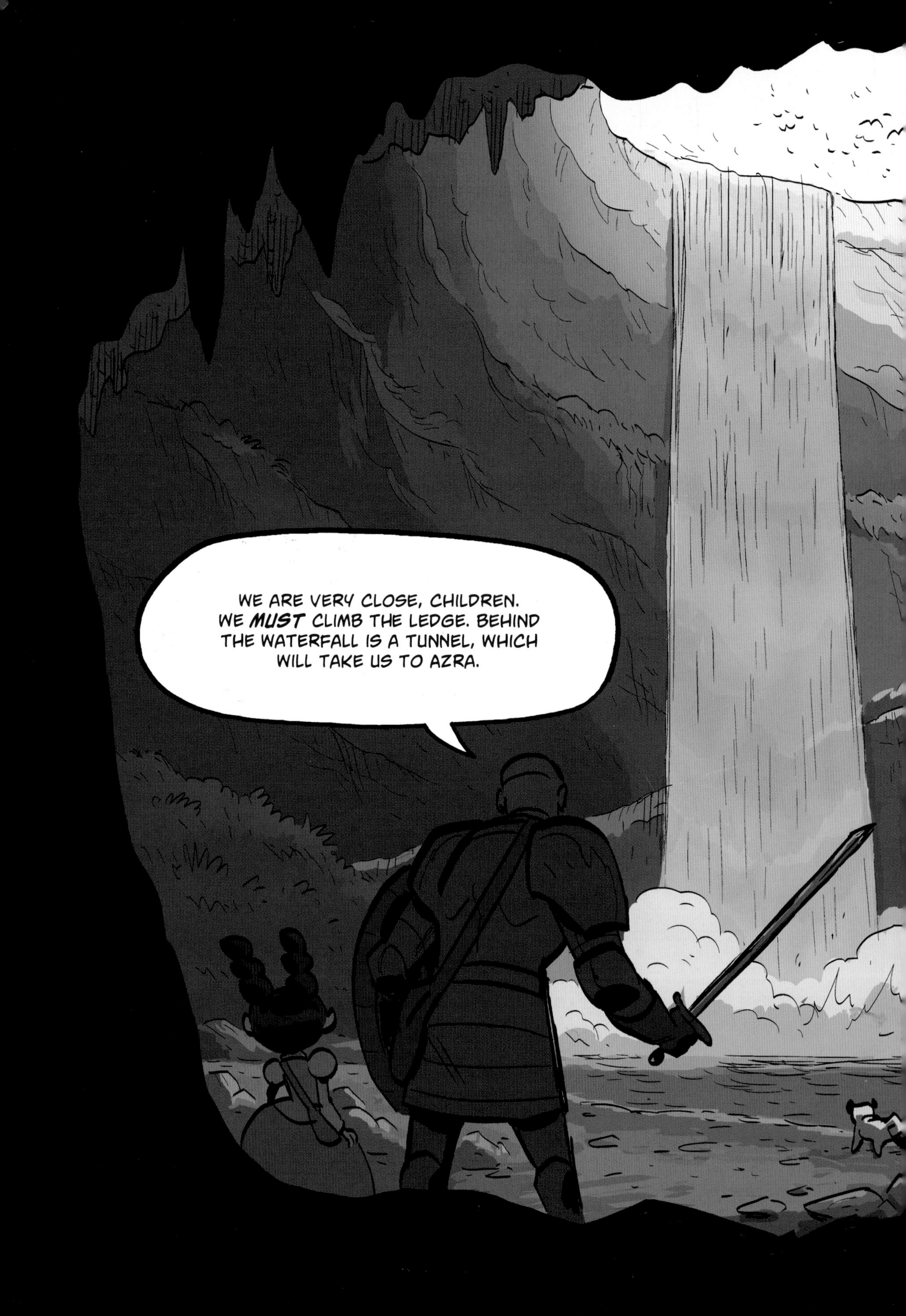
WE ARE VERY CLOSE, CHILDREN. WE *MUST* CLIMB THE LEDGE. BEHIND THE WATERFALL IS A TUNNEL, WHICH WILL TAKE US TO AZRA.

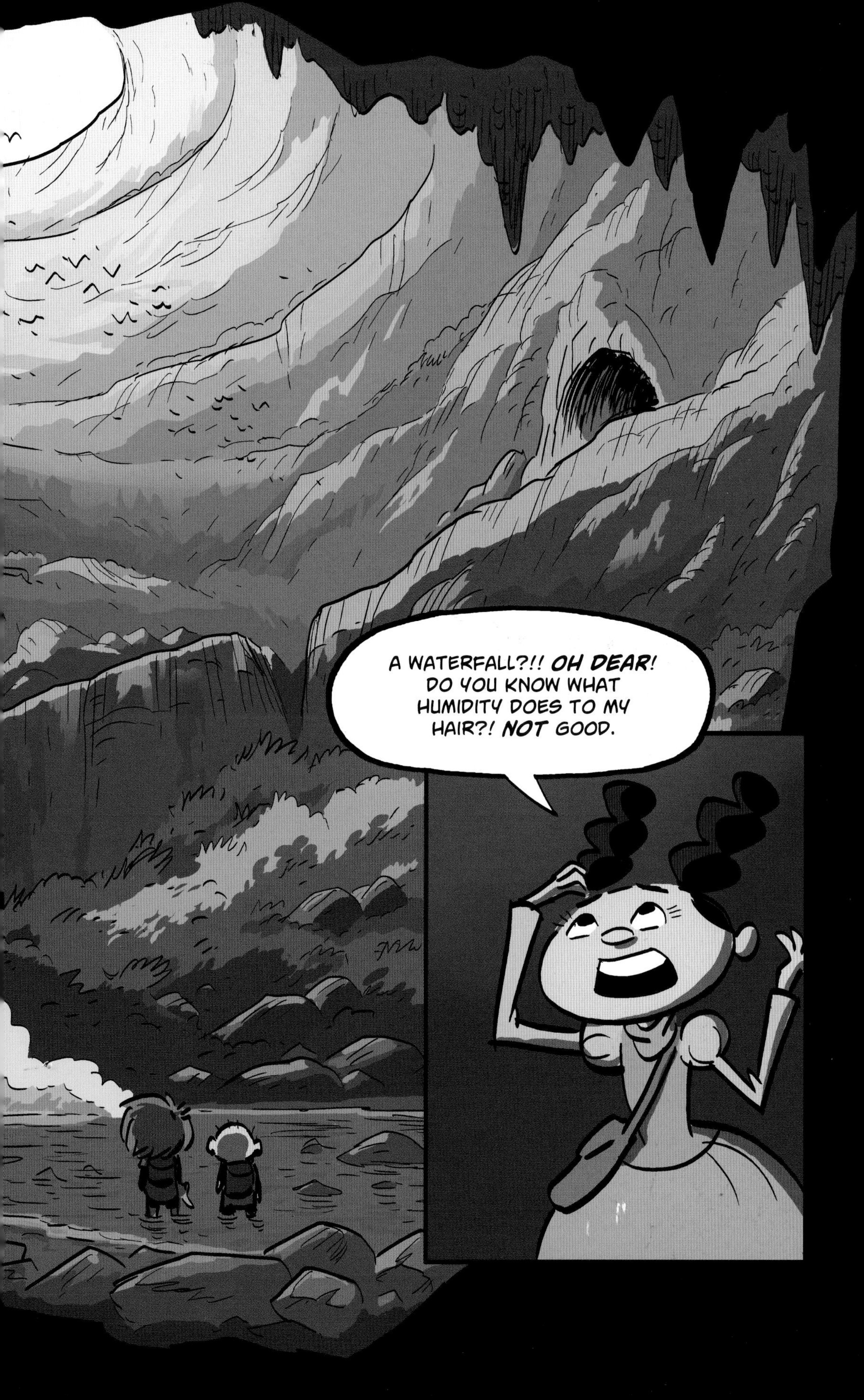
A WATERFALL?!! **OH DEAR**! DO YOU KNOW WHAT HUMIDITY DOES TO MY HAIR?! **NOT** GOOD.

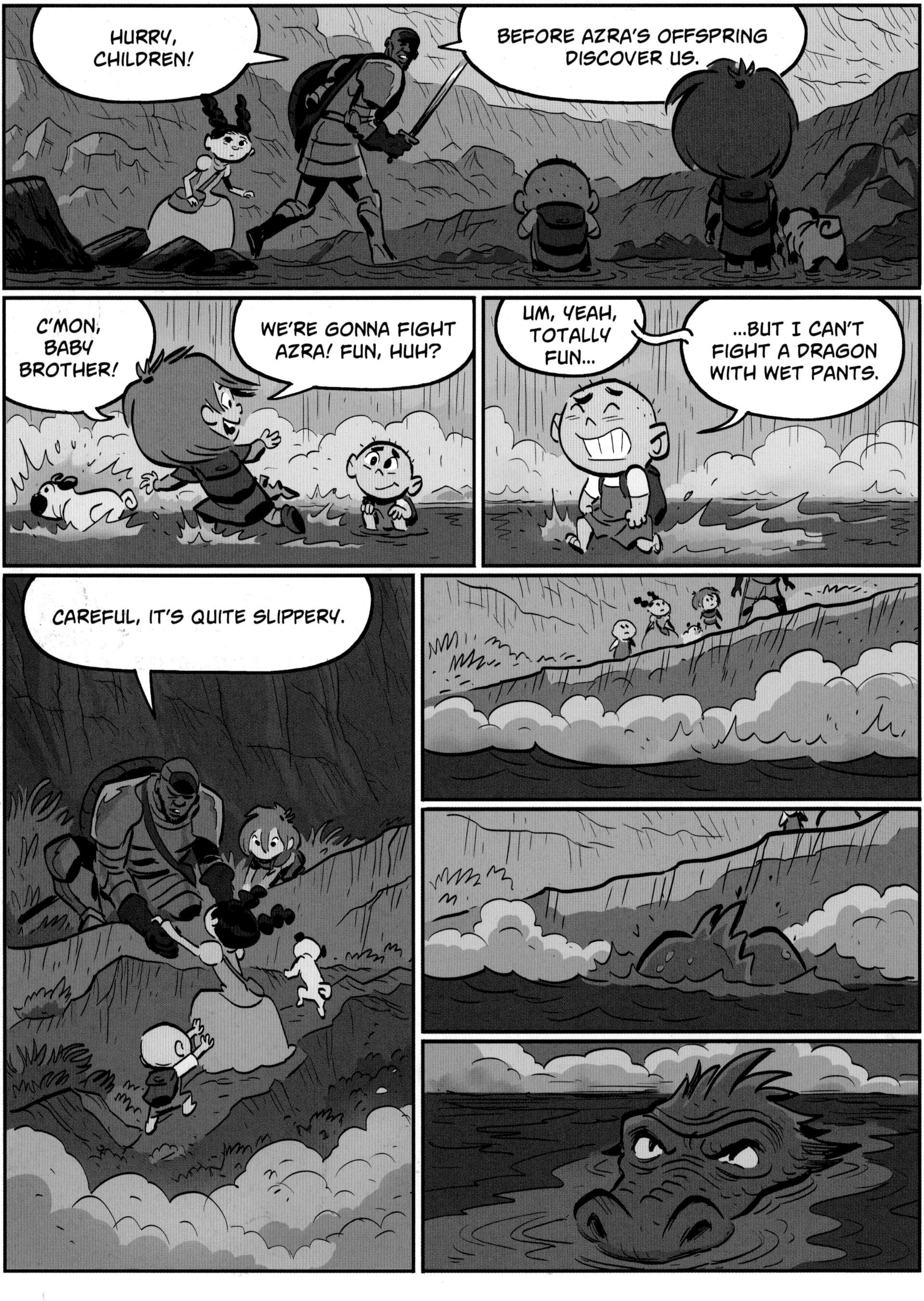
HURRY, CHILDREN!
BEFORE AZRA'S OFFSPRING DISCOVER US.
C'MON, BABY BROTHER!
WE'RE GONNA FIGHT AZRA! FUN, HUH?
UM, YEAH, TOTALLY FUN...
...BUT I CAN'T FIGHT A DRAGON WITH WET PANTS.
CAREFUL, IT'S QUITE SLIPPERY.

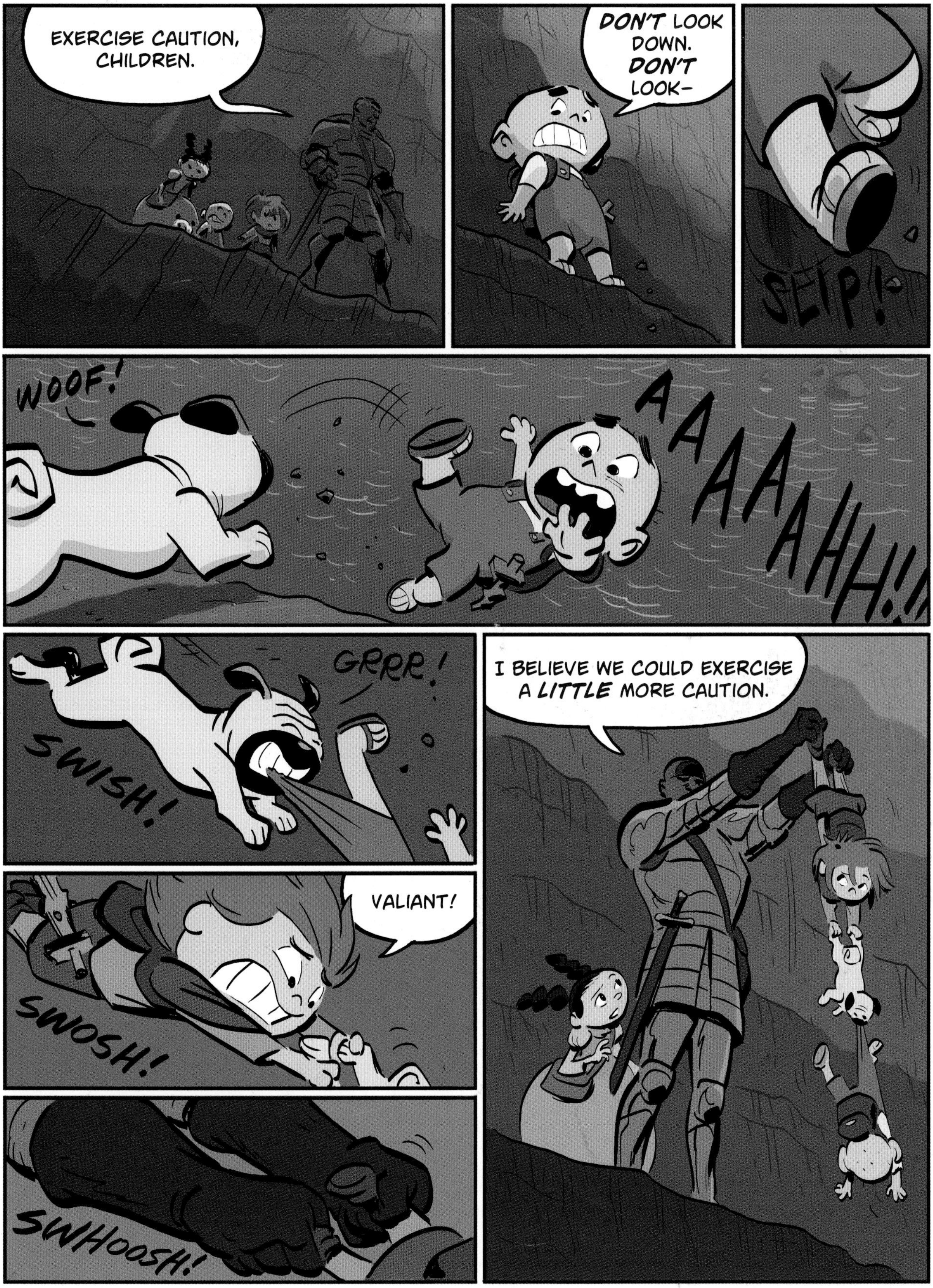
EXERCISE CAUTION, CHILDREN.
DON'T LOOK DOWN. DON'T LOOK-
SLIP!
WOOF!
AAAAAAHH!!!!
GRRR!
SWISH!
VALIANT!
SWOSH!
SWHOOSH!
I BELIEVE WE COULD EXERCISE A LITTLE MORE CAUTION.

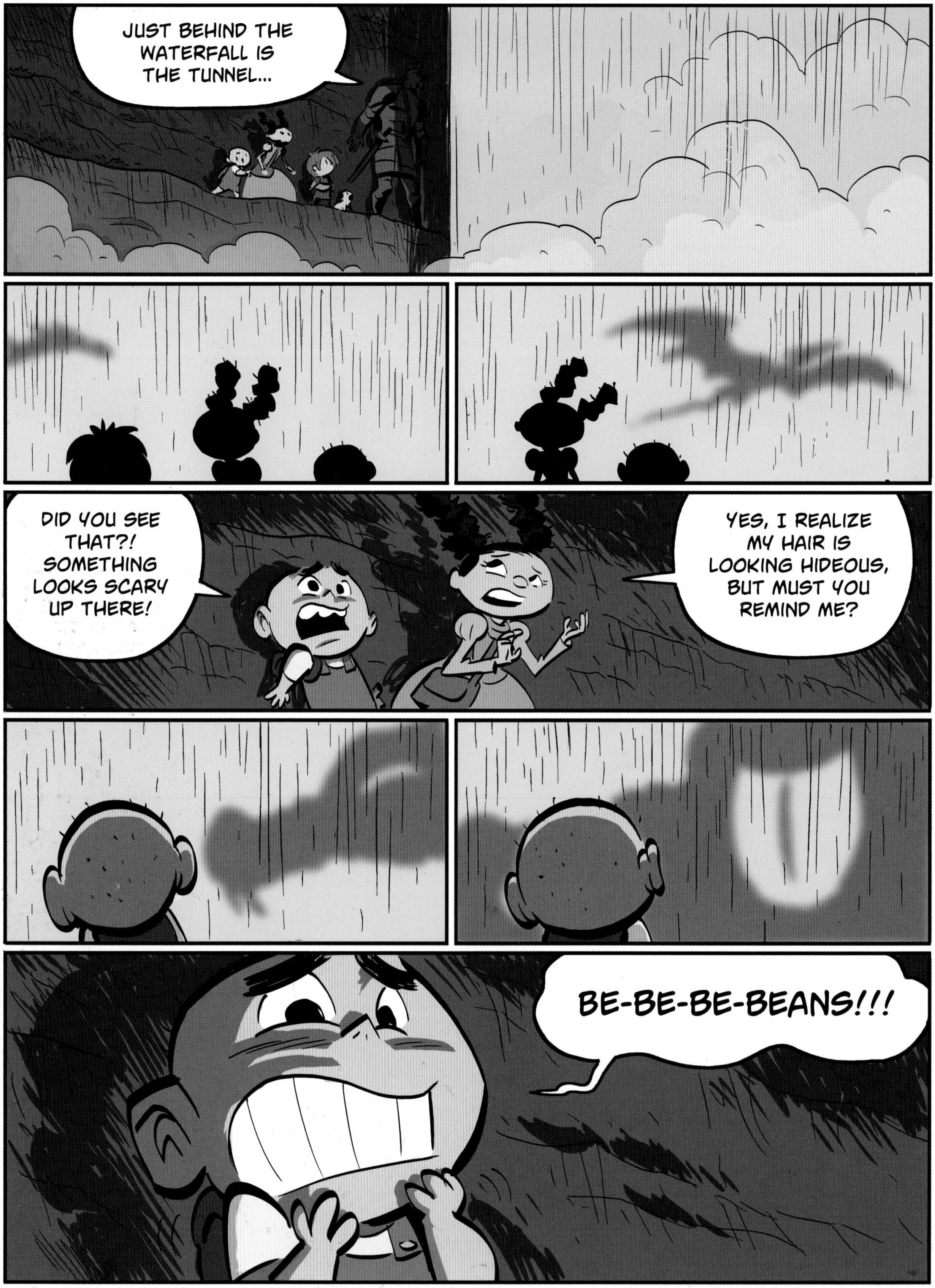
JUST BEHIND THE WATERFALL IS THE TUNNEL...
DID YOU SEE THAT?! SOMETHING LOOKS SCARY UP THERE!
YES, I REALIZE MY HAIR IS LOOKING HIDEOUS, BUT MUST YOU REMIND ME?
BE-BE-BE-BEANS!!!

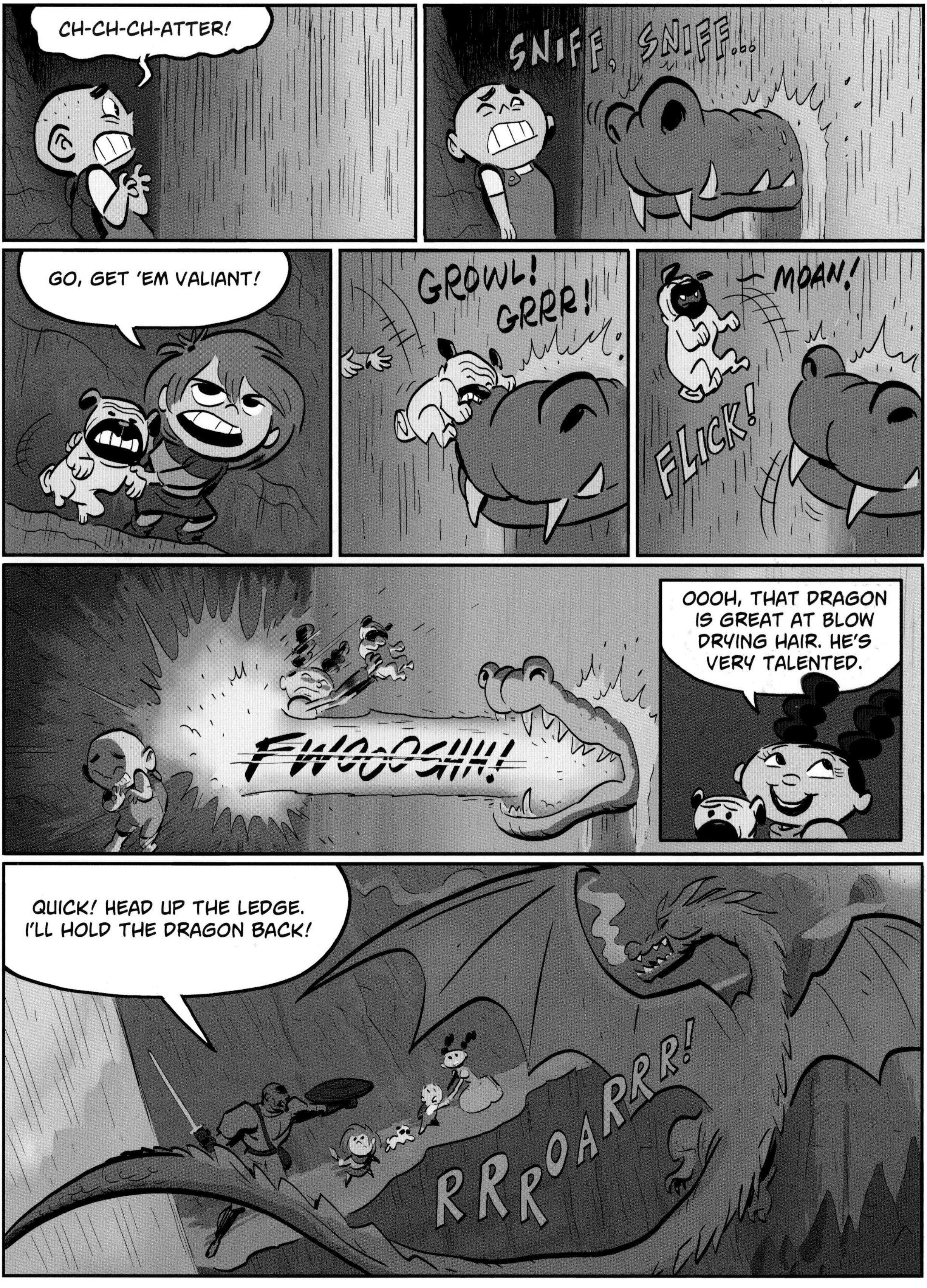
CH-CH-CH-ATTER!
SNIFF, SNIFF...
GO, GET 'EM VALIANT!
GROWL! GRRR!
MOAN!
FLICK!
FWOOOSHH!
OOOH, THAT DRAGON IS GREAT AT BLOW DRYING HAIR. HE'S VERY TALENTED.
QUICK! HEAD UP THE LEDGE. I'LL HOLD THE DRAGON BACK!
RRROARRR!

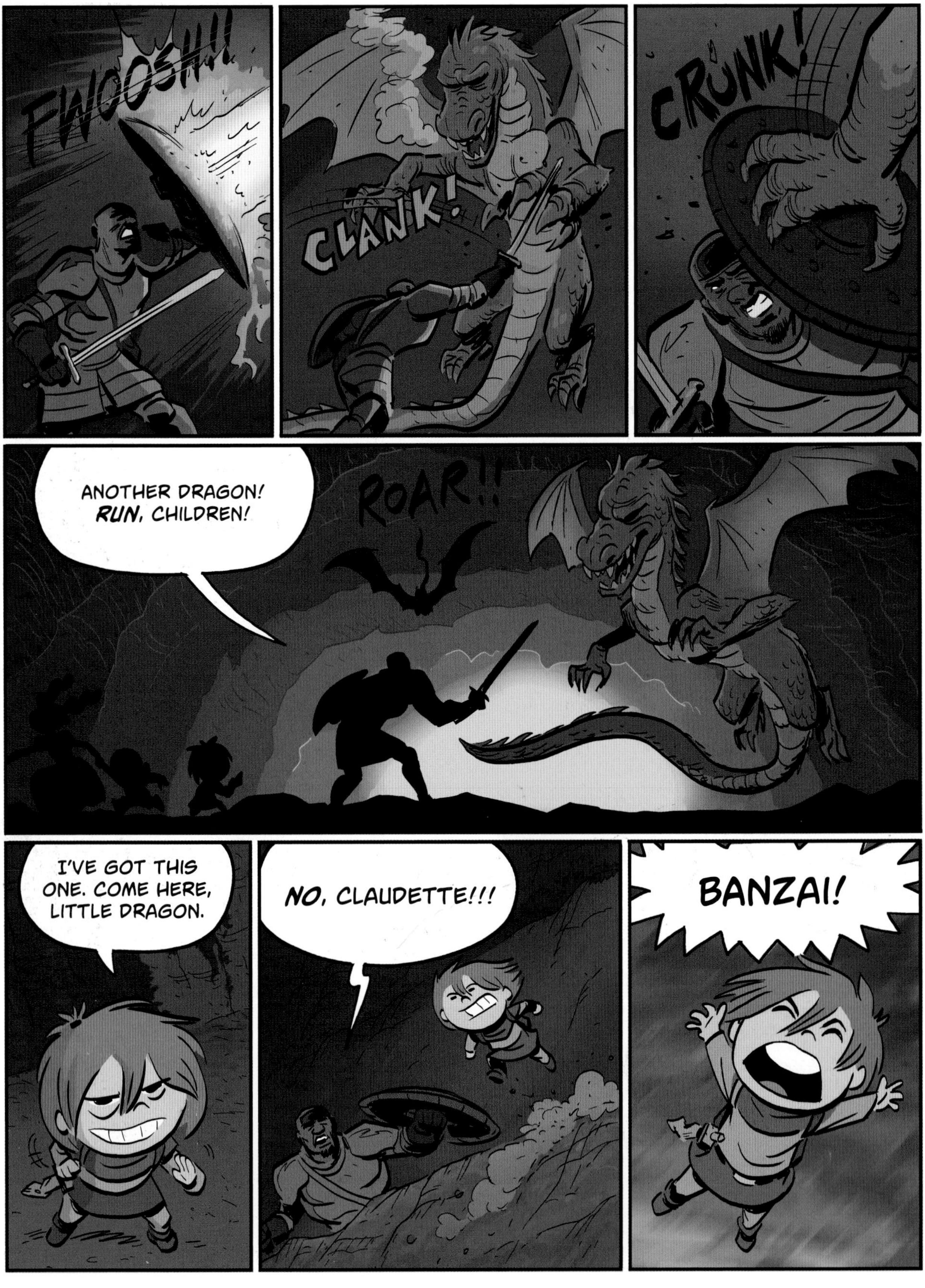
FWOOSH!!
CLANK!
CRUNK!
ANOTHER DRAGON! RUN, CHILDREN!
ROAR!!
I'VE GOT THIS ONE. COME HERE, LITTLE DRAGON.
NO, CLAUDETTE!!!
BANZAI!

HELLO, DUMB DRAGON!

SURRENDER!

PUFF!

HEY!

STOP MOVING!

WHOAAA!!!

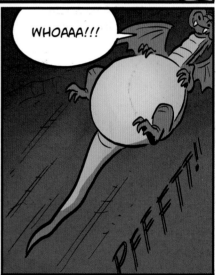

PUFFTTT....

HISS...

PFFFTTT!!

UM, ZUBAIR, WHAT SHOULD I DO NOW?

DON'T LET GO, CLAUDETTE! WE'RE COMING!

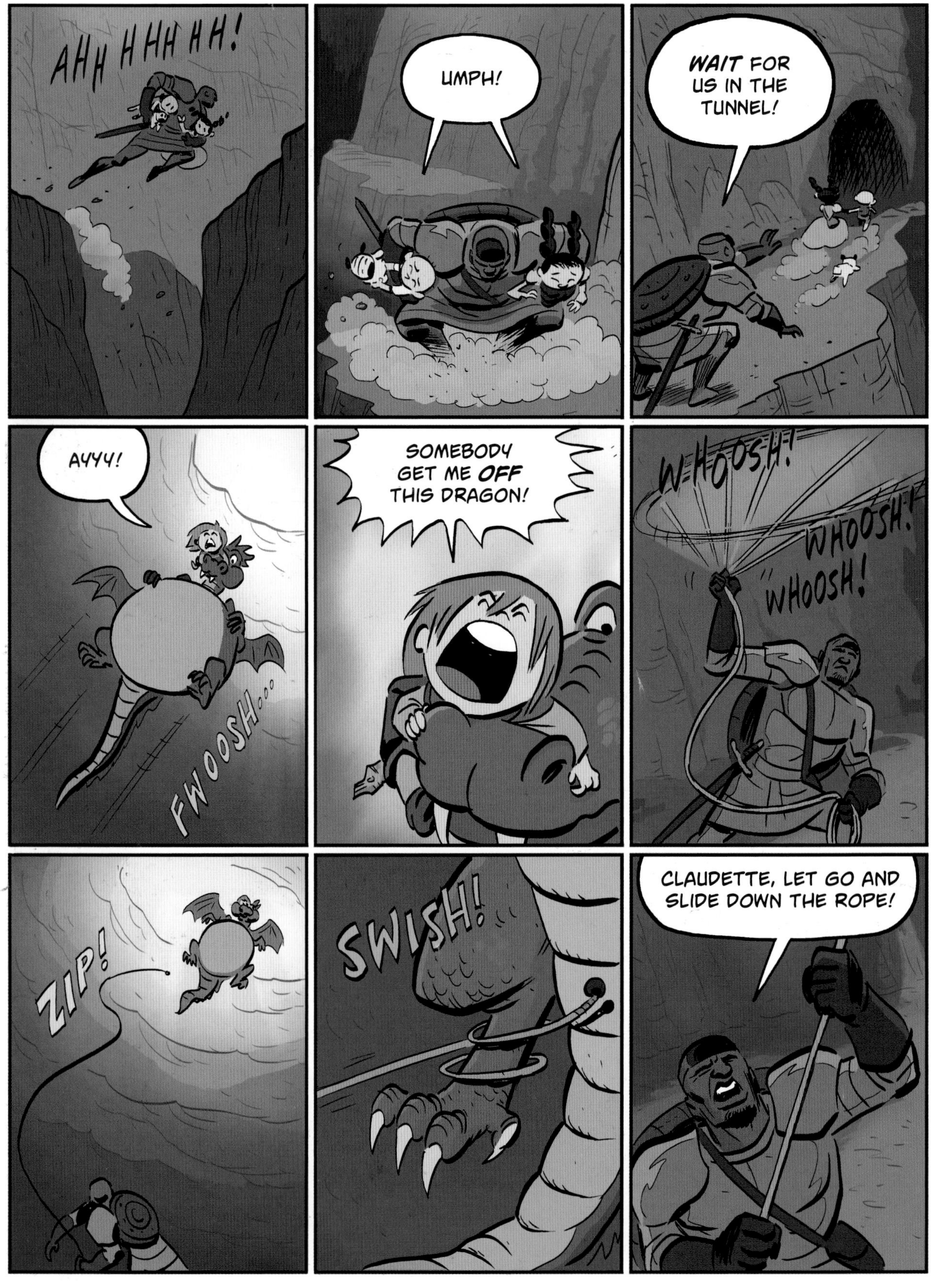

AHHHHHHH!
UMPH!
WAIT FOR US IN THE TUNNEL!
AYYY!
FWOOSH...
SOMEBODY GET ME OFF THIS DRAGON!
WHOOSH!
WHOOSH!
WHOOSH!
ZIP!
SWISH!
CLAUDETTE, LET GO AND SLIDE DOWN THE ROPE!

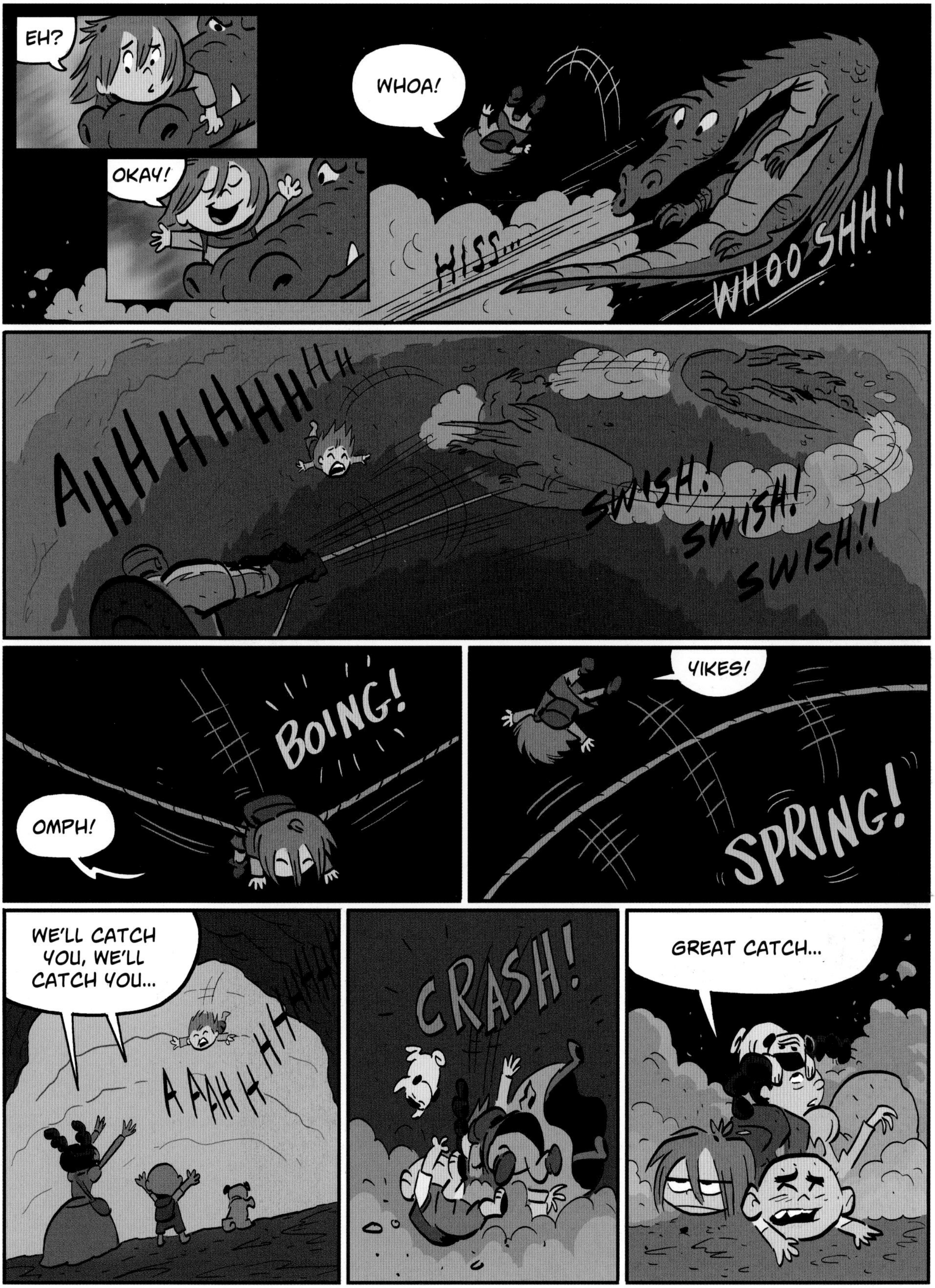
EH?
OKAY!
WHOA!
HISS...
WHOOSHH!!
AHHHHHHHHHH
SWISH!
SWISH!
SWISH!!
BOING!
OMPH!
YIKES!
SPRING!
WE'LL CATCH YOU, WE'LL CATCH YOU...
AAAHHHHHHH
CRASH!
GREAT CATCH...

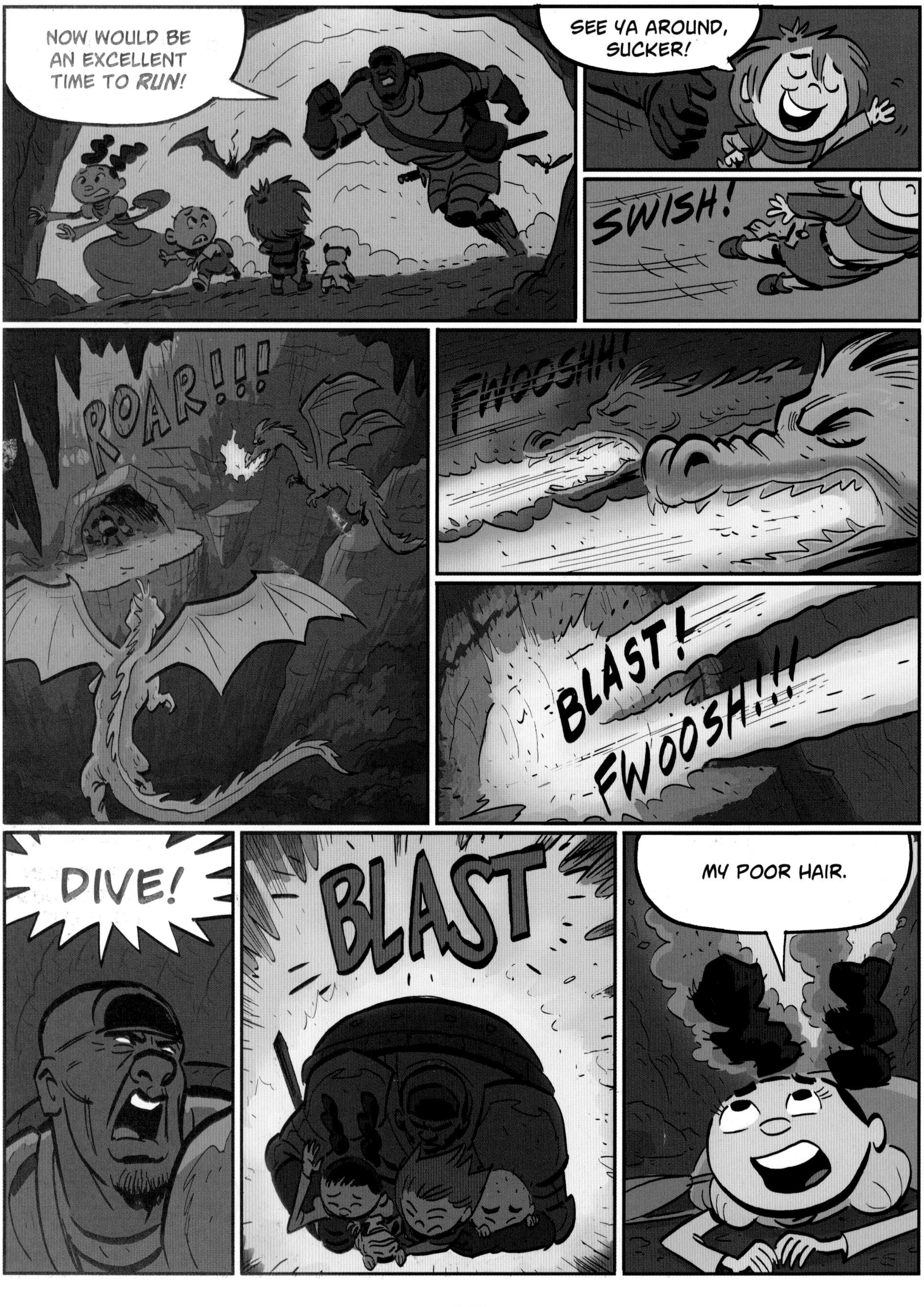
NOW WOULD BE AN EXCELLENT TIME TO RUN!
SEE YA AROUND, SUCKER!
SWISH!
ROAR!!!
FWOOSHH!
BLAST!
FWOOSH!!!
DIVE!
BLAST
MY POOR HAIR.

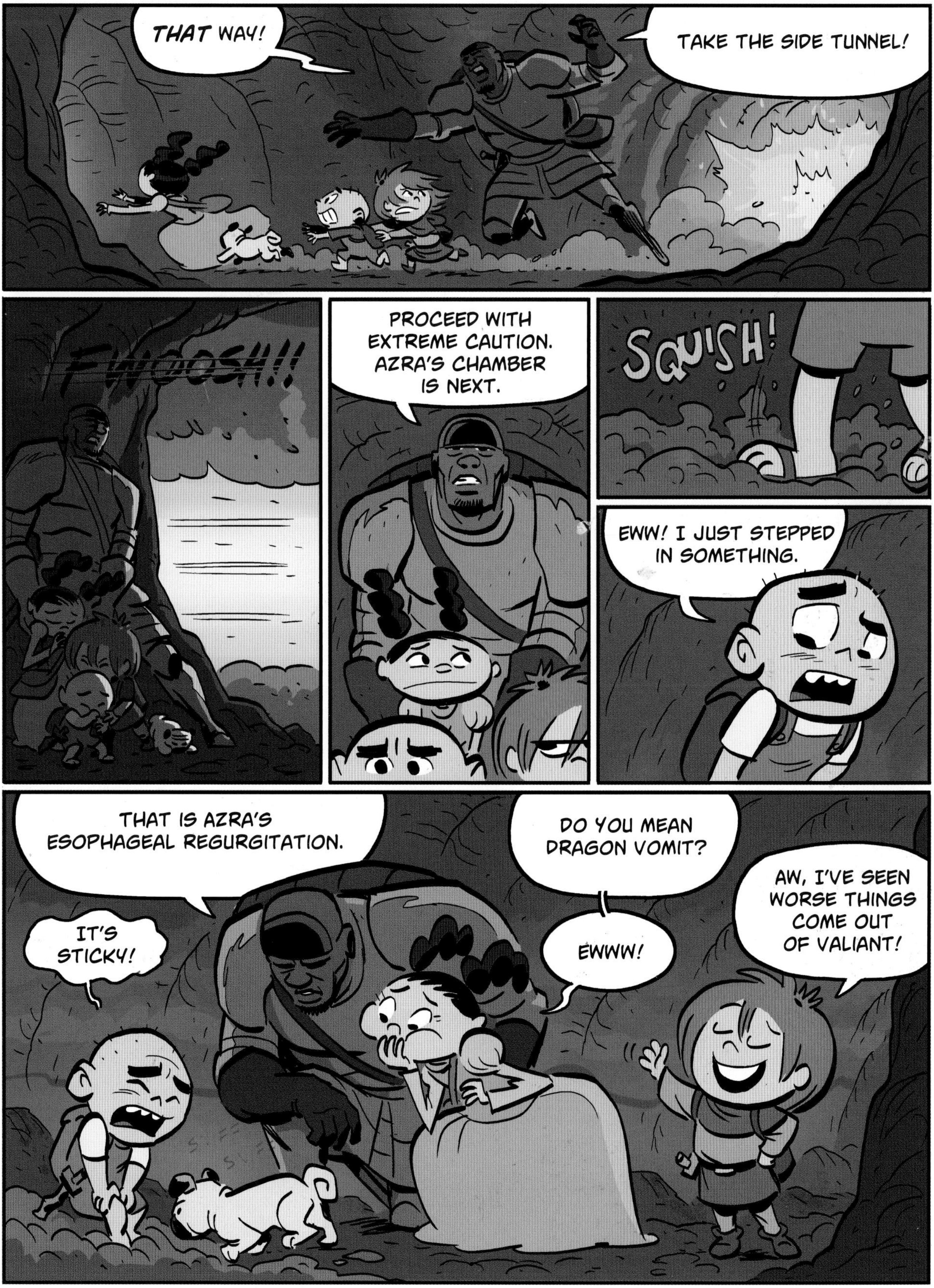
THAT WAY!
TAKE THE SIDE TUNNEL!
FWOOSH!!
PROCEED WITH EXTREME CAUTION. AZRA'S CHAMBER IS NEXT.
SQUISH!
EWW! I JUST STEPPED IN SOMETHING.
THAT IS AZRA'S ESOPHAGEAL REGURGITATION.
IT'S STICKY!
DO YOU MEAN DRAGON VOMIT?
EWWW!
AW, I'VE SEEN WORSE THINGS COME OUT OF VALIANT!

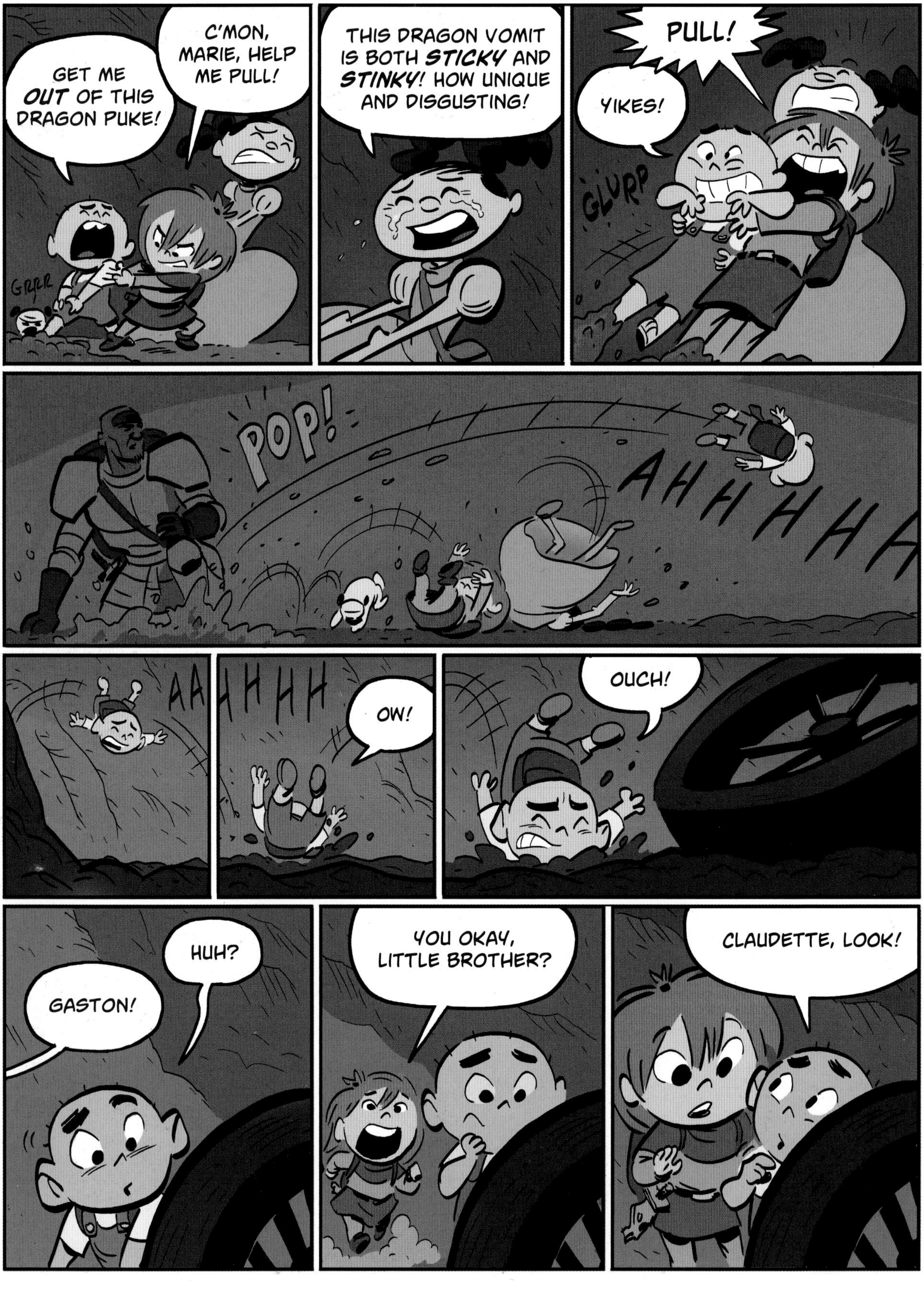
GET ME OUT OF THIS DRAGON PUKE!
C'MON, MARIE, HELP ME PULL!
GRRR
THIS DRAGON VOMIT IS BOTH **STICKY** AND **STINKY**! HOW UNIQUE AND DISGUSTING!
PULL!
YIKES!
GLURP
POP!
AHHHHHH
AAHHHHH
OW!
OUCH!
GASTON!
HUH?
YOU OKAY, LITTLE BROTHER?
CLAUDETTE, LOOK!

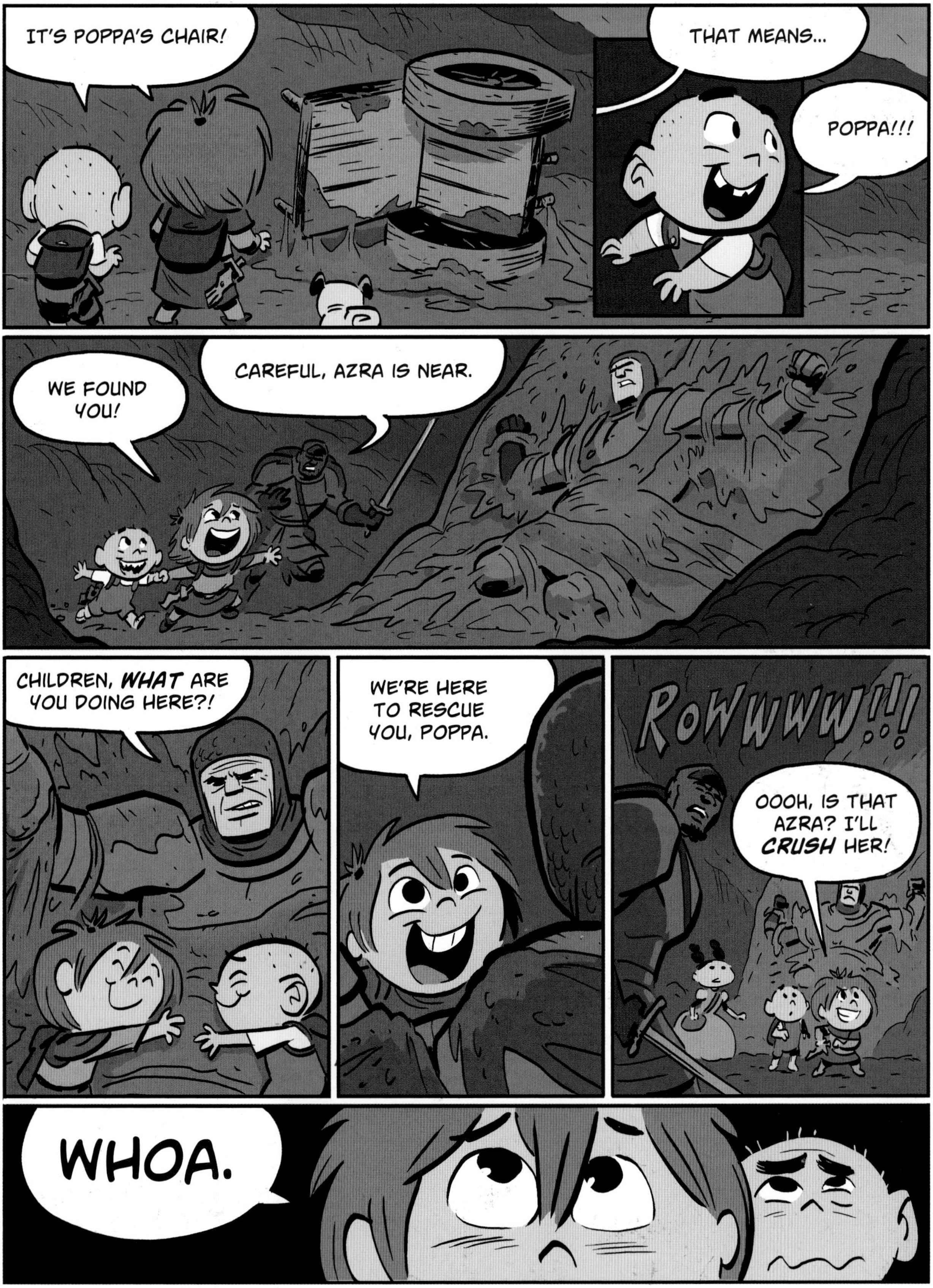
IT'S POPPA'S CHAIR!
THAT MEANS...
POPPA!!!
WE FOUND YOU!
CAREFUL, AZRA IS NEAR.
CHILDREN, *WHAT* ARE YOU DOING HERE?!
WE'RE HERE TO RESCUE YOU, POPPA.
ROWWWW!!!
OOOH, IS THAT AZRA? I'LL *CRUSH* HER!
WHOA.

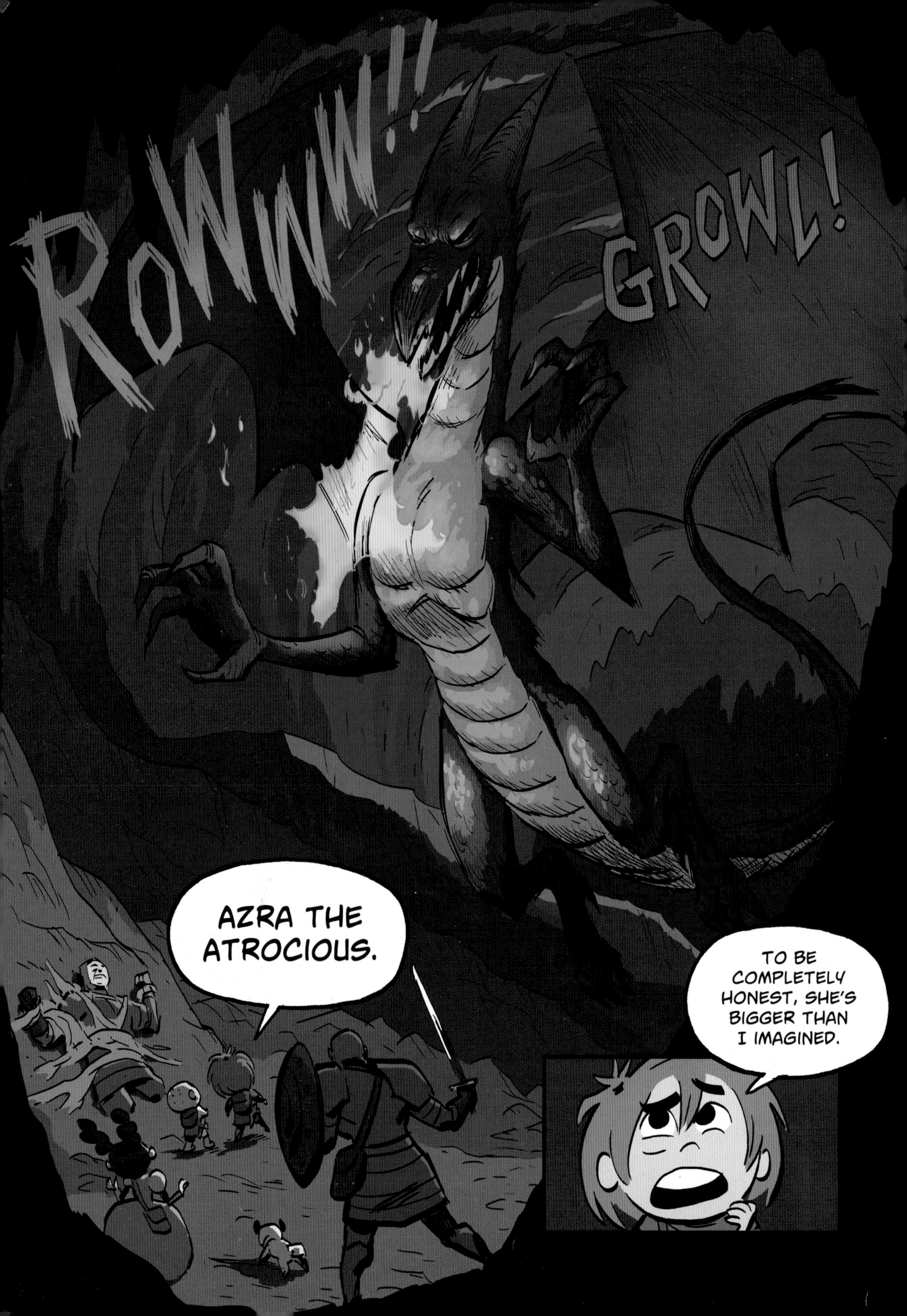

ROWWW!!
GROWL!
AZRA THE ATROCIOUS.
TO BE COMPLETELY HONEST, SHE'S BIGGER THAN I IMAGINED.

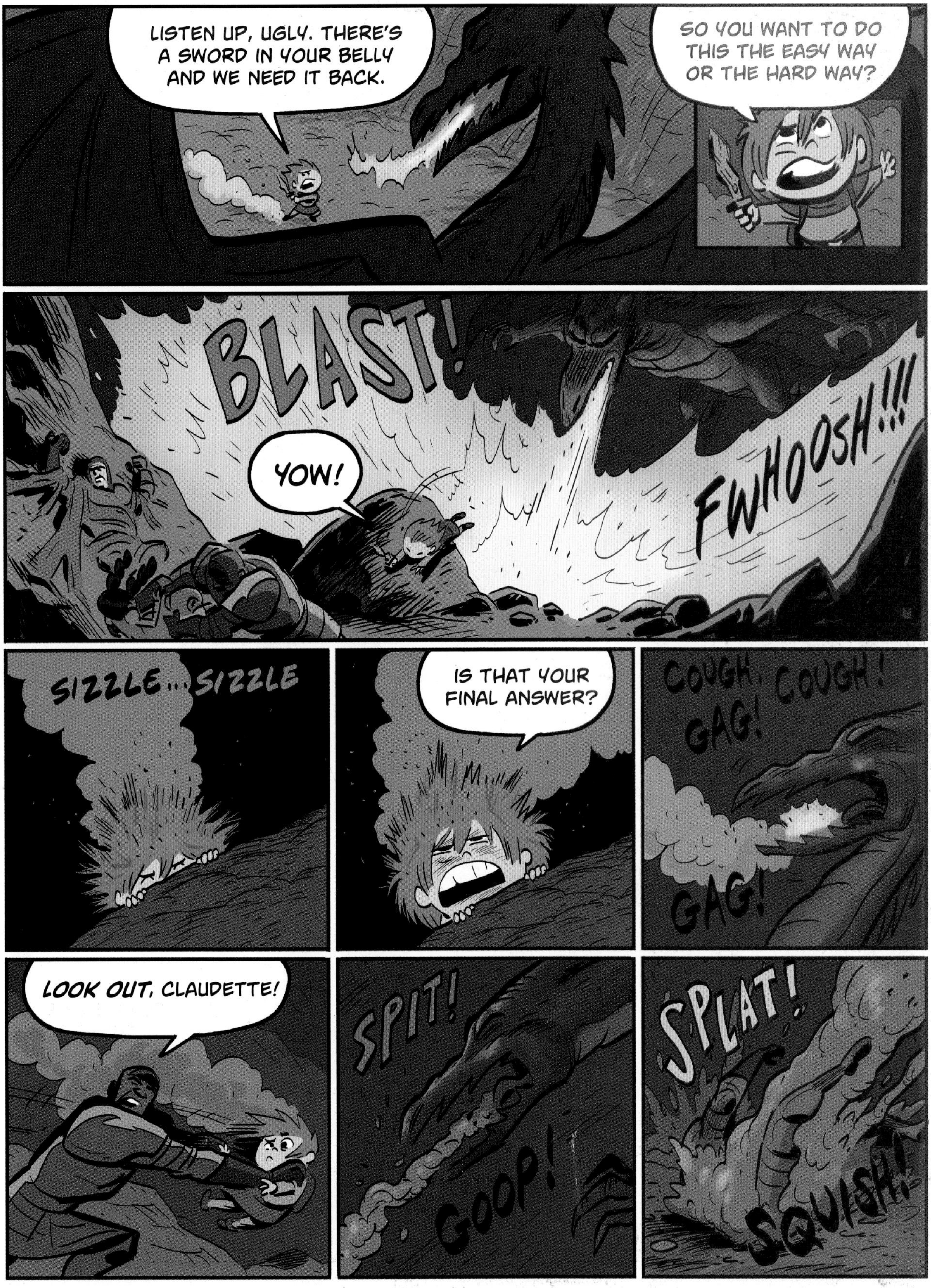
LISTEN UP, UGLY. THERE'S A SWORD IN YOUR BELLY AND WE NEED IT BACK.
SO YOU WANT TO DO THIS THE EASY WAY OR THE HARD WAY?
BLAST!
YOW!
FWHOOSH!!!
SIZZLE... SIZZLE
IS THAT YOUR FINAL ANSWER?
COUGH, COUGH!
GAG!
GAG!
LOOK OUT, CLAUDETTE!
SPIT!
GOOP!
SPLAT!
SQUISH!

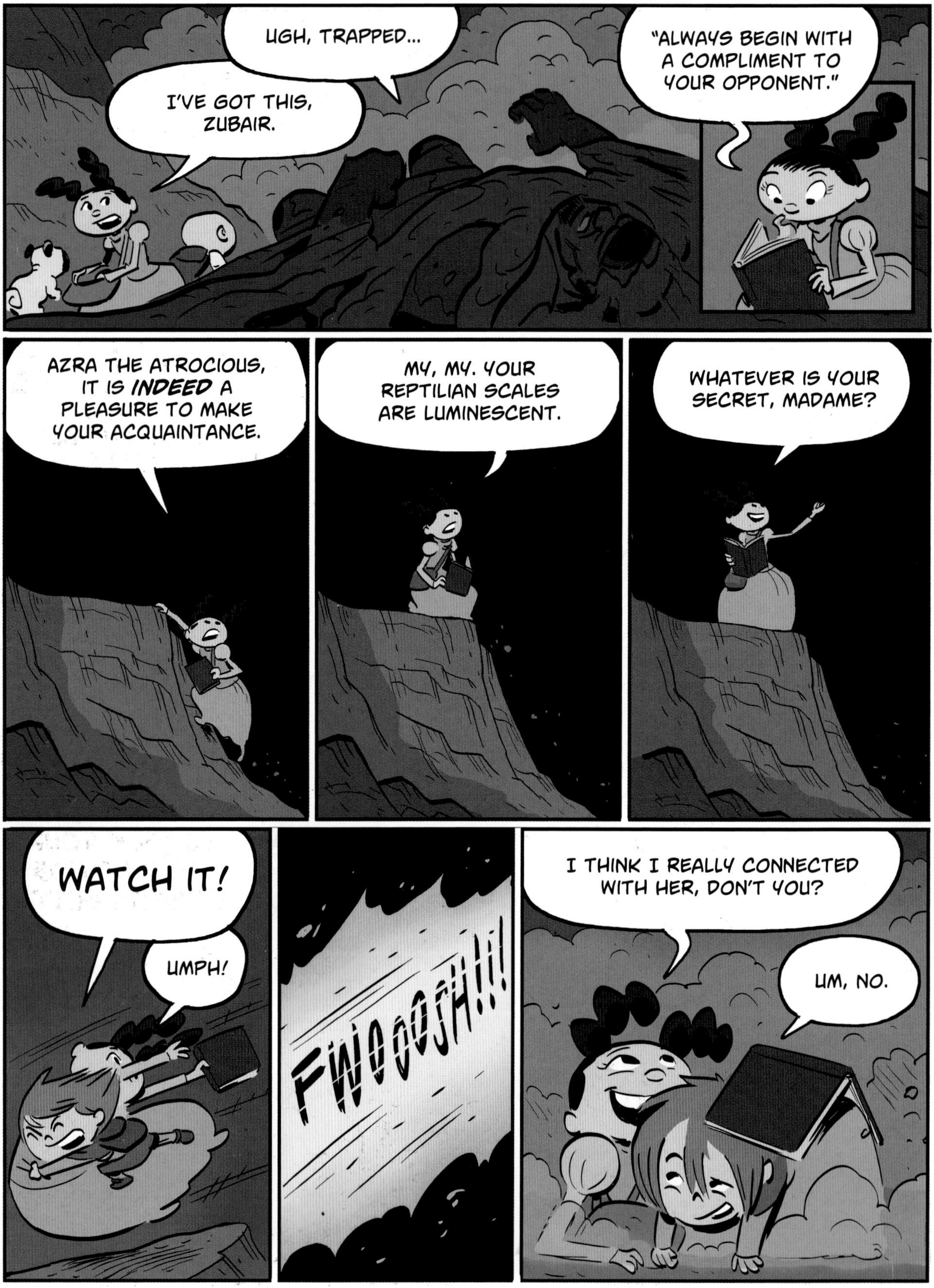
UGH, TRAPPED...
I'VE GOT THIS, ZUBAIR.
"ALWAYS BEGIN WITH A COMPLIMENT TO YOUR OPPONENT."
AZRA THE ATROCIOUS, IT IS *INDEED* A PLEASURE TO MAKE YOUR ACQUAINTANCE.
MY, MY. YOUR REPTILIAN SCALES ARE LUMINESCENT.
WHATEVER IS YOUR SECRET, MADAME?
WATCH IT!
UMPH!
FWOOOSH!!!
I THINK I REALLY CONNECTED WITH HER, DON'T YOU?
UM, NO.

CH-CH-CHATTER...

I AM A WARRIOR. I AM A WARRIOR.

...GONNA MAKE POPPA PROUD.

HURRY, CLAUDETTE!

GLAD TO SEE US, POPPA?

NO! YOU *SHOULDN'T BE HERE!*

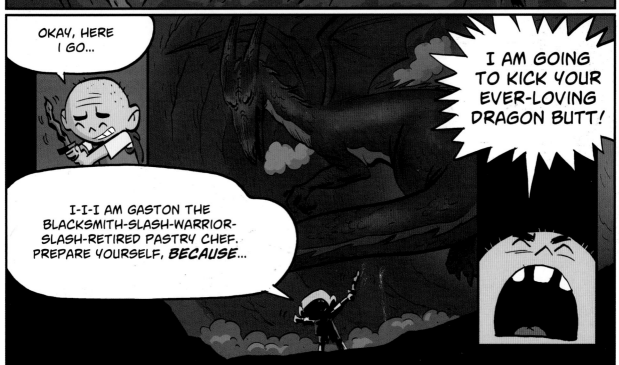

OKAY, HERE I GO...

I AM GOING TO KICK YOUR EVER-LOVING DRAGON BUTT!

I-I-I AM GASTON THE BLACKSMITH-SLASH-WARRIOR-SLASH-RETIRED PASTRY CHEF. PREPARE YOURSELF, *BECAUSE*...

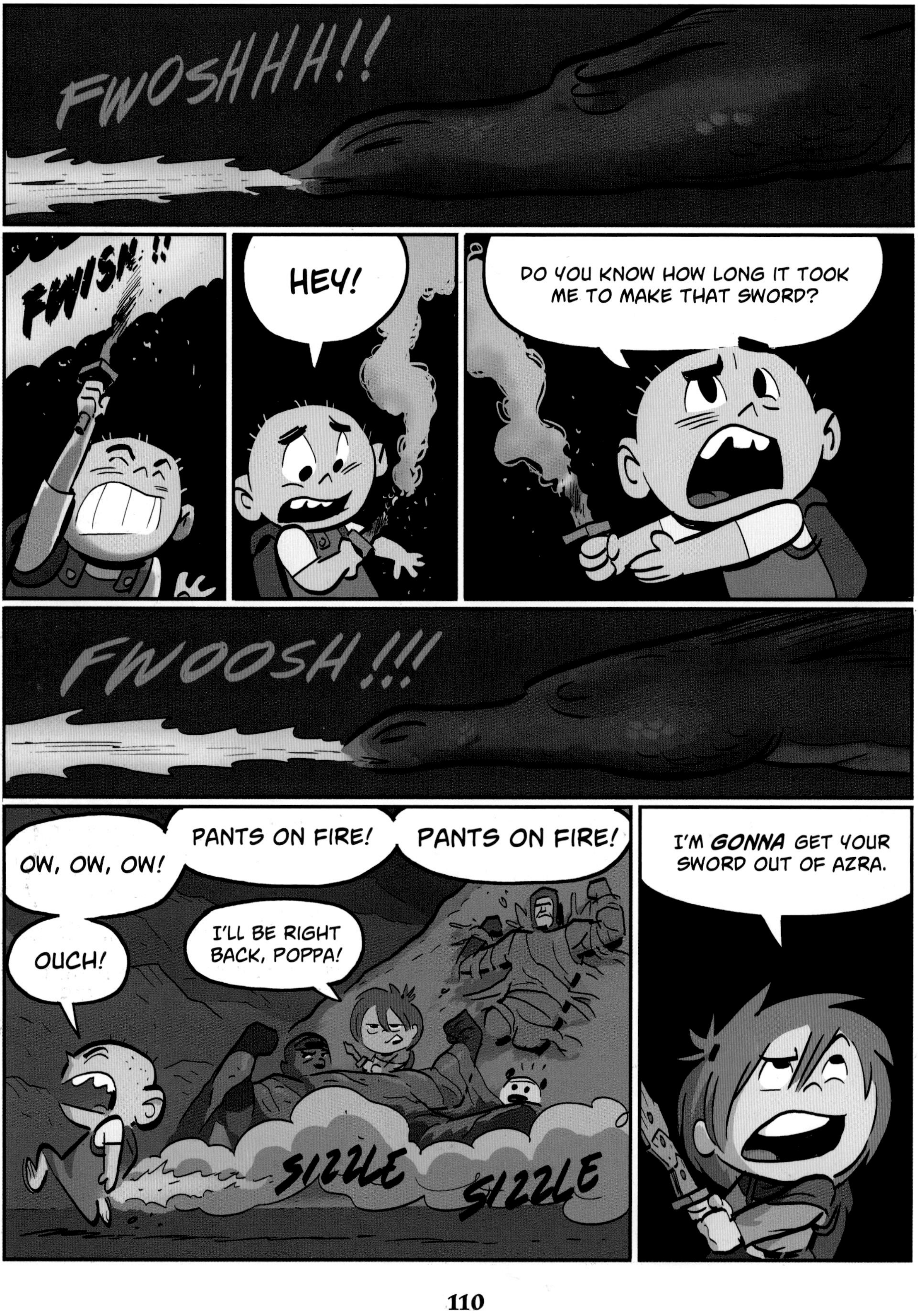

FWOSHHH!!
FWISH!!
HEY!
DO YOU KNOW HOW LONG IT TOOK ME TO MAKE THAT SWORD?
FWOOSH!!!
OW, OW, OW!
PANTS ON FIRE!
PANTS ON FIRE!
OUCH!
I'LL BE RIGHT BACK, POPPA!
SIZZLE
SIZZLE
I'M *GONNA* GET YOUR SWORD OUT OF AZRA.

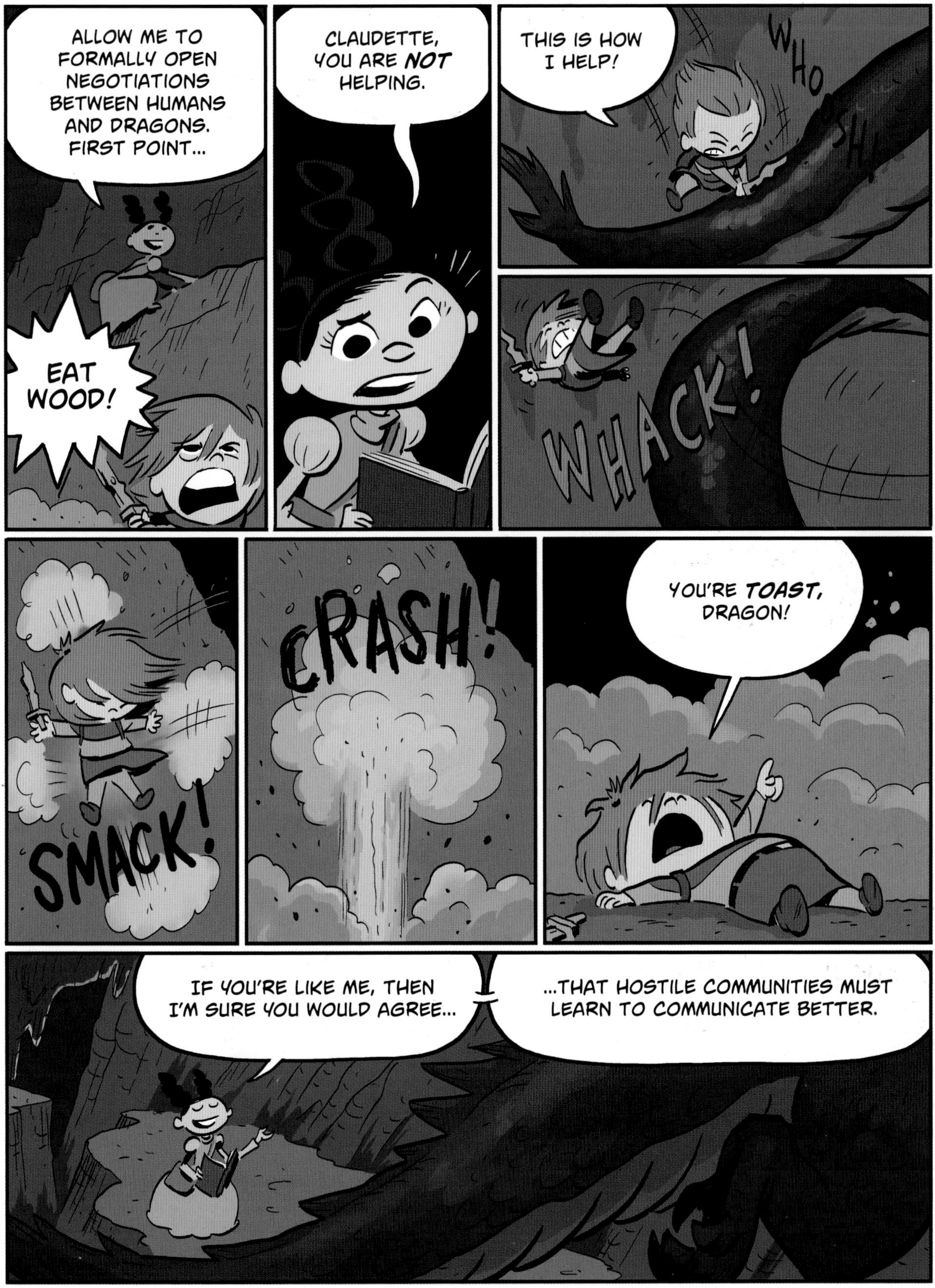
ALLOW ME TO FORMALLY OPEN NEGOTIATIONS BETWEEN HUMANS AND DRAGONS. FIRST POINT...
EAT WOOD!
CLAUDETTE, YOU ARE NOT HELPING.
THIS IS HOW I HELP!
WHOOSH!
WHACK!
SMACK!
CRASH!
YOU'RE TOAST, DRAGON!
IF YOU'RE LIKE ME, THEN I'M SURE YOU WOULD AGREE...
...THAT HOSTILE COMMUNITIES MUST LEARN TO COMMUNICATE BETTER.

GAG! GAG! GAG!

UH-OH.

SPIT!

SPLAT! GLURP!

ROLL, ROLL, ROLL...

DIPLOMATIC BREAKTHROUGH!

ROLL, ROLL, ROLL

REALLY?!

WE HAVE THAT DUMB DRAGON RIGHT WHERE WE WANT HER, RIGHT MARIE?

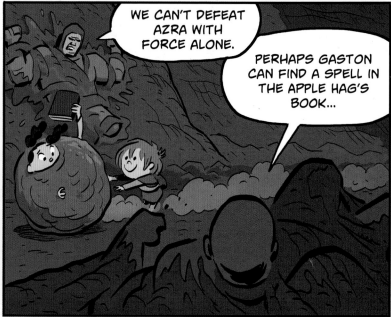

WE CAN'T DEFEAT AZRA WITH FORCE ALONE.

PERHAPS GASTON CAN FIND A SPELL IN THE APPLE HAG'S BOOK...

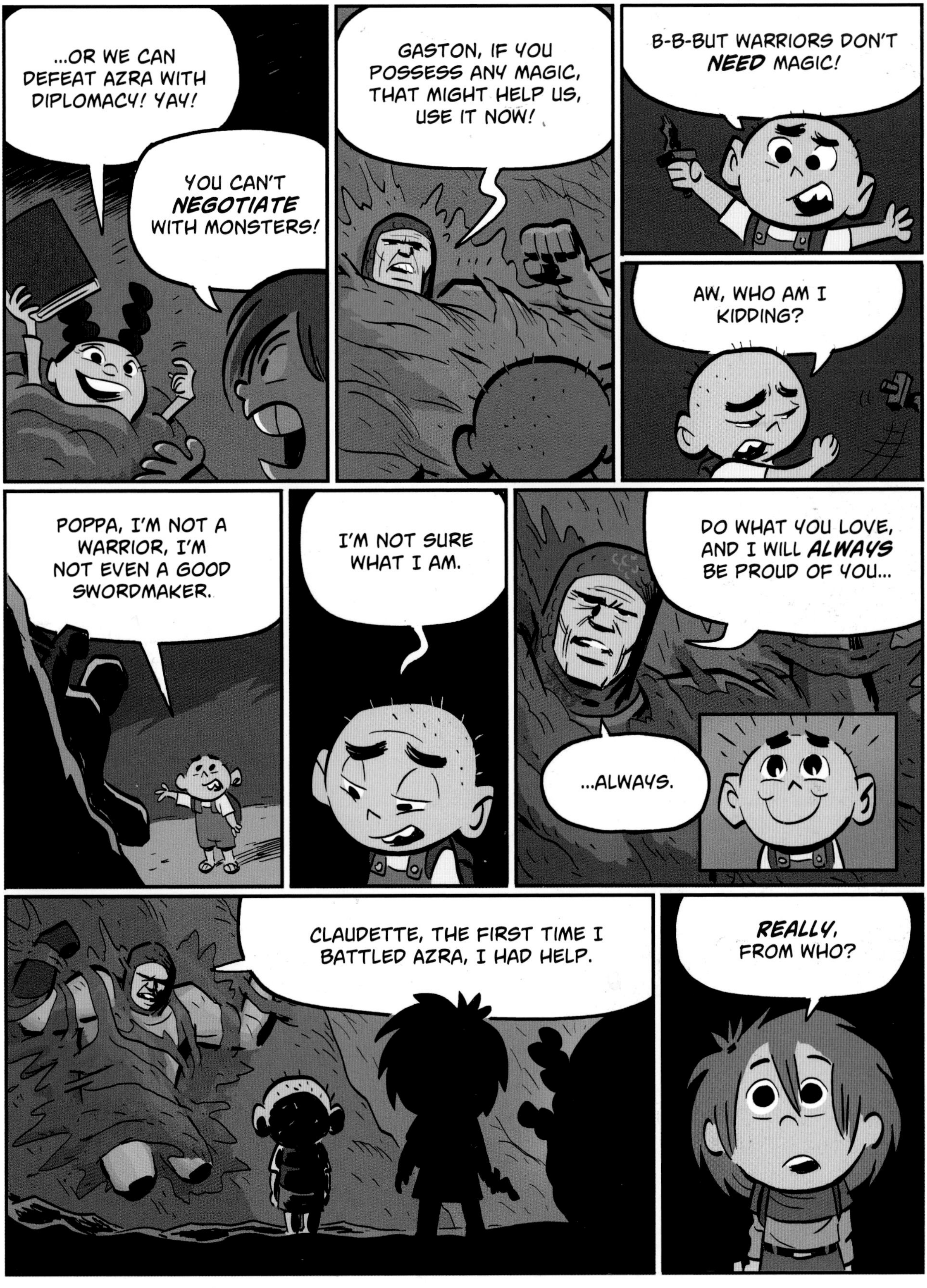
...OR WE CAN DEFEAT AZRA WITH DIPLOMACY! YAY!
YOU CAN'T **NEGOTIATE** WITH MONSTERS!
GASTON, IF YOU POSSESS ANY MAGIC, THAT MIGHT HELP US, USE IT NOW!
B-B-BUT WARRIORS DON'T **NEED** MAGIC!
AW, WHO AM I KIDDING?
POPPA, I'M NOT A WARRIOR, I'M NOT EVEN A GOOD SWORDMAKER.
I'M NOT SURE WHAT I AM.
DO WHAT YOU LOVE, AND I WILL **ALWAYS** BE PROUD OF YOU...
...ALWAYS.
CLAUDETTE, THE FIRST TIME I BATTLED AZRA, I HAD HELP.
REALLY, FROM WHO?

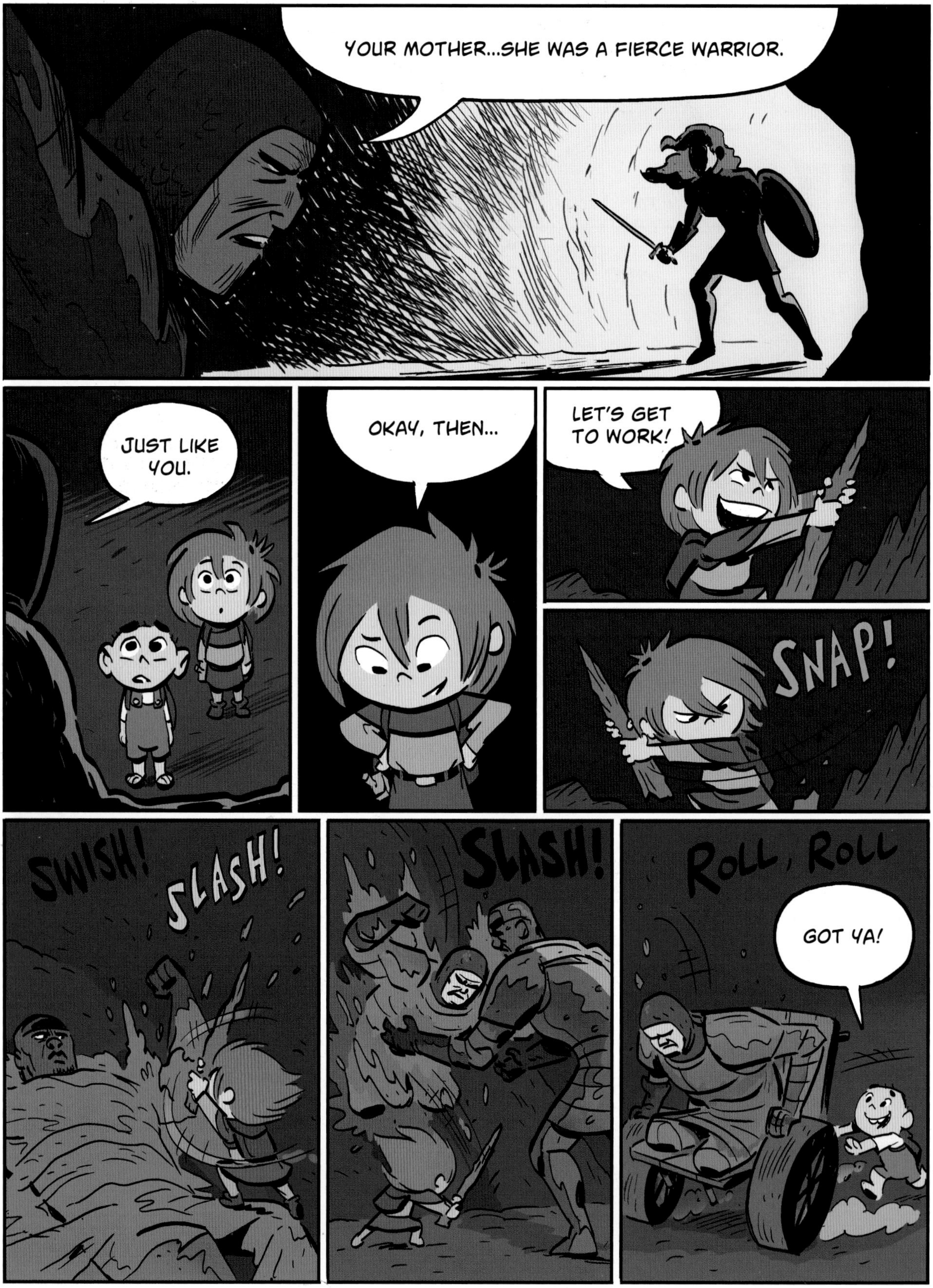
YOUR MOTHER...SHE WAS A FIERCE WARRIOR.
JUST LIKE YOU.
OKAY, THEN...
LET'S GET TO WORK!
SNAP!
SWISH!
SLASH!
SLASH!
ROLL, ROLL
GOT YA!

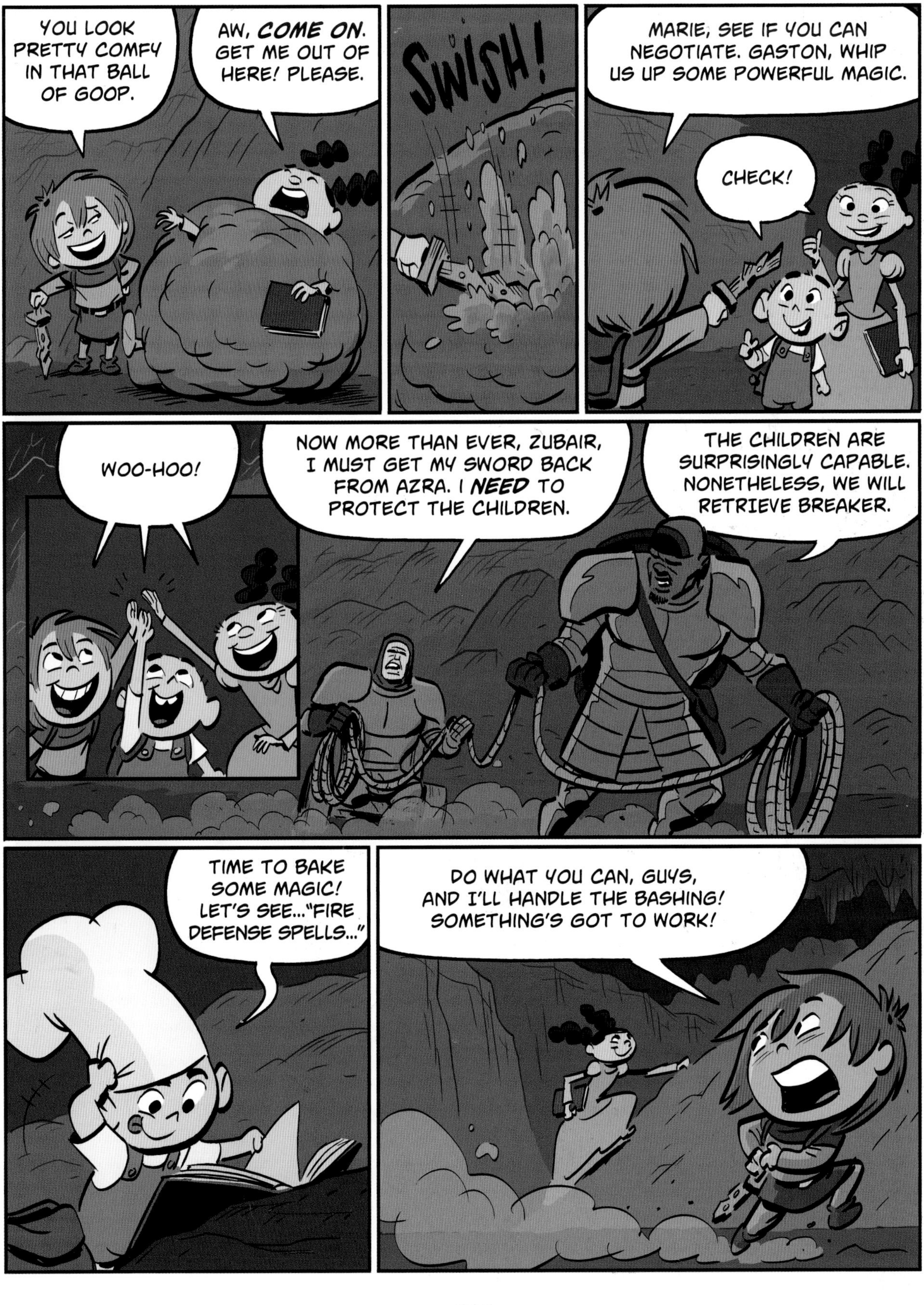

YOU LOOK PRETTY COMFY IN THAT BALL OF GOOP.
AW, COME ON. GET ME OUT OF HERE! PLEASE.
SWISH!
MARIE, SEE IF YOU CAN NEGOTIATE. GASTON, WHIP US UP SOME POWERFUL MAGIC.
CHECK!
WOO-HOO!
NOW MORE THAN EVER, ZUBAIR, I MUST GET MY SWORD BACK FROM AZRA. I NEED TO PROTECT THE CHILDREN.
THE CHILDREN ARE SURPRISINGLY CAPABLE. NONETHELESS, WE WILL RETRIEVE BREAKER.
TIME TO BAKE SOME MAGIC! LET'S SEE..."FIRE DEFENSE SPELLS..."
DO WHAT YOU CAN, GUYS, AND I'LL HANDLE THE BASHING! SOMETHING'S GOT TO WORK!

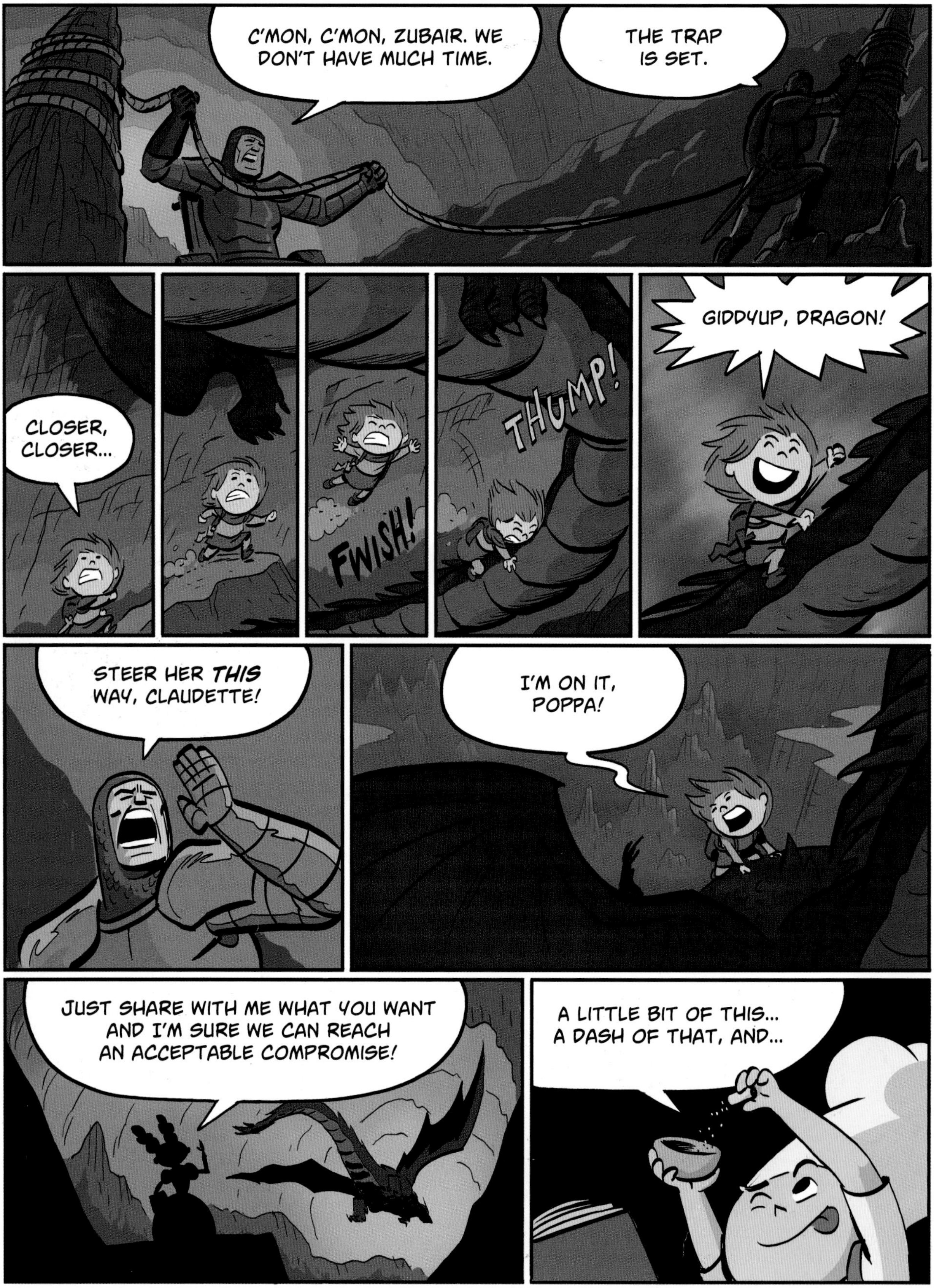
C'MON, C'MON, ZUBAIR. WE DON'T HAVE MUCH TIME.
THE TRAP IS SET.
CLOSER, CLOSER...
FWISH!
THUMP!
GIDDYUP, DRAGON!
STEER HER *THIS* WAY, CLAUDETTE!
I'M ON IT, POPPA!
JUST SHARE WITH ME WHAT YOU WANT AND I'M SURE WE CAN REACH AN ACCEPTABLE COMPROMISE!
A LITTLE BIT OF THIS... A DASH OF THAT, AND...

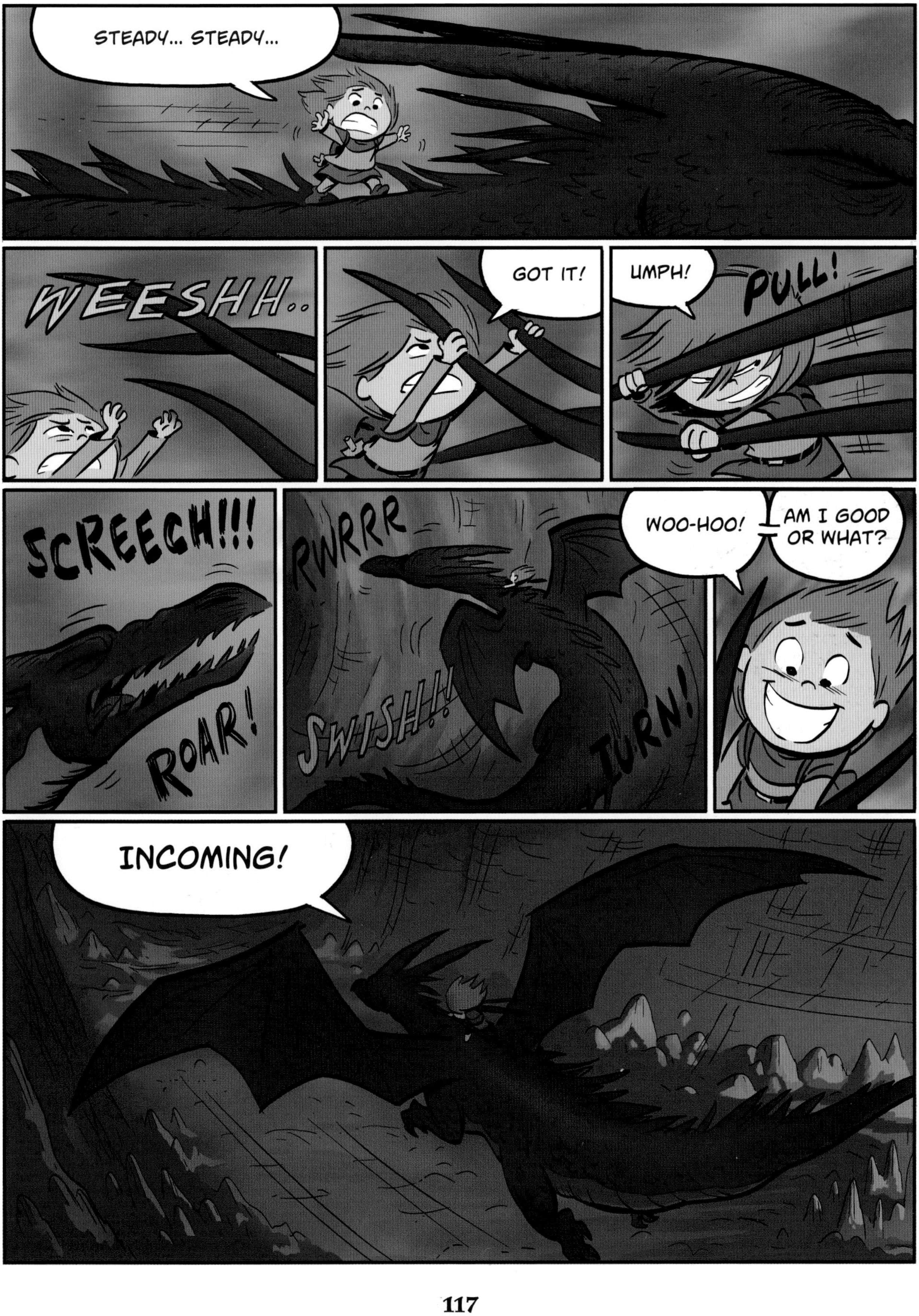
STEADY... STEADY...
WEESHH..
GOT IT!
UMPH!
PULL!
SCREECH!!!
ROAR!
RWRRR
SWISH!!
TURN!
WOO-HOO!
AM I GOOD OR WHAT?
INCOMING!

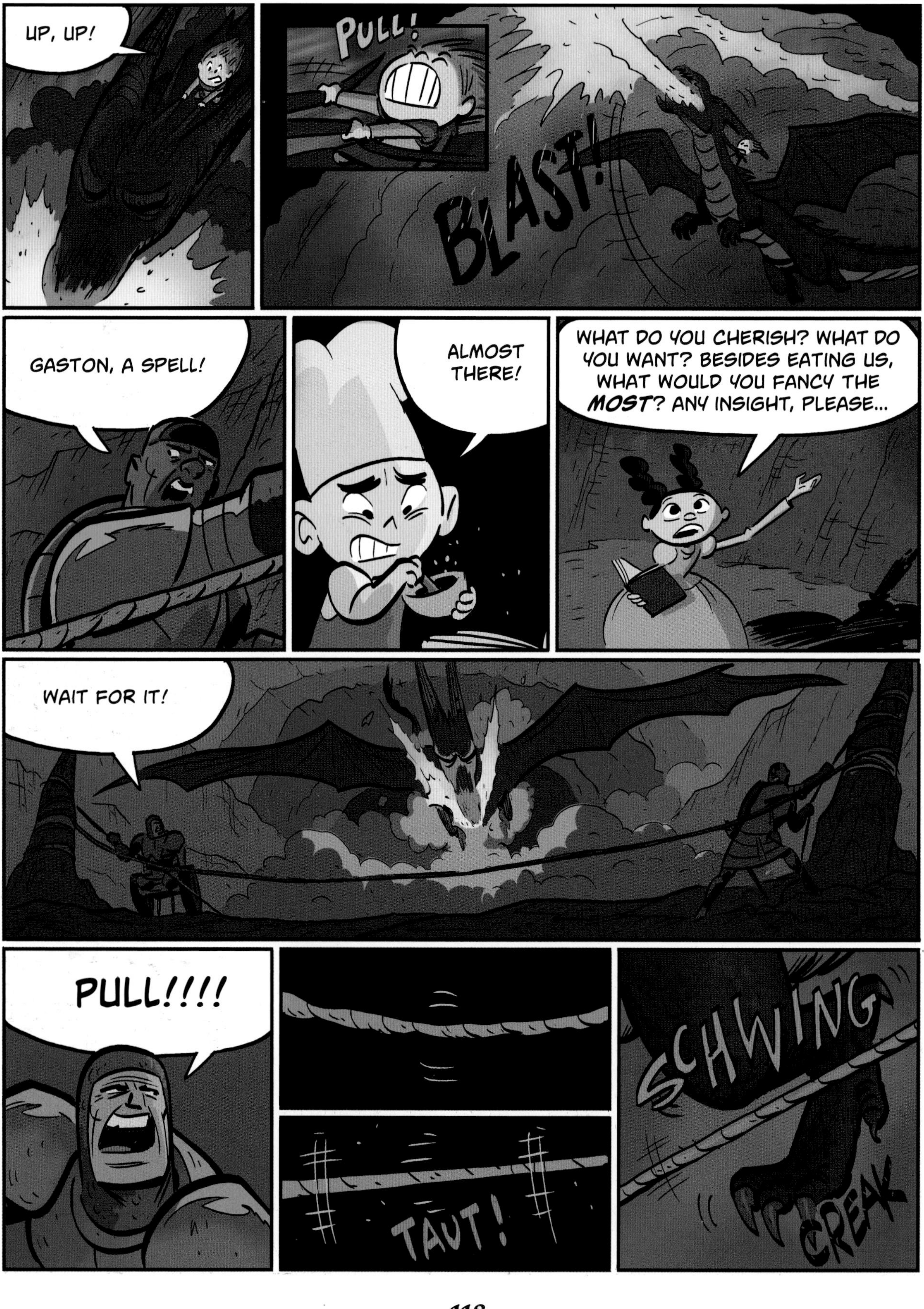
UP, UP!
PULL!
BLAST!
GASTON, A SPELL!
ALMOST THERE!
WHAT DO YOU CHERISH? WHAT DO YOU WANT? BESIDES EATING US, WHAT WOULD YOU FANCY THE *MOST*? ANY INSIGHT, PLEASE...
WAIT FOR IT!
PULL!!!!
TAUT!
SCHWING
CREAK

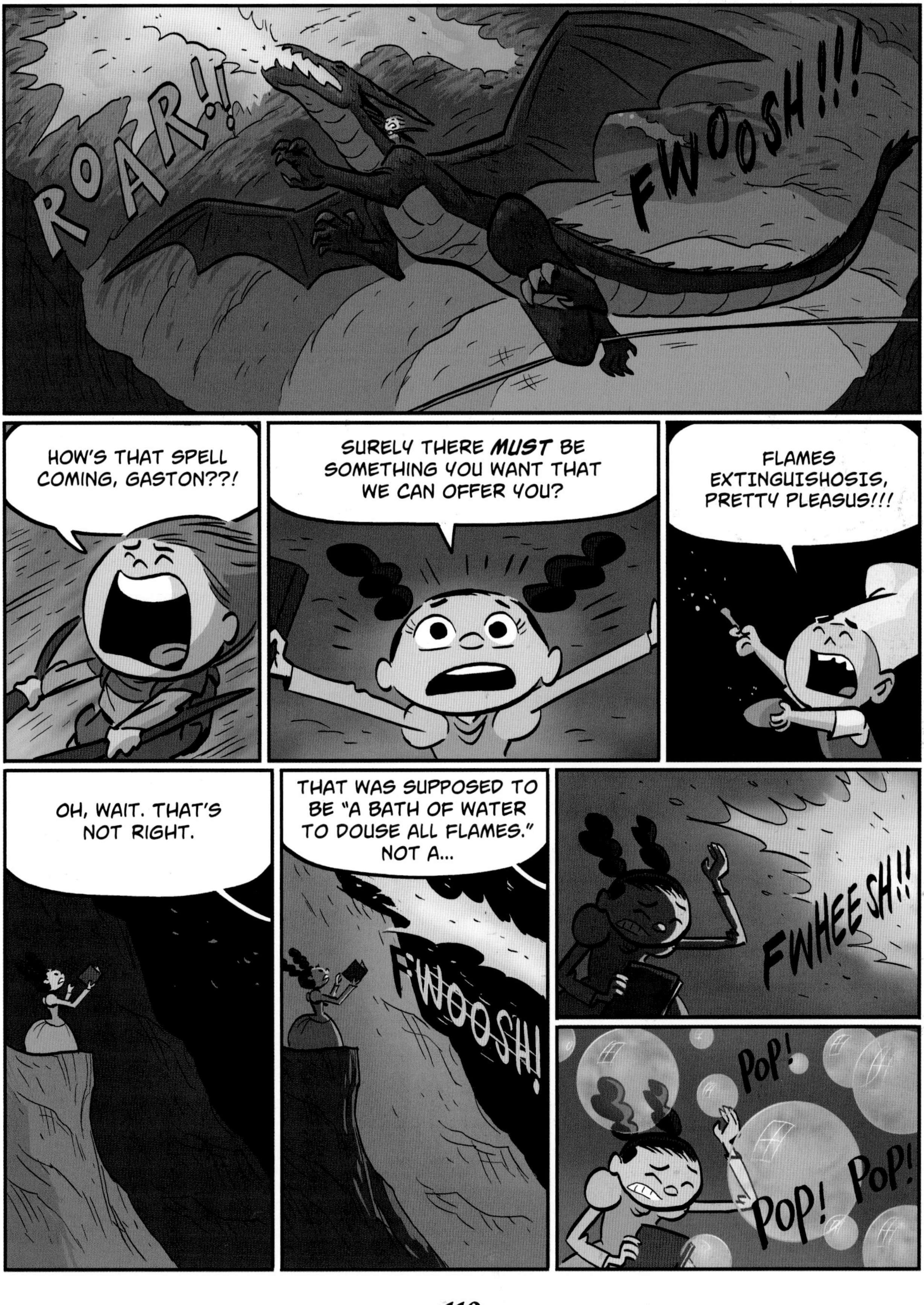
ROAR!!
FWOOSH!!!
HOW'S THAT SPELL COMING, GASTON??!
SURELY THERE MUST BE SOMETHING YOU WANT THAT WE CAN OFFER YOU?
FLAMES EXTINGUISHOSIS, PRETTY PLEASUS!!!
OH, WAIT. THAT'S NOT RIGHT.
THAT WAS SUPPOSED TO BE "A BATH OF WATER TO DOUSE ALL FLAMES." NOT A...
FWOOSH!
FWHEESH!!
POP!
POP! POP!

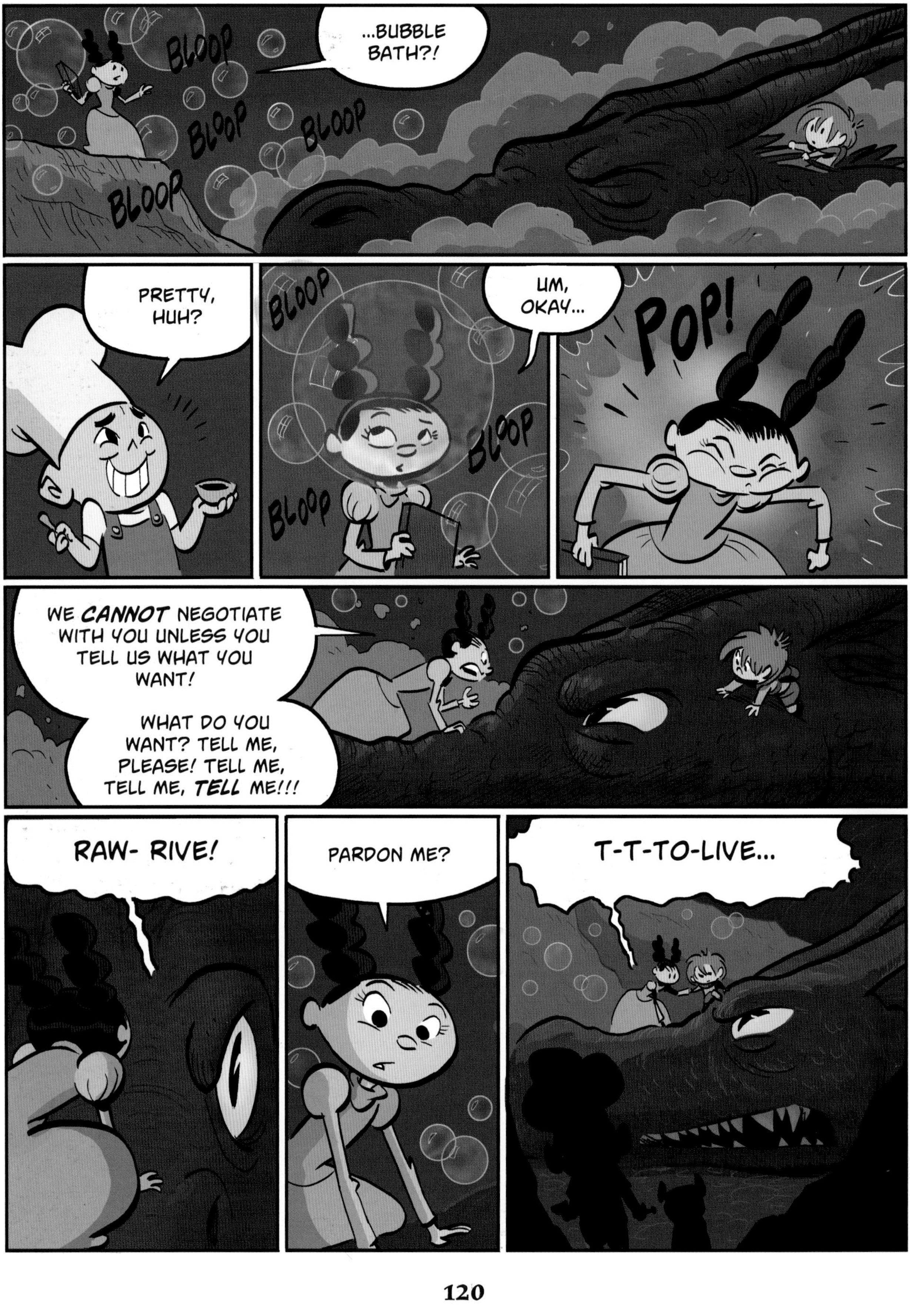
...BUBBLE BATH?!
BLOOP
BLOOP
BLOOP
BLOOP
PRETTY, HUH?
BLOOP
UM, OKAY...
BLOOP
BLOOP
POP!
WE CANNOT NEGOTIATE WITH YOU UNLESS YOU TELL US WHAT YOU WANT!
WHAT DO YOU WANT? TELL ME, PLEASE! TELL ME, TELL ME, TELL ME!!!
RAW- RIVE!
PARDON ME?
T-T-TO-LIVE...

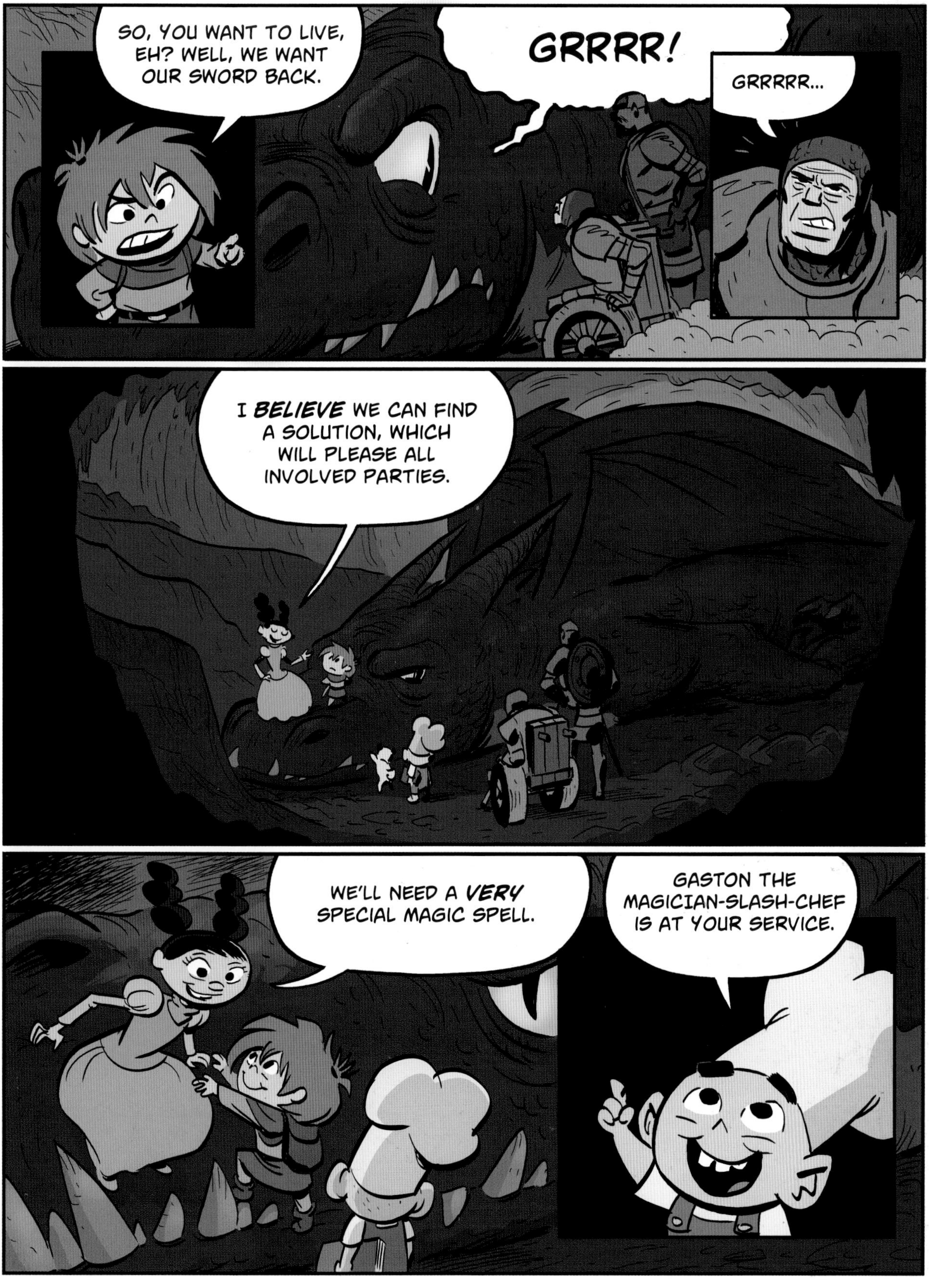
SO, YOU WANT TO LIVE, EH? WELL, WE WANT OUR SWORD BACK.
GRRRR!
GRRRRR...
I *BELIEVE* WE CAN FIND A SOLUTION, WHICH WILL PLEASE ALL INVOLVED PARTIES.
WE'LL NEED A *VERY* SPECIAL MAGIC SPELL.
GASTON THE MAGICIAN-SLASH-CHEF IS AT YOUR SERVICE.

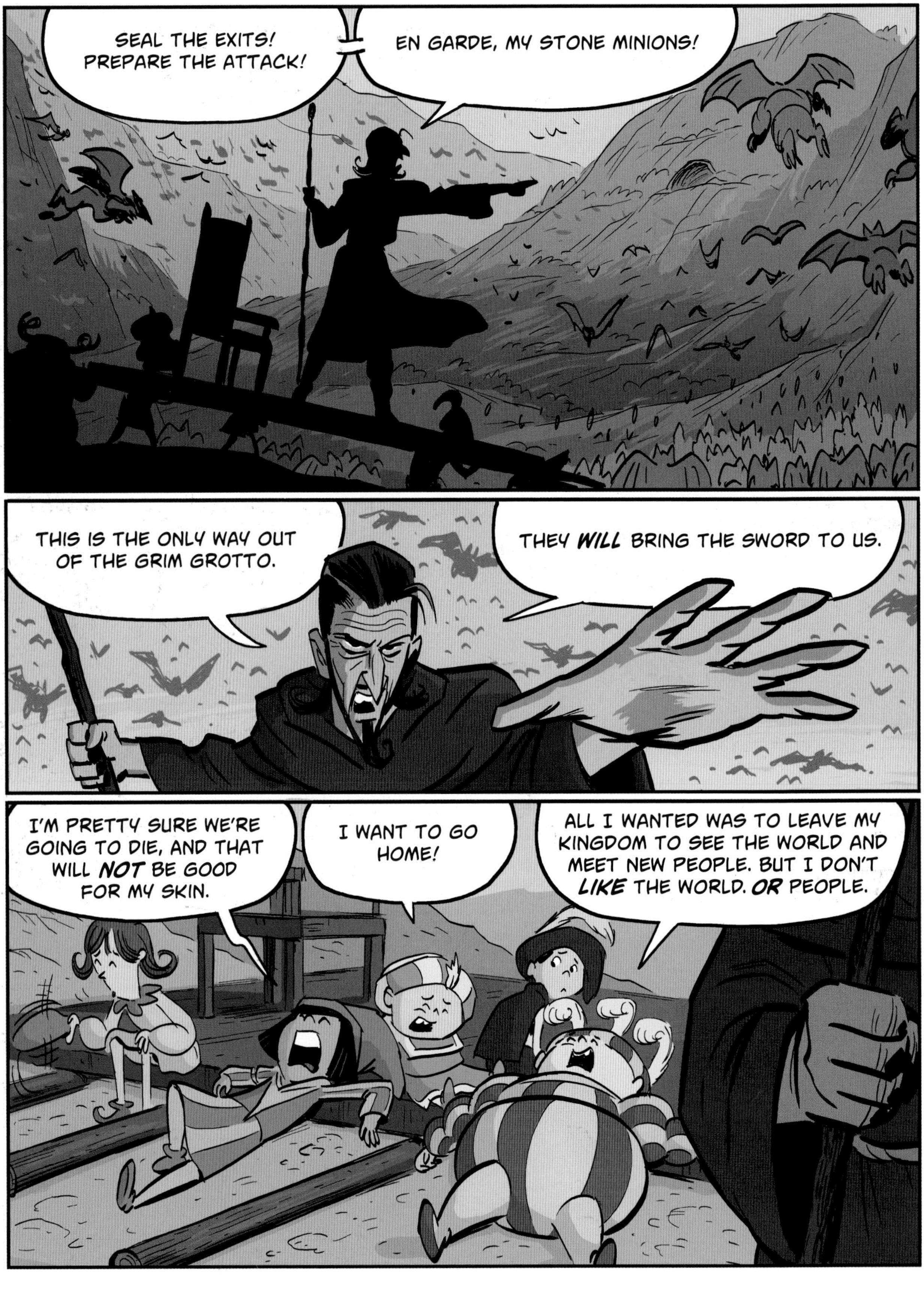
SEAL THE EXITS! PREPARE THE ATTACK!
EN GARDE, MY STONE MINIONS!
THIS IS THE ONLY WAY OUT OF THE GRIM GROTTO.
THEY *WILL* BRING THE SWORD TO US.
I'M PRETTY SURE WE'RE GOING TO DIE, AND THAT WILL *NOT* BE GOOD FOR MY SKIN.
I WANT TO GO HOME!
ALL I WANTED WAS TO LEAVE MY KINGDOM TO SEE THE WORLD AND MEET NEW PEOPLE. BUT I DON'T *LIKE* THE WORLD. *OR* PEOPLE.

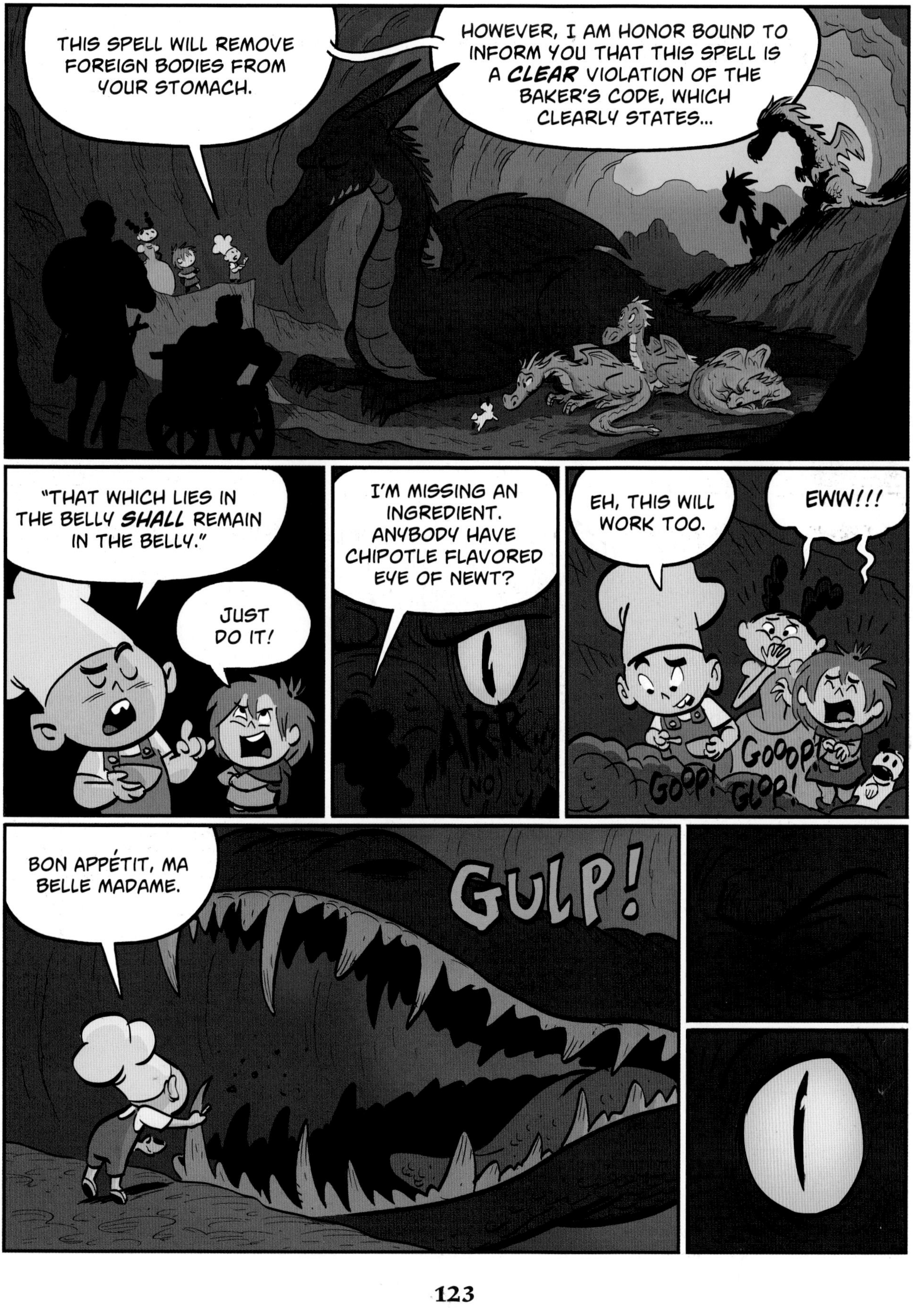

THIS SPELL WILL REMOVE FOREIGN BODIES FROM YOUR STOMACH.
HOWEVER, I AM HONOR BOUND TO INFORM YOU THAT THIS SPELL IS A ***CLEAR*** VIOLATION OF THE BAKER'S CODE, WHICH CLEARLY STATES...
"THAT WHICH LIES IN THE BELLY ***SHALL*** REMAIN IN THE BELLY."
JUST DO IT!
I'M MISSING AN INGREDIENT. ANYBODY HAVE CHIPOTLE FLAVORED EYE OF NEWT?
EH, THIS WILL WORK TOO.
EWW!!!
GOOP!
GOOOP!
GLOP!
BON APPÉTIT, MA BELLE MADAME.
GULP!

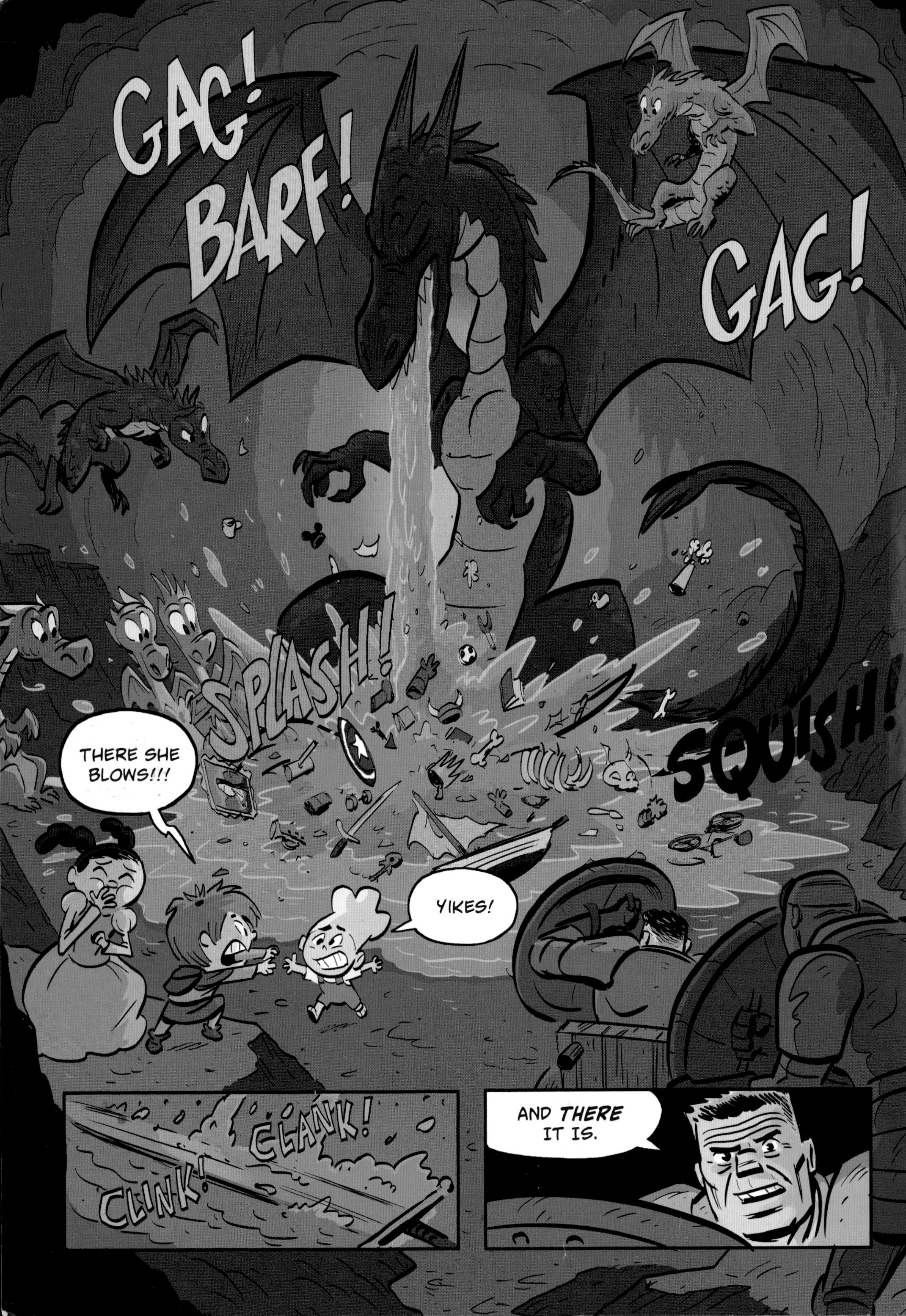
GAG!
BARF!
GAG!
SPLASH!
SQUISH!
THERE SHE BLOWS!!!
YIKES!
CLINK!
CLANK!
AND THERE IT IS.

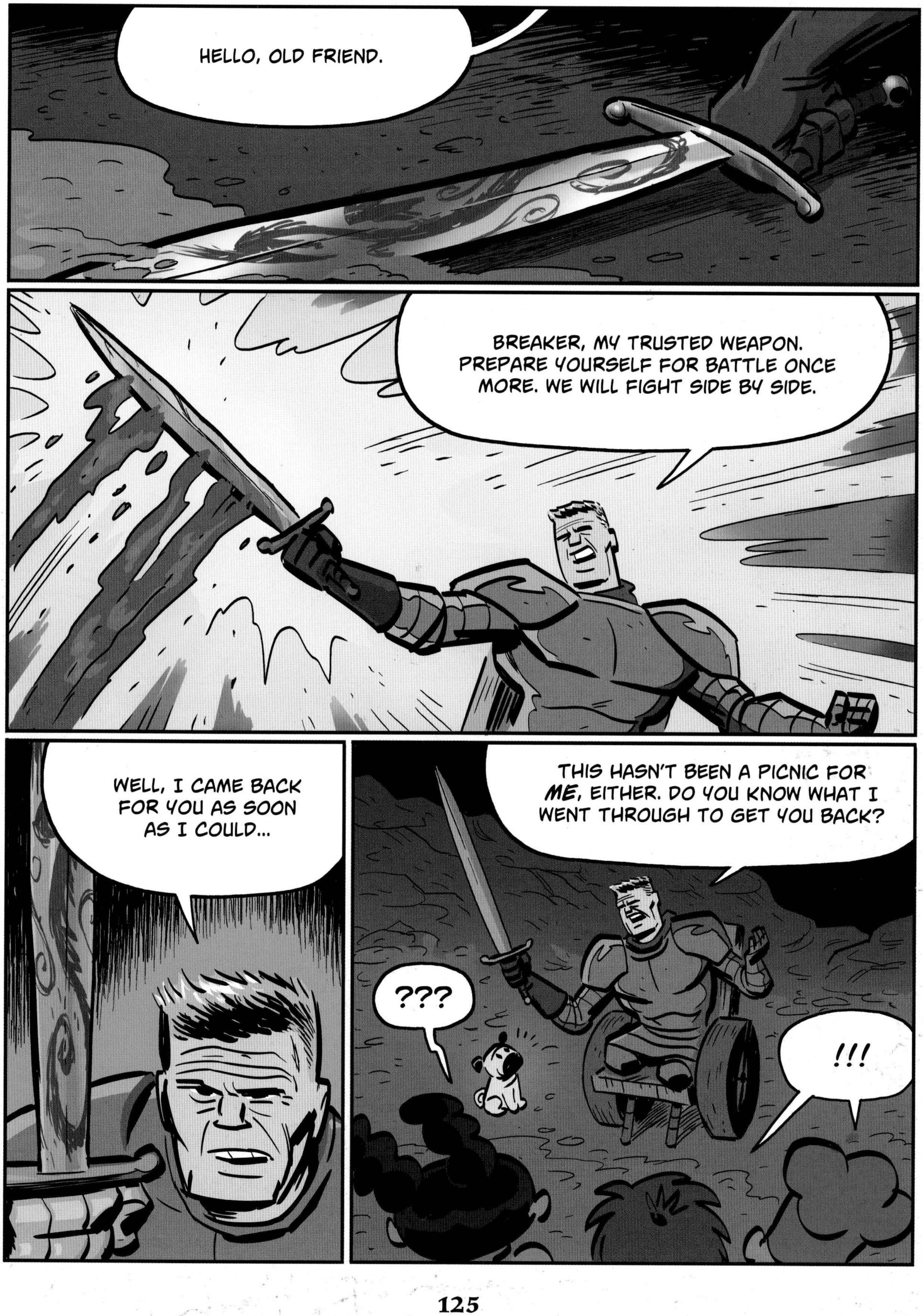
HELLO, OLD FRIEND.
BREAKER, MY TRUSTED WEAPON. PREPARE YOURSELF FOR BATTLE ONCE MORE. WE WILL FIGHT SIDE BY SIDE.
WELL, I CAME BACK FOR YOU AS SOON AS I COULD...
THIS HASN'T BEEN A PICNIC FOR *ME*, EITHER. DO YOU KNOW WHAT I WENT THROUGH TO GET YOU BACK?
???
!!!

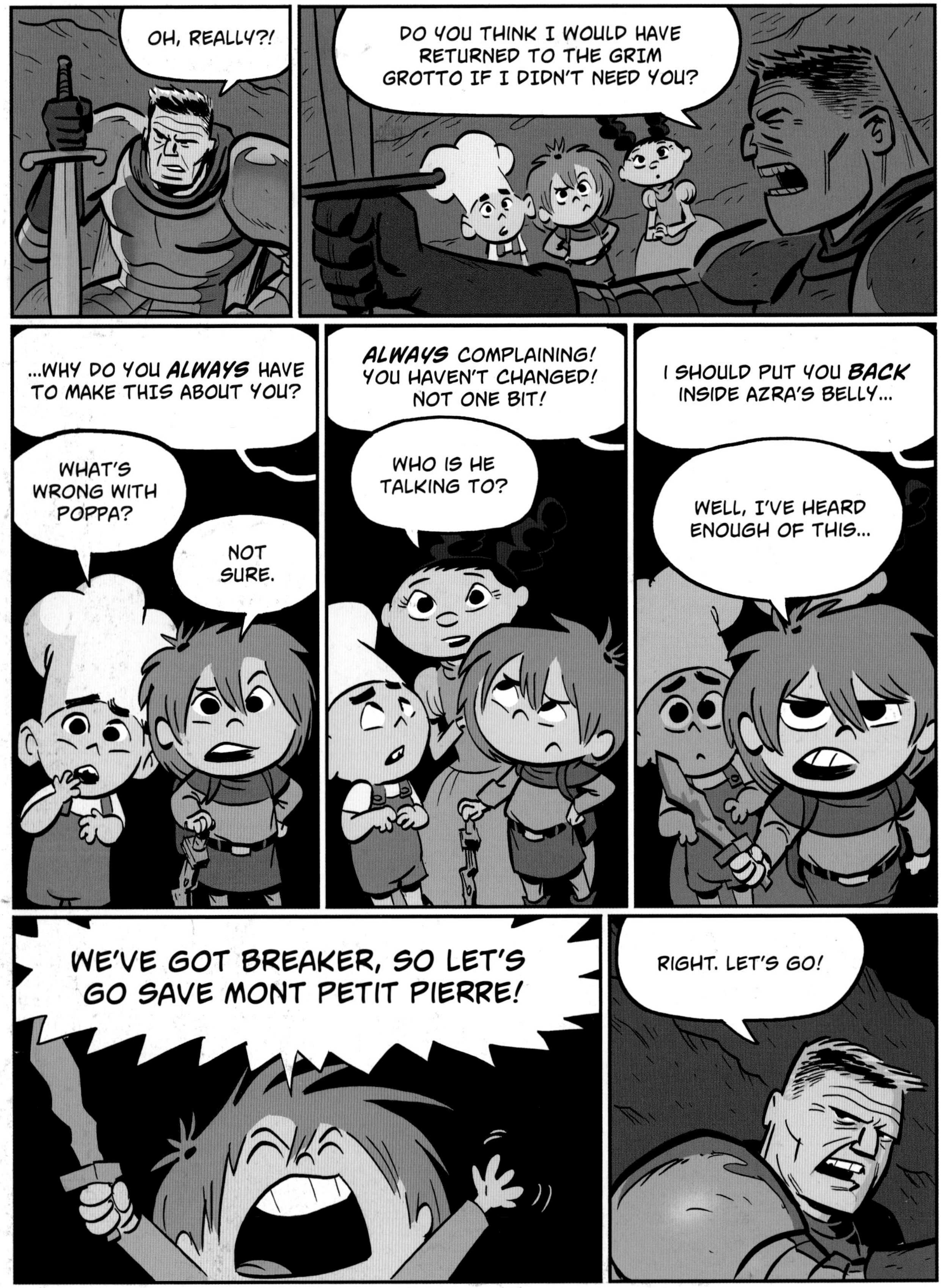
OH, REALLY?!
DO YOU THINK I WOULD HAVE RETURNED TO THE GRIM GROTTO IF I DIDN'T NEED YOU?
...WHY DO YOU ALWAYS HAVE TO MAKE THIS ABOUT YOU?
WHAT'S WRONG WITH POPPA?
NOT SURE.
ALWAYS COMPLAINING! YOU HAVEN'T CHANGED! NOT ONE BIT!
WHO IS HE TALKING TO?
I SHOULD PUT YOU BACK INSIDE AZRA'S BELLY...
WELL, I'VE HEARD ENOUGH OF THIS...
WE'VE GOT BREAKER, SO LET'S GO SAVE MONT PETIT PIERRE!
RIGHT. LET'S GO!

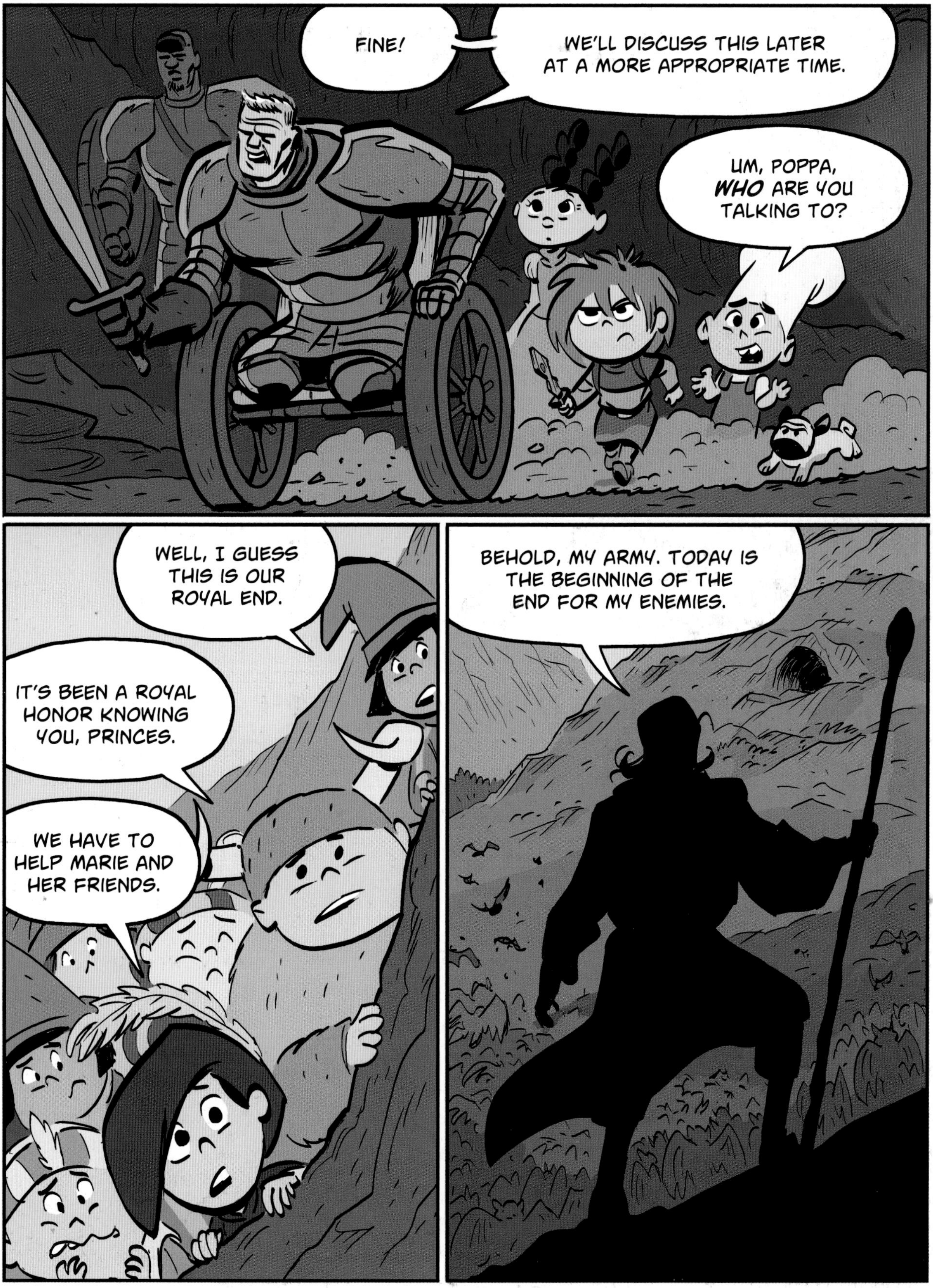
FINE!
WE'LL DISCUSS THIS LATER AT A MORE APPROPRIATE TIME.
UM, POPPA, ***WHO*** ARE YOU TALKING TO?
WELL, I GUESS THIS IS OUR ROYAL END.
IT'S BEEN A ROYAL HONOR KNOWING YOU, PRINCES.
WE HAVE TO HELP MARIE AND HER FRIENDS.
BEHOLD, MY ARMY. TODAY IS THE BEGINNING OF THE END FOR MY ENEMIES.

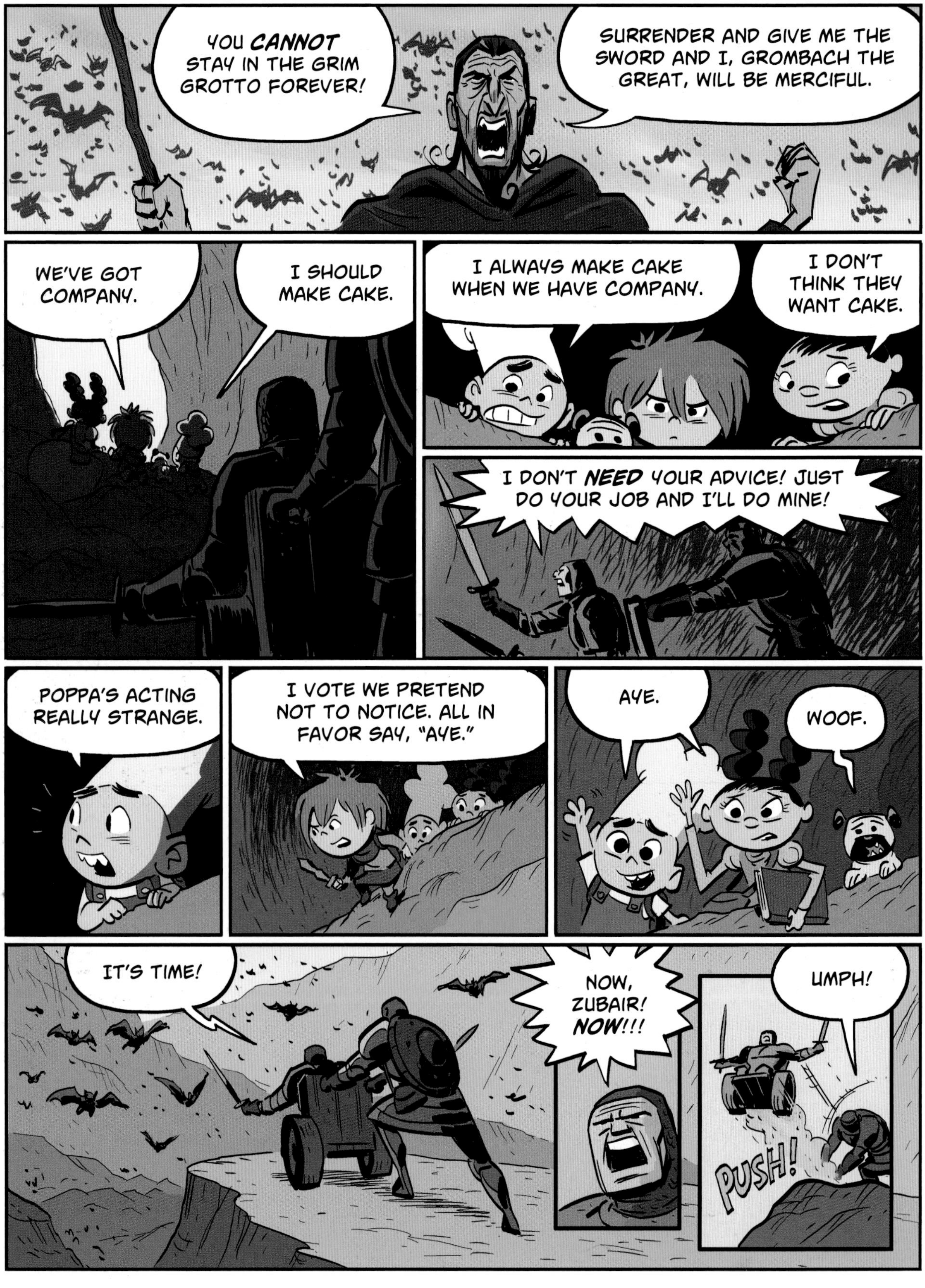
YOU CANNOT STAY IN THE GRIM GROTTO FOREVER!
SURRENDER AND GIVE ME THE SWORD AND I, GROMBACH THE GREAT, WILL BE MERCIFUL.
WE'VE GOT COMPANY.
I SHOULD MAKE CAKE.
I ALWAYS MAKE CAKE WHEN WE HAVE COMPANY.
I DON'T THINK THEY WANT CAKE.
I DON'T NEED YOUR ADVICE! JUST DO YOUR JOB AND I'LL DO MINE!
POPPA'S ACTING REALLY STRANGE.
I VOTE WE PRETEND NOT TO NOTICE. ALL IN FAVOR SAY, "AYE."
AYE.
WOOF.
IT'S TIME!
NOW, ZUBAIR! NOW!!!
UMPH!
PUSH!

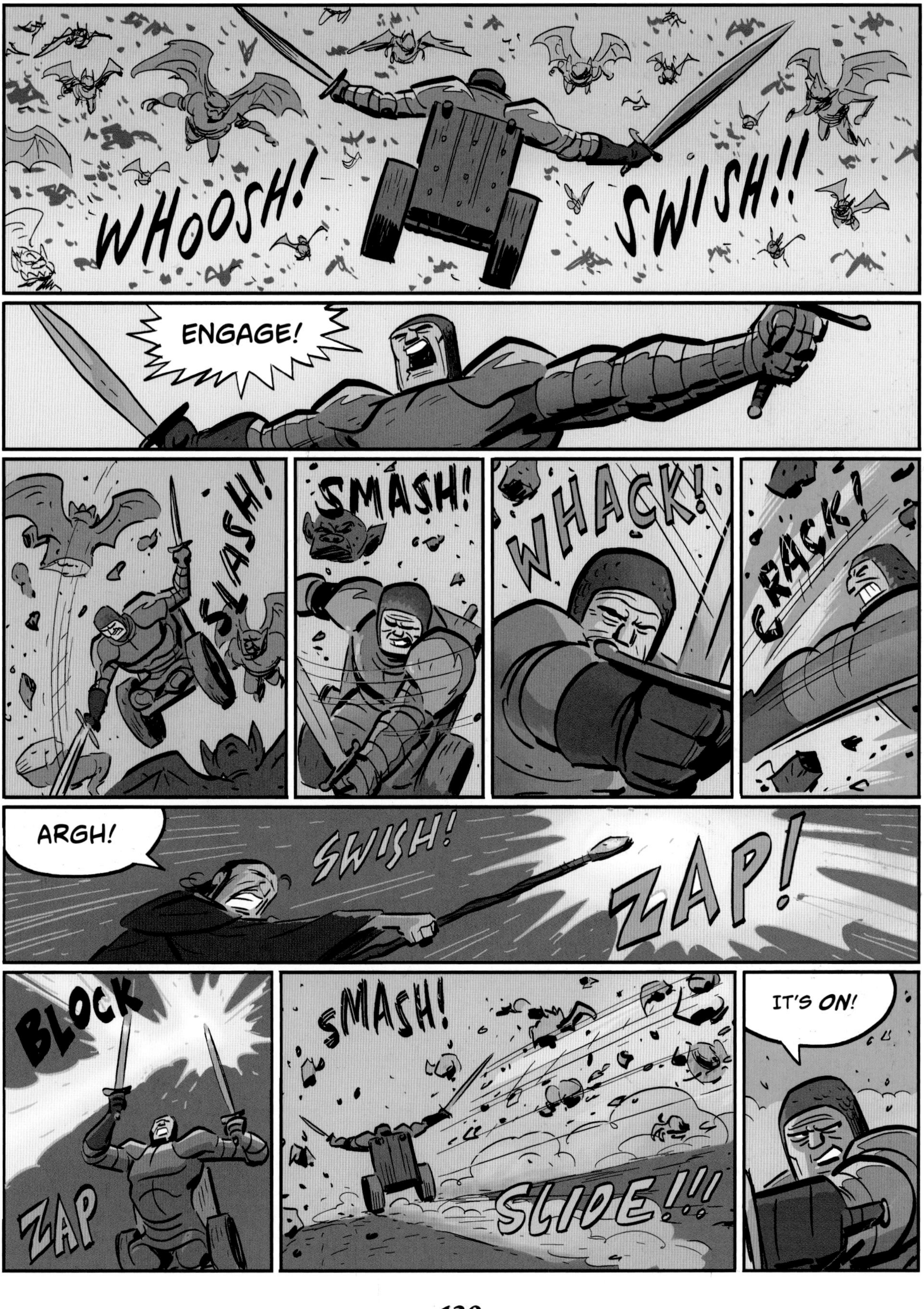

WHOOSH!
SWISH!!
ENGAGE!
SLASH!
SMASH!
WHACK!
CRACK!
ARGH!
SWISH!
ZAP!
BLOCK
ZAP
SMASH!
SLIDE!!!
IT'S ON!

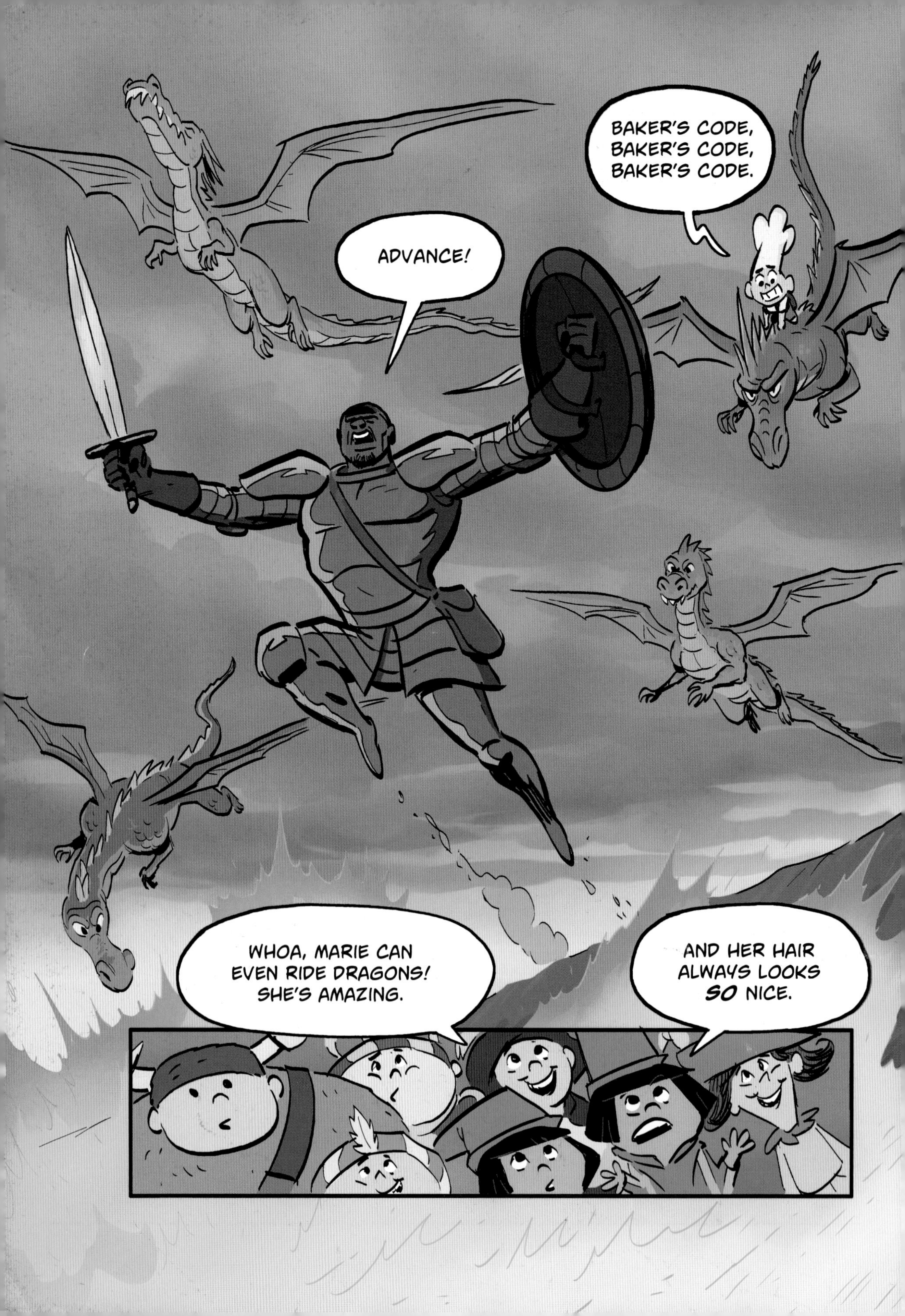
BAKER'S CODE, BAKER'S CODE, BAKER'S CODE.
ADVANCE!
WHOA, MARIE CAN EVEN RIDE DRAGONS! SHE'S AMAZING.
AND HER HAIR ALWAYS LOOKS SO NICE.

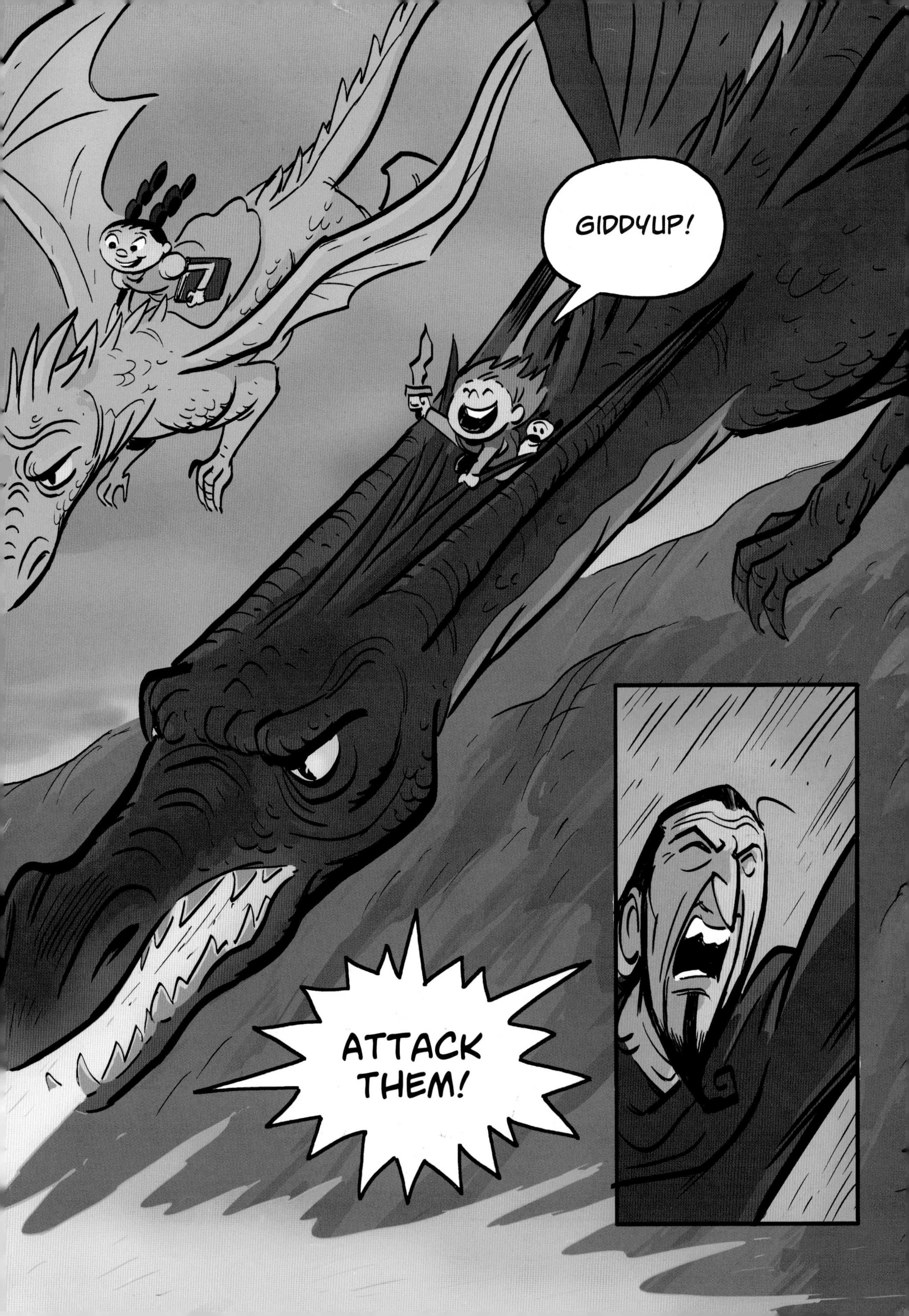
GIDDYUP!
ATTACK THEM!

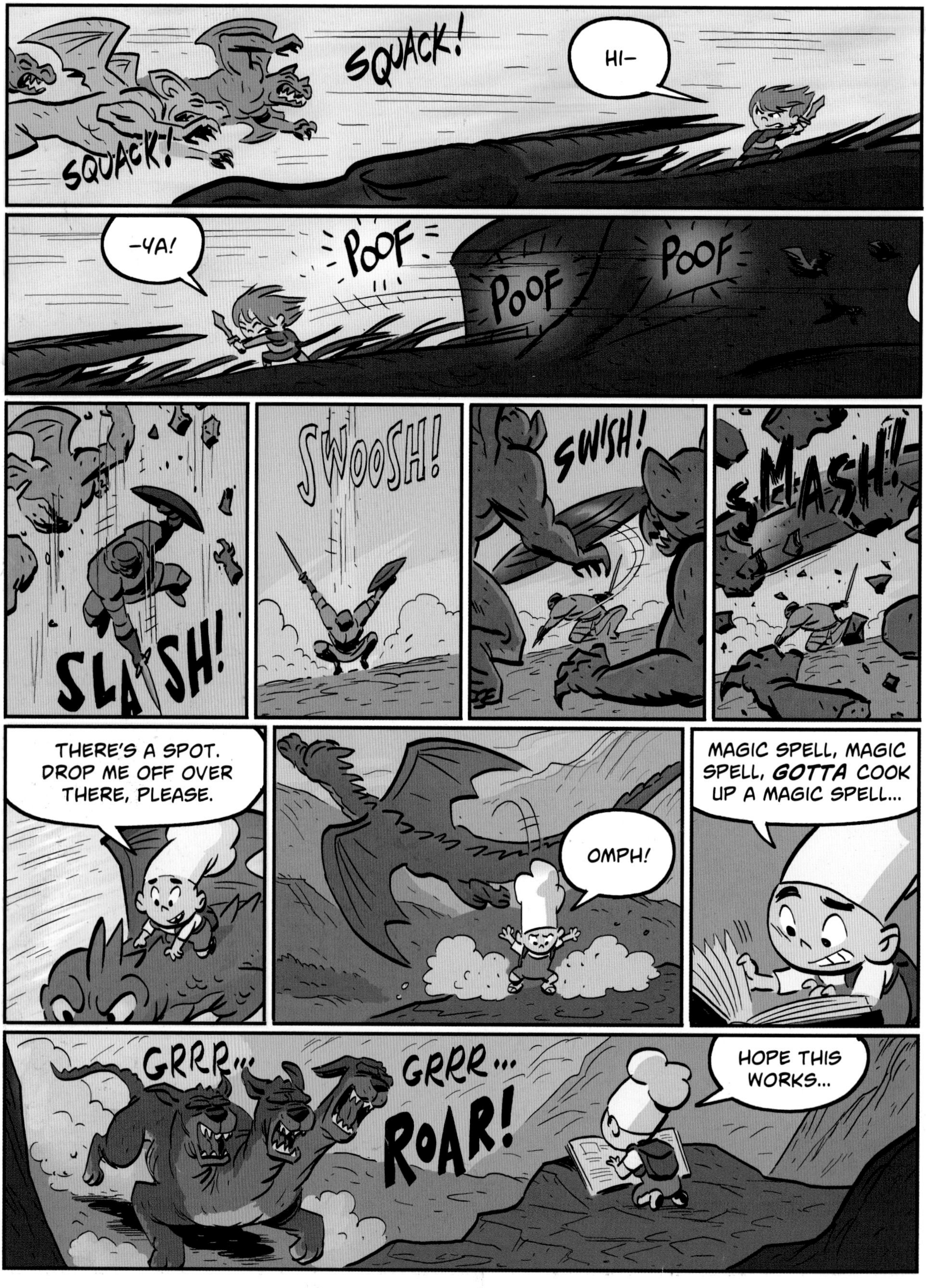
SQUACK!
SQUACK!
HI-
-YA!
POOF
POOF
POOF
SLASH!
SWOOSH!
SWISH!
SMASH!
THERE'S A SPOT. DROP ME OFF OVER THERE, PLEASE.
OMPH!
MAGIC SPELL, MAGIC SPELL, GOTTA COOK UP A MAGIC SPELL...
GRRR...
GRRR...
ROAR!
HOPE THIS WORKS...

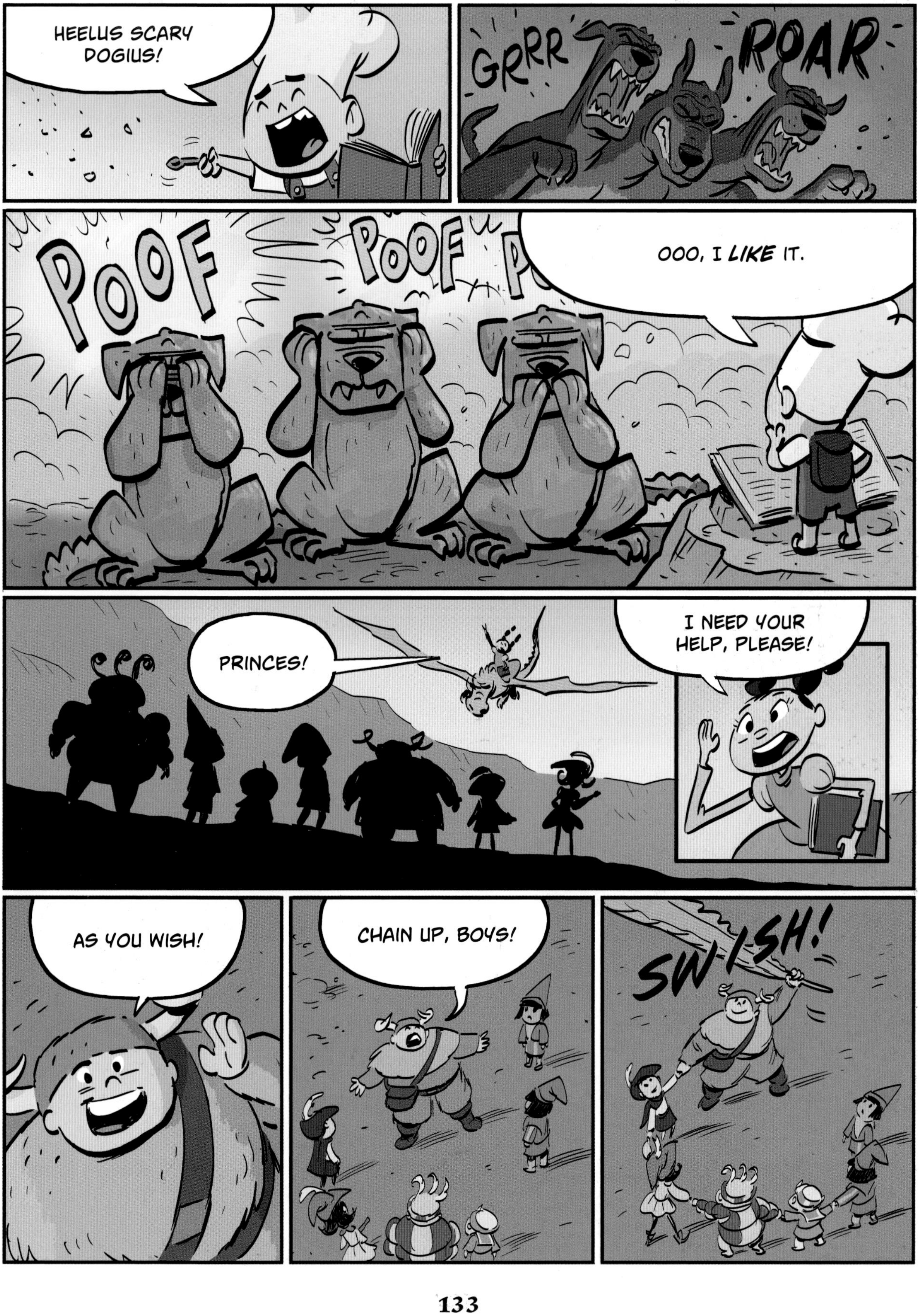
HEELUS SCARY DOGIUS!
GRRR
ROAR
POOF
POOF
OOO, I LIKE IT.
PRINCES!
I NEED YOUR HELP, PLEASE!
AS YOU WISH!
CHAIN UP, BOYS!
SWISH!

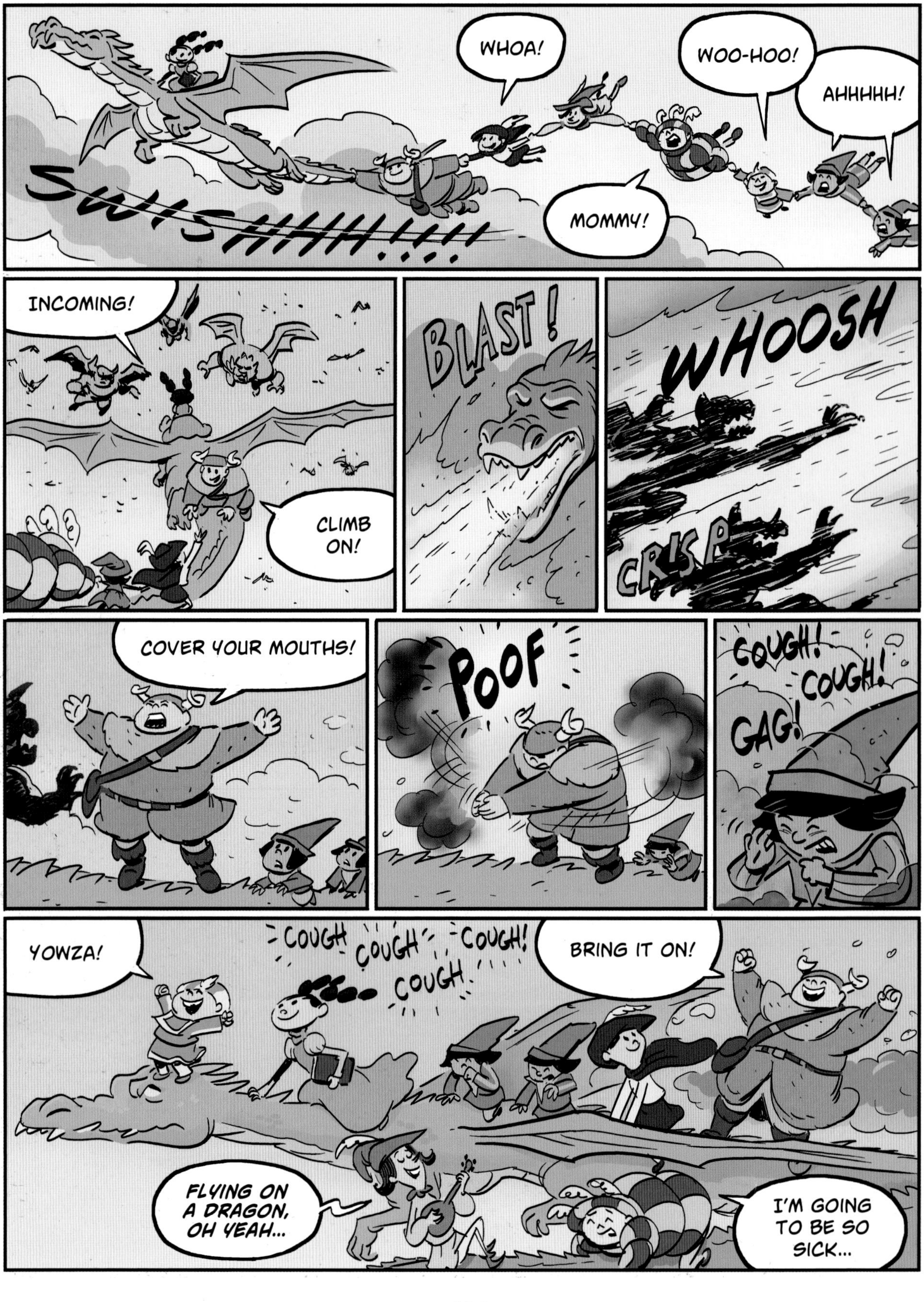
SWISHHHH!!!!!
WHOA!
WOO-HOO!
AHHHHH!
MOMMY!
INCOMING!
CLIMB ON!
BLAST!
WHOOSH
CRISP
COVER YOUR MOUTHS!
POOF
COUGH! COUGH!
GAG!
YOWZA!
COUGH COUGH COUGH! COUGH
BRING IT ON!
FLYING ON A DRAGON, OH YEAH...
I'M GOING TO BE SO SICK...

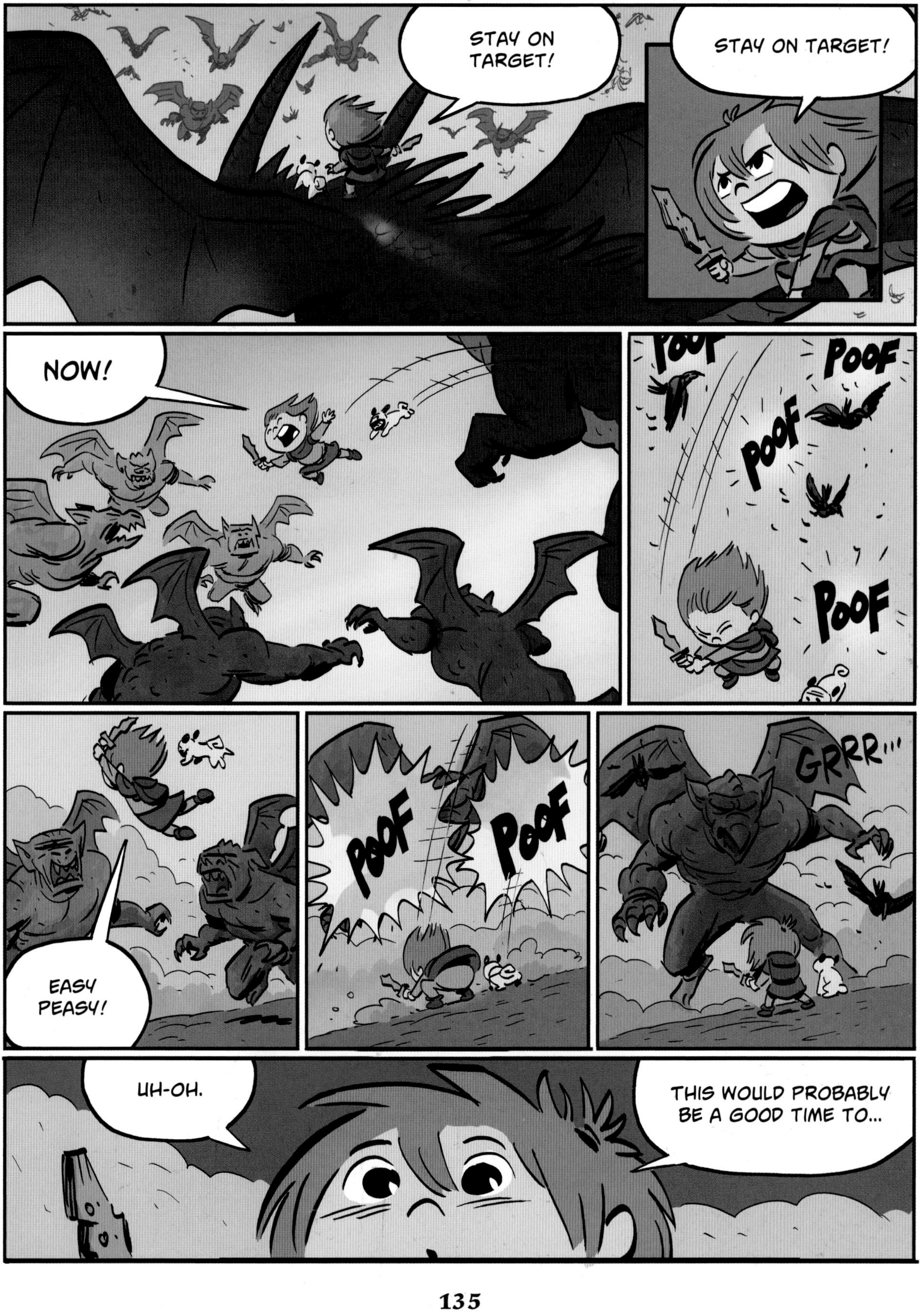
STAY ON TARGET!
STAY ON TARGET!
NOW!
POOF
POOF
POOF
POOF
EASY PEASY!
POOF
POOF
GRRR...
UH-OH.
THIS WOULD PROBABLY BE A GOOD TIME TO...

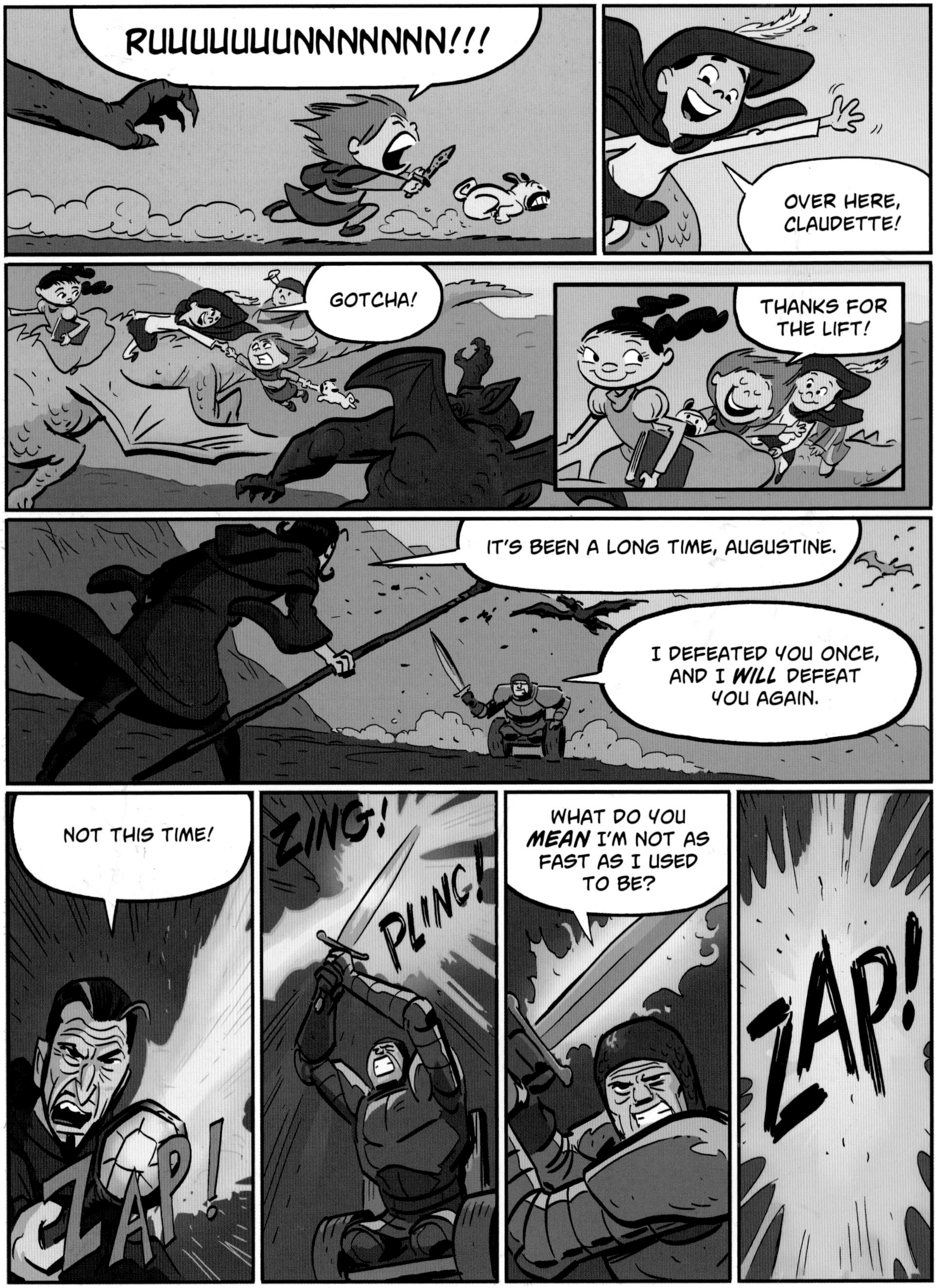
RUUUUUUUNNNNNNN!!!
OVER HERE, CLAUDETTE!
GOTCHA!
THANKS FOR THE LIFT!
IT'S BEEN A LONG TIME, AUGUSTINE.
I DEFEATED YOU ONCE, AND I WILL DEFEAT YOU AGAIN.
NOT THIS TIME!
ZAP!
ZING!
PLING!
WHAT DO YOU MEAN I'M NOT AS FAST AS I USED TO BE?
ZAP!

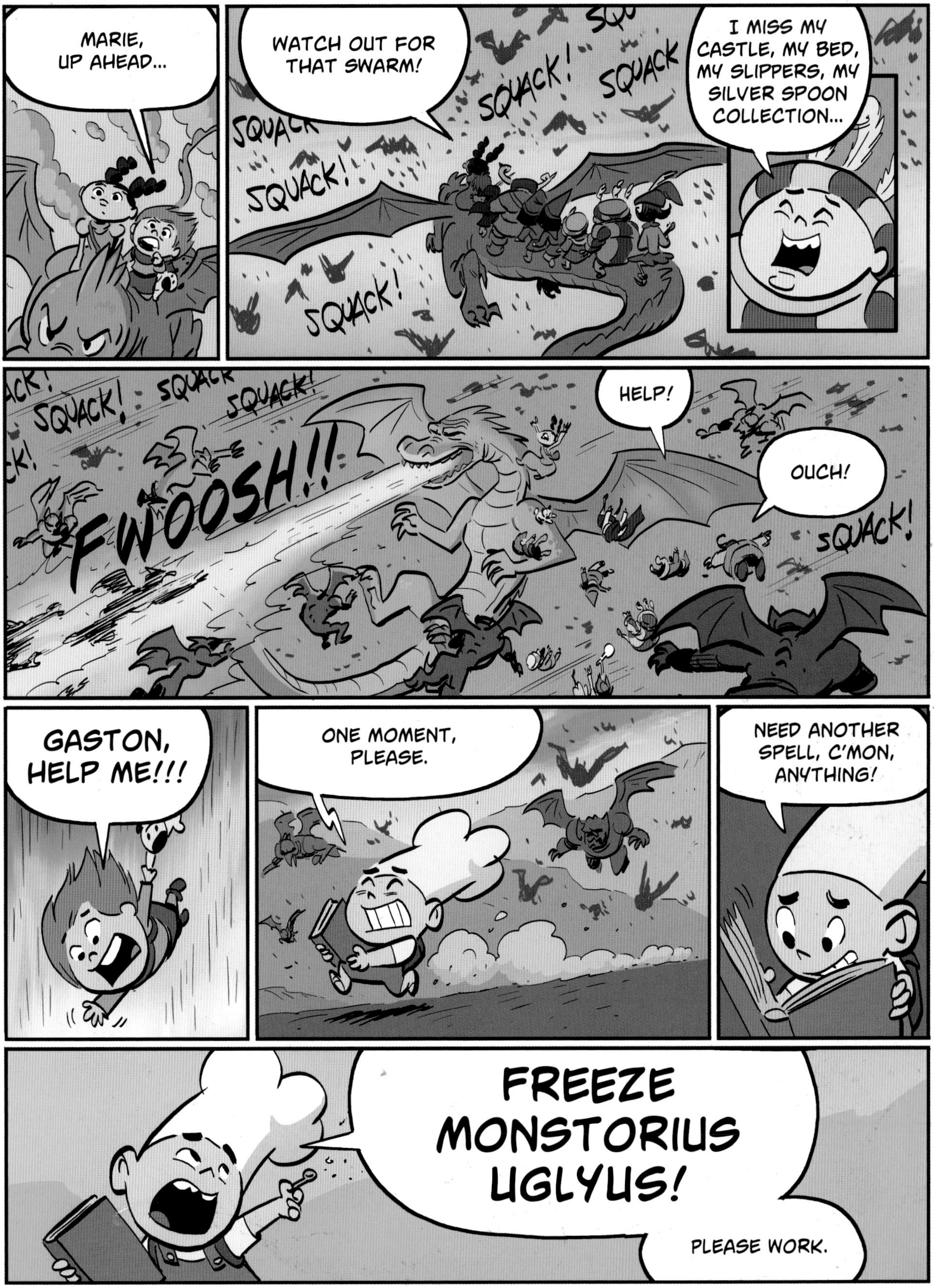
MARIE, UP AHEAD...
WATCH OUT FOR THAT SWARM!
SQUACK
SQUACK!
SQUACK!
SQUACK
SQUACK!
I MISS MY CASTLE, MY BED, MY SLIPPERS, MY SILVER SPOON COLLECTION...
SQUACK! SQUACK SQUACK!
HELP!
FWOOSH!!!
OUCH!
SQUACK!
GASTON, HELP ME!!!
ONE MOMENT, PLEASE.
NEED ANOTHER SPELL, C'MON, ANYTHING!
FREEZE MONSTORIUS UGLYUS!
PLEASE WORK.

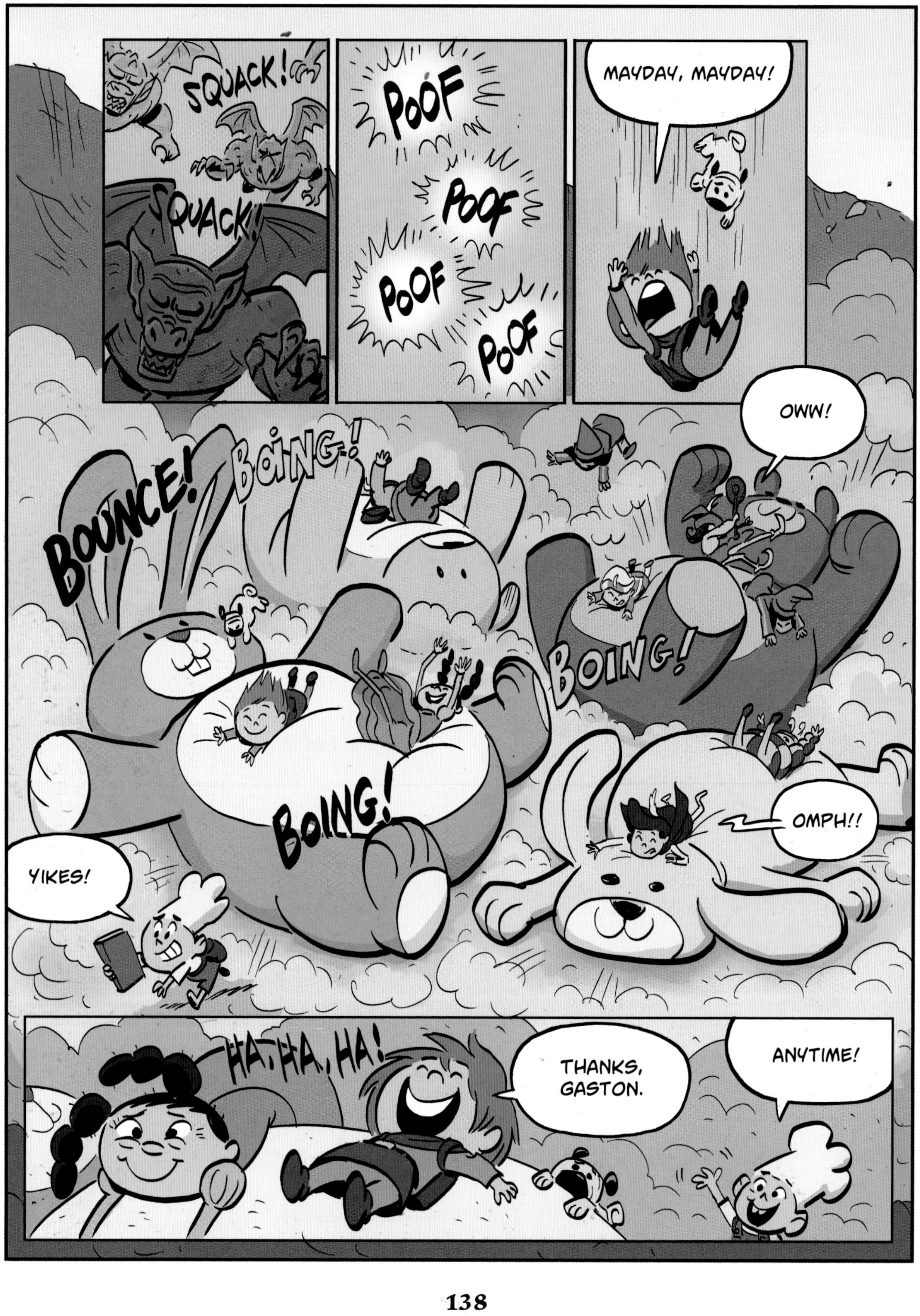
SQUACK!
SQUACK!
POOF
POOF
POOF
POOF
MAYDAY, MAYDAY!
BOUNCE!
BOING!
OWW!
BOING!
BOING!
OMPH!!
YIKES!
HA, HA, HA!
THANKS, GASTON.
ANYTIME!

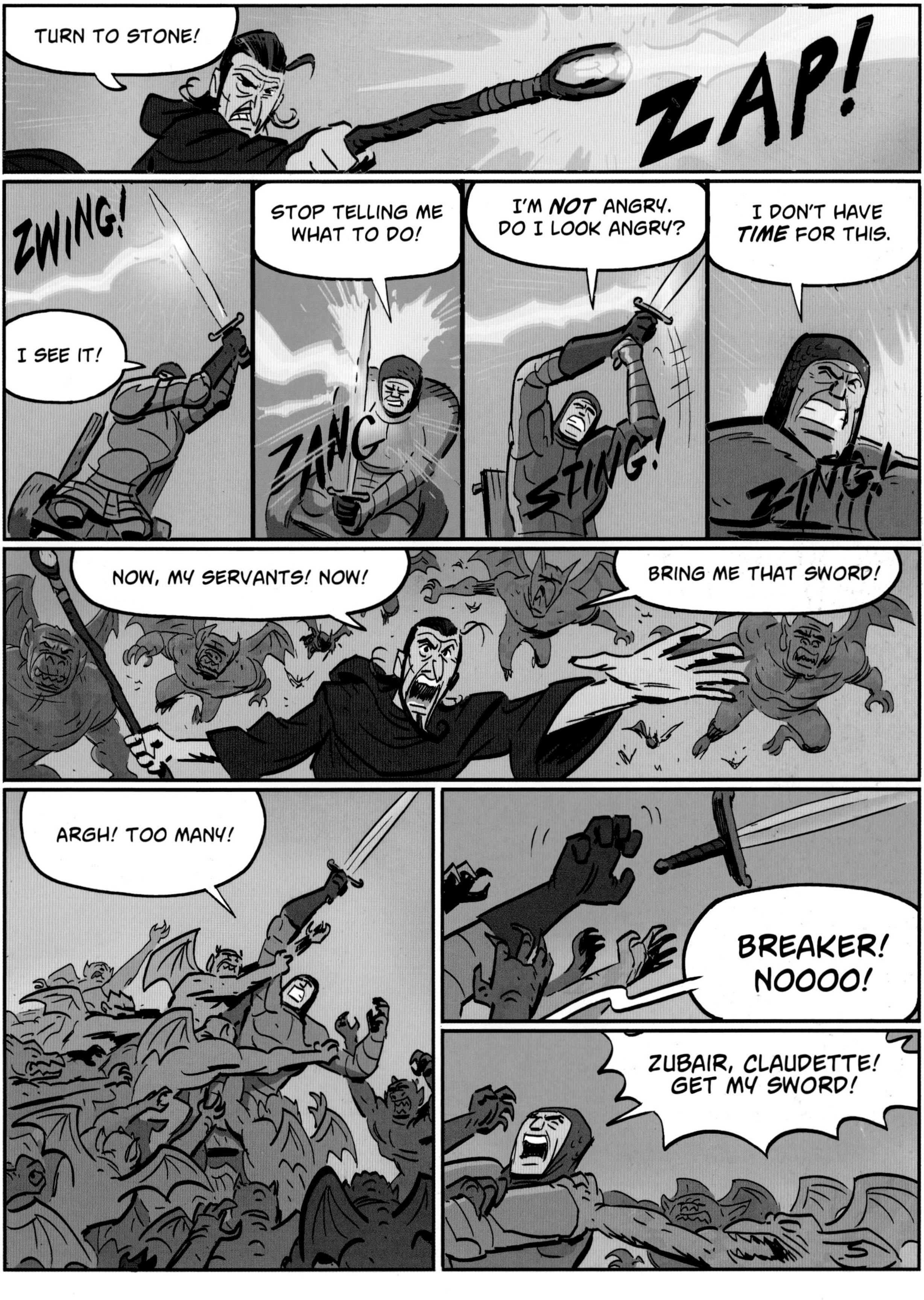
TURN TO STONE!
ZAP!
ZWING!
I SEE IT!
STOP TELLING ME WHAT TO DO!
ZANG
I'M NOT ANGRY. DO I LOOK ANGRY?
STING!
I DON'T HAVE TIME FOR THIS.
ZING!
NOW, MY SERVANTS! NOW!
BRING ME THAT SWORD!
ARGH! TOO MANY!
BREAKER! NOOOO!
ZUBAIR, CLAUDETTE! GET MY SWORD!

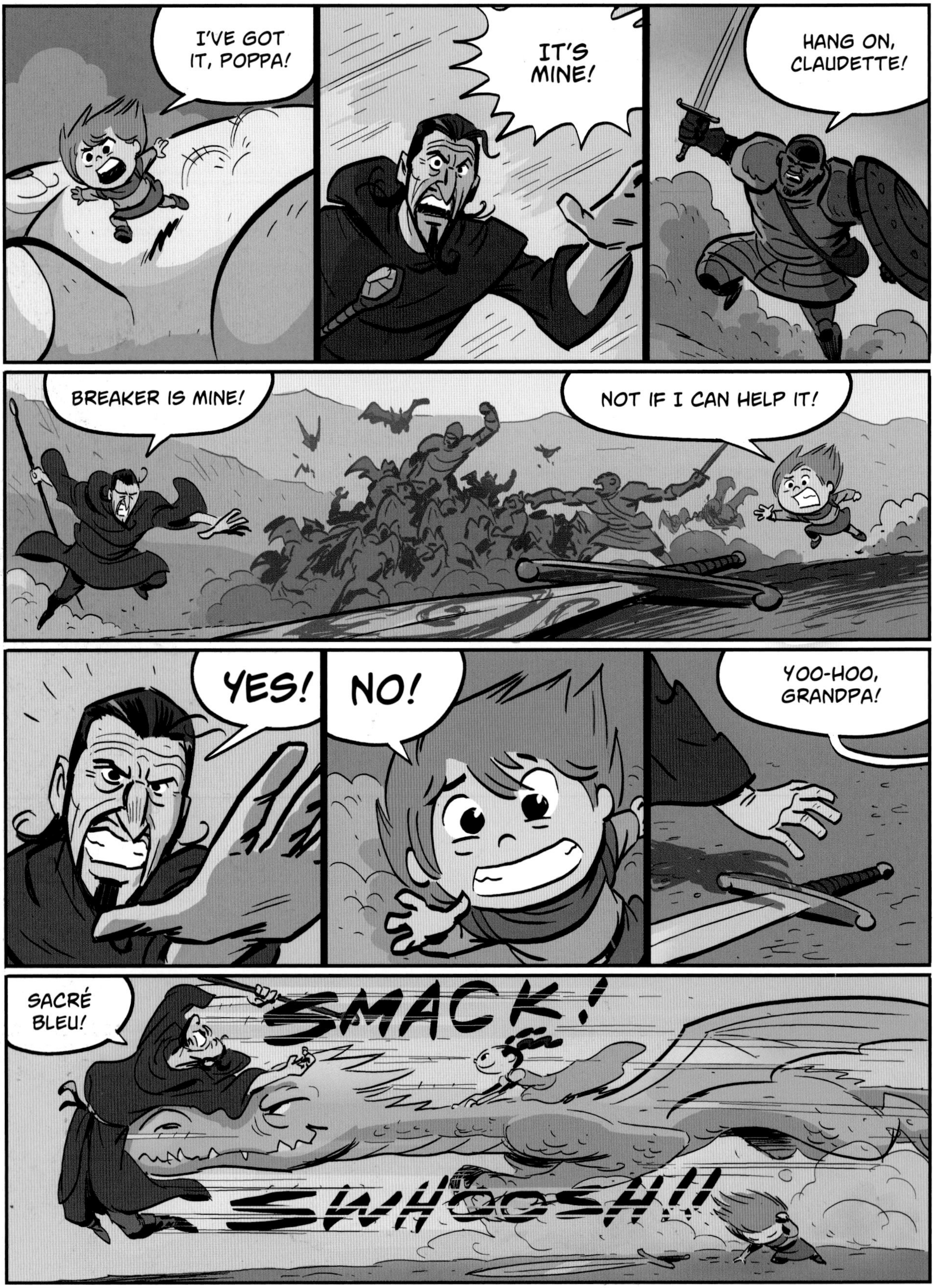
I'VE GOT IT, POPPA!
IT'S MINE!
HANG ON, CLAUDETTE!
BREAKER IS MINE!
NOT IF I CAN HELP IT!
YES!
NO!
YOO-HOO, GRANDPA!
SACRÉ BLEU!
SMACK!
SWHOOSH!!

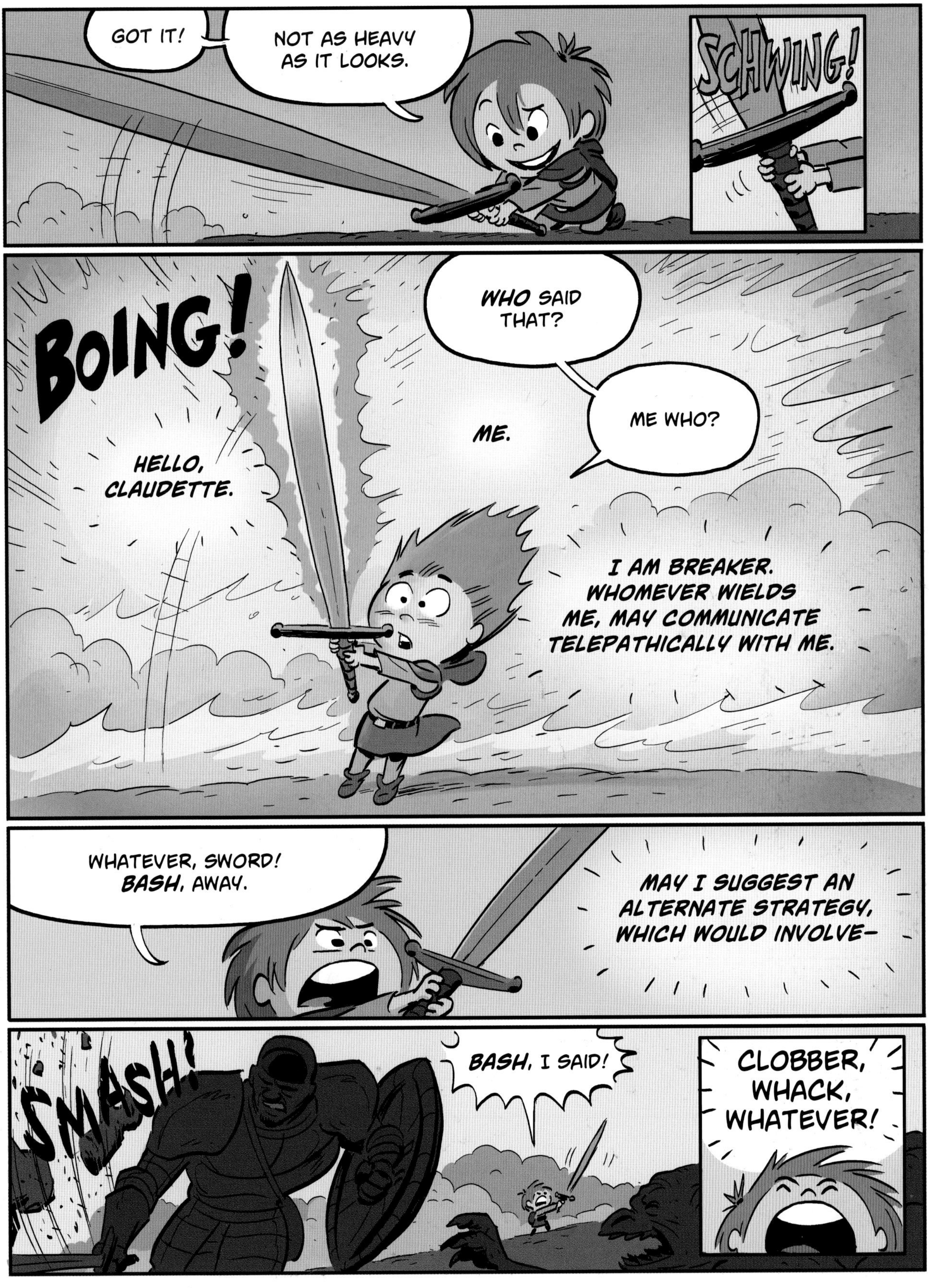
GOT IT!
NOT AS HEAVY AS IT LOOKS.
SCHWING!
BOING!
WHO SAID THAT?
ME WHO?
ME.
HELLO, CLAUDETTE.
I AM BREAKER. WHOMEVER WIELDS ME, MAY COMMUNICATE TELEPATHICALLY WITH ME.
WHATEVER, SWORD! BASH, AWAY.
MAY I SUGGEST AN ALTERNATE STRATEGY, WHICH WOULD INVOLVE–
SMASH!
BASH, I SAID!
CLOBBER, WHACK, WHATEVER!

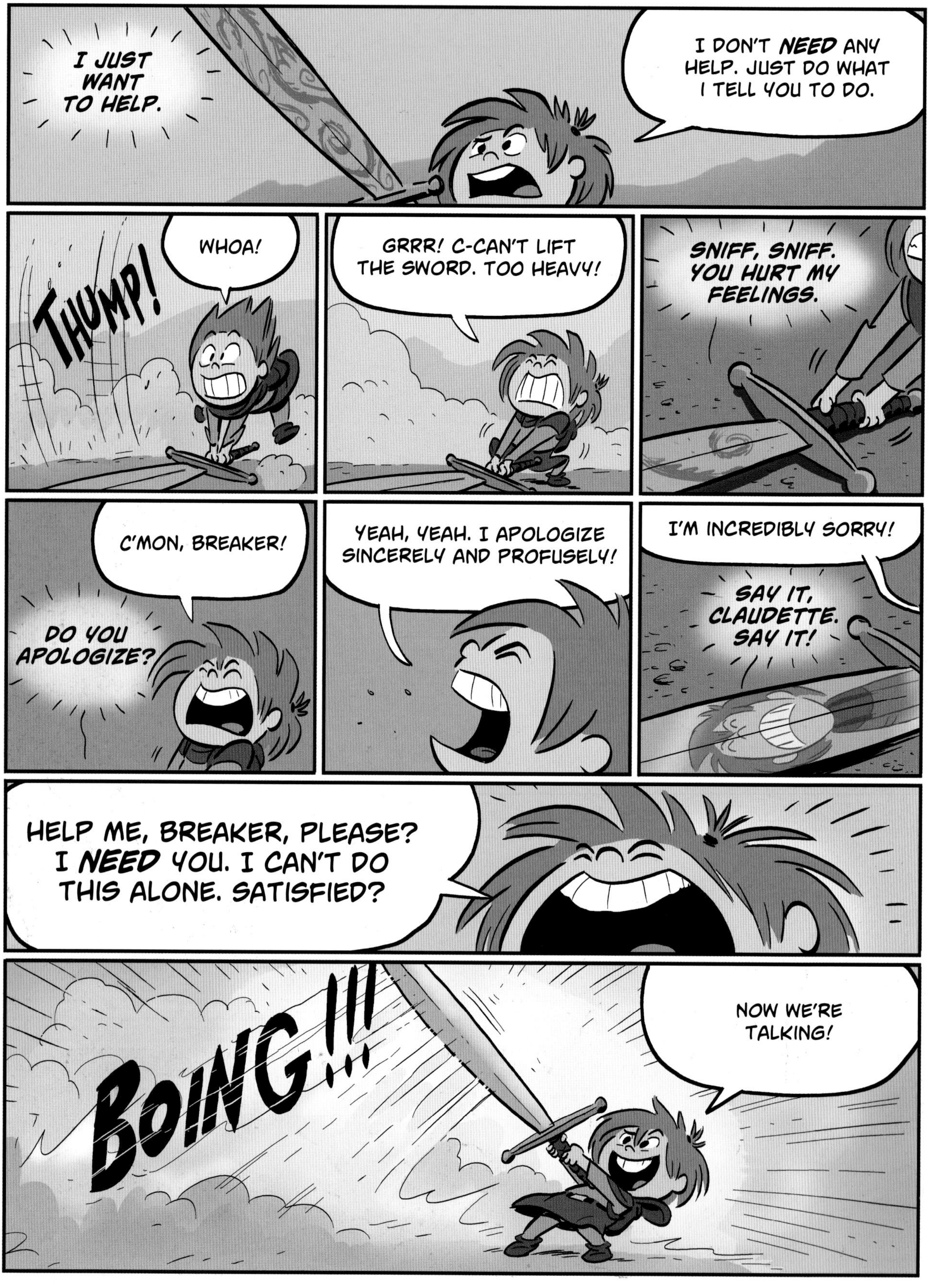
I JUST WANT TO HELP.
I DON'T **NEED** ANY HELP. JUST DO WHAT I TELL YOU TO DO.
THUMP!
WHOA!
GRRR! C-CAN'T LIFT THE SWORD. TOO HEAVY!
SNIFF, SNIFF. YOU HURT MY FEELINGS.
C'MON, BREAKER!
DO YOU APOLOGIZE?
YEAH, YEAH. I APOLOGIZE SINCERELY AND PROFUSELY!
I'M INCREDIBLY SORRY!
SAY IT, CLAUDETTE. SAY IT!
HELP ME, BREAKER, PLEASE? I **NEED** YOU. I CAN'T DO THIS ALONE. SATISFIED?
BOING!!!
NOW WE'RE TALKING!

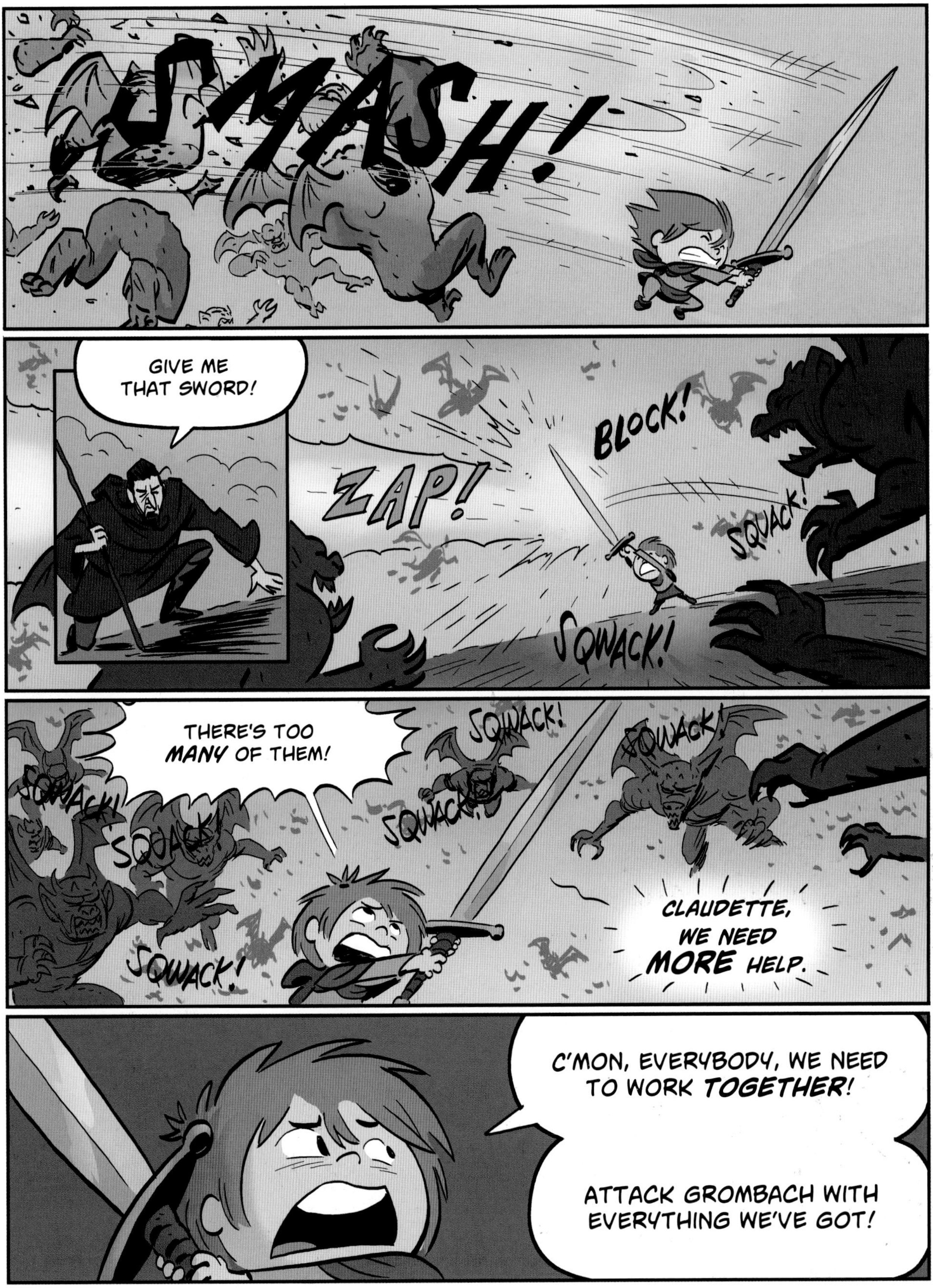
SMASH!
GIVE ME THAT SWORD!
ZAP!
BLOCK!
SQUACK!
SQWACK!
THERE'S TOO MANY OF THEM!
SQWACK!
SQWACK!
SQWACK!
SQWACK!
SQUACK!
SQWACK!
CLAUDETTE, WE NEED MORE HELP.
C'MON, EVERYBODY, WE NEED TO WORK TOGETHER!
ATTACK GROMBACH WITH EVERYTHING WE'VE GOT!

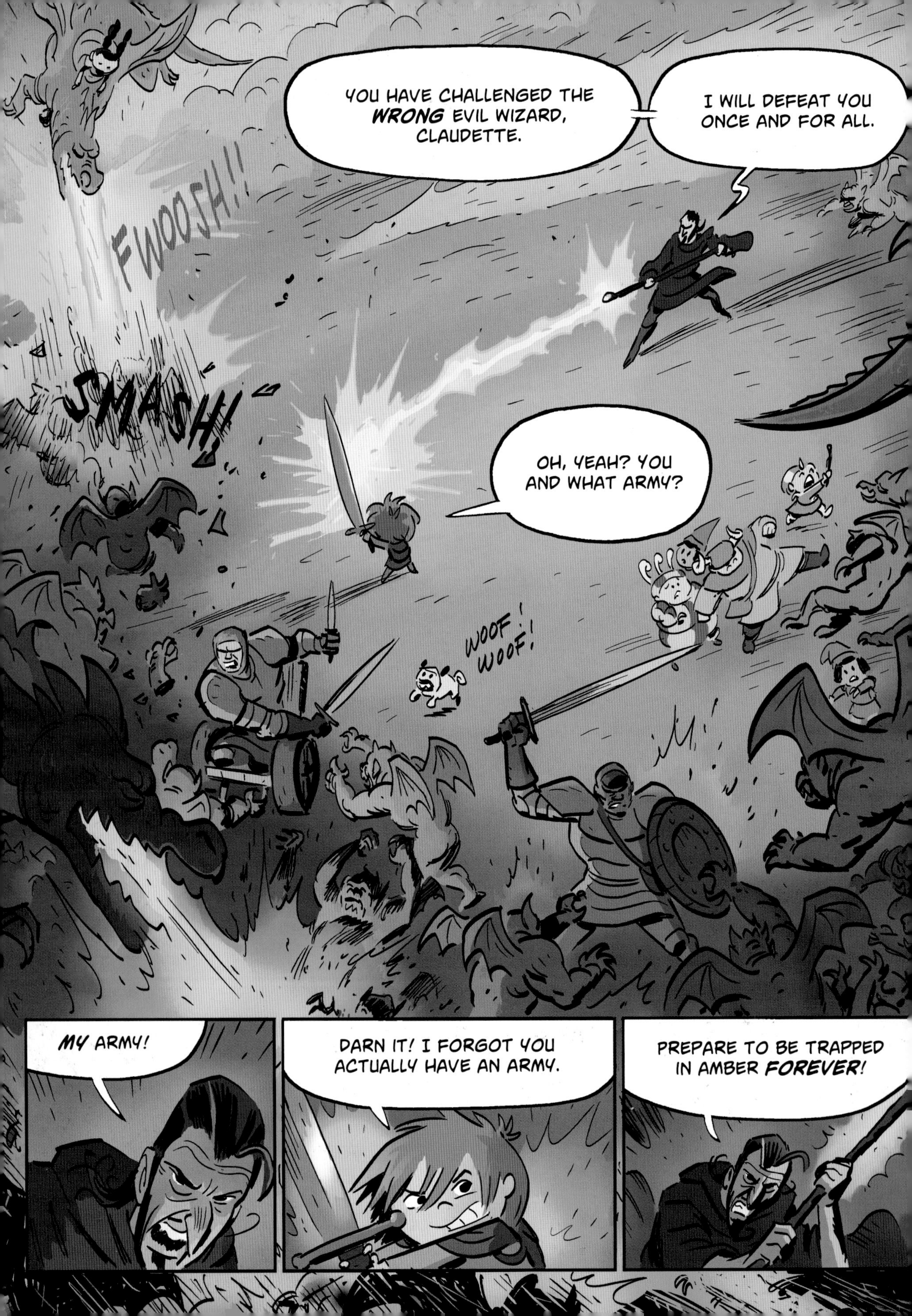
YOU HAVE CHALLENGED THE WRONG EVIL WIZARD, CLAUDETTE.
I WILL DEFEAT YOU ONCE AND FOR ALL.
FWOOSH!!
SMASH!
OH, YEAH? YOU AND WHAT ARMY?
WOOF! WOOF!
MY ARMY!
DARN IT! I FORGOT YOU ACTUALLY HAVE AN ARMY.
PREPARE TO BE TRAPPED IN AMBER FOREVER!

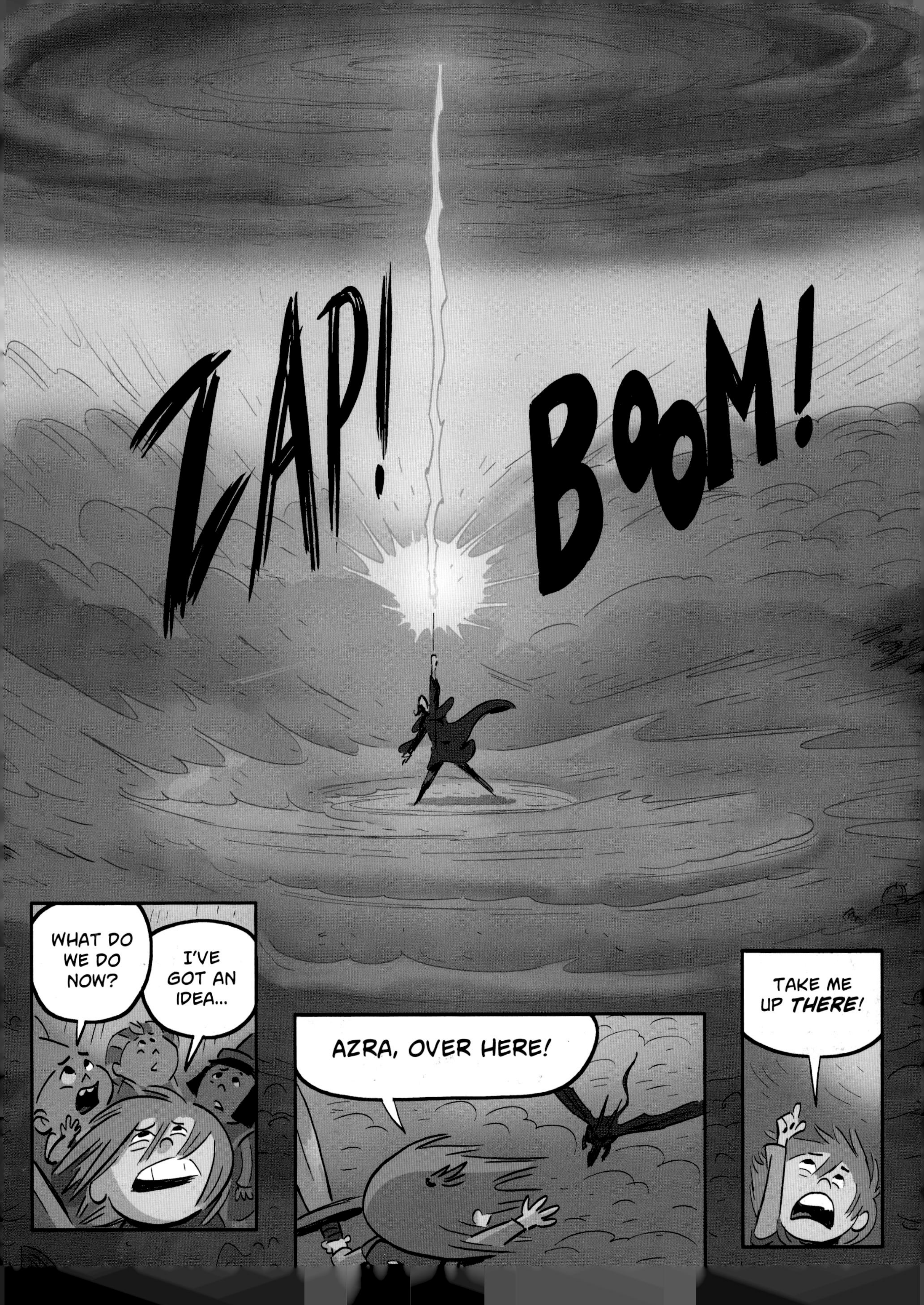

ZAP!
BOOM!
WHAT DO WE DO NOW?
I'VE GOT AN IDEA...
AZRA, OVER HERE!
TAKE ME UP *THERE*!

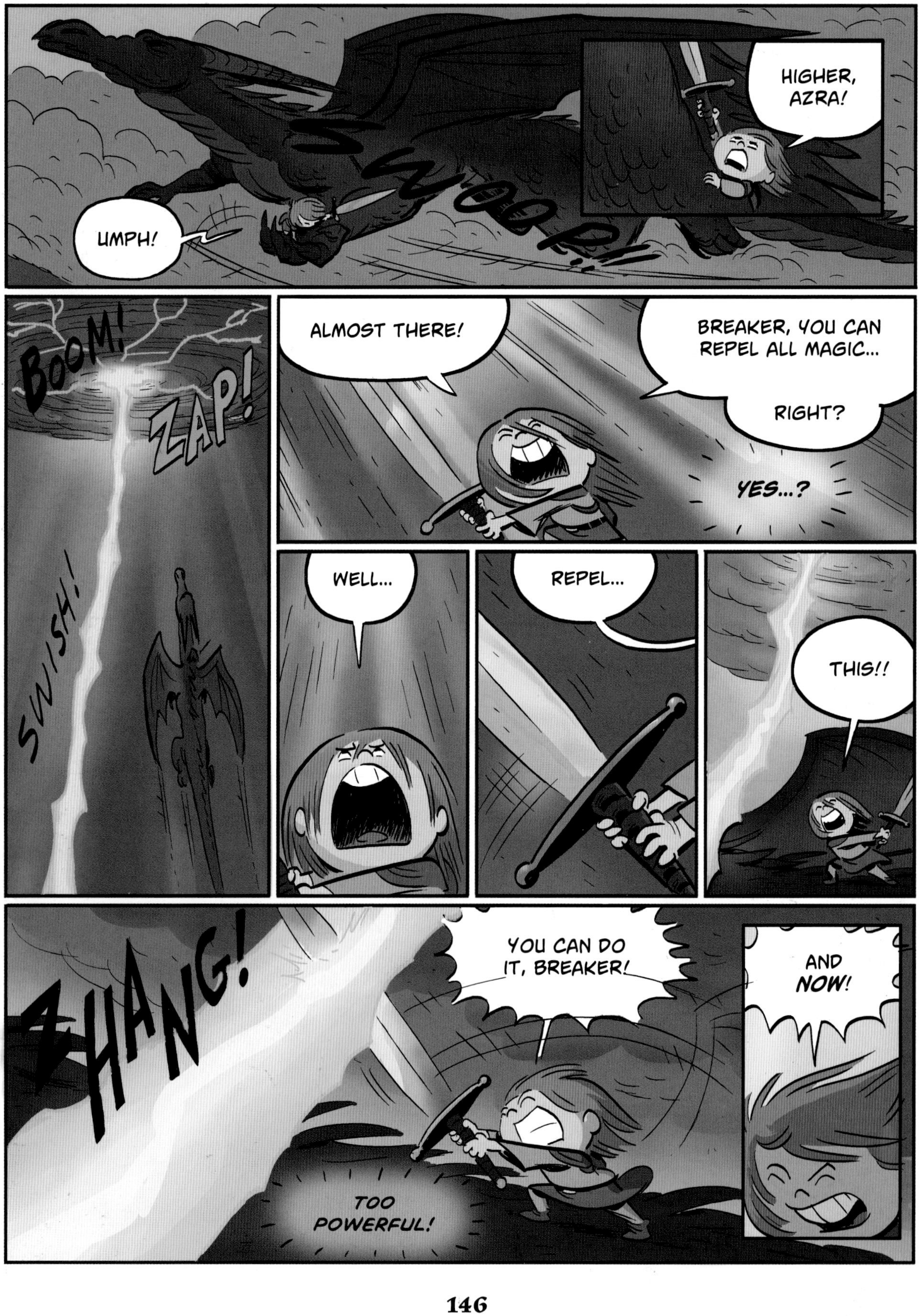
SWOOP!!
HIGHER, AZRA!
UMPH!
BOOM!
ZAP!
SWISH!
ALMOST THERE!
BREAKER, YOU CAN REPEL ALL MAGIC...
RIGHT?
YES...?
WELL...
REPEL...
THIS!!
ZHANG!
YOU CAN DO IT, BREAKER!
TOO POWERFUL!
AND NOW!

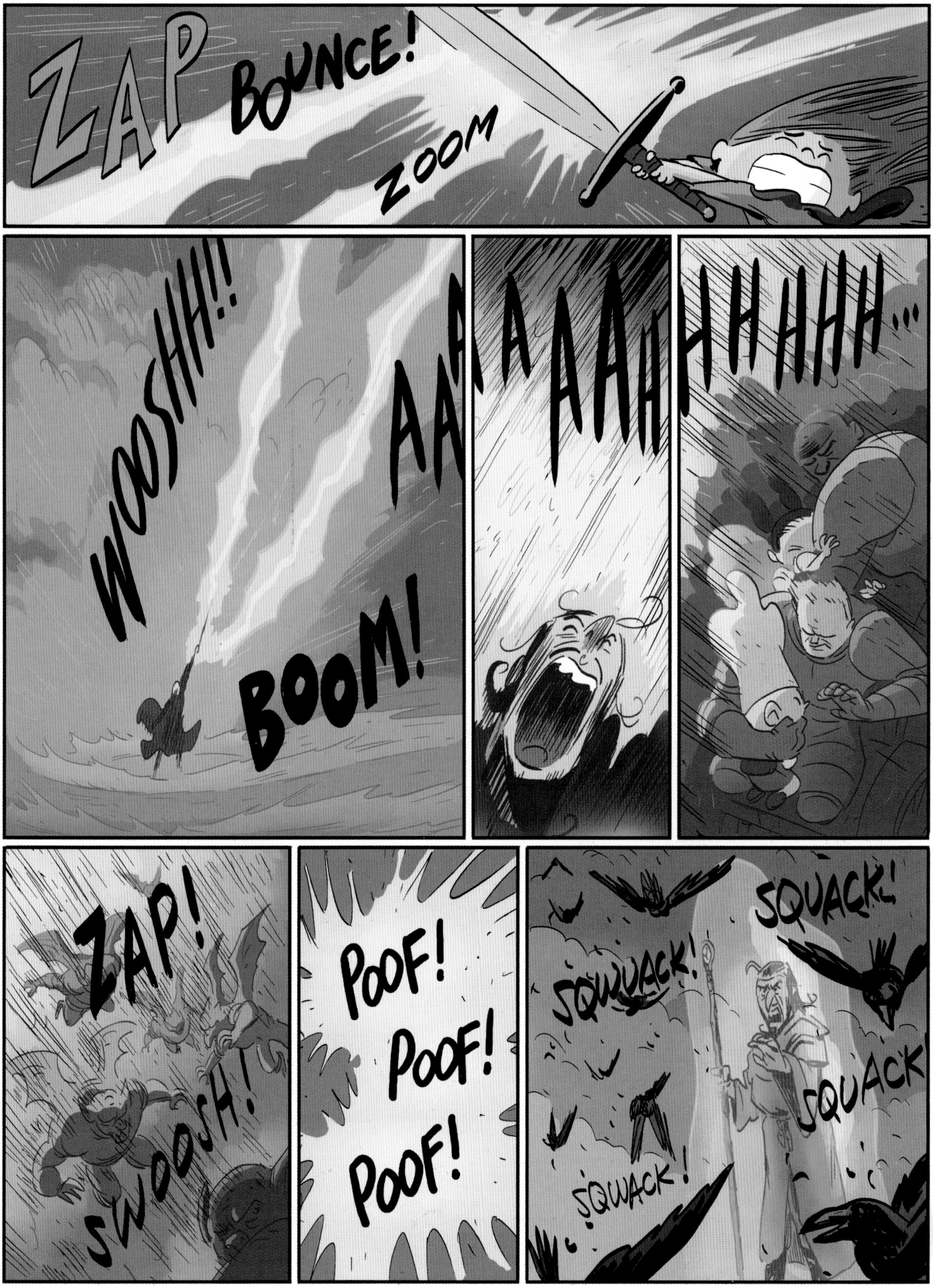
ZAP
BOUNCE!
ZOOM
WOOSHH!!
AAAAAHHHHHHH...
BOOM!
ZAP!
SWOOSH!
POOF!
POOF!
POOF!
SQUACK!
SQUACK!
SQUACK!
SQWACK!

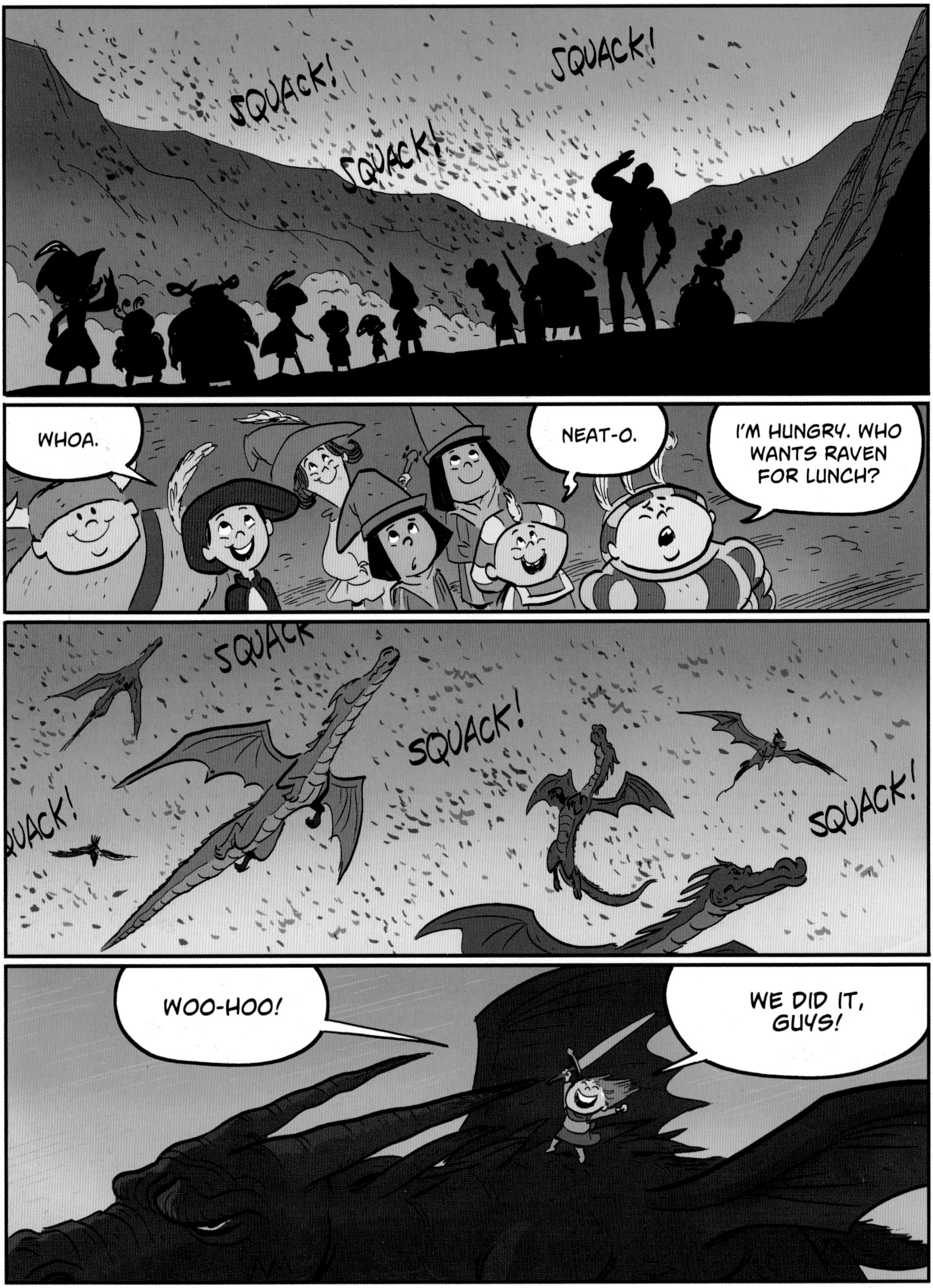
SQUACK!
SQUACK!
SQUACK!
WHOA.
NEAT-O.
I'M HUNGRY. WHO WANTS RAVEN FOR LUNCH?
SQUACK
SQUACK!
SQUACK!
SQUACK!
WOO-HOO!
WE DID IT, GUYS!

MEANWHILE...

SQUAWK! SQUAW SQUAWK! SQUAWK! SQUAWK! SQUAWK! SQUAWK! SQU

POOF!

SQUAWK! SQUACK!

?

SQUAW

SQUAWK SQUAWK SQUAWK SQU

SQUAWK SQUAWK SQUAWK

JUST AS I PREDICTED...

WE HAVE ROUNDLY AND SOUNDLY DEFEATED THE GARGOYLES. PIECE OF CAKE.

WHATEVER.

WHAT DO YOU KNOW, THOSE DUMB KIDS PULLED IT OFF. I'M **SURE** MARIE WAS BEHIND THEIR VICTORY.

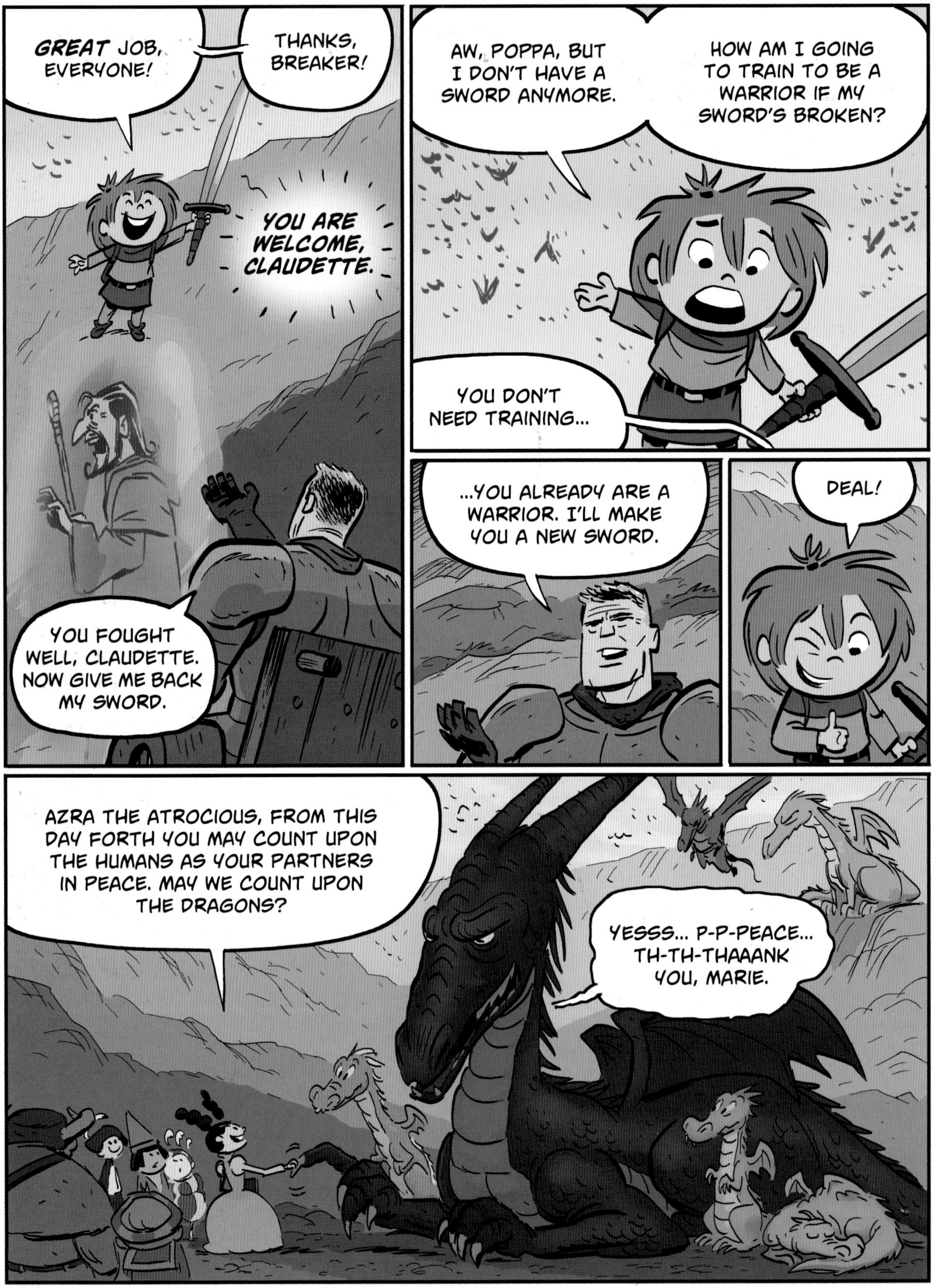
GREAT JOB, EVERYONE!
THANKS, BREAKER!
YOU ARE WELCOME, CLAUDETTE.
YOU FOUGHT WELL, CLAUDETTE. NOW GIVE ME BACK MY SWORD.
AW, POPPA, BUT I DON'T HAVE A SWORD ANYMORE.
HOW AM I GOING TO TRAIN TO BE A WARRIOR IF MY SWORD'S BROKEN?
YOU DON'T NEED TRAINING...
...YOU ALREADY ARE A WARRIOR. I'LL MAKE YOU A NEW SWORD.
DEAL!
AZRA THE ATROCIOUS, FROM THIS DAY FORTH YOU MAY COUNT UPON THE HUMANS AS YOUR PARTNERS IN PEACE. MAY WE COUNT UPON THE DRAGONS?
YESSS... P-P-PEACE... TH-TH-THAAANK YOU, MARIE.

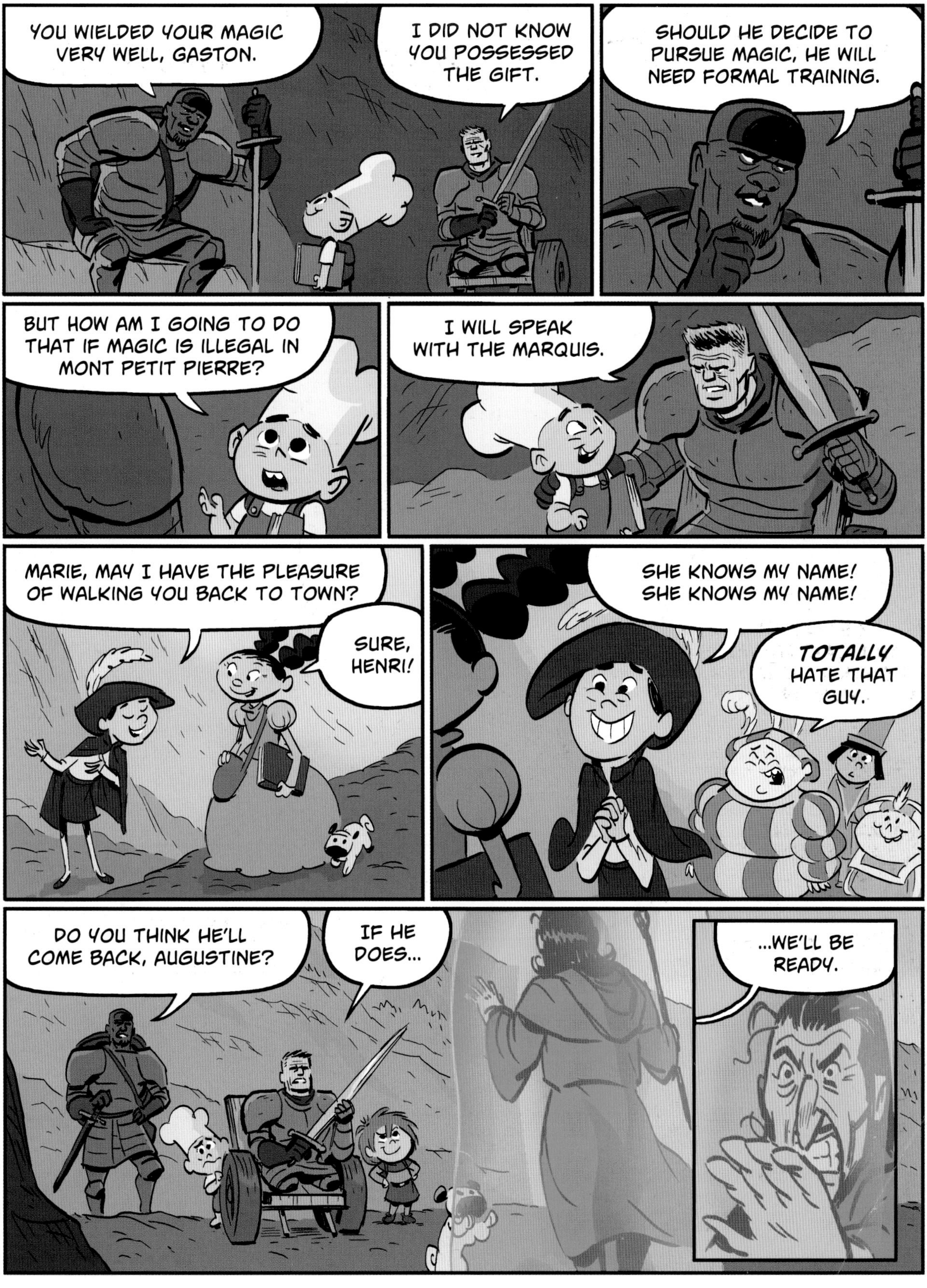

YOU WIELDED YOUR MAGIC VERY WELL, GASTON.
I DID NOT KNOW YOU POSSESSED THE GIFT.
SHOULD HE DECIDE TO PURSUE MAGIC, HE WILL NEED FORMAL TRAINING.
BUT HOW AM I GOING TO DO THAT IF MAGIC IS ILLEGAL IN MONT PETIT PIERRE?
I WILL SPEAK WITH THE MARQUIS.
MARIE, MAY I HAVE THE PLEASURE OF WALKING YOU BACK TO TOWN?
SURE, HENRI!
SHE KNOWS MY NAME! SHE KNOWS MY NAME!
TOTALLY HATE THAT GUY.
DO YOU THINK HE'LL COME BACK, AUGUSTINE?
IF HE DOES...
...WE'LL BE READY.

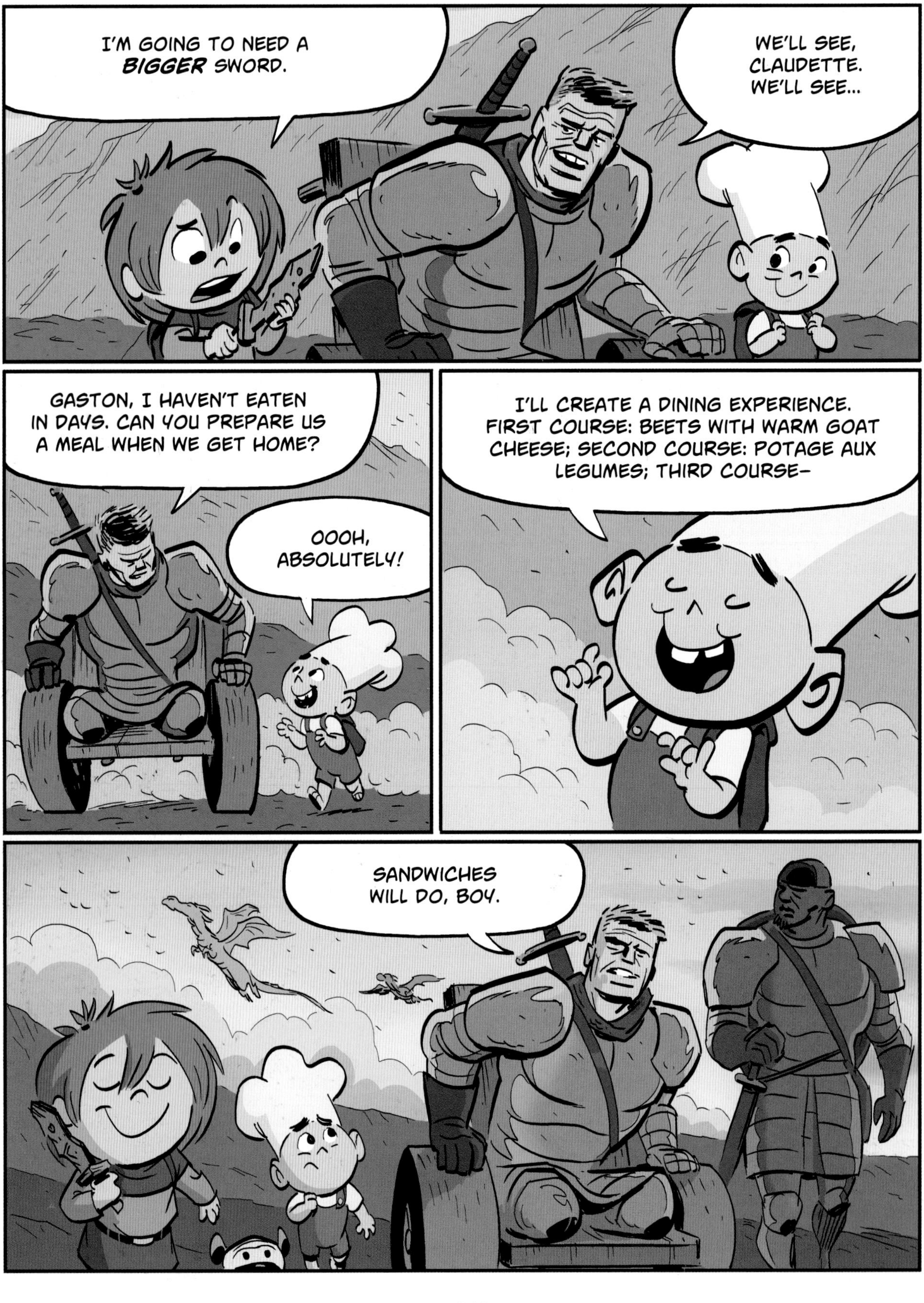
I'M GOING TO NEED A BIGGER SWORD.
WE'LL SEE, CLAUDETTE. WE'LL SEE...
GASTON, I HAVEN'T EATEN IN DAYS. CAN YOU PREPARE US A MEAL WHEN WE GET HOME?
OOOH, ABSOLUTELY!
I'LL CREATE A DINING EXPERIENCE. FIRST COURSE: BEETS WITH WARM GOAT CHEESE; SECOND COURSE: POTAGE AUX LEGUMES; THIRD COURSE–
SANDWICHES WILL DO, BOY.

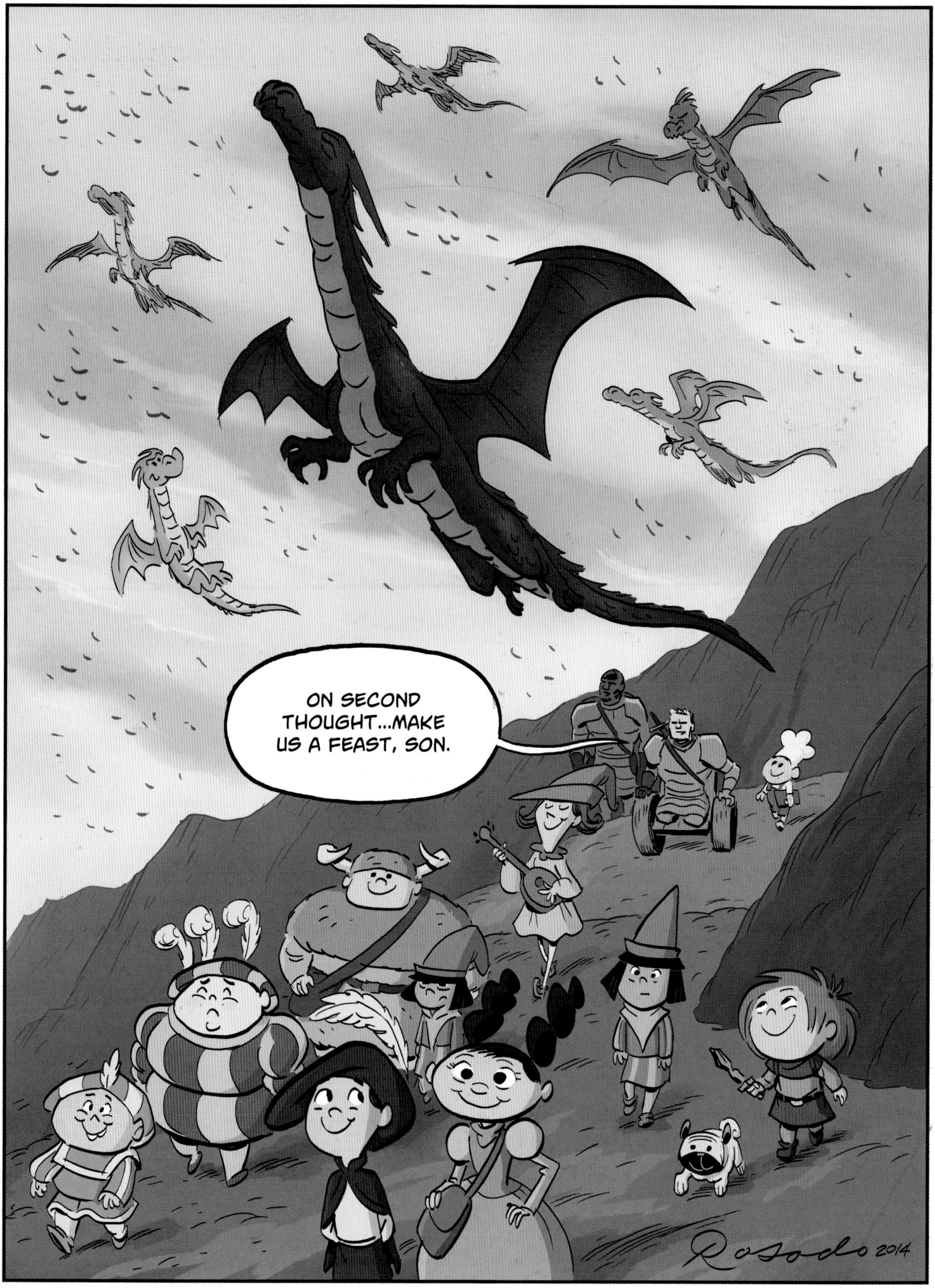
ON SECOND THOUGHT...MAKE US A FEAST, SON.
Rosado 2014

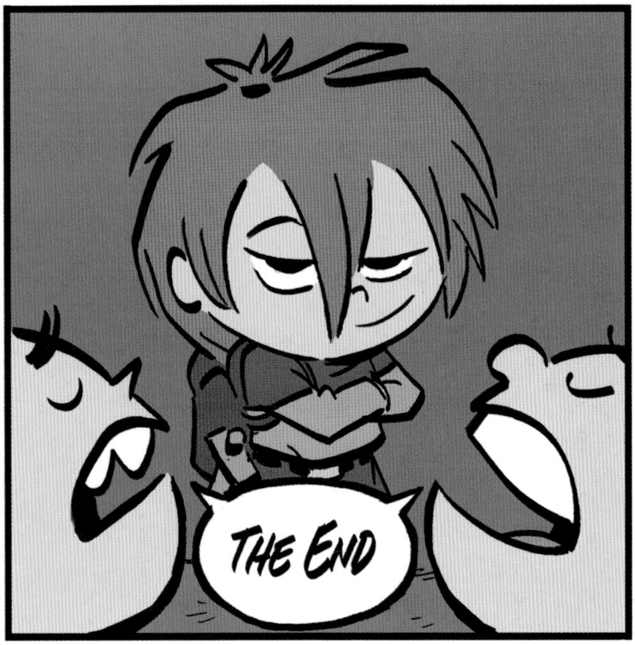
THE END

ROSADO/AGUIRRE - 2014